CONQUEST

Rise of the Rogues

KIRAN Ramchandran

Published by The Story Cure Press

Honolulu, Hawaii

ISBN: 978-1-970366-12-9 (Paperback)

Printed in the United States of America

Library of Congress Control Number: 2026938238

TheStoryCurePress.co

PRAISE FOR CONQUEST:

Rise of the Rogues

"A fantastic and well-researched adventure of international intrigue involving pirates, Maroons, slavers, Irish rebels and the fight for freedom."

Chris Blackwell, Producer of Bob Marley and U2, Founder of Island Outpost in Jamaica

"Conquest is wonderfully well-written, in parts prose and poetry. It is an enthralling, action-packed tale. Rooted in intensive research, the book highlights pivotal events that continue to shape our modern world."

Anil Kurian, Film Producer, The Walt Disney Company

"CONQUEST is a rollicking good story and very well told."

Phyllis Grann, former CEO of Penguin Putnam

"CONQUEST. The history, the empowerment, the people... a must-read adventurous movement!"

Mychal-Bella Bowman, Actor in Emmy-nominated series Underground Railroad

"This captivating tale of piracy and politics in the Caribbean turns on the irrepressible desire for freedom and equality in a world of empire, war, and human bondage."

Vincent Brown, Author of "Tacky's Revolt: The Story of an Atlantic Slave War" and Charles Warren Professor of African and African American Studies at Harvard University

"CONQUEST is a brilliant literary adventure that combines the tumult of pirates, invaders, and slaves with the vibrant history of the Caribbean and the enduring pursuit of freedom and equality. A masterful fusion of historical storytelling and timeless exploration of the human spirit."

David Eagleman, Professor of Neuroscience at Stanford University, Bestselling Author and Top 10 Podcaster of Inner Cosmos

"Deeply researched, CONQUEST engages the reader with an entertaining story while also enlightening them as to the historical roots of democracy, the profound culture of Jamaica's Maroon people, and the universal and relentless drive for freedom."

Henry Louis "Skip" Gates, Jr., Author, Filmmaker, English Professor at Harvard University, PEN Award recipient, MacArthur Fellow

Map of 17th Century Caribbean

Map of 17th Century Spanish Jamaica

Table of Contents

PROLOGUE........I

CHAPTER 1: JAMAICA........1

In which the way forward is doubted........1

In which sickness strikes........5

In which a crime is committed........6

In which Maroons & monkeys make mischief........10

CHAPTER 2: JAMAICA........19

In which a smuggler is drugged........19

In which a smuggler is bedded........22

In which a smuggler is trusted........26

In which a life is stolen........28

In which a smuggler claims a prize........33

CHAPTER 3: AT SEA........37

In which pyrates taunt their foes........37

In which bodies lie with bodies........40

In which a stranger scavenges........44

In which a bone cave offers shelter........47

In which strangers become friends........49

In which cannibals prepare to feast........52

CHAPTER 4: IRELAND 58

In which bogs are traversed..*58*

In which a beleaguered clan makes camp...............................*62*

In which a parley is convened...*64*

In which betrayal brings a bloodbath...................................*69*

In which all is lost..*73*

CHAPTER 5: JAMAICA...80

In which pyrates meet buccaneers..*80*

In which buccaneers define democracy...................................*85*

In which mates bicker..*88*

In which morals are questioned..*92*

In which a banQuet is consumed...*95*

In which pyrates are discovered amongst buccaneers...............*96*

In which defection is debated...*100*

In which pyrates are betrayed...*103*

CHAPTER 6: JAMAICA...110

In which rulers take a ride...*110*

In which a trial is held...*113*

In which a shipyard takes shape...*118*

In which the future of the world is plotted............................*121*

In which a lover is astounded...*131*

CHAPTER 7: JAMAICA...134

In which a monkey is a man...*134*

In which a man is no longer a monkey *138*

CHAPTER 8: IRELAND 142

In which orphans journey homeward *142*

In which orphans encounter an old enemy *149*

In which orphans are assaulted *152*

In which Irish orphans are captured *159*

In which prisoners dare escape *163*

In which prisoners are bought and sold *170*

CHAPTER 9: JAMAICA 173

In which tricks are played *173*

In which tricks are turned *175*

In which tricks are trounced *178*

In which a sewer is a gaol *179*

In which a quest is undertaken *184*

In which pyrates set sail *194*

CHAPTER 10: JAMAICA 198

In which Maroons seek Maroons *198*

In which magic is debated *205*

In which a god is summoned *209*

CHAPTER 11: ENGLAND 214

In which servants are purchased *214*

In which servants journey the Thames *221*

In which a servant meets a captain *225*

In which terms are defined 231
In which stories are shared 236
In which ladders are climbed 242

CHAPTER 12: JAMAICA 246
In which waterfalls are scaled 246
In which quarry is tracked 249
In which soldiers attack 251
In which a tribe is decimated 254
In which the sun shines again 257
In which strategy is spoken 261

CHAPTER 13: ST. KITTS 266
In which a pyrate is hanged 266
In which mistakes are made 270
In which a life is threatened 276
In which graves are robbed 281
In which a fight club is found 286

CHAPTER 14: JAMAICA 290
In which a life is revived 290
In which customs cause confusion 294
In which Maroons gather 296

CHAPTER 15: AT SEA 303
In which a bargain is struck 303
In which a man is murdered 307

In which an execution is ordered *311*

In which desires are fulfilled *313*

In which secrets are kept *317*

In which a crime is punished *319*

In which a storm strikes *320*

In which losses are calculated *323*

CHAPTER 16: JAMAICA 331

In which soldiers are smoked *331*

In which soldiers are surprised *333*

In which soldiers are spooked *336*

In which soldiers spar *340*

In which soldiers take refuge *344*

CHAPTER 17: CAPE VERDE 346

In which faith crumbles *346*

In which a governor presses his advantage *348*

In which a servant celebrates and a captain suffers *350*

In which an opportunity is presented *353*

In which Christmas is celebrated *357*

In which violence begets violence *361*

In which a mercy is done *366*

CHAPTER 18: JAMAICA 372

In which water breaks *372*

In which Maroons plot a raid *374*

In which prayers are recited 376

In which Maroons attack....................377

In which skills are revealed 380

In which Maroons deliver vengeance....................381

CHAPTER 19: JAMAICA....................385

In which a soldier is kidnapped 385

In which a truth is tested 388

CHAPTER 20: AT SEA....................398

In which a sail is spotted....................398

In which a sail is pursued....................401

In which a captain confronts his quartermaster....................410

In which a banner of blood is raised 417

EPILOGUE: ENGLAND 425

In which a conquest is ordained....................425

CAST OF CHARACTERS....................439

In Alphabetical Order by First Name 439

BIBLIOGRAPHY 444

Books....................444

Journal Articles....................454

Additional Sources 461

ABOUT THE AUTHOR....................462

PROLOGUE:
JAMAICA, 1653

IN WHICH A STRONGBOX SEALS SECRETS

The darkness concealed a necklace of scars circling his neck, the origin of his nickname Throat. It also masked the faces of the ne'er-do-wells skulking into the dicing, drinking, and whoring houses that littered the alleyways of King's Square in St. Jago de la Vega, the capital settlement of Jamaica.

Patrolling soldiers passed Throat with no more than a nod, unalarmed by the five pistols strapped to his jet-black doublet, the cutlash that rode his hip, and the amputated appendage he long ago had converted into a knife-hand. Hailing from the Plymouth Colony of New England and born Owen Butler, Throat had served don Francisco de Leiva, the wealthiest and most powerful man on the island, for years. Over time, he had won a position as the Señor's most trusted henchman. Thus, Throat understood better than any the gravity of a summons to de Leiva's personal quarters within the Cabildo at this late hour.

The sound of Throat's boots slapping against the brick stairs echoed down hallways embellished with arabesque archways. Enclosed within the two-story complex were the offices of Jamaica's rulers — Catholic men of *limpieza de sangre* whose pure-blooded ancestors had claimed the island for Spain following the arrival of Christopher Columbus. Though officially they paid deference to the *adelantado* or lieutenant governor of Jamaica, each one bent the knee before the individual who masterminded affairs of state: Don Francisco de Leiva. This man was, moreover, a *familiar* of the Spanish Inquisition. His holy title rendered him untouchable in politics, heavy in purse, beyond all mortal bothers, and terrifying to plain citizens.

The clock struck the third hour after midnight just as Throat entered the elaborate apartments that Señor de Leiva had constructed within Jamaica's municipal headquarters. These consisted of a council room, a salon, a spacious wardrobe, and a false door, behind which hid a decadent boudoir devoted to carnal recreations.

Throat delivered his secret knock: Five measured raps followed by three staccato notes. De Leiva swung the portal open, swishing a robe that was as red as the blood of Christ. Behind him, his concubine Maxi Supa reclined atop silk bedding imported from Paris. Dewdrops of perspiration trickled between her breasts, glistening evidence of their recent congress. Basking in her titillating form, petite and firm, she lay in the splendor of her nakedness whilst focusing upon the two male figures in the room.

De Leiva welcomed Throat to sit upon a mahogany chair that seemed to eat the light from the room's tapers. Once his eyes had adjusted, Throat noticed an ivory strongbox perched atop the nearby escritoire. "Be this the mission, then?" he asked.

"*Claro*, Puritan."

Throat bristled. "Why, after so many years beneath your feet, must you persist in molesting me with that title?"

"Because it exemplifies my dominance over all heretics. Entrusting my secrets to a Puritan elevates my currency amongst the elites and deepens the shivers I provoke amongst the low-born." His master beamed a wry smile.

Throat drew his intact hand across the scars at his wind pipe. "Pray, then, *Señor*, what does the strongbox contain?"

"For the present, that shall remain unknown to you."

"I easily could smash it open with a boot."

"Ahh, but you see?" de Leiva replied. "It may be paneled with elephant tusk, but the inner framework is made from Syrian steel. Furthermore, it is defended by an intricate lock of Moorish make."

"Which I could pick with this blade," Throat proclaimed, brandishing his knife-hand.

De Leiva narrowed his eyes, lifting the strongbox directly before Throat's face. "*Sí*. But that which provides my treasure its utmost protection is neither lock nor steel. Tis this sigil."

When Throat glimpsed the gold emblem, he reared back as if facing a furnace. He fathomed at once its meaning: The seal of the Inquisition struck dread into every heart.

"I place this critical item within your governance," de Leiva declared, handing the strongbox to Throat. "Within the fortnight, you must deliver it to the North Coast, whereupon the ruffian El Mulatto awaits its arrival. From there, the strongbox will sail to Veracruz."

"What smugglers call a ferreting," said Throat.

"I reckon you shall not fuck the swine on this simple task," his master growled.

Throat lowered his gaze. "Never, *Señor*." He wrapped the treasure in a woolen cloth. "I forgo my privilege to question its contents, but… May I ask why the strongbox must be transported northward with all haste?"

Don Francisco de Leiva, who scarcely ever indulged in fermented drink, quaffed a goblet of wine adulterated with water. "Take a mental walk with me," he said.

Throat centered his attention, as did Maxi Supa.

"I wager you know of the king-slayer of England, Lord Oliver Cromwell?" de Leiva questioned rhetorically. "Having committed atrocities upon the Irish, he delivers them as captives to the Caribbean islands, so that they might perish in neglect and poverty. But these indentured servants harbor the blood of the Gauls. Fighters they are, with courage and a craving for freedom in their own corner of the New World. Same holds true of the buccaneers who have occupied our North Coast."

"Because you, in your exclusive authority, invited them to settle there," interjected Throat.

"*Sí*. For the sake of spirited trade! Recall, Puritan, how entirely the Empire of Spain has strangulated commerce amongst these islands. I had no choice but to welcome the smugglers into our borders."

De Leiva paced three steps across the room. "But now the ungrateful buccaneer traitors have teamed up with disgruntled mariners to release a hideous scourge upon this New World – pyrates. And within our hinterland…? Something even worse. African servants have absconded into the mountains and assembled themselves into armed tribes. Imagine! Sea dogs, native Irish hellcats, and hostile blackamoor warriors preparing to battle against us."

De Leiva sank into a chair, pouring a fresh goblet of watery wine. "There is, as well, one other gang uniting with these dung-vermin. They trade in intelligence and multiply their wealth through shrouded wiles. Can you figure who they might be?" he asked.

"I cannot speak with certainty," admitted Throat.

His master scoffed. "The exiled Sephardic Jews, naturally. Who report on the happenings in every port of these West India Islands from *Terre Firme* to Europe and back again. No fox plots amidst the hedges without their knowing."

"Are you the fox, *Señor*?"

"One who wanders in the shadowed woods, but who searches for the hidden snares," de Leiva confirmed. Then he fell into a hush, consulting his worries before articulating their omen. "War is in the wind."

Throat scrutinized his master. "Tis a curse to live in such interesting times."

"Forsooth! All the countries of Europe race to declare themselves against Spain. They pine for a clash. But these outside perils increasingly are matched by hazards breeding within our domain. Hostiles surround us, Owen Butler." Don Francisco de Leiva downed his watery wine and charged his goblet once more. "The world is writing a new page. The Most Catholic Empire of Spain no longer can thrive by mining money straight from the earth in the shape of gold and silver dust. The Dutch have fashioned a republic, and also contrived a system of capital syndicates that permits people from any background to accumulate wealth. England has emptied its throne of a monarch. Enterprisers everywhere clamber for power. The French have coined a new term for these types: *entrepreneurs*."

"Arghh," Throat rumbled. "Tis the yearning for change that brings the terms for war."

"My darling Protestant, your eyes have opened." De Leiva's aspect had gone cold and hollow. "Approaching is a collision between autocrats and their challengers – those who say they are determined by equality and free will. Only the most ruthless shall win the future and stamp out the past."

Stowing the cloaked coffer beneath an arm, Throat asked, "I suspect there is no true treasure residing within this coffer? No gems nor glittery ore, eh?"

"It contains riches more valuable than coin. Get on before the end of night," de Leiva insisted. "Enemies circle us."

Throat threw a glance at the naked figure reclining upon the bed. "And what of her? She who has recorded our discourse?"

"Maxi?" de Leiva replied, eyebrows raised. "When I purchased that Quechua woman from the silver city of Potosí, I had her plead the blood of Christ. I can put my first and last trust in the *concubina*. She shall not sully her dignity in the dirt of men's ploys."

"But in that very dirt is where secrets are buried," Throat replied.

Don Francisco de Leiva grasped his elbow and steered his most trusted henchman out the chamber door toward the ink of dawn.

Chapter 1

JAMAICA

IN WHICH THE WAY FORWARD IS DOUBTED

Their scout, a scrawny indentured Taíno boy aged ten years, gawked at Throat's macabre features. The scars about the man's neck were chilling enough, but it was the stump of his right wrist that truly horrified the child. Where there ought to have been a hand was lashed a six-inch blade.

Their detachment had stalled ten miles following its departure from St. Jago de la Vega. Thirty men – baggage slaves, mercenaries, and musketeers – halted at the crossroads beneath the heights of Monte Diablo while Throat brushed against his apprehension. Troubled by their current course, don Francisco de Leiva's most prized henchman dismounted his mule, yanked off his leather hat, and spanked at the gnats vexing him. His black hair sprang skyward in a fuss.

For the first time, the full portrait of Throat's funerary features were exposed to the young Taíno tracker. Perhaps in honor of his terrifying anatomy, Santángel speculated,

Throat attired himself as an ominous entity. He rejected the customary stockings and shirt of the era, donning instead black breeches and a matching silk vest. His arms, untouched by the gunpowder tattoos preferred by many of his ilk, remained milky pale despite the pounding blaze of the tropical sun. To Santángel, Throat appeared as nothing less than the cousin of Lucifer.

"And?" Throat snarled at the *encomienda* in Spanish. "You are certain on this route?"

Santángel coughed the fright from his gullet. "All is well," he replied. "This ancient path was once a prime trade-way for my people. It will give us to Porto Anton before the week's end."

Throat grunted his mistrust. He stared into the distance, where the hills vibrated in prismatic greens, and beyond, to where saw-tooth pinnacles rose. Given the strict schedule, he determined it best to continue with Santángel's selected pathway. He dared not disappoint his master. He saddled his mule again and spurred the beast into movement.

Zacuto, a secondary *bravo* or henchman of don Francisco de Leiva, synchronized his mule's step alongside Throat's. "Are you certain you want to follow that mamey nut?" he asked in Spanish. "Although he swore his allegiance to the One True Faith, I doubt Santángel surrenders to Christ during Mass."

The Catholicized boy, marching on foot aside the two men, swiveled nervously. Zacuto snapped at him like a crocodile and began tinkering with his vermillion *faja*, a sash accommodating three blades: trencher, bodkin, and machete. "The choicest route would be to cut through the Boca and wind a way up Monte Diablo." He flicked a finger at the youth. "Only a bottled worm like this one would coax us through the windward ascendancies."

Throat controlled his response. Aside from feeling too heat-queasy to strain his elementary Spanish, he refrigerated an ample dose of derision for Zacuto. The *bravo*'s moniker meant left-handed, suggesting the man's sinister inclinations. Zacuto had a reputation for deciding disputes by pistol shot through the back.

"Clock my prophesy," Zacuto continued. "This polluted Indian will steer us into a forest grove where his blood-guzzling kind, wearing testicle bells squeezed into monkey girdles, aspire to kill us and make off with de Leiva's treasure."

Throat's eyes darkened. "Ho, is that the sneaking subject that has you babbling so?" He sent the accusation through an abrupt shift to English.

Zacuto squirmed. His gaze slid toward the mule secured at the middle of the train of four pack animals. Unlike the others, she was not burdened with weapons, drinking water, or provender for their journey. Fastened upon her saddle was nothing more than a pile of blankets concealing the ivory strongbox.

"Surely by this time you have inquired as to the contents of de Leiva's coffer?" Zacuto asked.

Throat spurred his ride onward.

Zacuto sped into pace. "No?" he needled. "Don Francisco discriminates against even you? Bitter pity!"

Neglecting subtlety, Throat raked the stub of his knife-hand.

"Listen here, good fellow. Why not solve the mystery now?" Zacuto urged. "We are entitled to know de Leiva's secret. It is our lives he has imperiled with this journey, not his own."

"Clap your trap," Throat growled. "I'm the wrong man to attempt as a friend."

Zacuto, still, would not relent. "Would you not like to swim in riches, Throat? Say we chop through that box and learn how it holds an extraordinary pile of silver coin. Diamonds. Jewels. Or greater even than that?"

Throat rounded on him. "*¿Incluso mayor que qué?*"

"*¿Qué?!*"

"Even greater than what? You said a thing 'greater than silver, diamonds or jewels.' What you reckon is more desirable than that?" Throat asked.

Zacuto stared blankly. "I... I..." he stammered, blushing. "I know nothing! Nothing at all, I swear to you. I only was conducting speculative talk for our amusement."

"Wiser not to," Throat snorted. "Do you sincerely believe that our master, the omnipotent don Francisco de Leiva, transports his fortune in a bin? You sand trout! Whatever is in this coffer is far more thunder-striking."

Red-faced, Zacuto retreated at last.

Throat paused to sup sweet wine from a leather blackjack hitched to his mule. It troubled him that his companion had uttered the fact of it: De Leiva had cloaked every detail of this errand in secrecy. Throat still knew nothing of the nature of the item he was porting. Naturally, he was burning to unveil its mystery, but opening the strongbox was a capital crime. He would not act. He was all too familiar with the brutal punishments his master extracted for even minor infractions.

IN WHICH SICKNESS STRIKES

The team lumbered forth another three days with mules battling through choking vegetation. Always they set out at first light. Always by mid-morning, the sun annihilated their senses. After 12 hours enduring heat compounded by stifling humidity and red dust, they were reduced to ragged puddles.

In a moment of weakness, a mixed Spanish-Taíno servant whined about his exhaustion. Throat responded by tying his wrists to a baggage mule and cinching the beast's weighty cargo around the miserable man's neck.

As they forded the Rio Cobre, two of the men's faces grew pale. Eyes marbled red. By nightfall, five in their convoy had begun vomiting a black, viscous fluid. Their wretching and groaning haunted the dark hours. At dawn, the *mestizo* whom Throat had shackled to the mule dropped dead. Soon, others lost strength. Within a few days, the plague had struck nine – more than a third of the troop.

Zacuto postulated that the party had been poisoned by a toxic leaf such as jimson weed.

"No, this is Barbados distemper," Santángel argued. The child reminded Zacuto that most Jamaican bondservants were conscripted from an area south of St. Jago de La Vega referred to as *La Otra Banda.* The Other Side was a fetid plot of land left to the most depraved and rebuked island residents. Outbreaks of diseases such as Barbados distemper, also known as yellow fever, were common.

Throat spurred Santángel to find a tolerable retreat. The boy led the group to a wan Taíno community. With musket and sword, the men drove the Amerindian natives shrieking from their village of eight circular dwellings.

By now, fully half the crew had fallen sick and two more had perished in agony. Those clinging to their health unloaded the mules and hauled the goods into the simple round *bohío* shelters constructed from wood and palm leaves. Throat secured de Leiva's chest within the eight-foot circumference of the hut he had preempted.

That night, Catholic men supplicated before the Blessed Virgin Mary and begged the protection of St. Michael the Archangel. Island natives and men hailing from the Guinea Coast of Africa invoked their tribal deities. All confronted desperation.

Upon the red-clay floor of his hijacked dwelling, Throat carved the shape of a scythe. Around the outside of his *bohío* he etched a pentagram. Born of Black Magic and scarred forever by it, he was more intimate with witchcraft than the others ever would have suspected. He felt it wise to take his own precautions.

IN WHICH A CRIME IS COMMITTED

Throat awakened with renewed vitality and called upon the hut of Zacuto. The Spanish *bravo* lulled atop a mat of plaited coconut fronds, exhibiting no symptoms aside from a cantankerous spirit.

"We ought forsake the afflicted," Throat suggested, his voice low so as not to prick the ears of those languishing close by. "We are but two days shy of Porto Anton. As I judge it, eleven men have stamina enough to continue. You?"

Without delay, Zacuto agreed. He and the healthiest cohorts proceeded to feed, water, and burden the mules. Afternoon sun-rays sliced through the treetops as they secured their weapons to the train.

It came time for Throat to hitch the portentous ivory chest to the center mule. But when he retreated to his *bohío*, he happened upon Santángel hunched over the strongbox. The *encomienda* had snapped a musket tamper into its lock.

"*Buenas*," Throat remarked casually.

The ten-year-old whirled round. "I have committed no offense!" he objected before having been accused.

"Shhhhh," Throat whispered.

"I am a simple child. Zacuto dragooned me!"

"Do you comprehend not the meaning of the escutcheon?" Throat asked. His voice was laced with an eerie tenderness affecting the nuances of parenting. He ticked his finger at the golden seal and stalked closer to the boy. "Look how Christ faces downward, his head pointing into the sun. The implication is stark: Those who defy the Lord shall be bound to the scaffold and condemned to the flames in a compulsory act of faith: the *auto-da-fé*."

Santángel backed against the hut's woven palm wall.

Throat continued. "Do you not fear the dire seal of the Tribunal, child? Tis a gold plate used only by familiars of the Holy Inquisition. The crest specifies that this strongbox is intended for none other than King Felipe IV of Spain."

Throat grazed the boy's chin with his blade-hand. "Not a soul amongst us is brave enough to tamper with it."

Santángel was shaking. "I had no choice," he squeaked. "Zacuto threatened to slay me if I did not open the box! He said he would unspool my bowels."

"Trust me, boy, your execution is a sure fact. Zacuto is the smallest of your worries now. Don Francisco de Leiva shall not grant you the kindness of gutting you, oh no. He shall burn you alive at the stake – a death far more..." Throat searched his mind for a comparison. "Let's just say that a broiled human is quite the shrieker. Tis the worst punishment humans have devised."

Tears rushed from Santángel's eyes. "Zacuto swore to secure my freedom if I accomplished this single deed for him. He swore upon Santa Maria!"

Throat consoled the boy by knuckling his soft cheek with his flesh-hand. "I shall not divulge your misdeed. Not to anyone," he promised.

"I will do anything you ask, *Señor*, anything," Santángel whimpered. Outside, they heard Zacuto punishing the lassitude of a stray servant with a whipping strap.

"I ought tell you something, boy," Throat said. "This freedom you pine over? Why, it exists not. There is no freedom from the regime of living. If I were to abolish your chains, how do you think it would alter your life?"

The *encomienda*'s eyes widened. "I would lark away my days taking siestas, gobbling cashews and bananas, and listening to the songs of doves. I would fish in cool streams, learn the pleasure of sailing a piragua upon a breezy sea... perhaps turn pyrate."

"No, Santángel, you would not," Throat snapped. "Even if I delivered you to freedom, you still would not qualify as free. You would remain an uneducated eyesore in the minds of the highborn. Your complexion still would be the incorrect color, proving your membership in a degenerate and unwanted race. No matter your situation nor the value of your youth, you again would be constrained, expended, and abused. In a handful of years, you would grow sickly, and when they deemed you an invalid, you would be thrown to the dogs for supper. Where is the saving in that?"

"You speak as an old hand on this subject. Is it correct, then, what is rumored about you?" Santángel asked. "That you, also, are the bonded property of don Francisco de Leiva?"

Throat cocked an eyebrow. "Every single one of us is confined by one condition or another. The only possible redemption comes from mounting the strength to widen our cage."

Santángel nodded weakly. Impatient mules brayed beyond the thatch walls. Zacuto sounded a whistle, indicating that they were ready to depart.

"Now give me a hand with this coveted chest," Throat said, pressing the treasure into Santángel's arms.

With newfound surety, the boy accepted the strongbox and stepped out from the *bohío*. Throat trailed, searching for Zacuto. The *bravo* scowled the moment he registered the child's cheerful demeanor and the ivory coffer – still sealed – cradled in his arms.

Raising his voice for all to hear, Throat declared, "We cannot be gracious to the meek." Abruptly, he plunged his poniard-hand into the back of Santángel's neck. The blade broke through the boy's trachea and popped out his mouth like a glistening tongue.

Santángel emitted a croak. Throat withdrew the knife and reclaimed the strongbox just before the child collapsed to the dirt gripping his blood-spurting larynx. The other men trembled, but Throat watched with fascination as Santángel tossed about in the grass, irrigating it with his life force. Moments later, the child expired.

Throat grunted his approval. He recovered his kerchief and used it to clean his dagger-hand before issuing a command. "*Vámanos*!"

IN WHICH MAROONS & MONKEYS MAKE MISCHIEF

Throat pressed his diminished crew of 12 onward. He was pleased with how the yellow fever had taken hold at the most effective moment thanks to his deliberate inclusion of the infected mestizo in their company. He himself already had suffered from yellow fever; he could not contract it again. By late the next morning, they would be close enough to Porto Anton for him to complete his pruning of the group, as de Leiva had instructed, thus ensuring the secrecy of the mission. Throat reckoned he would have the two remaining musketeers murder three servants a piece as an exercise in fidelity. Killing Zacuto would be Throat's gratifying task.

Mashed fools, he mused. *They are utterly unwise to the evidence: Masterpieces can be wrought more readily by the sudden grip of savagery than by the gentle caress of the brush.*

Zacuto deemed it judicious to make another bid for friendship. He spurred his mule alongside Throat's. "Have you newsed recently?" he queried in stumbling English.

Throat ignored the *bravo*, for at that moment, their cavalcade emerged from the woodlands. In an open glade, they were greeted by the scents of flowers and banana trees. Throat closed his eyes, reveling in the gusts of cool air blowing in from the sea.

"I've heard that some men loyal to the monarchy are plotting the assassination of the king-slayer Oliver Cromwell, the self-coronated Lord of England," Throat responded at last. He tossed Zacuto an expression of counterfeited conviviality.

"Shall we light a pipe?" Zacuto replied in Spanish, unable to interpret Throat's English. He rifled unsuccessfully through his *aparejo* in search of his paraphernalia.

They trotted a mile in silence whilst the others swapped tidings, bawdy stories, and cakes of *cazabe*. After an awkward breather, Zacuto resumed their socializing, this time in Spanish. "The scallywag Wim Jackson has been placed under arrest."

"Is that so?" The information blindsided Throat.

"*Verdad*," the Spanish *bravo* attested. "I hear it this way: He is to have his neck stretched upon the isle of Saint Kitts for crimes of rovering."

All of Jamaica recalled the tale of the notorious William "Wim" Jackson. Ten years earlier, in 1643, the pyrate – with nothing more than one hulk, a pinnace, and two pinks – had conquered Jamaica's capital of St. Jago de la Vega. The government had been forced to pay a ransom of 250 head of steer, a glut of cassava, and 8,000 pieces of eight in order to convince Wim to sail elsewhere. Some of his crew, having developed a love for Jamaica's bountiful hills and bays, had chosen to remain behind – including one Owen Butler, soon to be renamed Throat. Today, these rogues made up the majority of the island's English-speaking population.

Throat was unwilling to disclose his prior association with Wim Jackson, however. He said merely, "No. Not possible. The Englishmen of St. Kitts would never dance their hero from the gallows."

"Tis true, believe me," Zacuto maintained. "The English and the French of St. Kitts have determined that they must put an end to Wim Jackson. They are terrified of the contagion of pyracy spreading throughout West Indias. And amidst their shivers comes now a new rogue – the one called Iron Eyes. You have heard of him, no?"

Throat turned away from Zacuto, his interest pulled again to the path before them. They were entering into Jamaica's dangerous North Coast territory. Void of Spanish settlements and soldiers, it was here that daring runaways and ignoble smugglers, buccaneers, and pyrates ruled.

"Iron Eyes. *¡Madre, mia!* That rogue is calamity incarnate," Zacuto babbled. "Word of his triumph over the Treasure Fleet reverberates like thunder. The master countries of Europe are scrambling with alarm over news of this stunning scoundrel. He excites pyrates across all ports of the Caribbean."

The procession entered a field of bending elephant grass and towering kapok trees. Throat observed the two musketeers at the front of the line.

Zacuto jawed on, oblivious. "Iron Eyes and his men could bend entire islands to their knees, far outreaching any feat Wim Jackson performed. What if the reckoning of the damned be upon us?"

"Shut your blow-hole!" Throat snapped, spurring his mule forward.

He could not specify from whence the solitary figure had appeared, but there she stood in the middle of their pathway. Ahead of him, the musketeers hitched the four pack mules to the nearest tree and crept upon the Negro woman.

Although bowed slightly by the burden of a maiden's yoke, the pole across her shoulders bearing two ponderous pails, she strolled effortlessly. She was of modest stature, strong and bony. In spite of having aged some three decades, her skin was faultless. Her nose was broad, her lips full. Her finely-woven tresses, bound by a butterfly knot at the back of her head, contributed to her regal appearance, even though she was clothed in nothing more than a ragged smock.

Under the soldiers' covetous gaze, the woman froze. Yet she disclosed no fear. Nor did she lay down the staff crushing her shoulders.

Throat recognized a warrior when he saw one. This was no servant.

Enjoying the views exposed by her ramshackle dress, Zacuto's eyes feasted upon her body – the curve of her shoulder, the small soft round of her belly, the sidelong swell of her left breast. The others, too, were intoxicated. Throat discerned each of his men lusting for a turn with her. And after such a straining journey, it was customary that he should enable their cravings.

"This sleek and wild-eyed black mare is the exact type of beast I relish breaking," proclaimed the closest musketeer.

"Do so, and I reckon she will blast a new mouth into the back of your head," Throat retorted. Instead of approaching, he edged away.

Los Cimmarónes, it dawned upon him. The Maroons. The epithet had been smeared upon escaped slaves by the Spaniards, who likened the people to stray big-horns they had been tasked to retrieve. When they fled, the Maroons infiltrated the mountains, where they founded tribes amongst the island's most forbidding regions. Their existence tormented don Francisco de Leiva. They lived as inflammatory insurrectionists, raiding estates for weapons, freeing the enslaved, poaching cattle and hogs, and laying waste to Spanish landowners.

The most infamous leader of the three Maroons tribes of Jamaica was a woman who called herself Nani.

Throat yelled at the musketeer to fall back. But it was too late. Already he was reeling backwards. "*Bruja! Bruja*!" he shrieked. "Witch!"

Throat scarcely could track the implausible eruption of events. Nani's buckets somehow had begun to gurgle, as though steaming with piping hot water. They boiled over without any flame.

"Slay her!" Throat commanded his men. They loosed blunderbusses, but before a single shot was fired, Nani whirled and flung her scalding water upon the nearest musketeer. He dropped to his knees bawling in pain.

In one graceful stroke, Nani turned her shoulder pole into a lance. She gored the second musketeer as he flew at her, dispatching him on the spot.

Throat aimed his pistol and shot. Yanking a baggage slave in front of her, Nani used his body as armor. Throat's roundshot shattered the boy's sternum but left her untouched.

The mules were jabbering now with terror. Zacuto's animal hopped like an unsprung madcap, ejecting him onto the grass. Throat bit through a fresh cartridge as Nani closed upon him. There were still six uninjured men, including Zacuto. Several baggage-slaves fired from behind the barricade of animals. Nani speared one through the neck. Errant balls pelted the ground and whistled into the trees, but none grazed her.

More determined than ever, Throat tamped his barrel, slid away the rod, and sighted his target. He executed a flawless shot. Lead skimmed the Maroon queen's shoulder. Her clavicle spouted blood and she toppled to one knee. He closed in for the kill.

He was steadying his pistol for the fatal round when the trees shuddered and the canopy above broke open. Throat gaped as a living nightmare unfolded. Leaping black shapes blotted the sun-bleached sky – claws out, fanged and deadly.

He could not fathom what was happening. Monkeys? Yes, a horde of small drab grey and reddish-brown monkeys was sailing down from the treetops and attacking his men. In packs of three and four, the beasts jumped upon each human. They chewed at faces, gouged eyes, and dug yellowed claws into neck-sides. Screams pierced the ear like jagged icicles. Sighting a dark streak from the corner of his eye, he backhanded his cutlash and struck one down.

Throat was agog. He had heard the gossip that some still survived in the mountains, but not ever had he witnessed monkeys upon the isle of Jamaica. Certainly, no one ever had reported the rare, diminutive creatures attacking humans. Yet here they were, evidently having cast an intelligent allegiance with Nani. He counted 30 of them. They clambered and clung, swiping and biting. Those who were not shredding the men hurled coconuts and feces.

Within minutes, Throat's retinue was annihilated in rolling agonies. He thrust himself into the melee in search of Nani. There he encountered an even more bestial shape. It thudded out of the branches on four feet but quickly ascended onto two hind legs, standing taller than him by a foot. What Throat figured at first for bristly fur he quickly realized was a coat of grass and caked mud. The creature's eyes were wide and dark and it smelled of fruity rot.

Then, through a net of the creature's matted hair, Throat spied a face that looked and moved like his own. The aberration was as far removed from a monkey as his own self. It was human.

"Sasa!" Nani called. The monkey man edged past Throat and ran full speed in her direction. Suspended in awe, Throat judged the beast a hex conjured by her sorcery.

Zacuto, recovered from his fall, aimed his pistol at Nani's head. But the shot flew haywire as Sasa rammed into him. The mankey secured Zacuto's neck in his powerful grasp.

The Maroon leader snatched up the fallen guns as they bounced into the elephant grass, turning them upon the remaining men. Throat skewered monkeys with his blade-hand.

"God-a-mercy, we are but servants low-to-the ground! We beg for quarter!" plead the two baggage-drudgers still living, one of African origin, the other Arawak. Nani barked a clipped directive, and the monkeys tearing at their skin dispersed. Dumbstruck by the sudden grace, the men bolted for the mountains, hurrying, in all likelihood, to join the free Maroon peoples.

The field now bore a bloody display of carcasses both clothed and furred. The sole living participants – notwithstanding a score of monkeys – were Zacuto, Throat, Sasa and Nani. The Spanish *bravo* sputtered, still immobilized by the mankey's chokehold.

"Fetch the strongbox!" the Maroon queen directed Sasa in Spanish. This hurled Throat further into a state of mystification. How in Satan's name did she come to possess knowledge of de Leiva's precious coffer?

Zacuto saw a chance to rescue himself. He twitched his eyes, signaling the hiding place of the strongbox. It was tucked beneath the hefty woolen covers burdening the mule nearest them. At once, the mankey cast aside his quarry and aimed for the prize.

Throat, meanwhile, whirled his cutlash and harpooned the monkey that had been gnawing on his thigh. He stood no more than 20 paces afar from Nani. She appraised him coldly as she raised her voice to hasten Sasa's looting. It took Sasa mere seconds to bite through the lashings on the mule's saddle. He liberated de Leiva's chest just as Zacuto erupted with howls, a half dozen monkeys falling upon him.

Throat strode toward Nani, his left arm unfolding a pistol. *You shall not blunder this shot,* he assured himself. Blood trickled from her shoulder. Throat raised his arm. She glowered. The barrel kicked. The thumping of the shot echoed off the trees. Nani fell over.

Throat stood over her, triumphant. He reckoned the shot had punctured her lungs or possibly nicked her heart. But although Nani's filthy grey shift was stained with blood from the wound that had plastered her shoulder, there was no hole in her chest. No mark at all.

She fluttered her eyes open and locked them upon Throat. Then she unclasped her right hand, displaying a fist full of blood. Nestled within the red slick of her palm was the lead ball he had fired seconds ago.

Great Cronus! thought Throat. *She caught the shot in her bare hand?* He was speechless. In his 15 years of living amongst the witchery of Salem, never had he encountered or even conceived of such a possibility through the dark arts.

With all the other men now dead or having spirited into flight, the monkeys turned their attention upon Throat. Panicked by Nani's exhibits of necromancy, he raced as fast as his legs could carry. Tearing across the meadow, he anticipated the grunt of musket fire, the clawing hand of the mankey around his neck. Neither came.

Nani stood but did not give chase. Sasa questioned her with a look.

"No," she said. "Let him be. His telling of this event shall spark a crisis for *Señor* de Leiva. And with a touch of fortune, it shall draw forth another avenger of the dispossessed: the Jewish smuggler Gaspar Carvalhal."

Chapter 2

JAMAICA

IN WHICH A SMUGGLER IS DRUGGED

The Jewish smuggler Gaspar Carvalhal fretted impatiently at midnight on January 13, 1653, the date and hour dictated by the Maroons for their rendezvous. He and his complement of 30 contrabandistas remained aboard their ship as instructed. This month's full moon, revered by the Arawak and several African tribes as *the listening moon*, stared down upon them with particular intensity.

Their vessel, the Soltera, was the sleekest pinnace ever to have contested the Caribbean seas. Presently, she was moored upon Jamaica's North Coast just off the fledgling outpost of Las Chorréras, a location that modernity would rechristen as Ocho Rios. Her crew, tranquilized with boredom, yawned away the hours with dice and rounds of faro, their card game of choice. Consumption of distilled spirits was not permitted by their captain. Carvalhal, meanwhile, paced the planks, calming his turbulent nerves by suckling a clay pipe.

Just before the sun awakened, *abeng* horns – trumpets fashioned from the antlers of longhorn steers — sounded from the depths of nowhere. The ear-splitting alarm excited terror amongst the slumbering smugglers. But Carvalhal, who had educated himself as to the messages blasted from Maroon *abengs*, knew they blared not a warning but a welcome.

From the mist of daybreak three dugouts encroached upon the smuggler's vessel. Soon, Nani's delegation of 18 men had joined the *contrabandistas* in hauling two-score crates out of the Soltera's hold and onto the Maroon bacassas. The weight of the cargo caused the crafts to slouch into the sea.

Carvalhal left the labors to those in the bloom of youth. Having reached the remarkable age of 45, the smuggler was no longer held captive by his manhood. Whilst the years may have preyed upon his strength, they also had reinforced him with wisdom. His graying hair warned any feather-brains who crossed him that he was cunning enough to survive.

The sun had reached its zenith by the time the last chest of merchandise had been hefted. "Come you!" snarled JoJo. Even clothed in tatters, the 16-year-old was an obsidian spike of certitude whose musculature had been sculpted from a strenuous life. Head held high, prominent nose upturned, her tresses were tamed in a butterfly knot at the back of her head, mimicking the fashion preferred by her mother.

Carvalhal asked his crew to regroup 20 paces afar. This placed him in a vulnerable position – and, critically, demonstrated his respect for the Maroons.

For over a year before he had met them, the smuggler had studied the elusive mountain rebels, interrogating every person he encountered who possessed knowledge of them as to Maroon customs. His tactic had proven successful. Gaspar Carvalhal was presently the sole person of European descent to have secured recurring trade rights with the Windward Maroons. Beyond him, none outside their own tribe – no matter the tint of their skin, nor the story of their origin, nor the promise of their reward – ever enjoyed mingling directly with their leader, the Obiya sorceress Nani.

"The chieftain Nani requires your presence. By her authority, undertake the passage alone, with not one of your men," JoJo declared in Spanish.

"Aye, Josefina," Carvalhal conceded, observing the formality of her christened name, which had been pressed upon her from a birth in bondage.

JoJo bristled at its sound.

The Maroons fixed Gaspar Carvalhal upon the thwarts of a canoe between a gang of Africano and criollo warriors. The oarsmen raked the kapok dugout past churning waters where rivers emptied into the sea.

Nani's daughter presented a clenched hand.

"What is this?"

"You know, smuggler," JoJo replied. "Skullmurk."

Carvalhal snatched the crab claw from JoJo's palm and tilted its powder into his mouth. He grimaced at the skullmurk's tang of urine, bitter-root, and dead fish. For the space of a day, the plant medicine would rob him of his mental faculties. It certified that he would not recall the location of their encampment.

In minutes, his jaw turned to wood. By the time the canoe had touched shore, Carvalhal could not place their position. The Maroons stashed their vessels into hideaways of undergrowth, burdened a handful of mules with the crates he had provided, and commenced a hike into mountainous territory. Carvalhal stumbled clumsily behind them.

IN WHICH A SMUGGLER IS BEDDED

A whistle sounded in the darkness. Carvalhal startled. "Where went the sun?" he slurred through tangled thickets of thought. The usually dapper runagate resembled a crumpled poem — slack-jawed, doublet askew, his tousled locks a windblown battlefield. A ring of Maroon chuckles buzzed through his ears.

From behind the trees, 20 more Maroon rebels crept into sight. Carvalhal blinked through the phantom moonlight. He could not find Nani amongst the crowd. The skullmurk tenaciously gripped his senses.

The Maroons got to alighting the burros. JoJo snatched an adze, twirled the instrument overhead and, with blade reversed, crashed it through the chests. The tribe dug the treasures out from the straw bedding.

Displeasure dimmed into scowls as the Maroons surveyed the goods. "These are not the sterling commodities of Bordeaux and Nantes," complained the giant Alzo. "The muskets are of irregular length. The flintlocks lack springs."

"They're all crank," jeered Santo. "These guns are Spanish rejects. Carvalhal, you insult us with a stock of cow-turd!"

JoJo glared at her companions, eyes webbed red from exhaustion. "You done with your bellyaching? Do you forget how dire is our need for weapons?" She approached the smuggler, speaking slowly. "We accept these tarnished arms with gratitude. Now my mother demands a private audience."

Carvalhal smiled. The circuits between his mind and mouth had been disconnected.

"Don't act a child," JoJo growled. "Your capacities of deduction may have curdled into a lumpy gruel, but you're no boor. Behave, Gaspar, else you'll face the hex of a most inconvenient Obiya curse." She teased her finger at him with a wry grin.

He followed her into the foliage. Some half hour later, they came upon a lonely dale.

"I leave you here," JoJo said, pointing at an *ajoupa*. The traditional Caribbean thatch-roofed dwelling was boned by bamboo and clothed with banana leaves. Traditional Taíno construction always left one wall open. This one, Carvalhal noted, was enclosed on all sides, affording privacy. Through spaces in the thatch, he detected the sultry dance of shimmering candles.

He circled the dwelling until he came upon a small opening. Entering, he saw Nani standing alone against a wall beamed by coconut branches. She was garbed in her customary gossamer shift, and from her neck hung a cord of white caiman teeth. A fire played in the small stone pit at the structure's center. Upon a desiccated tree stump that served as a table she had lit a dozen tapers. The effect was mesmerizing. The flickering light built her already elevated status to that of Goddess.

The Maroon chieftain had covered the floor with soft animal hides. Upon a second stump table in the far corner, Carvalhal could make out a rectangular white object. He took several steps closer, mouth hanging open.

Atop the coffer's lid was emblazoned the symbol of the Spanish Inquisition. *Could it be?* he marveled. Nabbing the strongbox had been a far-fetched possibility. *Is this truly don Francisco de Leiva's most mysterious parcel?*

But he did not voice the question. Instead, he pointed at the bandages on Nani's shoulder and hand. "What wounds are these? What happened?" he asked with mounting concern.

She probed the dressings of rusted blood on her right hand, and shrugged. "Tis no matter."

He squinted, attempting to expel the last drops of skullmurk from his mind. He desired terribly to visit her with capacities intact.

As if reading his thoughts, Nani gave him a calabash of fragrant liquid. "Drink."

"Thank you!" Carvalhal grasped the gourd and gulped and gulped. Within minutes, his clarity was restored. He motioned to the ivory chest. "I see you have greeted success in our quest. Tis beyond belief."

She ignored him. Moving about the hut, she anointed each of its four posts with a splash of blood and rum drawn from a bark bowl.

"Truly you have retrieved from don Francisco de Leiva a crucial object, my queen," he pushed. "It shall be my pleasure to turn it against him."

"It shall be my pleasure for you to make naked," Nani replied, eyes frisking him. With a swoop, she undid her knotted tresses, allowing them to tumble over her sculpted shoulders.

He offered a sheepish look.

"Now you."

Carvalhal hesitated.

"Make naked now," Nani ordered. Her voice was carnal, greedy.

He renounced his weapons, slithered off his shirt, and dropped his breeches to reveal a penis fully erect. From the *ajoupa*'s opposite wall, she feasted upon his swollen manhood and the straps that decorated his torso where it met his thighs. "Fetch me your pistol."

He complied.

She grasped the gun in her capable hand and aimed it at his chest. His heart felt as though it were stampeding horses – but not from fear. Those seconds revealed to him how deeply he had come to trust Nani in their three years of knowing one another. Stalking him in concentric circles, she roamed his pistol over his body. His breathing escalated to a pant. She was, he thought, beautiful in the most terrifying manner.

With the steel of the barrel pressing against his temple, she commanded Gaspar to drop to his knees. Then, hoisting her smock, she moved in front of him. She bumped his head forward with the pistol so that he crouched directly between her legs, filling his face with her swollen wetness. When his tongue drew designs upon her pleasure spot, her breath tightened. His hands swam over her firm buttocks and up her back as the flintlock clapped against his ear. Gaspar's heart leaped. The livened weapon injected a distinct drama into their union.

Now Nani moved him away. Whilst still training the weapon upon Gaspar, she peeled the chemise off her shoulders with her injured hand and dropped it to the ground.

For half a second, Carvalhal studied the merchant's mark upon her belly that had, two decades ago, branded her as enslaved property. He touched it delicately, but she grabbed his hand and moved it to her nipples. He encircled them until they hardened.

When at last she prompted him to the floor of cattle skins, his cock was roaring stiff to the point of aching. She laughed softly, licked the droplet that beaded its tip, and climbed atop him, slipping his substantial length inside her.

His hunger fevered. Perfumed with sweat and vanilla bean, her tits brushed him. The need to feel them plunging within his mouth overwhelmed him. As he sucked, he heard her slide away the gun. Enthralled by bliss, Nani bit his neck. When she grasped his penis in the molten vise of her pelvic muscles, it sent his mind into orbit. He nearly fired.

"No, wait," she commanded, grinding atop him. Her ass heaved. She yearned for no sensation beyond that of her feminine depths filled by his cock. He grew thicker. She moaned in waves of ecstasy. Her quim was spanking wet upon his balls.

The banging turned frantic, their fucking rampant. The Devil was pouring paradise into her soul. God was irrelevant. She worked madness upon his organ until she crashed atop him. He climaxed with the grunt of a boar, she with a strange howl. Together they flopped satiated upon the animal-skin floor.

IN WHICH A SMUGGLER IS TRUSTED

The dawn was awakening the wilderness with song when Nani returned to the hut, bathed and bearing slaughtered wood-pigeon and partridge for breakfast. Carvalhal, who had slept the dreamless slumber of the drugged, fastened his breeches and stood wide-eyed before her, shirtless, unshod, and vulnerable. His desire churned with a different hunger at the site of the freshly-killed foul.

Carvalhal and Nani stared silently at one another, unmoving. Despite their turbulent existences, each of them had clung to a desire for partnership true and equal. But this was always left unspoken. Every time Gaspar Carvalhal lay with Nani, he surrendered his adoration at her feet. He expanded her trust, and each time chipped away the armor that sheltered her own heart. Was it possible they had chanced upon the culmination of their deepest desires, one in the other?

Nani felt the pull of an anguished longing to ask him, "Do you view any belief as truth?"

He took her in with tender eyes. "Yes. Love. Love is truth."

His words decimated her. *Love? Love!* She began to sob. Water rained from her eyes.

Carvalhal seized her with panic at having upset her so. He drew her to the cushioned floor and took her upon his lap. "Hush, hush," he whispered into her ear.

Nani, engulfed by grief and rage, was robbed of speech. The simple sincerity of Carvalhal's statement was too strong for her to bear after a lifetime scarred by betrayal and outright abuse. Romantic love was impractical. She could not sneak love from out her dreams and into the beating light of day. She despised his mere mentioning of it.

Carvalhal remained calm in the face of her hurricane. From the core of his being, he believed that nothing could trample their feelings for one another. Their love belonged to them and them alone. He breathed through her explosions, holding her tight in his arms.

When her rancor waned, Nani softened into his embrace. She surprised herself by confessing aloud, "Never will I stop loving you, Gaspar Carvalhal. That is a truth of mine."

"As it is with me," he replied, lifting her lips to meet his in a deep kiss.

And yet.

Each lover tacitly accepted that wishful reveries of a life together could only rouse the frowning fates. Nani and Gaspar had no choice but to forbid romantic love a place in their lives. They could not spare the effort required for intimacy nor heartbreak. Both had actual empires to topple and tribes of beloved followers to lead. Both faced a future rampant with risk, in which every outcome was uncertain other than a violent death.

Emancipating herself at last from his arms, Nani reflected. Even though deprived of his daily partnership, Carvalhal's presence in her life still served a transcendent purpose. It gave her hope. *Hope is a seed*, she thought. *And from that seed, virtue and decency can flower within even the most malnourished garden.*

IN WHICH A LIFE IS STOLEN

They stepped outside the *ajoupa*. Carvalhal tackled the task of collecting fuel for a fire. Nani stationed herself upon a mahoe tree stump and trussed the birds for roasting.

Gazing at her authoritative beauty, Carvalhal sighed, once again enchanted and troubled by the radiance of her strength. How many times has she been betrayed by force and violated? He worried. He knew her courage had been forged from broken pieces.

He summoned his own grit and braved the inquiry. "I long to feel closer to you, Nani." He took a seat upon a neighboring stump, leaning forward so that his arm brushed hers. "Might you share your tale with me? Or will you decline my inquiries again? Throughout this province of Jamaica, fables are traded like sustenance. Whilst some malign your name out of fright, many more believe you are nothing but a myth."

Plucking two feathers from the partridge, she leaned them in his direction, tickling his chin. "You speak first. Why do you keep bestowing guns upon people such as us, Gaspar?"

"Not people *such as* you. No other people. I forge no connections with those two other Maroon clans. I am committed solely to you and those who stand by you," he replied, infusing his gaze with a gentle look.

"Hup! I asked you for the *reason.* Why?"

Carvalhal fished into his leather *gargoussier* bag for gunpowder in order to light the fire. "Those arms are not alms," he quipped.

"Speak plainly this second, Gaspar Carvalhal – most wealthy, famous, and feared running trader of the West India islands!" she clucked. "Every other moon, you top us off with your guns. Why?"

"We are allies, Nani. Our objectives are one and the same. I am a Jew. My people have been outcast from our homelands – the kingdoms of Spain and Portugal. Europe's masters strip us of our dignity. So it is that we seek a haven where we may settle in freedom and worship without worry. If I may venture so bold a comparison, your people, too, were separated from your homelands."

"Kidnapped gets at the truer sense of it," she corrected sharply.

"Kidnapped," he adjusted his phrasing. "Wrenched from home and families, you were oppressed by greed in the form of masters. I reckon you, equally, pine for a refuge, a corner of the world where you may live in sovereign peace."

Nani studied the smuggler. "I see. Tis your wish to unite with us against the Spanish masters? To battle beside us in ejecting them from Jamaica?"

"Yes, quite simply that," Carvalhal replied, stoking the cooking fire.

Nani turned the skewered birds upon the spit and stared at the flames as though retrieving her memories from waves of heat and light. She began to speak a story she never before had told.

"My birth name, Anané, means Fourth Child – such are we named in my Akan village. One day, my farmer father goes to work, but it is not the field that he meets; it is a band of roaming slavers. He is drowning in impossible debt. Me, a girl aged nine years, I am the answer to his failings – like so many children of every place and time. With hope beaten out of him, he sells me as captive property. My father's running debts are thus absolved.

"He sheds no tears when the ruffians bind me in chains. Only my mother cries for me. She embraces me one final time and says: *The worth of a woman is no more than dirt. We are bought, bartered, cut-down, plowed, implanted, and reaped for profit.* Then the slavers snatch me out of her arms."

His fingers met hers with featherlight love. "I do not know how to impart my sorrow. Each syllable I ponder seems barren."

She allowed him to take her hand. Then she persisted. "Alongside a herd of other captives, the slavers ferry me down a web of rivers to the coast. They cram us into a fortress termed a *slave factory*. We persevere in squalor. In one corner, an open pit of feces. Everywhere, armies of rats. And always the aroma of death catches me. By the day, more captives die. Their flyblown corpses collapse into the muck. They are left there to rot. Soon, a fever falls upon me. For weeks, it will not relent. But then I realize: My illness is not a fever of the body. It is a fever of terror, hatred, and disgust."

Her voice stumbled. She saw the compassion glistening in Gaspar's soft eyes. Her hand gripped his with such force that her fingernails drew blood. "The worst nightmare I can envision. It occurs. Caboceers – hirelings of the Kingdom of Dahomey – they fall upon me like wild dogs, desecrating my sacred depths. *Speak one word, and we cut out your tongue!* they threaten, the repugnance of heavy drink polluting their breath."

Ever bereft of language, he held her gaze, slowing his breathing to quell the rage rising within him.

"We endure there, dungeoned in Ouidah, till the new moon opens. The slavers press this into my belly," she lifted her chemise, rubbing her fingers across the umbrella-shaped scar. "Iron ripened in blazing coals, and I am branded. Shackled, I am loaded into the hold. Next, the vessel carries me over the western ocean."

"The Middle Passage," said Carvalhal.

"No imagination can form more of a Hell on Earth than those nine weeks!" Her entire body tightened and she gnashed her teeth. "When, finally, our ship arrives at Porto Esquivel, 20 are dead and we all look like zombies. The traders auction us to landowners. We learn how they make themselves wealthy upon our sweat, our tears, our blood. How they own us and control every piece of our lives.

"Sold to a *hato* here in Jamaica, I choose not to talk and also not to eat. The only control I have. The taskmasters force mashed manioc down my throat. But I grind leaves from cassava, which grows all over this island, into Obiya poison. It helps me spew forth the manioc. I starve."

Carvalhal was still as a stone, embedded in the stream of her recollections. "What, finally, made you eat?"

"Nature spirits. They entered my anguish and beseeched me to choose living. They chanted of a future ordained for me." She lifted herself and ascended her arms toward the heights of the enveloping mahoe trees. "Obiya swapped my weakness with courage. I perceive its power even in this New World. No day travels by without the ancient science of my ancestor mothers guiding me. Christian believers may have dipped me in the water of Christ, but my soul was annealed by the flames of the Serpent."

Gaspar Carvalhal found himself bankrupt of words. He reached forward, drawing Nani into an embrace. She battled her desire to collapse once more into sobs, taking long, steady breaths instead. When she felt herself calm, she released herself.

Pulling the game off the spit, she certified that it was flawless in succulence. In silence they sat upon the forest earth, sharing a warm and lovely breakfast. For an instant, they were the very thing they could never be.

IN WHICH A SMUGGLER CLAIMS A PRIZE

For hours, they made love with the passion of paramours denying time. Against a tree. In the mud beside the river. Once more upon the soft animal skins of the *ajoupa*. The sun had climbed well past its apex when at last Carvalhal sighed, "My men await…"

"And so, too, do my people. We must get on," the Maroon chieftain concurred. Begrudgingly, she took four steps to cross the hut. When she turned back to face him, she held in her hands don Francisco de Leiva's ivory chest. "Take this."

His wide-eyed expression communicated his awe at both her achievement and the offering of it. He took hold of the box. Roughly the volume of a coal sack, it weighed two stones.

"De Leiva's men nearly took my life when I captured this! This I did for you. In faith."

"My queen, I have no ability to thank you. The troves of weapons I give you represent but a pittance of my gratitude." He laid the parcel on the ground. "See here, this item is a key. It opens a door for you and your people, for me and my people, and for many more who are oppressed. With it, your fugitive nation might stand a chance of winning the freedom everlasting of which you dream."

"But how?" she fired back. "What does it contain?"

"Aye, I beg your faith, my love. Allow me to explain. I view this chest of don Francisco de Leiva as a grenade sent by the armory of angels. It shall break Spain's 160-year supreme authority over the New World." Clasping her hand, he brought it down upon the strongbox. "Fathom that."

"Tis naught but a box."

"Within is the bait that shall lure one arrogant nation against another," Carvalhal elaborated. "I suspect it is England, foremost, which smolders with a burning ambition to topple Spain from the New World. Once one power is pitted against the other, the alliances between rebel entities will shift in the wind."

"You speak of Maroon and Jew?"

"And others," stated Carvalhal. "Make no doubt that the moment word of the unholy theft of his coffer has reached don Francisco de Leiva's ears, all his wrath opened. The High-Sheriff of the Holy Crusade will unleash the island's militia, and likely clamor for further backing from La Isla de Cuba and even Santo Domingo. Such a force of Spanish horse and gun will prove insurmountable – unless we, too, multiply our numbers." His fingers gardened his whiskers as he calibrated a thorny proposal. "While I pursue the friendship of fellow demeaned outcasts, both Irish indentureds and pyrates, you might rally Lubolo and Juan de Serras, the captains of the two Leeward Maroons clans."

Nani snorted. "Ock! Lubolo and Juan de Serras? I trust those two lumps like crocodiles in the mud. As far as the stout Irish, I know spit about them. And as for the mercenary freebooters? They worship only greed."

"You're a fugitive. You can't remain an orphaned island in an ocean of enemies."

"It suits this fugitive well and fine."

"But by Jove, tell me your ears have not been tickled by the legendary name of Iron Eyes? He is of character and courage set apart from pyrates past. Dedicated to more than death and spoils, he has sworn his blade to shattering the shackles of oppression. His confederacy of sea rovers, alongside the Irish, Maroons, and Jews, are four factions viewed by Europe's high-born as lepers. Together in alliance, we can tip the martial contest between the master countries of Europe in our direction. Specifically, we might orchestrate a clash between England and Spain, the outcome of which delivers our freedom."

Nani measured Gaspar, trying to ford the span of his ploys. "I want to meet this Iron Eyes," she relented.

Carvalhal let out a breath. "As do I. But every Spaniard is also on the hunt for him. Our next step resides here," he rapped the ivory chest. "This is manna from heaven; the keystone for making our destiny!"

"I have no faith in your Biblical God," Nani clucked, casting her cynicism once more upon the coffer. "How this box should do as you say, I do not grasp." She lifted the box, spinning it in her hands before carrying it outside and placing it firmly upon a stump. "Open it," she commanded.

Carvalhal complied. He worked a fistful of gunpowder into a bit of canvas. He jammed this packet within the lock. When he lit it, the nails screeched and the strongbox top flew free. Eagerly, he reached inside and extracted a heap of knotted wool that resembled nothing more than a bird's nest. Upon shaking it out, it revealed nothing of interest.

"Tis a mass of rubbish, that which you entrust to transform the world!" Nani cackled.

"Not at all. It is merely beyond our comprehension. Tis a missive from a familiar of the Inquisition crafted in a secret code."

"A code?" she asked.

"Aye," he confirmed, shaking the knotted wool once more. "Tis a message written in a form of language so protected that only Inquisitors possess the knowledge required for its translation. And this message is destined exclusively for the king of Spain."

Nani continued to gaze at him with skepticism bordering on derision.

"It may appear of no consequence to you," he urged. "Yet believe me, my queen and darling, I shall gain a translation. Then we shall step through the portal of a new existence – one in which we may live as lovers and leaders of our own free and bountiful domain."

"You gamble too much with my patience, Gaspar Carvalhal," she retorted. "And my life."

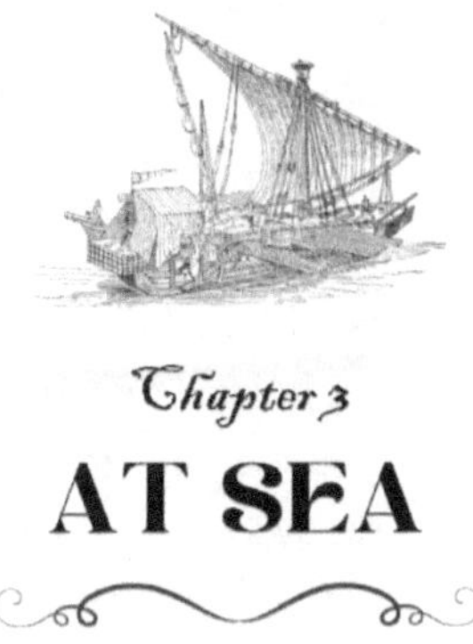

Chapter 3

AT SEA

IN WHICH PYRATES TAUNT THEIR FOES

The pyrate captain hurled obscenities at the six Spanish coastguard boats chasing them through the turquoise waves. He double-cocked his cherrywood pistol and blasted lead at his enemies.

"Zounds!" he shouted at the 50 men cowered before him in their fleeing longboat. "Recall, my roaring hearts, how we snatched from these foul Spaniards a utopian life. If we survive, we steal our freedom once again. If we perish, then huzzah and to hell! Who amongst us denies that these past 12 months have been his most splendid?"

None tendered a croak. His audience was snagged at the throat by terror. Behind the captain, their pyrate ship burned.

In March 1652, whilst impressed into servitude upon a merchant vessel sailing for the English colony of Barbados, Damien Baines had provoked 20-odd tars into winning their ship through mutiny. He had insisted that they anoint him captain only if he earned it through a common vote. He had called them "brethren — brothers equal in all ways." Hours later, they had christened him Captain Iron Eyes, for his eyes brimmed with liquid night. Yet all the same, he was prone to spells of jesting and kindness. In the year since, he had forged a company of pyrates 200 strong.

As more salvos burst upon them, Iron Eyes frisked his pockets for a smack of tobacco. Locating none, he mimed such exasperation that it served to belittle the horrors lunging their way. Several tars guffawed loudly. Such was the flair of Captain Damien Baines, who married rugged mystique with polished confidence.

The pyrates could not sweep the oars fast enough. Bodies crumpled or flipped overboard. At the floor of the longboat, viscera and fissured limbs stewed in pink bilge water.

The Boatswain trembled at the bloodbath. He attempted to wriggle forward, but his grasp on the bulwark slipped and he splashed into the butcher's soup. In shock, he noted rather scientifically that slivers of human bone float whereas scattered teeth do not.

"Suck my marbles, you anus-cleaners!" Iron Eyes shouted at the Spaniards, who had released a fleet of longboats from their mighty ships. "May the Devil spit syphilis upon you!" He was the only pyrate who dared parade his full height above the gunnels.

The Spanish soldiers repaid his tribute with blunderbuss shots. The pyrates fired muskets and pistols. The warring parties fouled the air until it was so thick with ash that it could more easily be eaten than breathed.

Suddenly, Iron Eyes crouched before the Boatswain. "Been worrying about you," the captain said, his voice tender. "We shall live."

Just then, their boat pitched, colliding with bellicose swells at the coastline. The pyrates shoveled their oars frantically. If they were to stand any chance at fending off their executioners, they had to nab the first foothold upon this puny and exposed island.

From its outset, Iron Eyes had discerned the ferocious onslaught as one led by none other than Araña Sangrienta. His name meant *one who relishes the spill of blood*. Although only 25 years old, the commander of the Spanish West Indies *guardacosta* waged battle with the zeal of a Christian soldier. His mandate had been issued by none other than don Francisco de Leiva, the most magnificent individual on the isle of Jamaica. De Leiva had granted Sangrienta impunity to "ravage and commit any indecency desired against heretic violators."

As soon as the pyrates' longboat neared the shore, Iron Eyes led his surviving 30-odd men in a sprint through the shallows. Reaching the sand, they were driven to the ground by shot and forced to crawl upon their bellies like crabs.

The Boatswain watched in horror as the Spanish soldiers landed the first of their six longboats. Then came Sangrienta himself. Small in stature but lit with fanaticism, his uniform boasting a dozen medals and his necklace adorned by a diamond crucifix, the squadron commander waded to shore. His *soldados* followed, guns spitting lead. Another boat landed. Then another.

Escape could not be found. Chosen by Sangrienta as the ideal venue upon which to entrap the pyrates, the islet offered no defense. It consisted of nothing more than a few starved acres of soil and Bermuda grass.

Musket shot slugged the Boatswain in the thigh and tore into his calf. He faltered, crashing face down upon the sand. Everywhere around him, necks burst with blood. Skulls were blasted into puzzle pieces. Soon the beachhead was littered with pyrate cadavers.

"Amass the bodies of the infidels here!" Sangrienta instructed his soldiers from a bluff of parched grass.

The Boatswain could not locate Iron Eyes, nor could he detect more than a handful of men still living. Muttering a last litany to the saints he long since had deserted, he wormed his way up the final lengths of sand and onto the scrubland.

The heap of stinking corpses offered the sole possibility of concealment. When the closest *soldados* turned away, he squeezed himself into the mound of cadavers, balling up in agony.

IN WHICH BODIES LIE WITH BODIES

He suffered disassociations with time. When he awoke beneath the wretched mound of bodies, the Boatswain had no idea how long he might have lain there. With his right hand, he probed the wounds in his left arm and leg. Death was inhabiting his flesh.

Victorious, Araña Sangrienta unfurled a scroll proofed with the sealing wax of the king of Spain and read aloud. "I hereby declare that an egregious act of hostility was committed against His Most Catholic Majesty Felipe IV, our Lord the King – God preserve him, we kiss his hand – and his subjects upon the twelfth day of June, 1652, amongst the waters of the Yucatan Channel. For the theft of the flagship of the Spanish armada, El León de Oro, the enemy captain known throughout the West Indies as Iron Eyes and all his men shall be killed with no mercy."

Sangrienta's voice rose in tenor and gained in sanctimony. "Let this divine retribution for maligning the Empire of Spain warn the entire world: When man abandons himself to evil, the pain shall be death!"

In the silence that followed, a furnace of memories raged through the Boatswain's mind. Three months into their career of pillaging coastal trading vessels throughout the Caribbee Sea, Iron Eyes and his gang had stumbled across Spain's famed Treasure Fleet. Due to either providence or blind luck, *La Flota de Indias* had misinterpreted the wind. The flagship, El León de Oro, had deviated too far from the men-of-war intended to protect her.

Hotly, the pyrates had raised sail and taken their prey with ease. Iron Eyes and his brethren had plundered the Spanish vessel of its sterling, gold-dust and 100,000 pieces of eight. Kinked with manic glee, they had put flame to their own ragged ship and adopted the handsome Spanish galleon for themselves.

Fast as a tempest, the name Iron Eyes had spread, until it was greeted by panic, dread, and envy throughout every public house in the region. The invincibility of the Treasure Fleet – whose 20 to 30 wealth-laden vessels always were guarded by six mighty warships – had been defied.

Not only was this story inflated into myth, but so were Iron Eyes' convictions. He preached a new framework for living, in which each person was endowed with an equal voice – no matter his social station, tint of skin, religious creed, or criminal violations. The commoners were ensorcelled by the talk, which built up force so rapidly that it portended a tidal wave breaking upon the shores of history.

For the next year, the pyrates had, with their stolen treasures, pursued the pleasures of dicing, whoring, and drinking throughout the West Indies. Upon many a sultry Caribbean night, Iron Eyes had lain beside the Boatswain atop the deck, contemplating their destiny as they gazed upon the stars.

Both men traced their origins to Wales, though to different regions. Damien Baines had been reared in the uplands, the Boatswain in the south near the River Teifi. Neither bore any fondness for their former merchant masters, who had hailed from London. Following the conquest of Wales 300 years past, the English had compelled the local people to genuflect and forbidden them to speak in their native Welsh tongue.

As history would have it, the English had reprised these tactics ten years ere, this time in the kingdom of Ireland. Few dared mutter the word aloud, but in clenched whispers many a Welshman labeled Lord General Oliver Cromwell's treatment of the Irish people *genocide*. The Boatswain and Iron Eyes differed not in this opinion.

Whenever the two Welshmen spoke, they displayed their loathing for the English by settling into their traditional language, in spite of the legal ban.

"Tis a biting irony," Iron Eyes had remarked one eve in their common tongue, his gaze piercing the vast darkness speckled with gold as if decoding a mystery. "We are so insignificant, yet driven by such exorbitant desires." He turned to look the Boatswain in the eyes. "We must fight to preserve our noble ideals. Trust none and no one, but have faith that the best resides in everyone."

"And when we fall shy of our ambitions, let us perish amongst our own," the Boatswain added.

"Swear you'll dedicate yourself beside me, inspiring these renegades into a fellowship of self-determined men? One day, we might stand together strong as any kingdom. That is my most daring dream."

"My word," pledged the Boatswain.

"Dignity demands freedom," Iron Eyes pronounced solemnly.

A soft rain began to fall. The Boatswain inhaled the scent of freshly rained-upon wood.

"I was birthed into circumstances bereft of prospects," the pyrate captain confessed. "And I was taught not to nourish a single yearning."

"From the time I was a youngling, my kin also muzzled my cries for a better life," the Boatswain agreed. "I reckon all who choose this ship as their home come from similarly wretched beginnings."

"The mere impulse of wanting felt hazardous."

"Criminal, even."

"But what if we change that," Iron Eyes suggested. "We educate our men to be unafraid of their desires. We give them heart to chase their ambitions. Think on it…" He inhaled deeply. "Men such as us might finally lead a life. Not simply suffer one."

IN WHICH A STRANGER SCAVENGES

The present was like a chamber with many doors. The Boatswain could not distinguish what was here and now from what was reverie. *Perhaps,* the Boatswain hypothesized, *all of life is but a waking dream.*

And yet here was Iron Eyes lying beside him – his skin roughened by sun and sea, his cheekbones striking. *My eyes do not perceive this*, the Boatswain corrected himself, until there was no refuting reality. This was not dream. It was Iron Eyes. But he was a corpse.

Mist seeped into the Boatswain's eyes. Holding his breath, he dove into the putridness and felt for the captain's cherrywood pistol. Even in death, Iron Eyes aimed it in optimism. The Boatswain plucked it from the captain's dead hand before drowning in darkness once more.

When again he awoke, there was nothing to hear but his own ragged breath. Then, concentrating, he heard the panting of a dog rooting about the charnel heap. The animal was not feral, nor was the encroacher a Spanish soldier. A voice spoke to the dog in a tongue foreign to the pyrate, its tone bright and musical.

Ever fearful, the Boatswain slid a corpse further over himself. But the movement served to agitate a rat. The dog reacted instantly and the scavenger followed, pushing aside rotting bodies.

First came a stream of words in Spanish, which the Boatswain, in his injured state, failed to comprehend. When the stranger spoke again, it was in a coarse form of English that came off as unplanned poetry. "Twas me who scented you living still. Not the hound."

The Boatswain fumbled for Iron Eyes' pistol. But in the seconds it took him to level the hefty weapon, the scavenger removed a rolled plug of tobacco from his pouch, kindled its tip with a smoldering match drawn from a wooden box, and began smoking the makeshift cigar through a nostril. With nonchalance, he kicked the gun from out the invalid's hand. His brown eyes assessed the man.

The Boatswain exhaled a heavy draft of resignation. As his gaze adjusted to the radiance of the morning, he compiled a better portrait of the stranger. A burst of wild brown hair surrounded his face like a halo. Muscles cut his lean form with rivers and canyons of striations. He was attired in billowing short breeches, with a bolt of linen wound tightly around his torso and a rag-tag calfskin vest. He was neat-shaved, his pierced septum adorned with a splinter of bone.

The scavenger yanked the Boatswain out of the death mound and into the sunlight. "You look chewed up by tragedy," he said. Then he returned to work. Nimbly, he excavated from the corpses rings and silver neck chains, cutlashes, hangers, and Waloon blades. He seized dirty apparel, discarding items that smelled unbearably of feces. He unplugged daggers from spines.

Nearby, the tan and white-spotted hound also sought treasure. In spite of her colossal stature, she bore evidence of a rough-hewn existence – a chewed-up ear, scarred nose, and crooked hind leg.

"*Vaya*, Zemi. Good girl!" the scavenger praised when the dog scented a shooting iron.

The sun sparked green upon the horizon. In the gloaming, the scavenger hauled Iron Eyes' corpse onto the grass and began to dig him a grave in the mounting darkness. The Boatswain reckoned crabs would vandalize the body that very night. Gulls would pluck it to the bone. But for a few hours, Captain Damien Baines would be consecrated to the earth, his life bid farewell with honor. For this, the Boatswain felt immense gratitude to the stranger.

At moonrise, the scavenger lifted the Boatswain into the stern of his canoe. The craft had been hewn from a kapok tree and fitted with a triangular sail. Her master whistled, and the hound sprung aboard. As they shoved off from the shallows, the Boatswain was visited by a fresh bout of agues. Zemi curled beside him, donating her warmth.

With alacrity, the scavenger harnessed the wind. Drawing upon the last of his strength, the Boatswain propped himself against the gunnels. "How may I call you?" he croaked.

"Tiburon," the stranger replied.

"As for me, I hail from the headlands of county Cardiganshire," the Boatswain volunteered. "Twas christened as—"

"Hush it," Tiburon curtly rejected the disclosure, his gaze focused upon the nighttime sea.

"What moved you to save me?" the Boatswain sputtered.

The scavenger did not answer. The Boatswain found his remoteness alluring.

Moments passed. From his vest, Tiburon withdrew the cherrywood pistol that had belonged to Iron Eyes. He handed it to the pyrate.

The Boatswain coughed in surprise. Seldom had he witnessed such an act of trust, much less one so immediate. The small gun of Captain Damien Baines was an exquisite appliance. Double-barreled, it measured a whopping 24 inches. Its iron was engraved with the fleur-de-lis, indicating that it had been forged in Dieppe, France by Brachie – arguably the finest manufacturer of firearms in the Western world.

"You ain't its original owner," Tiburon charged.

"True," admitted the Boatswain.

The scavenger turned his back to his companion, ending the conversation.

"How, in the grisly aftermath of that wild whirl with the Spanish, did you figure which was the corpse of Iron Eyes, our cherished captain?" the Boatswain asked.

Tiburon meditated upon a faint horizon.

"He alone you took special pains to bury," the pyrate pursued.

The scavenger glanced over his shoulder. "Apart from your own self, he alone was not shot through the back."

IN WHICH A BONE CAVE OFFERS SHELTER

Two days later, the canoe touched upon the shores of another lonely but more spacious island. Rising from cruel cliffs, dense woods cloaked its interior.

Tiburon moved with certainty, whilst the wounded man languished. The scavenger hefted his boat to the far side of the rocky shingle and hid it with branches fetched by Zemi.

Then, in a remarkable display of brawn given his slender form, he hauled the invalid up the sheer rock face.

They established quarters in the one place Tiburon trusted: A bone cave carpeted with human skeletons. Spines, ribs, femurs, and skulls were strewn about like kindling. The Boatswain speculated that over 100 souls had perished here.

Tiburon explained the cave's genesis. Native inhabitants – Taíno people like himself, and as well those of Arawak and Carib origin – once had thrived throughout the Caribbee region. Many had opposed the *encomienda* system, which conferred upon Spaniards the "right" to enslave and extract tribute from any conquered non-Christian people.

"With packs of mastiffs snarling at their heels, miserable islanders made their way here, to Navassa," Tiburon said. "But the refuge they found was brief. The Spaniards drafted more dogs and better trackers to terrorize them. Those who persevered chose the finality of *Las Rocas Suicidas* – the Suicide Rocks, as these dreary bluffs now are known." He scratched Zemi's nicked ear. "Rather than abide enslavement by the conquistadors, thousands of our people ingested poisonous manioc root to end their lives. Such caves can be found all over our lands."

In the silence that followed, the Boatswain reevaluated his companion's melancholy nature.

Employing his sail canvas, Tiburon formed a hammock in the cave. He undressed the invalid and treated his wounds with poultices drawn from a cow-hide sack. "These plant medicines will ease your frightful torments. Not certain they shall thwart the onset of death, however."

His patient nodded.

Tiburon spat into the wounds, causing the pyrate to rear back. "We must stifle the corruption," Tiburon explained. He proceeded to rub his saliva into the festering injuries, ignoring the Boatswain's hot tears.

As the hours passed, the pyrate wrestled with disbelief. He could not comprehend the reason behind Tiburon's kindness. "My sorry condition imposes a dire – no, a deadly weight upon you. Yet still you work to save my life. Why?" he asked. Later, he questioned Tiburon again. "Pray speak your business with me. Spit it out!"

Tiburon refused to respond to the interrogation.

When night dropped, pain carried the Boatswain down another dreamless tunnel. He heard Tiburon say, "Listen you, we are bargaining for time in these parts, chancing untold odds."

"I've been drilled by the shot of a hundred Spaniards. Why worry?"

"A horrid breed dwell here," Tiburon replied. "They dine upon human flesh."

IN WHICH STRANGERS BECOME FRIENDS

Days passed, then weeks. By virtue of Tiburon's patient administrations, the Boatswain's health bettered. He bolstered his gains in strength through a regime of physical exertion. Yet the more he recovered, the more he questioned *why*. Why had he alone survived, amongst all his crew? Why had Tiburon materialized to rescue him?

Tiburon applied his days to hunting turtle and runty swine, fetching fresh water from a nearby stream, foraging fruit and edible plants, fishing, and spurring his hound to uncover eggs that wood-fowl laid in the undergrowth. He dared not fire a shot for fear of alerting the maniacal inhabitants of the island. So, from the ocean he snared stingrays and cured their tails into arrows for his bow. When able, he gathered fresh cashew nuts, which he roasted from out their poisonous shells.

Most evenings were lost to the cadence of flaking stone into arrowheads. The Boatswain would attempt to decrypt the curious history of his companion. Never did he succeed.

One sweltering afternoon as they neared a second full moon upon Navassa, the invalid managed to take several steps. Tiburon celebrated the achievement, but the Boatswain scoffed.

Tiburon handed him a calabash of hog lard. As instructed, the Boatswain lathered it upon limbs decorated by fibrous lesions. The salve was a saving grace in fending off the ever-present battalions of mosquitoes.

"Blasted fucks, we smell like privies now, no different than the cannibals," the Boatswain quipped.

"Aye, and the weeks of sweat and grot caking your hide place you further at odds with civilized man," Tiburon chuckled. His companion bathed frequently, the Boatswain had observed.

Upon gaining his permission, Tiburon deluged the pyrate with river water from a basin. The Boatswain scrubbed his bushy copper-blonde beard and hair with digo, an herb that generated cleansing suds. Then he clubbed his locks behind his head and started to shave with Tiburon's shark tooth.

In the Boatswain's view, the scavenger could not have possessed a more superfluous tool. Tiburon's elegant face lacked whiskers. In fact, he was hairless aside from the mass of tresses tumbling from his head.

Focusing upon the task at hand, the Boatswain traced the line of his jaw with his index finger. He startled, nicking himself when Tiburon announced, "Jamaica."

"Burning quim," he muttered, dabbing blood from his chin.

"Jamaica."

The Boatswain issued a quizzical look.

"You asked my homeland. That's the where."

The Boatswain welcomed the detail but vibrated with further questions. "Tis why you speak Spanish so well. But what's the reason for your wielding English with such ease?"

Tiburon appeared struck by the obvious nature of the answer. "Because so many of your type roam the Jamaica island, pyrate. The North Coast is the rallying ground for buccaneers who track and trade. Yet also south, where sits the capital township of St. Jago de La Vega, a number of English residents prosper. They ply their trades beside Spaniards, Portuguese, free Blacks, *manso* Indians, Lutherans, Jews, infidels, and Christians. Among Spain's Windward colonies, Jamaica is a bona fide original."

The Boatswain considered this remarkable notion as he splashed water upon his face.

"We cast off upon the morrow," Tiburon said.

"For which place?"

"Jamaica, I'm telling you!" Tiburon replied, exasperated.

"In this state? I still rate as pitiful," the Boatswain objected.

"As is, we go." He exited the bone cave to rouse the piragua, his sail empowered canoe.

"Harr! Not so hot, Tiburon. You may flatter that island, but every sea rover worth his salt knows how it slumps in neglect."

"Precisely," Tiburon said, walking away. "We are more apt to succeed where we are ignored."

"Succeed in what?" the pyrate called out.

"Be a friend. Dismantle our lodgings," Tiburon ordered and marched off toward the shore.

Slowly, the Boatswain bundled blunderbuss, musket, and cooking implements into a canvas pack. He wove a sling for his captain's cherrywood pistol. He packed dried fruit and fish. But just as he was beginning to confront the cartouche boxes and powder horns, weariness overcame him. He sank into slumber.

IN WHICH CANNIBALS PREPARE TO FEAST

Zemi's hysterical barks jerked the Boatswain awake. He leapt up from the bone-strewn floor and, banishing a grimed coverlet, stood half-naked and confused. He searched for his shirt but could not locate it in the dark.

The hound's obstinacy was non-negotiable. She snapped at his ankles, herding him out of the cave.

"Owza! Back off, you scold!" the Boatswain shouted. Groping hastily in the blackness, he found three items he had not yet stowed. He lurched into the moonlight with wad, shot, and the double-barrel pistol of his foregone hero, Captain Damien Baines.

The steep, broken descent was overshadowed by trees. Zemi drove him forward with snapping leaps. When she rammed him from behind, he entered a runaway tumble down the cliff, his legs straining to uphold him. Before long, he tripped and fell face-down upon the stony earth.

"Stuffed fucks!" he cried.

Zemi barked.

"God above, spare me from this cantankerous bitch," he groaned.

From below, the Boatswain heard Tiburon unleash a wail that turned his blood to ice. It was followed by deranged howls. The pyrate doubled his urgency and sprinted down the ridge with Zemi driving ahead. By the trees nearest the beachfront, he counted six cannibals.

Tiburon had been stripped of his clothes. His body was covered with gashes. Blood dripped from his temples. Distressed yet defiant, he thrust a puncheon pole at his assailants. The cannibals mocked him.

The Boatswain stood just inside 100 yards - the maximum reach of musket shot. By the timid light of the moon, his odds were minuscule. The fact that he bore a pistol and not a musket rendered his chances close to nil. Thankfully, he was a prodigy when it came to small arms.

He bit through a wad and loaded the cherrywood gun with shot. His eyes fixed upon the target. His finger followed instinct. The trigger clicked, the weapon jumped, and the first cannibal fell, a hole blasted through his forehead. With incredible agility, the Boatswain charged his gun and fired again. Before the abusers even realized what was happening, a second man had lost his life.

Tiburon looked into the trees as flustered reprisals banged blindly in the Boatswain's direction. Zemi stayed hunched in the undergrowth, growling.

Then, from the base of the furthest cliff, the Boatswain discerned a terrific hubbub. Forty men carrying torches had broken forth. In mere seconds, the mob would pour over them.

The Boatswain again loaded his pistol. One of the tormentors pounced upon Tiburon. The Taíno scavenger slugged the man-eater in the nether-realms. The distraction halted the rampaging gang for a moment.

"Flee!" the Boatswain shouted at Tiburon, revealing his own position. As the men launched at the Boatswain, Tiburon slithered past his attackers and aimed for shore. The Boatswain caught a glimmer of moonlight off the piragua just before a barrage of shot burst through the eucalyptus inches above him.

"Come, you both," Tiburon cried. "Haul with Satan at your heels!"

Zemi bolted and the Boatswain followed, pistol and powder-horn pumping in his arms. Tiburon heaved the small craft into the shallows. Seconds later, Zemi bounded aboard. The Boatswain crashed forward, ramming his weight against the stern and launching the hefty canoe afloat. He clambered in and dove aft to claim the oars seconds before the cannibals reached the shoreline. The most incorrigible of them tripped through the water in pursuit of the Taíno man, the pyrate, and the hound.

Tiburon bent a sail upon the wind and the piragua sliced safely out to sea. Under the sheen of the moon, he and the Boatswain peered back across crashing black waves, mesmerized by their attackers. Flickering beneath their torches, they resembled gargoyles brought to life – encased in filth with wiry hair and fibrous skin.

The Boatswain sighed in relief against the gunnels. Tiburon slumped at the bow. Zemi curled close.

That was when the pyrate began chuckling. The ordeal had left Tiburon without a stitch of clothing. Granted a moment beyond peril, he noted his companion's naked form for the first time. "It appears you've been beguiling me all this while," he said.

"On which subject?" Tiburon asked, matter of fact.

"On the subject of being a man."

"Never said I was," Tiburon shrugged. "Tis like this, mate. My soul craves equal to any man's."

"Except there ain't no cock and balls swinging from between your legs!"

Tiburon turned to face the salt breeze. "Tis my choice to present as a man on account of the way this world is tailored for men. I thank you for guarding this secret in confidence."

The Boatswain ducked his head with respect. "Shan't mention one word to anyone. Tis the smallest due for what you have granted me. I remain beholden to you, my friend."

The surf sparkled. The Boatswain supposed the conversation complete. He was by this time accustomed to the quiet habits of his comrade. It was a surprise, then, when Tiburon spoke again. "None of us are what we appear to be. You follow?"

The Boatswain cocked a brow.

"Some fathom from the start who they be. Others shape themselves to match the moment. What matters is that you are ready when the occasion calls for you."

The pyrate stalled in silence. Instinct informed him more was coming.

"You mustn't let *him* perish from the hope of this world," Tiburon beseeched. "His testament surpasses flesh and bone. Once a man of spirit, he arises again as the spirit of man. Do you fathom me, Captain Damien Baines?"

The Boatswain gulped.

"None can place his likeness. None can confirm his fate. You sailed with him. With your crew, he shared his dreams. You are more familiar with Iron Eyes than any other. What say you, pyrate? Are you ready to rise?"

Understanding dawned upon the Boatswain at last. "Tis why you did not ever want to learn my name…" he murmured, drifting in uncertainty. Then his demeanor turned stern. "None can stand beside Captain Damien Baines. None are equal."

"Look, you. Iron Eyes lives on in the hearts of many."

"Iron Eyes is dead!" the Boatswain shouted, his voice bitter.

Zemi sprang forward in defense of her companion. Tiburon quieted the dog. "You grieve him."

"Above all others I have lost," the Boatswain confessed. "Also, there is one other man who can paint Iron Eyes' true portrait. The same man who laid him to waste. The commander of the first *guardacosta*: Araña Sangrienta."

"No lone man can halt the surge of freedom."

The darkness absorbed their private thoughts. Then the Boatswain clapped his hands to his thighs. "By God, of what use are my past and my birth name? Come closer, mate of mine."

Tiburon leaned in. The Boatswain fixed his friend with motley irises – one blue as the northern sky, the second hazel as autumn grass. "I am a filibuster of the sea in quest of sovereign rights for all men – all people," he corrected himself.

"And by what name do you call yourself?"

The Boatswain faltered.

Peaked with intensity, Tiburon demanded, "I say, speak your name!"

The man before him grasped Tiburon's hand. "I am Captain Damien Baines," he declared, "a renegade pyrate and freedom-fighter better known to the world as Iron Eyes."

He boasted a heroic aura, Tiburon decided. And despite his tawny blonde hair and mismatched eyes – one azure, the other olive green – it was possible that this man embodied the character created for him better than the original Iron Eyes ever had.

Chapter 4

IRELAND

IN WHICH BOGS ARE TRAVERSED

They were ancient creatures, the bogs – vast open bellies that widened for miles across the Irish landscape, digesting the events of eternity. They entombed slain warriors, drowned Celts, and deposed chieftains. They engulfed the robbed, the raped, the crippled, and the misbegotten. Any traveler who took an idle step and fell into a bog hole might remain preserved in the airless peat for a thousand years.

Rory O'Lorcan adjusted his mantle to better guard against the lashing wind, provoking a stench of putrescence and toadstool. His breath had grown skunky, indicating the onset of starvation. For months, he and his clan of Irish rebels had subsisted upon little more than root gruel, lichen, and moldered lilac bulbs. Rarely had they shared so much as a morsel of hunted bird or lake trout.

Rory hastened his younger sister nigh. He always bid Aisling keep him company at the front of the caravan. Back amongst the group's straggling members, too many erratic minds feasted upon her newly-awakening womanhood.

The girl tongue-clicked her bay to trot alongside Rory's horse, both of them leading their animals on foot. The clan claimed only three horses as mounts and five bog ponies for hauling burden. Marred by flea bites, lice sores, and jutting ribs, each beast was more miserable than the last. Yet so were their keepers. Clan Lorcan offered a portrait of privation. Skeletons scurrying toward their graves, all.

"Tis not the worst we've endured," Aisling chimed in their native Gaelic tongue, trying to lift Rory's sour spirits.

Always the bogs berated them with wetness until they felt like amphibians. Yet traveling through the squelchy terrain was necessary in order to evade the English Parliamentarian regiments pursuing them.

Three years past in 1650, Lord General Oliver Cromwell, who now fancied himself Lord Protector of England, had declared Ireland a conquered land. By then, he had massacred every native person at Drogheda, 2,000 more at Wexford, and even more at Clonmel. But the Irish Confederates had refused to submit. Cromwell had countered with wrath, commanding his troops to destroy crops, slaughter livestock, and hang opponents without quarter. A great famine had ensued, bringing with it dysentery, typhus, and the black plague. By 1652, the vast majority of the native Irish population had either perished or been displaced.

"Word is Major-General Venables has returned," Rory commented.

"May he grow a cunt of teeth," Aisling snorted.

"Ock! Watch your mouth, Ash," he joked.

"Seldom is there a holy person in a holy war," she retorted. "Besides, prim is for prods. I'd rather not be a princess, but a pyrate queen like Grace O'Malley."

"No doubt about that," Rory chuckled, mussing her hair.

The 18-year-old admired his sister, three years his junior. Her gumption dwarfed her stature. Aisling was quick to learn and an excellent horseman. But her most darling quality, in Rory's view, was that no matter the family's burdens, she never succumbed to despair. She had decided early in life to love more strenuously than to loathe. It was not just for her protection that Rory wished her to walk nearby; Ash offered rare comfort to him.

A sheet of rain cleaved from the sky. Rory craned round to survey the trailing members of Clan Lorcan. Their momentum flagged as their every step became imprisoned by the spongey heather.

"Bustle up!" he entreated. "Recollect '49, when five of our kinsmen, myself included, tasted the horrors of Drogheda." He waved in the direction of their chieftain Cormac the Younger and his father Morrough. "Two never returned, and only by God's miracles did we three survive."

Acknowledged by mere mumbles, Rory raised his voice further. "But did the English dogs dampen our fortitude? Did they curb our convictions? Did they stifle the great daring soul of the Irish?"

A few men hooted.

"No!" Rory rallied. "Traveling northward, we scattered into the bogs. Here we abide with faith, trusting that we shall continue the fight along with other Native clans."

"Clear their way!" shouted several in the group.

"Death in hell!" returned a smattering of others.

"Today, we have garrisons in Galway, Sligo, Roscommon, and Jamestown!" Rory continued. "Thirty thousand strong, we stand on equal footing with our enemy. One day soon, we shall oust the foreign dogs from our lands once and forever!"

"Clear their way to death in Hell! Clear their way to death in Hell!" the clansmen cheered, their voices growing louder.

"Onward, my kin," Rory concluded. "Let us make for the parley. By the grace of God, we shall join forces with our brethren and banish these rancid English zealots from our shores!"

The company roared.

"Tis as they say," Ash smirked, "nothing riles a clan more than a good craic." She swatted her brother affectionately. In so doing, she jerked her horse's bridle. The animal nickered before dashing away.

"Agra!" Ash cried as she chased the bay, planting her feet upon the peat with the agility of one who has cultivated the habit since infancy.

Rory hauled his dun after them. When he was installed alongside Ash and her darling Agra once more, he confessed, "I fret this parley will not answer our prayers, Sister."

"Yet if it does not, we die," she said simply, her green eyes fixed upon the grey horizon. Rory saw no value in continuing the conversation. For the next six miles, the siblings trudged in silence.

The *tulach dála* was an ancient Gaelic tradition as hallowed as Brehon law. For generations, the ruling septs had gathered at a decreed place upon a certain date so as to remedy feuds, settle agreements, divide territories, and forge alliances. But this parley worried Rory, for it would be like none other. This parley would be led by a murky figure who controlled the final Irish garrison in northeast Ulster – a man called Seneschal the Black.

Little was known of his history. Rory had heard only that he had fought in the Irish Confederate War of 1641. Some argued that he was a clergyman who had been divested of his holy orders. Regardless, the conspicuous truth, Rory had concluded, was this: Seneschal the Black was a warlord who had risen to power upon a wave of desperation that tumbled forth from all the devastated Irish lands west of the River Shannon. And it was upon this unpleasant fellow that Clan Lorcan was wagering their last slice of bread.

IN WHICH A BELEAGUERED CLAN MAKES CAMP

Ever was the night most treacherous. Clan Lorcan made camp upon domed ground of moss and mire. They attempted to spark the peat they had cut and dried weeks ago, but after days of watery skies, it had turned dank again. A few sputtering fires begrudged them comfort. In the shivering cold, afflictions relapsed, hope thinned, acrimonies festered, and the weakest, eldest, and youngest succumbed to eternal darkness.

Rory sought each eve to account for his most intimate kin. He found his father Morrough devotedly cleaning his boots. Rory stood opposite, shuffling his feet awkwardly.

Searching for a topic, he asked, "How many days till we reach the parley, do you reckon?"

His father's focus remained fixed upon his pointless contest with the muck.

"Seven is my guess," his son volunteered.

Morrough only grunted.

Disheartened, Rory drew nearer to his mother. Even from afar he could hear her helpless keening. In her arms lay Baby Grace, his youngest sister, who had lived a mere thirteen months upon this earth. Máthair swayed as she implored her little one to abide. Two days past, Baby Grace had ceased to utter a sound. There was not a drop more milk to be coaxed from her mother's bosom. Máthair's agony at this was unimaginable.

As Rory turned to leave, he detected two bronze eyes blinking at him from beneath Máthair's sleeve. His middle sister Beatha had taken up residence inside her mother's cloak. No occasion, not even the promise of cheer upon her recent eighth birthday, could propel her from her hiding place.

"Where is Fin?" Rory asked her, inquiring after his little brother.

"Scavenging," Beatha muttered.

Rory hesitated. His heart was leaping toward his loved ones, yet if he moved any closer, he feared it would fracture. "Good Lord, the weather!" he commented superfluously before receding into the shadows.

Maintaining a freezing wet vigil that night, Rory thawed himself with recollections of a more gladsome time when Irish fields had burst with grain and young lovers had courted upon hills of bell-heather. The only commotion encountered had been Mass bells praising Sundays in Christ. The only agitation felt had been the turning of the seasons. But no longer did such dreamy simplicity exist. England, in its fresh Commonwealth, had declared the Irish peoples barbarous and determined to systematically eradicate their way of life.

IN WHICH A PARLEY IS CONVENED

Platinum clouds decorated the sky one week later when, at a rise upon the northern horizon of an otherwise flat landscape, Rory detected a pile of stones. "Feast your eyes. Tis the parley, there!" he cried out.

Baby Grace had drawn her last breath that very sunrise, and Máthair, in her grief, seemed no more than a ghost. But with the promise of novel companionship and desperately needed sustenance, the other ragged members of Clan Lorcan quickened their pace. Even the horses and mules seemed heartened.

Atop the hill, Irish families assembled amongst the remnants of an ancient village. The location, a bygone seat of giant kings, was a strategic venue for a parley, indeed. Its rock walls had derided eons of decay and offered a still durable defense.

Canvassing the scene, Rory counted a greater number of clans in attendance than he had predicted. Some derived from the Scottish Galloglass and others boasted a Redshank pedigree. These men painted their bearded faces with crosses of blood purged from their chieftains. Their *glibs*, sections of hair grown long from the front and top so as to fall across the face, were clotted with filth.

Although the elder council would lead the discourse at the rake, Brehon law ensured that everyone was free to attend. Most of Rory's kinsmen, however, dissipated into the crowd, peddling stolen English blankets, frieze cloaks, linen headdresses, crucifixes, and wolf pelts as trade for food and other pleasures. All across the hill, giddy folk unlidded casks of *usquebagh* or whiskey donated by Seneschal the Black. The liege lord's largesse contributed to a festive air.

As the sun slumped, Rory set off to the hall, where he found the chieftains throwing themselves at the feet of the Seneschal, groveling for aid. The warlord's face, when it emerged from the smoke of his clay pipe, was waxy and pocked. His coils of hair were slickened with scalp varnish. He favored a plain, rough-woven cassock, simulating the attire of a bishop. Half listening, his gaze trivialized his male guests and made overtures at the few women present.

"We grant you a conditional partnership," the Seneschal offered at last, voice mud-thick with condescension. "You might garrison here for a week's time. Our grace ends there."

Rory sprang up from the straw strewn across the stone floor. "I beg the lord to speak."

Seneschal the Black's icy eyes raked him up and down.

Rory signaled for the speaking rod, gaining several minutes to plead his case uninterrupted. "Rory am I, tanist of Clan Loran with family seat in Galway," he stated. "We must commit to fighting Major-General Robert Venables of the New Model Army. He is bent upon destroying us. Two months past, our clan attacked 60 of his soldiers, wiping out his supply convoy."

"This declaration is irrelevant to us," the Seneschal sniped.

"Why, my lord, I swear tis otherwise," Rory refuted. "Major-General Venables is coming upon us with an army 2,000 strong. Steeped in righteous judgment like Lord Oliver Cromwell before him, he thirsts to extirpate every Native son and daughter. You, Sir, might cast open the sanctum of the church. You might establish a refuge therein for our wives, mothers, sisters, and wee ones while we men fight."

Silence enveloped the chamber. The Seneschal toked from his pipe. "Purely by payment of a tribute shall you gain this security."

The remark sparked new rounds of debate. Rory shrank from the ruckus, his gut tumbling with disdain for Seneschal the Black.

Under the aura of the gibbous moon, he investigated the happenings upon the hillside. Rutting noises drifted from behind trees. Several women approached, seeking to arouse his animalistic cravings. A soothsayer volunteered visions of salvation and damnation. A bard enticed a small crowd with mythic tales of triumph in days of yore. Dancers spun as pipes, flutes, and fiddles blasted lively reels.

Further down the slope, open fires burned. A gang of young people hurled peat at one another in a Celtic version of a snowball fight. Others tripped and spasmed, deranged by whiskey and more provocative plant medicines. Everywhere the gatherers gloried in consumption. None, it was clear, anticipated living longer than their meekest regrets.

Along the river's brink, Rory glimpsed a figure silhouetted against moon-frosted clouds. It was his only brother, Fintan. At age 12, the lad's limbs were gangly, yet already his shoulders suggested a man emerging.

"How's the lad?" Rory shouted above the din. The sounds claiming the dark were as raving mad as upon the eve of Beltane, the annual spring festival.

"You vanished for hours," Fin remarked. "I suppose you were stirring your pert pole in a friendly bog hole all the while?"

Rory smile faintly. "Aye, I might see if I can win a dalliance from one of these lasses."

"Why not five?" Fin fired back. Like a swift contagion, giggles claimed them. Each was eased by the presence of the other.

As with Aisling, Rory was protective of his little brother. Fintan, unlike most ripening men, bore no menace. Given a choice, he would rather smooth a dispute with his wit than with his fist. Even so, he had been reared a stalwart member of Clan Lorcan. Flawlessly he could hit a target with his pistol in the dark or, with a sweep of his skene, slice the wings off a gnat.

The boy hassled a grease-smeared clout between his fingers, working his way toward a tiny treasure twisted inside. When he loosened the cloth, he displayed to Rory the treasure it contained. "Dear Brother, feast on this. Have ever you seen a thing more splendid?"

Rory peered at the several oily morsels of meat in Fin's hand. His brow raised.

"Partake of this bit of lamb with me," the younger boy insisted. "My belly shrieks and I reckon yours does, also."

Without warning, Rory rushed his brother, swatting the bits of nourishment away.

"Oy, you cracked bastard!" Fin screamed, throwing himself at Rory's neck. The two of them thrashed in the sedge grass till Rory managed to blunt Fin's nose with his fist.

"From whom did you purchase this indecent flesh?" Rory demanded.

Fin tamped the blood dribbling from his nose. "This or that straggler amongst the O'Neills. What does it matter?" he answered ferociously. "I traded him for three brass buttons I snatched off a dead English trooper."

"And what was his route to the meat?" Rory asked.

"Crikey, Rory! Beat off," Fin growled. "Why do you care? Are you planning to find me a replacement? My guts are in roils because of you, you dried cunt."

"Hearken, boy," Rory said. "You know not the unrelenting extent of this famine. There so rarely is a Godsend. Even a rat, if a person gets lucky enough to trap one, won't be shared with a stranger."

"The man welcomed a bargain. It can happen," Fin answered bitterly.

"No, Fin. It cannot," Rory said, temper still flaring.

Upon Clan Lorcan's most recent flight through the bogs, Rory had not discerned a single living presence beyond the occasional bird. The English had slaughtered every livestock and burned every field in Ireland over the past dozen years, rendering their home country a wasteland. He also knew, in his decade of wisdom over his brother, how desperation encouraged people to seek out solutions previously deemed inconceivable. "The meat was unnatural," he said.

"You don't know that," Fin defended.

"Yes, I do."

Fin studied his brother's face in earnest till he grasped Rory's meaning. Then, all at once, he was reduced to sobs. Rory grabbed the boy, enclosing him in his arms. Fin just wanted to eat. The hunger was so cruel. The lad's wails burst with the agony of perpetual suffering. In that instant, he appeared young and fragile, just a bundle of frosted blue eyes and bones.

As he coddled his wee brother to his smock, Rory recalled the corpses he had counted blackening in the bogs. Easy enough to fashion a trade in human flesh when no other sustenance could be scrounged. If a husband might stave off his family's hunger pangs, if a mother might save her children – dying, as they were, far before their time – who could fault them? It was either nothing or this, this meat scavenged from the most unthinkable source.

IN WHICH BETRAYAL BRINGS A BLOODBATH

The English New Model Army had been pursuing the fractured Irish clans like bloodhounds. Major-General Robert Venables and his soldiers were keen to annihilate the stubborn Celts, but with patience they waited for the full gathering to amass.

Their initial incursion preempted daybreak. One thousand English foot soldiers and 200 horsemen swarmed the forward position of the hill. Upon hearing the hooves rumbling in the lavender light of dawn, the Irish clans leapt into action. The men possessed few horses and even less gunpowder. They brandished mostly broadsword and axe, with only the occasional small arm to support their courage. Yet simply by roaring, "Clear their way to death in Hell!" and clashing their steel, they succeeded in disheartening the enemy long enough to hasten their eldest, youngest, and sickest to the church, where Seneschal the Black had granted them asylum.

Fin scoffed when Rory commanded him to follow his mother and sisters into the holy keep. "I shall fight alongside you!" the boy cried, stabbing his skene against the sunrise. It was the knife his father Morrough had bestowed upon him the previous year at his Ceremony of Kings. But Rory insisted he go, and Aisling dragged Fin after her.

As the English fired cannons upon the hillside, the Seneschal proposed a scheme to falter the enemy. "During Hugh O'Neill's last stand at Clonmel in 1650, our fighters took advantage of blind alleyways within the keep, from behind which they could launch their fire," he explained. "Never shall we survive the onslaught of cannons, which already have begun to turn our garrison walls to rubble. But with only a light vanguard of men, we can bait Venables' thousands into the keep. There, the majority of our forces hide behind the walls, ready to launch a surprise counterattack."

The chieftains concurred that Seneschal the Black's plan might just work. Anyway, they were but a piddling militia facing an exceptionally paid, outfitted, and trained army. What choice did they have?

The clans agreed to draw lots in order to determine who would act as the decoys. The chieftains huddled round. When Cormac the Younger, the leader of Clan Lorcan, pulled his poplar rod, he grimaced. It was the only one that had been peeled of its bark. The worst luck had fallen upon them.

Rory traced a cross in the earth with his broadsword before slinging the blade at his side. He embedded a pistol in his mantle. Upon the Seneschal's signal, he, Morrough, Cormac the Younger, and their 20 surviving kindred rallied beneath their standard. They put heels to their horses and raced from behind the protection of the garrison walls.

The English soldiers took the bait. They soared after Clan Lorcan at once, chasing the riders back through the wide-open garrison gates and down its constricted alleyways. The Clan Lorcan fighters had only to defy the English onrush for a minute or two. Then their Irish brethren would break forth from behind the tumbling stone walls and massacre the foreign invaders.

Rory and his kin fired into the surging throng, the report of their arms reverberating against the stone-works. Soon, smoke obscured the passageway. He split a wad between his teeth, tamped the barrel, and blindly cracked his pistol. Nearby, he heard his family members discharging flurries of shot.

Suddenly, a chill gripped Rory's heart. Had they timed their run incorrectly? All about him, his kin were falling. Already exhausted of powder, those still standing were turning to their lances and swords. "I spy not one Irish soul atop the walls," he shouted.

The eyes of Cormac the Younger were raccooned with musket ash. "Entirely vacant," he gasped in agreement.

"Where are the drenching rounds of lead from our brethren?" hollered Morrough.

Rory discerned another voice, incorporeal in the charcoal air. "Tis a farce, Cousins. We have been betrayed!"

Those men nearest the jagged embankments began clambering upwards. It was the only escape. The English plucked their lives instantly. Fathoming the futility of that course of action, the others mustered reserves of fortitude. They accelerated with blades thrusting into the fatal phalanx of horse-mounted enemy soldiers.

For a few seconds, Rory witnessed him: Major-General Robert Venables, stout in the saddle, deep in the fray, and he understood why the commander's troops pledged themselves so ferociously to him. Venables battled alongside the humblest conscripts. Tragically, Rory also noted that Venables would have made an easy target for Irish snipers, had a single one fired from behind the garrison walls. But no one did.

Rory resumed the fight. Seconds later, his dappled gray mare collapsed upon her flank, studded with shot. Through the smoke, Rory watched a musket ball punch his father in the throat. At first Morrough appeared insulted, his eyes startled wide. Then he moaned and lurched to the dirt, dead.

Rory sprang for his father. As he bounded forward, sensation melted from his legs. He spilled to the dirt. Just a few feet away, he saw Cormac the Younger sink to his knees, a sword planted in his ribs.

Gunpowder diffusions obscured the sunlight, weakening day into twilight. Rory groaned and chewed his lip. He felt his hunger seep away like a silly nuisance. His smock was heavy. He placed a hand upon the strange heat at his chest and gazed as it became gloved in blood.

In all these long years of war, Rory had anticipated dying, but never once had he imagined not living. It was a strange thought, this distinction. Now, dying surprised him as simply another obligation of life, no more complex than the urge to eat or sleep. He hoped he would dream. Wonder washed over his face. Then, swiftly, his corpse was trampled by the rushing English hordes.

IN WHICH ALL IS LOST

Deep within the garrison walls, the churchyard was pandemonium. "Lord save us. The English executioners bear down upon us!" screeched Seneschal the Black, revealing his blackened teeth.

Guardsmen of the overlord prodded the frantic Irish kinsfolk into the safety of the church's basement. "Swift into the kennel, you pups," sneered a brute with a maimed leg.

Petrified mothers hastened their children down into the cellar. Tripping, they struck the stone floor with howls and bawling. Ash no sooner had hit the granite plinth than Fin came banging down on top of her.

"Slurp my juice, you apes," he cursed the guards.

"Hush, Brother."

Fin peeled himself from her. "Bleed me." He favored the unapologetic truth, no matter its costliness. For this, Ash could not fault the lad. "The Seneschal is a piss artist," he rumbled. "Bagpipe spit. And those two underlings—" his finger accused the scoffing faces at the entry, "they're a pair of fartleberries!"

An imperious woman, plump unlike the rest, spilled down the staircase. At its base, her sturdy figure skidded and her chin smacked the floor. A flurry of gems and trinkets of beaten gold scattered across the stone. As the final jewel tinkled, the crowd fell silent. The guards halted the stairway procession.

The Seneschal glared at the sneaky matron with despotic ice. He told his guards to haul her back up the staircase. She was tossed from the hideaway like excrement from a chamber pot, her gilded necklace and jewels confiscated.

The inward stream of vulnerable Catholic mothers, children, and the elderly resumed. Their numbers quickly surpassed the capacity of the underground larder. Yet the guards allowed more, stuffing the cellar past its last cranny. Aisling reckoned 200 or more souls seethed within, crying with fright.

When she spotted the long tartan garb of her mother, Ash jerked Fin by the arm. Together, they wormed their way toward her. But Máthair, lost in her mourning of Baby Grace, issued no response.

Just then, a terrific blast jounced the church. English cannons were beating down the Irish stone of the town walls. The church steeple imploded. Mortar crumbled loose and the underground vault of the church filled with noxious smoke. The crowd convulsed into fits of coughing. Pleading eyes solicited Heaven. Screeching voices prayed for the mercy of God.

Ash turned to Fin who was gagging beside her, the color in his face draining rapidly from pink to bone white. "Can't…" the boy gasped, "… breathe." His eyes rolled into their whites and he hitched backwards.

Aisling caught his collapsing body. Fin jerked in her arms. He kept trying to sound her name, but his tongue just clattered against his teeth.

"Máthair, speed! Fin is failing!" Ash cried out. Her mother's face remained a barren slate.

Then their sister Beatha poked from out the protection of Máthair's cloak. The eight-year-old fished inside her mother's chemise and plucked out a slim pouch. "Go on. Take this. The Seneschal will not otherwise be courteous."

Ash smothered the small clink of coin in her fist. For a second, she wavered. These were the very last of the family's meager funds.

"Clap a step, Ash," her younger sister brayed. "Take Fin outdoors so that he might gain air!" With more vitality than she had displayed in weeks, Beatha pressed Ash forward with tiny fingers. "Catch the Lord, Sister."

Fin slumped like a broken toy, his consciousness adrift. Ash hefted his malnourished frame in both arms. She combatted the tightly woven herd to force their way to the exit. At the top of the stairs, she pounded the door.

The lame-legged warden of Seneschal the Black opened it and scowled. "Cower and listen. If you hope to protect your spot in this last refuge, you need cough up a toll."

Ash handed him the coin purse. "Please, spare us a minute. My brother is dying." The guard snatched the bribe but committed to nothing.

In the jaundiced sunlight, Ash hauled Fin around a corner of the church. All creation seemed turned to rust with shot and fire. In every direction, curdling bawls collided with the clang of swords and barking muskets.

Ash towed her brother toward an empty lane where the rooftops coiled with fire. In a small courtyard stood a well. She hauled up the dangling bucket, but it presented only brine. The stream had been corked. Pouring out the fetid water, she sopped Fin's face and slaked his lips.

"Have mercy! Do you seek to murder me with this-" the boy sputtered, "this swamp puss?" He heaved until his wan complexion sucked back his usual rosy gleam. Then he scrutinized the world as if born anew.

Helping her brother to his feet, she anointed him with a kiss. "Now get to it. Move."

Fin did not budge. He dug his feet into the dirt. "What of Rory and Athair? We must lend them a hand."

"We must insist upon living," she retorted, jerking him toward the church.

Still his footsteps contravened. "And if already they have perished, what then?" she asked.

"Burn your mouth, Ash."

"Peer round you, boy. Heaven and earth tumble into Hell. Venables' army is thousands strong. Do you believe a miracle will befall us, is that it?"

His eyes turned acidic.

"The church's hold is our one and only hope." Then, sweetening, she put a hand to his back. "Live past this day, Brother, so that we might serve Rory and Morrough and all our family. We can tend their wounds and shower upon them more affection than ever they have known."

The defiance in the boy's face drained. He knew he was powerless. A seedling in a storm. No matter how much Fintan O'Lorcan wished to assert his burgeoning power, his youth could not be denied. "I only wish to tell Rory that I forgive him. He lessons me sternly because he wishes me to grow into a worthy man. This I know, and I am grateful for it."

She ruffled his hair. "Well, think on that, little peg. Let us be wise today, and tomorrow express our feelings, declaring their worth for all time."

They sped back toward the church basement, passing a clot of Irish Confederates falling to the blades of English soldiers. "Waver not, Fin," Ash instructed.

When they arrived at the front entryway, however, a strikingly contrary version of events awaited. The churchyard was swarmed with English forces. Ash shunted Fin toward a thin copse of trees. Their cover was flimsy, but by the grace of God, the sun had surrendered below the horizon.

English troops ignited torches to surmount the gloom. The flames flounced, disfiguring faces, multiplying size to monstrous dimensions. Ash and Fin witnessed as men lugged wooden pews outside the church and smashed them into shards.

Lurching forth, the shadowy appearance of a horse and rider unleashed a dark energy. Ash recognized the figure as he healed his mare to standing before the church door. "Tis him," she muttered, "Major-General Venables."

A gowned figure scurried to greet the English commander. His vesture was refreshed. His hair, varnished anew, was so black and shiny that it seemed to be crowned by an eggplant. But there was no mistaking the culprit's rude face.

Seneschal the Black, oily with obsequiousness, had his guardsmen bring a wagon. It was loaded with coerced treasures – a chest of coin, rolls of pelt, and kilderkins of butter, tallow and peat. He passed the tribute on to Major-General Venables. The warlord was compensating the English commander with the very goods he had leached from the Irish families in exchange for protecting them.

"Did I not speak it earlier in the church cellar?" Fin whispered. "That pork stump Seneschal the Black is a raging perfidy." She smothered his mouth.

Venables rewarded the turncoat with a carriage and three horses. He allowed the Seneschal to recuse himself along with two women and a measure of personal belongings.

Without a glance back at his soldiers, kinsman, or the sobbing emitted from the church, Seneschal the Black struck the horses. The beasts brayed, gouging the earth with their hooves. The carriage lurched into motion, and that was that. the Irish clans' final prospect of deliverance disappeared into the night. Their entrusted leader had betrayed them.

Enraged, Ash watched the Seneschal fade into obscurity. But the atrocities did not end there.

"Ash!" Fin gasped, scraping his nails across her arm.

She gazed back at the yard and realized that the church was aflame. Fire raced to the sky. The English soldiers were using the shattered church pews as kindling. As their torches awoke the wood, the blaze ramped into a funeral pyre.

Aisling could not block out the horrific cries from the church's basement, women and children begging and howling. "Damn us! Confound me! I burn, I burn!"

She surged from the trees, pitching toward the blaze, but Fin snagged her legs. "Máthair… Beatha…" she panted, hysterical.

He contained her, buckling her head between his grimy hands. "Hearken, Sister," he hissed, and pressed his face close upon hers till she was falling into his blue eyes. "We must insist upon living."

Her lips trembled and she was overpowered by tears. She turned a narrowed glower upon Major-General Robert Venables. The man reviewed the inferno serenely till convinced that not one Irish innocent would survive. Then he spurred his painted mare to a trot and galloped off.

Aisling O'Lorcan clawed a rock from the dirt and hurled it in his direction. "May every curse ever uttered haunt you. May the day come when I, by my own pleasure, unload you into the Devil's arms."

Chapter 5
JAMAICA

IN WHICH PYRATES MEET BUCCANEERS

As they sailed near the north coast of Jamaica, the man now called Iron Eyes asked his companion if he might tackle the seas as captain of the piragua. Tiburon waved him on. Zemi cozied up next to her master, relishing the tickle of wind over her muzzle.

"So, Tibbs," Iron Eyes asked, employing the term of endearment he had hatched for his cherished chum. "Tell me, then, the story of your homeland. Why do we aim for its North Coast? Reveal at last your intentions, I beg you."

"Tis a bellwether where buccaneers enjoy new modes of living, shattering traditions that have reigned over your 'civilized' nations across the sea for centuries," Tiburon proclaimed. He cushioned himself more comfortably against the till and gazed upon the emerging coastline, which was etched by rocky prominences and idyllic vales. Slowly, he strove to put into words the island's history as he grasped it.

Those who knew the Caribbean region well realized that Spain's mastery did not extend completely over Jamaica, Tiburon explained. Possession of the island had been awarded to Cristóbal Colón, the original conquistador. But his heirs governed like Medieval liege lords, directing profits from the colony into their private coffers and inspiring flat-out disinterest on the part of the Spanish Crown. Ignored by its custodians and its king, Jamaica had been orphaned.

Into this quagmire had entered the genius of don Francisco de Leiva. With coercive tactics, he dominated the colony. Three years prior, he had worked the actual governor of Jamaica, don Juan Ramírez de Arellano, into obedience. Then, he had enticed visionary fugitives to populate the island – men who schemed not simply to escape the societies that had inflicted wounds upon them, but to dismember entirely the systems that had rubbed salt into their wounds. He relied upon the buccaneers in two matters. First, they spread terror against foreign enemies who sailed too near this unguarded side of the island. Second, they brought wealth through their illicit trafficking of goods.

The presence of the Brethren of the North Coast – as the *contrabandistas,* conscript defectors, escaped slaves, original *Yndio* inhabitants of the region, displaced Jews, and marauders had classified themselves – provided the true motivation for Tiburon to return to his birthplace. "They are men of eleventh-hour valor," he said.

"And what shall we do when we find them?" Iron Eyes asked, befuddled.

"Aha!" his companion replied, face aglow. "Why, tis the ideal population from which to gather a fresh pyrate crew, Captain Iron Eyes!"

"We shall require a ship, also," his friend replied, mocking Tiburon gently. "Do your plans include that detail?"

But their conversation ended as, with scant warning, the clouds intensified into a squall. Waves broke over their tiny craft. Iron Eyes maintained a look of nonchalance as Tiburon scurried beneath a tarp and Zemi moved to share the shelter. The man flowed with the sea, Tiburon mused, like a true pyrate captain.

"What, Tibbs? Gone so long without a word?" Iron Eyes teased as the heavy skies dissipated.

"Was noticing omens in the gulls and clouds. Hasten us a league short of Santa Ana." His finger directed Iron Eyes toward a harbor of peacock blue and green. "By yonder shore, we ought encounter the buccaneers."

"Can we trust them?"

"Harr, dear Damien," Tiburon chuckled. "From the language of the North Coast Brethren, *trust* is a word expunged."

Iron Eyes tidied his whiskers with smutty fingers. "Can they aid us, then?"

"Based on the talk reaching my ears, one sight of the masterless men burns away any living doubt," Tibbs replied. "And their leader, Mota Sinan? Why he boasts the fame of a gladiator."

Upon landing at Las Chorréras, a vault of trees and brush provided protection for the piragua. The setting sun cast a golden hue across the rolling savannahs and steep limestone ridges that stretched east to west across the center of the island. Bats twirled. Owls repeated their one eternal question.

These serene sounds soon were eclipsed by eerie cries, which escalated over the next hour into blood-curdling shrieks. Zemi howled when cutlashes clanged like cymbals.

They sound like convicts rioting at Newgate Prison, thought Iron Eyes. "Reckon there are thirty," he said aloud.

A sudden colossal crack of muskets caused Zemi to protest again, this time with a disgruntled yelp. Tiburon swayed his head. "More like a force nearing fifty."

Once the commotion had ebbed, Tibbs spoke again. "Tis the hour for our approach." The frogs and cicadas approved by returning to their thrumming.

When the strangers entered the clearing, they were met by a terrifying sight: More than three dozen hunters – almost all decorated upon chests, arms, and necks by gunpowder spots or *tattoos* – aimed their pistols and muskets at Iron Eyes, Tiburon and Zemi. They resembled, Iron Eyes though, the villains of folktales.

"Throw down your arms," their leader commanded. The two visitors obliged, allowing cutlash, pistol, musket, and daggers to thud to the ground. An enormous dark-skinned fellow grasped Zemi firmly by her neck. Tiburon signaled her not to fight.

The man who spoke was dumpy, his blockish form draped in horse hides and dowsed with mud, blood, and hog grease. A wilderness of beard hid much of his face, but any hair he might once have possessed atop his head had fled. Suctioning phlegm up a nose that had been disfigured by countless skirmishes, he demanded, "Identify yourselves."

"The Jamaican islander Tiburon. And this here man? Why, this be the famed pyrate captain Iron Eyes."

"Hold now," the leader replied, slurring his words. He moved so close that they could smell the stench of his breath. "*You* are Iron Eyes? The genuine article? Why, eat a house of cunts! How is it that not a scrap of iron glints in your eyes?" He turned to face the rogues standing behind him and continued with a sneer. "Lads, back my observance. The pigments of his two peepers quarrel, do they not? One is the color of sapphire, the other brown as manure." He spun to scowl once more at the pair. "Are you throwing an egg on me?"

"I'm feeling equally disillusioned," Iron Eyes retorted with a frown. "Tibbs, tell me again what's been said about the legendary buccaneer commander Mota Sinan? The gent you've been lauding cannot possibly be the pickled runt standing before us now!"

"Seems we've been led off a cliff," Tiburon said with chagrin.

"Aye to that."

Seemingly as an afterthought, Tibbs added, "In his favor, note the age of this scrunchy toad. I'd place it around 50 years. Not measly. Here prevails a wild man who has for decades confounded death in a savage habitat. Quite a feat, is it not?"

Iron Eyes raised an eyebrow. "Do you mean to say, Tibbs, that this fellow is the bona fide Mota Sinan? And that he promotes a flabby impression so that others might underestimate him? That would indeed be a savvy strategy."

For the span of several breaths, the crowd of buccaneers stood silent, guns aimed upon the visitors' chests. Then their leader burst into laughter. "Fopdoodles! Triptakers! Saddle geese!" he roared, eyes glinting. "You're speaking with the great Mota Sinan and none other! Come, sit with us, Iron Eyes and Tiburon, and have us swap tales of our quests for freedom."

IN WHICH BUCCANEERS DEFINE DEMOCRACY

A blaze raged at the center of the encampment. The men downed bowls of rum punch with heads thrown back. They ingested giant slabs of beef as if they were but table scraps. Their flintlocks popped unprovoked. Yet they cavorted intimately with one another despite their divergent origins.

They dressed in cured animal hides, binding these also around their feet to serve as shoes. By a cincture of bull's hide at the waist, each harbored three or four lengthy knives as well as a *gargoussier* or cartouche box for the preservation of wad, shot, and slow-match. Many had bored holes through their ears, noses, and lips. All were damaged by battle wounds.

Mota Sinan furnished Iron Eyes and Tiburon with cups of fermented tipple brewed from bananas and sweet potatoes. "Here's to cursing kings, crushing Spaniards, and sticking our steel through all their laws," he cheered them. Then he strengthened his voice and raised a cup to his men. "Revile the past. Disrupt the present. Revoke the eternal!"

"Dignity demands freedom!" Iron Eyes contributed.

The men burst into *huzzahs*. Basking in solidarity, Mota plopped cross-legged beside the strangers.

"You reckoned correctly, Tibbs," Iron Eyes said to his companion, who sat at his side. He turned to Mota. "Your gang of scoundrels numbers near fifty. A notable collection."

Turning his attention away from the pyrate captain, Mota pled in Spanish for more drink from a man he hailed as Toulouk. The Carib warrior was lean, hewn entirely from muscle. With alarmingly sharp teeth that he had filed into points, the man resembled a shark. After distributing drinks, Toulouk sat with them.

"Rarely do we unite into a full complement," Mota clarified. "Usully, 15 to 25 men mingle at a time, and all depart whenever they please. Ain't none conscripted. We operate entirely by cooperation."

Most of the buccaneers, Iron Eyes noted, like many inhabitants of the region, could flit with respectable ease between English and Spanish. Toulouk continued the conversation in Spanish.

"The Brethren draw from the principles of this land's first people – *our* kind," he said, raising his cup to Tiburon. "We thrived upon these islands long before Cristóbal Colón invaded our quiet world with greed and carnage. Our ancestors were not without blood spilling and warfare, mind you. But they lived nevertheless by a creed of compromise, generosity, and care for the community. Our elders taught that people may be trusted as rulers over themselves. Long have we lived as individuals united in common pursuits, each with an equal voice."

"Aye!" Tibbs seconded, touching his mug to Toulouk's.

"Harr, elaborating on the ways of our Arawak, Carib and Taíno friends..." Mota toasted with his punch, "we have forged codes to regulate our quarrels and decide our future direction. From first to last, every man recognizes that these contracts must remain pliable, shifting as our wisdom gathers."

"The true diamond of the glittering charter of the North Coast Brethren," Toulouk attempted English now, "is that any color or kind of person may partake of…" he winced. The word he desired refused to come to mind.

Mota intervened. "Partake of the polity."

"Aye, partake of the polity," Toulouk nodded, planting a beholden hand on Mota's shoulder. "Which means, any man may rise even to the seat of leader."

"Our covenant stands upon free choice through the determination of the common vote. Every member's voice carries identical weight." Mota drowned his cup to culminate the dissertation.

"Tis much the same for us pyrates, who live and fight by a common code and equal vote," Iron Eyes said, though the velvety tipple had begun to muffle his wits and drag down his eyelids.

"Some have called these tropical islands of the Spanish Americas *the Kingdom of Cockaigne*. We live in a real-world Utopia," Mota purred. Fending off a yawn, he quoted the verse of John Donne:

License my roving hands, and let them go,

Before, behind, between, above, below,

O my America! My new-found-land,

my Kingdom's safest when with one man man'd.

He closed with his own stanza. "And why should *we* not be the ones to suck from out this land all its marrow?"

IN WHICH MATES BICKER

The fire had mellowed by morning. Although three simple shacks stood about the clearing, a vast share of the buccaneers slept outside with no covering, cozied into bushes or flattened against raw earth. Iron Eyes and Tiburon stumbled back to the hearth along with a smattering of other puffy-eyed men, their wits still rubbery from the buccaneer punch. They swapped mugs of swill for the coffee brewing in the cauldron.

Pulling Zemi close for warmth, Tibbs fell into conversation with an aqua-eyed lank who followed the good faith of a handshake.

"Winter Seasal," he introduced himself.

"I detect a lilt to your English," Tiburon said. "How did you come to these parts?"

"I renounced the miserable colony of Jamestown in Virginia for these sultry climes and the promise of an easygoing life," Winter replied.

A jolt of bawling broke the peace. A buccaneer rocketed out of a wattle shack. "The curse of marriage!" he keened in conspicuously elegant Spanish. "Tis like the dead man's jig beneath the gallows. Furious fuck! Diabolical bones! Divest me, holy God, of my appetite for love and turn that Judas into a rotted chunk of cow!"

Skulking to a place around the firepit, the love-ravaged Dario Colón downed a bowl of palm wine, insouciant as to the early hour. "Pray how the sky, no matter day or night, is eternally black when one is murdered in the heart."

"Oh, tears of tragedy! How arduous it is to be a descendent of Admiral Christopher Columbus!" ribbed Winter Seasal. "If only you had kept that peanut-sized pecker in your trousers, Dario, you would be feasting upon delicacies this very morn, a prince lolling about his mansion."

"Aww *Señor* Seasal, never doubt my love for you," Dario retorted. "But as an illiterate sailor who cannot even swim, your comments amount to nothing more than ass gas."

Winter chuckled. Iron Eyes snorted. He found himself swept by affection for these two men of acidic charms.

Witnessing the bemused glint in the pyrate's eyes, Winter shed a light on Dario's background and the nature of his thorny marriage to Huracán. The Spanish heir and the African titan had been betrothed for nearly a year, he said, yet they suffered from chronic explosive disputes.

"My lover is a jealous man of beastly stature whose forbears were stolen from Dahomey," Dario said. "He roars with righteous rage."

As for Dario Colón, he appeared the most incongruent person ever to have graced the barbaric, smutty ranks of Mota's Brethren. A thoroughbred noble, he really could trace his bloodlines to Cristóbal Colón. But his family had disowned him due to his homosexuality. Fortunately, Dario enjoyed chasing adventure. He had won a place among Mota's men by proving himself an undisputed maestro of the *boucan*, upon which he barbequed the most delectable meat.

"And you two men are actually married?" Iron Eyes asked, gaping with wonderment.

"*Matelotage*," Dario answered, demonstrating equal grace with English as with Spanish., "is a union of shared property grounded – if one commands a modicum of dignity – in mutual affection and welfare. The compact is recognized by us buccaneers as similar to any union between two people under God." He retreated into his palm wine. "Yet seeing that our kind is considered *diseased* by Christian minds, our arrangement is not honored by any kingly law. As such, it takes a place on the lengthy list of innovations promoted by us Brethren – free people unencumbered by society's judgments."

In that instant, Iron Eyes realized that the term *matelotage* must have sprung from *mate*, a term of endearment amongst sailors. He drifted into remembrances of his namesake, envisioning the true Damien Baines swimming through the surf, naked and beckoning. Fantasizing, he saw the two of them aging gently together in their own *matelotage* here amongst the Brethren of the North Coast.

Mota approached the firepit and stoked the flames. Iron Eyes studied the buccaneer through the shimmering heat. The pyrate captain cleared his throat. "I was mistaken, *camarado*. I out retract last night's remarks about you."

"How now?" cracked Mota. "An apology?"

Iron Eyes smirked. "It strikes me that your men bear feisty and admirable credentials. And that you are a noble defender of the common man."

"You don't curtsy to kingly laws, either," Tibbs concurred.

"My prejudice against you was undeserved, as well," Mota said to Iron Eyes. "You came upon us after rumors of your death. To witness you, a rising legend, in the flesh… ho now! My mates were smacked sideways in awe." His laughter emerged with a belch. "If you'd like to join our fellowship, I welcome you both. But every last rogue wields a ballot, as I mentioned. We scratch our *yea* or *naye* upon a round-ball, toss it into the calabash, and then tally the vote."

"Just the chance of it brings us joy," thanked Tiburon.

"Huzzah!" Iron Eyes cheered.

Mota Sinan rose to fetch the calabash, but then stopped. He peered back at Iron Eyes.

"Something is troubling you?" the pyrate captain questioned.

"I have no doubt that our pack will admit you. But… Well, we know of warrants flying about these parts. The Crown of Spain wants you dead. We enjoy a peaceful relationship with don Francisco de Leiva and the Jamaica islanders. So, do you see my worry?"

"My mere breathing near you places you in peril," Iron Eyes acknowledged.

Mota allocated a second for the pyrate to feel the gravity of his position. Then crinkles contracted the edges of his eyes. "But what is living without a dab of lunacy?"

Later that morning, the buccaneers favored admitting the fresh arrivals by a rare unanimous vote. They initiated Iron Eyes and Tiburon into the North Coast Brethren by pouring down their gullets rum infused with gunpowder, a drink they called *kill-devil.* Before noon, both recruits lay pancaked upon the dirt.

Similar antics knitted days into weeks, though the intoxicated buccaneers could not testify as to the precise passage of time. Just like pyrates, Iron Eyes noted, Mota Sinan's men pledged themselves to hedonism. They would sober only when the final bowl of punch, clink of coin, and portion of charred boar had been exhausted.

IN WHICH MORALS ARE QUESTIONED

With long faces, the men braved several days in poverty, their stores of smoked meat and punch depleted. It was the custom of the buccaneers to raze and resurrect their encampment in relation to the caprices of ranging longhorn cattle, wild horses, and boar.

Finally, upon a balmy morning, Huracán came whooping into the clearing. "Heigho! Hogsteers! Wild boar scour the western savannah!"

Mota Sinan was in the midst of sanitizing his teeth with a sassafras stick. He flung it into the fire and rejoiced. "Strap on your pikes and dash after the Devil, my fighting cocks. We ride!"

All but a handful of men catapulted into motion. This, after all, was the buccaneers' passion. When not destroying their senses with drink or lusting after Taíno whores who strained to support the perishing nearby settlements, the hunters worshipped the hunt. They readied guns, dogs, and horses.

Tiburon and Iron Eyes voiced their keenness to join. A soft-spoken Taíno man named Bequo broached a potential friendship by offering them *jungas.* The Maroon weapons were nine-foot pikes pronged with four steel daggers. Bequo had won the appliances by trading with the renegades. Every fortnight or so, the Maroons would slink down from their rocky bulwarks offering herbal medicaments, spices, and stoutly-crafted lances in exchange for tallow hides and smoked animal flesh. Above all, they adored Dario Colón's richly spiced meat, which they called *jerked*.

Within the hour, the *chasseurs* sallied forth. Never before had Iron Eyes witnessed such roaring horsemanship. Awesome to behold, it eluded description. Tiburon, too, was mesmerized by the symphony of thundering hooves and buccaneer athleticism. He soon learned, however, that he had leaped headfirst into the wrong activity for his composition.

At a distance of three leagues from their encampment, Huracán gestured the men to halt by the edge of a woodland. He enforced a slow gait with hushed steps through the tall grass. At his whistle, the hounds, who had been reared as malicious beasts, tore into the forest. Zemi, with a snap of her massive jaws, insinuated herself into the crazed melee.

From out the shrubbery, two dozen spiny black hogs came racing. An eruption of fusee shots, snarling dogs, and squealing pigs devastated the senses, jangling Tiburon's nerves.

The tusked males proved impervious to fright. They gorged the horses at the legs. One man, thrown from his saddle, soared into a rock outcropping. The impact split his head. Another was fortunate enough to land on soft earth, but a hysterical horse crushed his lungs with its thrashing hooves.

In their breakneck pursuit, the buccaneers slowed not to inventory the loss of life. On the contrary, they redoubled their efforts. Huracán whistled again at the canines, urging them to fall upon the sows and separate female boars from male.

Goaded into terror, the female pigs hurried to their dens, thereby leading the hunters directly to their broods. The *chasseurs* gleefully clubbed every piglet to death as their hounds jugulated the screaming mothers.

The buccaneers repeated the gruesome activity for the next several days until they had collected over 100 kills. These they hauled back to the camp's *abattoir* site, where Dario Colón had readied the finely-wrought, tempered wooden frames of the *boucans*. Just now, he was fanning the flames of the so-called Brethren fire. It would continue to blaze for nearly a week.

Tiburon, ornamented in boar blood, sought out Iron Eyes. "Pig-murdering with these furies is no stroll in the lilies," he confessed, feeling a weight upon his heart. "Which is worse? That they slaughter powerless babes and call it bravery? Or that they forsake their own dead without sentiment or the honor of final rites?"

"This is a clan of wild men, Tibbs," Iron Eyes shrugged.

Tiburon shook his head, eyes tightening. "You have come to appreciate the person who stands before you, Damien. Hand me a knife, and I shall sever any creature who intends to harm you from balls to throat. But this is not that. The North Coast Brethren may be visionaries with pounding spirits, but they amount to no more than mauling reptiles if they live without dignity. Even they ought to respect helpless creatures and honor their dead friends, do you not concur? Otherwise, how can their fellowship endure? Especially one that aims to meet the intricate demands of self-rule?"

Iron Eyes gazed with soft eyes upon his friend. "Your wisdom extends far beyond your years."

A gaggle of Mota's men shuffled toward the fire. Tiburon lowered his voice. "To me, they act as menaces with the coldest hearts."

IN WHICH A BANQUET IS CONSUMED

Dario Colón always attired himself elaborately. His hide trousers he embellished with silver and copper thread. A doublet of the softest calfskin he complimented with strings of tortoise shell. But within ten minutes of commencing his labors at the boucan, he was spattered with grease and pig viscera. His hands were seared, his creamy complexion charred. Nonetheless, he travailed amongst the carcass fumes for days, until the butchering grounds had devolved into a bog of blood and entrails. His devotion delivered toothsome morsels of meat swimming in tangy drippings.

As soon as Dario had completed his task, the buccaneers gathered for a banquet with great cheer. Clouds of flies had descended upon the huts where the supplemental flesh hung drying, but even they quit harassing the Brethren for the night.

Mota Sinan sucked marrow from a loin bone, then extended the treat to Iron Eyes. "Go on. Lay into it. We call this delicacy *the brandy*."

Iron Eyes set the bone to his lips and savored its ambrosia. The remnants he tossed to Zemi. When the boisterous glee lulled, he roused a conversation. "What are your thoughts on Jamaica?"

Mota answered in an instant. "It excels thanks to the sloop trade, which don Francisco de Leiva himself promotes."

"To de Leiva's cunning!" Tiburon lofted his cup in agreement. "Nowhere amidst *Las Islas de Barlovento* does there exist a more bustling contraband trade."

"Don't forget that our Jamaica is the sole Spanish possession in the world willing to absorb a citizenry of open Jews!" Mota cheered. "My people desire a cornerstone of this New World."

Iron Eyes scrutinized the buccaneer leader. Lit by the glowing coals, he seemed suddenly ancient and fatigued. "Is this your crusade, then? A thirst to rout the Spaniards from the isle of Jamaica?"

"My crusade is that which has been carried by generations of Sephardic Jews for the past 150 years," Mota replied. "We seek a home."

IN WHICH PYRATES ARE DISCOVERED AMONGST BUCCANEERS

Embedded with the North Coast Brethren, Tiburon and Iron Eyes encountered sensible policies and illuminating maxims alongside grotesque indulgence and ranting imbecility. They binged upon both for a period of three moons.

Tiburon widened his friendship with Toulouk and Bequo. One afternoon, they invited him to join them in shaping a dugout canoe in the manner of their forefathers. A felled cottonwood tree would be transformed, through the employment of naught else but adze and fire, into a vessel that could skim elegantly the water's surface.

Four others petitioned to participate in the sacred labor. The previous summer, these men had fled enslavement upon de Leiva's sugar estate in Guanaboa. Though he found them dully stoic in bearing, Toulouk motioned them to come along.

The elderly Ibrahim Reis was the patriarchal figure. His henna-colored skin was eroded more from life's ordeals than the passage of time. His scarred backside testified to the brutality he had endured. Scipio and Xiki both had been kidnapped from the Kingdom of Angola. Although they called themselves brothers, Xiki was shaped like a flour sack, whereas Scipio maintained the lean form of a plank. Their fourth companion, Chucho, was of Taíno origin, like Tiburon. Notably, he lacked a right ear. Upon an earlier attempt at freedom, *blackshots* – mercenary Negro servants who worked as bounty hunters – had nabbed him and claimed the ear as a trophy.

As they worked, Tiburon marveled at the choreography of the two native islander craftsmen. Toulouk sparked a fire at the center of the massive cottonwood trunk, while Bequo pacified the flames at the ends. They did not pause, even as they crisped their hands and singed their hair in order to scrape at the simmering wood. Before long it cleaved, willing as clay.

"Strangle the fire there!" Toulouk bellowed. A tail of flame had come whipping at Tiburon with the fury of a caiman. Tibbs hurled half a calabash of water on the torrent.

The smoke sent Scipio into a coughing fit. He dove his head into a tub of spring water, then sagged onto the grass. "My story is a summation of slavery's woes," he volunteered.

Silently, the other men created space for Scipio to unload his darkest recollections. "I took Nucay as my wife for one day. For one day, our covenant was blessed." His gentle smile faded. "Upon the second night of our marriage, the drover came visiting our quarters, his face shining with greed. He placed a gun barrel between my eyes and commanded me to keep out of the hutch. It was his turn in our marriage bed, he said. And the next night, and the next night, and the next."

Scipio shook his head, as if hoping to free himself of the images. "Sunday comes. For the two hours of Matin and Mass, we are not forced to work. I snatch a blade from the scullery. When the drover comes again that night, I slice open his guts. Before dawn, the master of the manor peels me open with the cat-o'-nine-tails. I am not meant to live. And Nucay, my innocent beauty? He shoots her in the head."

Toulouk bent to offer him a sup of fresh water from the calabash. Scipio drank, then forged on. "For two weeks, I could not move. Locked in the hell-heat of the boiling house, I lay balled up in a fever, shitting my insides out. The very day I was able to walk into the cane fields, I ran." A mist glazed his eyes. He stared at his hands. "My beloved, my Nucay. She was a butterfly trapped in the hatred of this world."

Bats began circling in the gloaming. The men returned to their task. Soon, the innards of the cottonwood trunk had been evicted and the timber miraculously formed into a roughhewn canoe. Later, they would harness adzes to shape an elegant stem and stern.

Tiburon gauged the carbon-coated group with a grin. *Toulouk is a tremendous shipwright. Artistry flows through Bequo's hands. The other four men crave to burn this world down and forge it anew. Such is the substance of fine pyrates.*

Iron Eyes, meanwhile, joined Winter Seasal and half a dozen more men on a coastal excursion. They launched a humble squad of canoes from Las Chorréras and traveled eastward, oaring into bays in search of susceptible trading ships.

All seagoing vessels periodically were confined on shore for the tedious yet requisite chore of caulking and careening their hulls. The procedure rendered the ships paralyzed. Plundering them was a child's game. Upon the rare occasion when the ill-paid, overworked merchant sailors roused themselves to mount a defense, the buccaneers had only to pop their muskets to end their lives.

They encountered just such a situation at Santa Gloria. When several sailors fired from the sand, Iron Eyes was able to witness the buccaneer sharpshooters' response. Their skills rivaled his own. The Low-Dutch sailors quickly surrendered, and the North Coast Brethren collected a significant haul. Iron Eyes salivated at the thought of these men joining his company of sea rovers.

They returned to camp with a generous spread of gold dust, ready money, jewels, and trading wares in the form of sandalwood, sugar, and cacao. These prizes far supplanted the value of the hides, meat, and tallow that the Brethren produced. A chorus of *huzzahs* erupted.

The only matter that caused Iron Eyes and Tiburon concern as they entered their fourth month as buccaneers was Mota Sinan's reaction to them. His attitude grew progressively less warm. These days, they noticed, he offered but a wooden smile, improvising always an excuse to turn to some urgent task. As the pyrates rose to eminence, Mota seemed to tabulate their every move as if playing a high-stakes game of cards.

IN WHICH DEFECTION IS DEBATED

Tensions within the camp escalated rapidly. Events reached a crucible the day before Easter 1653.

It began when Mota Sinan entreated Iron Eyes for an intimate audience. He selected for their caucus a lush vale that stood a pleasant distance from camp. Here rested the forgotten ruins of Nueva Sevilla, the original Spanish settlement upon the island. It consisted of no more than a few crumbling stone walls, which rapidly were being reclaimed by the jungle.

"I shall cut to the core, Iron Eyes," Mota said. "A faction of my men speak of defecting from our landed society to form a free nation upon the sea – under your leadership."

"Ho, I prompted no such rumblings, Mota, my oath to that. But say it is so. Still, we need not end with severing from you," Iron Eyes reasoned. "We remain united in purpose."

"See now, Damien, we have no use for your unicorn fancies. We North Coast Brethren are fulfilled by our present arrangement, carefree as Adams in Paradise."

"You're speaking of the stilted deal thrown your direction by don Francisco de Leiva?"

"What of our compact appears flawed to you?" Mota questioned back. "The Inquisition confers the title of High Sheriff of the Holy Crusade upon a few select men. De Leiva holds unbounded power over the region. With his steel clout and crystal vision, he unlocked Jamaica's north coast for us. He gives us reign to operate with scarce regulation. We live already as a free nation."

"A false Utopia."

"A bed of velvet that deserves to be kissed all over," Mota argued.

Iron Eyes fell silent. Mota unsheathed a nine-inch dagger better known as a *buccaneer's toothpick* and explored casually the sharpness of the blade.

Iron Eyes laughed and offered a dram of rum from his leather pouch. "If I may speak with no shackles upon my tongue?"

Mota took the pouch and supped heartily.

"You have bent the knee to de Leiva, Mota Sinan. You no longer act the hero. You have shrunk to the size of a grub, eyes to the ground seeking shit upon which to feast."

"Harr!" Mota barked, spewing rum. "And you, Iron Eyes, you flightless fledgling? The words you prattle are no more than infant sputter."

"I am only petitioning for plain talk, one Brethren to another," Iron Eyes hastened.

Mota pointed his blade at the pyrate's chest, shaking. "Shut your mouth, or I shall plunge this dagger through it and shut it forever."

"Let us take our debate before the men, then," Iron Eyes returned serenely. "Tis the Brethren way, is it not?"

Less than an hour later, the two leaders stood before the fire. Fifty rugged souls had gathered. They sat upon the ground quietly, captivated by the prospect of a debate.

Mota started. "Damien Baines, though entrusted with considerable talents and bold in temper, lacks seasoned grit. He has not the gumption to face the adversities he so frantically pursues. Whereas we, my friends, enjoy a free and easy existence under the protection of the most powerful man in the region – the best of all possible worlds."

Iron Eyes snatched his moment. "Master Mota is the King of Rogues, no one can argue that fact. But his years of striving have suffocated his fire." Iron Eyes circulated amongst the crowd. "Tiburon brought us here to move as a force. And although Master Sinan joins me in the cry for freedom, he has grown tired of the struggle and taken up shelter in the bosom of the enemy. Like the dirt beneath our feet, Mota Sinan suffers the trampling of his guarantor, don Francisco de Leiva. Who of you roaring rovers admires such meek obedience? Here, you live as servants clad in invisible irons."

"I am a friend of safety and preservation, that is true," Mota hissed, cheeks firing red. "You might try living past all that has broken me."

Iron Eyes held his attention upon the men. "Lounging about the North Coast from month to month, acting as pawns to a Spaniard… Is this your destiny? You, whose hearts are so relentless and unafraid? You might inspire freedom seekers the world over, seeding hope amongst those who have suffered agony at the hands of the entitled!"

"And you, Iron Eyes. You trust the high seas to bring you terrific freedom?"

"Aye, mate, and more!" the pyrate captain proclaimed. "We can create a sovereign state upon the seas. We can stamp our names into the history books. While you cast aside immortality in favor of a few scruffy acres of land?"

Mota's cackles devolved into a coughing fit. He sleeved the lather bunching at the corners of his mouth. "If you proceed at your present trajectory, you will accomplish nothing more than the murder of every unfortunate man who votes to take your side," he admonished. "Such a pity, captain. Your ideals leave you strangled in the weeds."

Iron Eyes thrust forth his chin and reflexively gripped his pistol. "You are an apology of a rebel."

Tibbs winced at the rashness of the man's words. Yet silently, he applauded the transformation unfolding before him. Iron Eyes was, in that moment, the very incarnation of the pyrate captain whose name he now wore with pride.

Mota tore his pistol free of its sling. Tiburon at once leapt at the iron and shoved it away from Iron Eyes.

Reluctantly, the buccaneer leader retired his weapon and subdued his anger. "Freedom is but an illusion. All of us are vassals to greater masters. Even King Felipe IV of Spain negotiates with other rulers. Even he bows before the Pope and God. We are wise to take compromises where we may."

Not one sound arose from the usually rowdy crowd. Mota Sinan drew a regrettable breath before offering a hand to Iron Eyes. With his words, he formed a pact. "A poll shall reveal which of my hard-won brothers casts their lot with you, and thus discards me. Let us part as opponents in doctrine, but friends in purpose."

IN WHICH PYRATES ARE BETRAYED

The tabulation of ballots proved Mota Sinan triumphant. Only a few buccaneers voted to defect from the Brethren of the North Coast in order to join Iron Eyes and Tiburon as sea rovers. Mota asked those who remained loyal to him to ready their horses for a hunt the next morning. At dawn on Easter Day, they slipped away from the encampment without a parting word.

Daylight, when it trudged across the sky, was capable of no more than a wooly gloom, contributing a desolate air to the settlement. Huracán blasted from out his *bohío* bare-naked, a tempest with manhood still alert. "Fuck a fish! The hunt departed hours past." He reeled back upon the shack and bellowed, "I ought trepan you, Dario!"

His lover crept from out the thatched shelter. Dario Colón yawned extravagantly, kneaded a crick from his neck, and slipped into a set of shorn breeches. "Am *I* to be blamed for *your* goatish lust? Tsk and toss off."

"Bastard!" Huracán snapped.

Iron Eyes, Tibbs, and Zemi, seeking a better view of the entertainment, sat upon a log by the dying fire. "Their coupling is a riddle," Iron Eyes commented.

Ibrahim, Scipio, Xiki, and Chucho, the four men who recently had escaped enslavement upon de Leiva's estate, lounged on an adjacent plot of grass. Toulouk, the shipwright, was filing his teeth into needles by dint of a stone arrowhead. His companion Bequo was breakfasting upon forgotten cakes of cassava. The New Englander Winter Seasal rubbed sleep from his eyes.

Iron Eyes digested the final tally. Of the roughly 50 buccaneers, only these seven had enlisted with himself and Tiburon. And yet, appreciating the skills and traits of each one, he remained impervious to disappointment.

"Don't figure me an ally, Iron Eyes!" Huracán shouted, causing the pyrate captain to grin. "I had no mind to stand by you yesterday, and even less desire to befriend you this morning. A stupid blunder caused me to tarry, on account of this voracious bugger." He jabbed a thumb at his mate.

"Calk your hole," Dario cracked.

Tiburon flung at Huracán a horse blanket with which to cover his muscle-striated frame. The giant man twisted it about his waist without ceasing to grumble. "It was never my plan to lark with you acorns."

"Hey ho!" Iron Eyes cheered Huracán with his coffee tin, smiling still. "Cease cringing like some enslaved knockabout. You're a damn North Coast Brethren, Huracán – a rare and lucky lad with every chance in the world. If you so desire, then scuttle off after Mota's clan. He'll embrace you yet."

Dario planted himself upon the log beside Tiburon and lent Zemi his affection. "You *chicas* have space for one more?"

Huracán glared at his lover. The disinherited Spanish nobleman shrugged. "Alas, my darling civet cat, ours was never a starry marriage, merely a galactic fuck affair."

With that, Huracán exited their consortium sporting nothing more than a toga. The men chuckled.

Then Tiburon went quiet.

Iron Eyes was the first to discern the eerie transformation. "Seen a ghost?" he asked.

"Look around. Where are our weapons?" Tiburon said. He could not locate his musket nor the guns of the other men, which ought to have been stowed about the camp.

Iron Eyes wrapped his hand about the hilt of his cherry wood pistol. He always slept on it for precisely this reason.

In that second, Zemi started barking in the direction of the trees. She snarled, pinned back her ears, and burst with full-throated mania. But it was only Huracán emerging from the woods. The large man staggered forward, babbling something incomprehensible.

"Back so soon, my love?" Dario tutted.

Huracán did not reply. He struggled another foot toward his partner in *matelotage* before blowing over like a candle flame. His immense body met the earth with a thud.

"Goat of Ghenna!" Dario shivered. Iron Eyes, Tiburon, and the others reared back in shock. A small hatchet was plugged into Huracán's spine.

"Mota, you motherless runt cock!" Dario sizzled. "That scurvy-infested rogue has betrayed us!"

"Fuck bricks," Winter Seasal muttered.

"Get moving, gents. We must leave this camp at once!" Iron Eyes shouted.

"Head to where the land downslopes!" Tiburon yelled. "Flee to the basin so we can gather our vessels and escape down the river!"

At that moment, an onslaught of salvoes began to batter the pasture. Within seconds, the air was a blizzard of wood shards, gunpowder smoke, and whirling lead balls. A bullet skimmed Iron Eyes' still weaker left leg. It went gummy and he crumpled.

A hand hoisted him up. With a surge of power, someone heaved him away from the devastation. Iron Eyes recognized his redeemer. It was Tiburon, blood trickling from his right ear and powder burns scarring his previously smooth cheek.

"The others…?" Iron Eyes gasped.

Keeping a steady arm around Iron Eyes, Tiburon ran fast as he was able through the woodland, heart pumping. Round-shots banged from across the meadow. Musket balls nipped at their heels. At the downgrade, they made out the forms of Bequo, Toulouk, Dario, and Scipio. Just behind them, Winter fought to escape the madness. They skidded down the lichen-carpeted slope with bullets chasing.

"There!" Tiburon commanded the men.

The path terminated abruptly. "Tibbs, you mentioned nothing about killing ourselves on suicide cliffs!" Iron Eyes protested.

"Just shut your eyes," Tiburon hollered as he flung them both over the ledge.

"Ahhhh!" In quick succession, Iron Eyes and his nine companions plunged 76 feet to fates unknown.

Iron Eyes smashed through branches until he landed upon what he was certain to be rock. The impact incited agony. Craving breath, he realized he was underwater. He exploded to the surface a gasping shamble.

Once he had regained his breathing and his eyesight, he discovered the worst. His friends already were being lined up along the far side of the riverbank. Tiburon, Bequo, Toulouk, Dario, Winter, Scipio, Ibrahim, Chucho and Xiki all had been captured and forced upon their knees. A coalition of degenerates held flintlocks to their temples, threatening execution. It puzzled Iron Eyes, however, that not one of the nine buccaneers had been killed.

A man with a face of gnarled rubble shouted in Spanish over the rumbling of the waterfall. "If you aim to avoid a massacre, do not attempt escape. With joy, I shall blast your companions from life, one after the other."

Conceding, Iron Eyes trod through the heavy currents at the foot of the rapids and towards the riverbank.

The bounty hunter strode into the flow of water to meet him. "Iron Eyes, the pyrate captain. Tis you?"

"Who yearns to know?" Iron Eyes questioned gamily, pushing himself onto the sodden clay of the bankside.

"I am El Mulato, but that is of no concern to you. I am but an implement of a potentate. *His* name should haunt you."

"To that end, speak *his* name."

"Oh, with pleasure," responded El Mulato, stepping nearer. "Don Francisco de Leiva."

Iron Eyes grimaced, scenting again the vinegar of Mota's betrayal.

"Don Francisco de Leiva has known for many weeks that you were inhabiting the North Coast of his island. Also, His Most Catholic Majesty has condemned you to death as punishment for indignities perpetrated upon La Flota and her flagship, El Lion del Oro." The bounty hunter turned to one of his minions. "Have I recited it as we rehearsed?"

"Perfectly," praised the younger man.

El Mulato beamed. "Get to it, then. We aim south, for the capital of Jamaica." His pack of knaves grappled Iron Eyes to the ground and tied up all the captives with tightly-wound cord.

Dario's face purpled with rage. "That ass-ache Mota Sinan, may he be nailed to the stoop of purgatory! How dare he hand us to the gallows only to further ingratiate himself to de Leiva!"

But again, Iron Eyes questioned the strange circumstances, wondering about de Leiva's motives. If de Leiva had wanted him dead, would he not be dead?

Chapter 6
JAMAICA

IN WHICH RULERS TAKE A RIDE

Don Francisco de Leiva's carriage scoured the dusty roadway, aiming toward Jamaica's capital settlement of St. Jago de la Vega. The hillocks it traversed boasted numerous *rancheros*, where fields of tobacco and cane were marked by the occasional sugar mill and refinery. It was a pleasing parade of enterprise, he thought, for each asset contributed to his astronomical wealth.

For the Spanish citizenry who plied the seven estates of this sprawling *hato* – a land grant dominating the southern portion of the island – the sight of de Leiva's trundling vehicle elicited tense whispers. The malignantly-styled sedan was varnished black with window-glass draped by dark, heavy damask. Emblazoned in gold leaf upon the side panels was the family's coat of arms. The plate inscribed at the rear heralded de Leiva as a High Sheriff of the Holy Inquisition. It proclaimed itself a chariot of the Underworld.

De Leiva reveled in the fearful looks from passersby as his carriage shoved past. Hawkers, muleteers, fruit vendors, and fish mongers scurried out of the way. Yet he also enjoyed witnessing the industry burgeoning upon his island. In a gesture that belied his prejudices, he waved at everyone from Jewish blade grinders, to free Black men or *horas* licensed as copper menders, to English brickmakers traveling to town on foot.

Opposite him, Maxi Supa upon the black velvet cushions of the cabin, her nose turned up at the vulgar castes outside. She sipped from a jug of coffee flavored by tamarind. "Do tell me, my champion and love, has any word come from your *soldados*?" she inquired in a dulcet voice.

"I have sent my finest after the Maroons. Before the next full moon crowns, Nani, that black whore, shall be quartered and her head rammed upon a spike," he declared, gesturing for Maxi to share her beverage.

"And what of that bleached cockroach, your servant Throat? I never did comprehend your faith in him." She handed him a mug of coffee with a scowl.

"Imagine this. Throat hails from Salem, a town in the English colony of Plymouth. His mother was a witch."

"Eww," she replied. "Never."

The carriage bounced over a boulder, causing de Leiva to sputter a sup of coffee. "Alas, Throat holidays at present in the gaol, where he suffers alongside the felons of the month."

"Mm-hmm," Maxi murmured. "A solid man for trifling thuggery; a trifling man for battles of state."

De Leiva chuckled, drinking up the nectar of her enormous honey eyes. His wits seized whenever he locked his gaze upon her. He could not say that he loved his mistress, but he desired her like a fiend starving for sin. Maxi Supa was uncompromising in her demand that he prettify her with the latest fashions from France. Yet she enjoyed painting her face with intricate maquillage in the fashion of her Amerindian mother and grandmothers. As a result, she appeared to him like an exotic bird.

"But have you recovered the strongbox that Throat lost on your behalf?" she admonished him. "I did not deliver myself spitting and cursing to your roughcast island so that I might trail your coffin in tears."

"No need for you to worry, my starling."

"I suggest you look truth in the face and ready yourself to die, my prince. For if you fail to recover the strongbox, that is your certain fate."

His vitality slipping, de Leiva fell back against the couch. He recalled the journey during which he had found his mistress and brought her home.

Three years ago, he had voyaged to Potosí as a newly-minted Familiar of the Holy Inquisition. The so-called *silver city that transformed the world* was mythic from Beijing to Byzantium. For more than a century, the wealth mined from the Bolivian highlands had provided half the silver known to humankind. Meanwhile, enslaved under the Spanish Empire's *repartimiento* policy, the Native people suffered endless abuse at the hands of the very men who relied so completely upon them and the treasures buried in their stolen lands.

De Leiva's Church-appointed mission had been twofold: He was to fathom the economics of the mines, and also to procure a servant from the region. Maxi Supa's tribe spoke and wrote in a language incomprehensible to the rest of the world. The Inquisitors had decided to rely upon them to encrypt all correspondence between one another and with the Crown, so that their messages could be deciphered only by Quechuans. De Leiva had thrilled in finding a conspirator not only sharp in wit, but also stunning in physical attributes. He had not, however, anticipated falling so completely for her charms.

IN WHICH A TRIAL IS HELD

The La Vega church, Jamaica's squat enforcer of the One True Faith, was pealing her bells by the time de Leiva's coach arrived at the capital settlement. The summons for Vespers, the evening devotional, reverberated as far as the seaside shanties of *La Otra Banda*. A whiff of chemicals, grease, and putrid hides from the tannery district breezed across the main plaza.

Friars trod scrupulously into the abbey. Women scampered behind, attracting the interest of militia men who whistled at the youngest and most flirtatious. Furtive men of sufficient means, recognizing an opportunity to escape God and family, hustled downriver to the brothels.

Statues at the center of the square honored his Most Catholic Majesty and the *conquistadores* Francisco Pizarro and Hernán Cortés. Beneath them, upon a bed of satin grass, drudgers retired from the day's toils with tokes of baccy and nips of sherry. Baggage slaves and porters napped in dust and horse dung at the edge of the roadway.

Behind the stables were less charming scenes of public urination, defecation, and vomiting due to inebriation. Howling and banging arose from the prisoners restrained in the public goal, their ruckus doing battle with the tinkling notes of a lone guitarist who played from the Cabildo stairs.

As a way to remind citizens of his eminence, don Francisco de Leiva dismounted from his carriage with a flourish of his purple cape and strutted alone up the stairs of the *audencia*. Here, he reaffirmed monthly his dominion over the island.

The grand room of the government building was illuminated by 100 tapers. The candlelight served to flaunt his height, nobly chiseled features, spotless complexion, and shoulder-length flow of brown ringlets brindled with gray. A distressingly handsome figure, his conduct was nonetheless ruthless.

He sat at the head of a vast teak table, his fellow leading men populating either side of its monumental length. The fact that the governor was not present at this assembly surprised no one. All the *alcade* officers recognized that Governor Juan Ramírez de Arellano ruled from de Leiva's kennel. It was don Francisco who determined the fabric of life, the fortunes of enterprises, the course of law, and the retaliations of the Church upon the isle of Jamaica.

Outcast to the far end of the table where they sat shrouded in darkness were the men who championed the opinions of the governor and remained loyal to the Colón heirs. Paco de Proenza, head of the island militia, held the seat of honor beside his patron on the right. On de Leiva's left sat his son Justo. The 18-year-old detested anyone ever mistaking him for his slightly older uncle, Cristó. Aged 20 years, Cristó showed interest only in merry diversions. His effete tendencies – the way he laughed easily and compulsively expressed gratitude – drove Justo mad. And the sorest part, well, that was how Cristó displayed tender emotions. It was too much for Justo to bear. Point of fact, Cristó's place remained vacant still.

Without preliminary drivel, the nine-strong *alcalde* commenced to rule upon the misdeeds perpetrated by the populace during the previous four weeks. The warden banged into the room yanking a bedraggled lad who had, in a fit of hostility, spat upon militia captain Joseph Pavón.

"In keeping with the Seven-Part Code of Andaluz, you are found guilty of dishonoring a member of our military service," don Francisco ruled. "For this, you shall have your cutlash and one of your pistols blasted to bits." Drawing from the ancient Roman law, de Leiva could hew any situation to his advantage.

The subsequent case concerned a barber who recklessly had shorn his customer's whiskers alongside an open roadway. His hand had been jarred by a passerby, and the client had lost a morsel of his left ear. For this, de Leiva concluded, the barber must concede to also being shaved alongside the open roadway – but by a blind man.

Cristó slunk at last into the chamber, the chestnut-toned skin of his face flushed pink. Perspiration glued his mop of frizzy dark hair to his temples. De Leiva, gnashing his teeth, disregarded his prodigal newphew and persisted with official business.

Next, a ribald young man appeared before the officers. He confessed to having insulted another nobleman by shouting, "You are a repellent mule who swives with his own sister!" According to de Leiva, the Law of Andaluz demanded snipping the tail off the young man's horse. The lad broke into fervent pleas to avoid such humiliation. Summarily, he was dismissed.

As a middle-aged woman was ushered into the chamber, de Leiva took a moment to inspect Cristó more closely. "You are swimming in the cups!" he accused.

"And yet, Uncle, I am far too sober to endure this legislative performance, in which you rely upon a 400-year-old document to dispense justice," Cristó sassed. "I'd rather be sloshed to oblivion, not knowing my arm from my arse, than live backwards like you."

"You dare blaspheme me upon this day?" de Leiva questioned loudly enough for the other *alcalde* members to hear.

"No more than I dare blaspheme the shiny minds of those us, about us… I mean around us," Cristó slurred, glancing at the faces judging him from across the length of the table. "Why do you not speak against the use of this Medieval law code? How long will you continue to suckle from a nag's teat? Especially one aged past four centuries?" He laughed at the scowls thrown his direction.

The bailiff interrupted, announcing that the woman before them had been implicated for spinning prophecies. Without ado, de Leiva remanded the witch to his private dungeon, known as *the wolf jaws*. The Tribunal of the Inquisition would rule against her heresy.

In last place, Throat was chaperoned into the hall in shackles. His eyes baited them, the haunt of a smirk flickering across his lips.

From the room's dark reaches, don Bastía Cartagena de Agramonte, a *hidalgo* who was friendly with Governor

Ramírez, asked haughtily, "How is it that we must pronounce judgment upon your favored *bravo, Señor* de Leiva? What crime has he committed?"

De Leiva was in a quandary. He could not name the exact nature of the prize Throat had lost to Nani, as it bore fatal secrets intended solely for His Majesty the King of Spain. Furthermore, inventorying Throat's cruel features, don Francisco felt reluctant to execute his loyal servant. The rogue was his most artful weapon.

"Dereliction," de Leiva said carefully. "Owen Butler neglected his duties and lost a property that I had entrusted to him."

"What was the waylaid belonging? How can we make a verdict if we do not know the value of the prize?" de Agramonte questioned.

De Leiva grumbled. "An *aviso* for the Catholic Majesty of the globe, His Excellency King Felipe."

"A warning?" de Agramonte clarified. "What peril befalls us?"

De Leiva searched his mind for a canny escape. "Don Paco, have I mentioned peril?"

"No, Patrón," replied Paco de Proenza, the militia commander seated at his side.

"Belched it?"

"Nay, Patrón."

"Farted it?"

"Nay. And neither has your tongue uttered it."

"Holy is the valley of Josaphat. Enough!" begged de Agramonte.

The drink-fuddled Cristó inserted himself into the tumult. "Uncle, this servant merits punishment by drowning. Shall we not pronounce it?"

De Leiva's eyes softened at the dilettante's timely support. He turned his glare upon Throat. "Owen Butler, your crime is blundering daftness. By the Law of Andaluz, you must be tested by drowning. Should God grant you His mercy, do not try me with such flimsy outcomes ever again."

"Sword to heart, not ever again, Patrón," Throat avowed.

Upon the subsequent daybreak, Throat was marched to the rickety quay at the port of Cagua where he was bound inside a leather sack along with a hound, a snake, two agouti, and a rooster. The mouth of the voluminous bag was sewn closed and tossed deep into the waves. It was upon Throat to win an escape or else perish. Such was the penalty demanded by the Seven-Part Code.

IN WHICH A SHIPYARD TAKES SHAPE

"Jesus enlightened us as to the dignities of labor. Widely known as a carpenter's son, he demonstrated the Godliness of performing simple tasks by hand," intoned Father Alonso Tello, the dull bishop of Jamaica's Catholic church. His house of worship was no more than a crumbling stone structure with a failing rooftop, but Tello served his master well, providing the rubber stamp of religion upon all of de Leiva's schemes. Furthermore, he shared any sensitive information that crossed his ears – even when obtained in the sacred space of the confessional.

"By the labor of our hands, we invite the Lord's blessing upon ourselves and all," the priest concluded at last, sprinkling the beach with holy water. Tello's ritual anointed the shipyard that de Leiva was constructing upon the shoreline of Guadibocoa. In his mind, it would determine the entire fortune of Jamaica, establishing the island as the seat of the New World.

In order to execute his vision, de Leiva had to efface eight swampy hectares filled with lavender jacarandas, swaying coconut trees, and berry-producing pimentos. None present that morning had courage enough to question his sanity. A consequential exchange of silver had secured the cooperation of Jamaica's governor and *alcaldes*, even though not one of them had dignified this blessing ceremony.

Porto Esquivel stood several leagues large of La Vega. For months, de Leiva painstakingly had evaluated every foot of the site. Visiting during all hours of day and night, he had noted the moon's impact upon the tides, when the sea shrank into hazardous toothed shoals. He had observed how two noble rivers generated a rare depth of between three and four fathoms when the waters peaked. All told, he calculated, the shipyard might accommodate vessels as herculean as three-deck, 70-gun men-of-war.

Immediately inland, the island was dominated by woodlands – which, naturally, counted in de Leiva's vast holdings. An endless supply of timber could be felled and herded down current to the yard. Not only that, but the native tree species were famed the world over. They endured tropical heat and the ravening of *teredidae* or shipworms, which, no matter the precautions taken, chewed through the hulls of ships hewed in Europe.

Don Francisco de Leiva was fit with both the bottomless purse and the obsessive mind demanded to execute such a colossal project. This would be no ordinary shipyard. Porto

Esquivel would dominate all others, to the point where every first-class shipwright in the West Indies would beg to work here. It would be admired as the golden standard of a galleon factory.

Tipping back a cavalier hat jeweled with diamonds and spruced with parrot plumes, de Leiva allowed the late morning sun to fondle his finely-featured face. He exhaled certitude as he envisioned his creation, paying no mind to the commotion convulsing around him. Mauls pummeled, saws rasped, and chisels clinked. Overseers barked at drudgers. De Leiva's smile was so wide that his face ached. His shipyard would blossom an entirely new route to power and prosperity.

When he opened his eyes, his attention was drawn upon a meek craft being sailed into the mooring by a handful of sailors. He fetched his steed and rode down the hillside to where the vessel christened *La Nuestra Señora de Magdalena*, Our Lady Magdalene, was docking. Soon, drudgers would begin the process of dismantling her so as to cannibalize every bit of metal and raw material she had to offer.

"Your name?" he called out to the slender, copper-haired lad who was securing the vessel.

"Komeet Jutte, Sir. But those who know me call me Comet," the youth replied in Spanish muddied by a Dutch accent.

"The ship. Is she a patache?"

The youth looked at him with a blank freckled face.

De Leiva continued his inquiry. "Her contours and sail plan lead me to believe that she might also be a lightweight frigate?"

"Harr! Doubtless she's a queer one," Comet replied. "However you may classify her, I tell you this for free: She moves like a scalpel through the sea, dissecting the wind with utmost finesse."

De Leiva nodded slowly. "Rescue this sloop from the chop."

Comet returned a surprised look. It was an aberrant request given de Leiva's ruthless devotion to profit.

"I have plans for her. Fetch at once the principal shipwright."

IN WHICH THE FUTURE OF THE WORLD IS PLOTTED

For the next half hour, don Francisco de Leiva consulted with the shipwright, setting him upon his new task. Following their conference, he rode back up the hillside so as to enjoy the fresher breeze and shade furnished by a grove of palm trees.

It was 11 o'clock precisely when don Paco de Proenza hurtled into the harbor grounds, navigating past mammoth pieces of equipment and 300 haggard workers of mixed color and race. An illustrious horseman, the *sargento mayor* of Jamaica's militia mounted a snowy Andalusian mare with chocolate feet. Per usual, he donned a parakeet-green military costume with two muskets strapped crosswise over his back. At his side, he tucked both a sword and a brace of pistols. A cord of bandoleers jounced from his stout chest.

"Greetings, don Francisco," he said after sliding off his horse and securing her to a palm tree.

"You stink of sex," de Leiva stated.

"There are worse fates in this strife-filled life, are there not, Sir?" Proenza winked.

"And yet," de Leiva scolded, "I am aware of your chosen partner in these scandalous activities. If you would like for your arrangements with my wife to continue, don Paco, please do arrive cleansed of body and soul. Your obligations to God and Jamaica come before your earthly hungers."

"Verily, *Patrón*," Proenza agreed, cheeks tinging red. "I shall straighten my wayward behavior at once. Not one sniff of your dissatisfaction shall remain."

De Leiva warmed, slamming a fist upon his companion's shoulder so forcefully that the sturdy man stumbled backward. Beyond them, a fresh matter captured their attention. A carriage of chartreuse and gold crunched its rococo wheels through the shipyard. Moments later, de Leiva's nephew and ward Cristóbal de Ysassi disembarked in a costume decorated by frills, brocade, a resplendent buckle, white stockings, and a doublet of fuchsia silk. De Leiva measured the lad with disdain.

"My, my, Cristó. You resemble a powder puff," Proenza ridiculed.

Cristó brushed away the aspersion. "Pray, Uncle, I owe you an apology for my belated arrival at this terribly exciting conference of yours."

"*Again* you are overdue, just as you were yesterday at the *alcalde* assemby," de Leiva snarled.

"If it is obedience that you crave, Uncle, then buy yourself a hound who worships your tedious discipline," Cristó quipped, snapping a judgmental look at Proenza.

"For such surliness, I ought shove you upon your knees and jam my iron into your mouth," Proenza retorted.

"Have I chipped your famous swagger?"

Proenza bit down hard. "You fluff puppet, it is not possible for you to make a monkey out of me."

"No, for you already are one!" Cristó laughed.

"How's this? The cup of pudding calls the dish of meat soft?"

Cristó giggled, his entire body vibrating. "You're the one with lint in his cranium."

"You're the one with a piss-pot skull and pygmy brain."

"Enough!" de Leiva boomed. But neither party paid heed.

"You're a toothless termite," Cristó snapped.

"You, a bout of syphilis!" said Proenza.

"You, a crime on the eyes."

"Ha! That's the piss calling the rain wet," Proenza remarked with glee. "You're the one with skin so dark it appears scrubbed in dirt."

The remark silenced Cristó for a moment. Rage streaked across his face. "I ought beat you for questioning my lineage."

"But you do not boast the butter-cream complexion of a proven Spaniard, don Cristóbal. People talk about you. Surely you are not deaf to the gossip?" answered Proenza cheekily.

"They distrust his *limpieza de sangre*, is that it?" barked de Leiva, stepping between the two men. "Do you, don Paco, question the purity of his Spanish blood?"

"Strike me dead this second," Proenza stuttered. "I hold no such belief, *Señor*."

De Leiva sucked air between teeth, hissing scorn. He was, of course, conscious of the chatter. A significant portion of Jamaica's elite questioned the young scion's lineage – the reasons for which were obvious. Cristó's dark locks bunched around his head in kinks. His vaunted cheekbones, large eyes, and soft nose were complimented by a rich skin tone. It seemed apparent he was of mixed-race heritage. But that was not the story told by the Ysassi-de Leiva family.

Without another word, de Leiva began studying the golden ring that adorned the third finger of his right hand. It boasted a crucifix of pink diamonds set before a flaring sun, proclaiming him a sanctified soldier of Christ. Glowering, he thrust the all-powerful token before Proenza and awaited the ceremonial obligation due to him. The *sargento mayor* bowed and placed his lips to the ring.

"If the *limpieza de sangre* of my ward is challenged by men under your command, you have my word that they shall be strung from the gallows. As a courtesy to my treasured wife, you, however, will have your guts busted by water. Doña Zora relishes your winsome looks, and I prefer not to tolerate her blubbering when your face is disfigured by the rope. Understood, dear Paco?" De Leiva patted the man upon the cheek with his bejeweled hand.

"I request, Patrón, the heavenly sympathy of your forgiveness," Proenza answered. "*I have applied mine heart to know, and to search, and to seek out wisdom and the reason of things, and to know the wickedness of folly, even of foolishness and madness.*"

"Pfft, Ecclesiastes," Cristó tutted. "Now you fancy yourself a bishop with a gun?"

"Glory be," de Leiva said with a roll of his eyes. "I desire not bickering runts by my side, but righteous Templars thirsting to charge into the fray!"

"I am just such a man," avowed Proenza.

"And I… uhh… well, I am more self-ruled," Cristó responded with an uneasy titter.

But de Leiva had become distracted. He swooped his face an inch from his nephew's. "While every noble Spaniard acknowledges your skin color as authentic for southern breeds – you nevertheless seem to be donning a mask, Cristó."

"What?"

"There is paste upon your face." De Leiva poked Cristó's cheek with his pointer finger and swiped up a glob of white goo.

Proenza leaned in to interrogate. "Aye, sure enough," he said, bemused. "My, don Cristóbal, are you spending nights as a harlot?"

"Almighty angels, have mercy upon us!" de Leiva cried. "You are madder than a medicine show, boy."

Cristó crinkled his nose, attempting a truthful reply. "Tis but theatrical tincture. Or rather the residue of it. We employ it for depicting our characters…"

"*We?*" De Leiva wondered, aghast.

"*Characters?*" snickered Proenza.

"For my opera," Cristó explained, slumping. "I have composed the music and written the book."

De Leiva searched the sky. "Unstrap a razor and slice it across my neck!"

"But Uncle!" Cristó entreated. "Every composer alive quests for a residence in Sevilla. Spain is arising as the kingdom of masterworks. Already, the divine Monteverdi and Cavalli – both Italians, no less – have described Sevilla as a paradise of poetry and music."

Don Francisco harnessed his tongue for nearly a minute. *"This* is your pursuit? Opera?"

"*Sí, Señor,"* Cristó confessed, his voice merely a whisper.

"Quit dreaming, child. If you submit to ambition, as compelled by the Lord, and live within His wisdom and strength, then like a mastiff you shall snap up your fate. But this pursuit of opera? It humiliates our lauded name."

Cristó wobbled a nod. He could not argue any longer. "I wonder why, exactly, you have brought me and don Paco together upon this fine day, Uncle?"

De Leiva smiled. "Finally, I might quench your belated curiosity." He frisked his pockets for his *petite lunette.* Extending the telescopic lens, he steered it across the offing. His tenor turned teacherly. "Don Paco, observe the budding shipyard. Speak sincerely. What do you make of it?"

Proenza knew better than to stall. His praise rushed forth. "Tis as if I were an audience to a reenactment of Genesis. You, Señor de Leiva, have spoken: *Let there be a shipyard.* And behold! Your creation bursts forth with magnificence!"

"Indeed," de Leiva agreed, his gloomy mood clearing. He turned to his nephew. "And you, Cristó? What is your opinion?"

"Handle my commentary as you are able," the youth shrugged. "I perceive the stink of tar, the clank of mauls, and hordes of drudgers fading from existence. I note several frigates coarsely built, which are likely to drop to the bottom of the blue before attaining Porto Rico."

De Leiva glowered.

"Yet also," Cristó injected rapidly, "I observe the bustle of innovation. The birth of trade and enterprise, which may very well establish this corner of the globe as a capital port above any other. I sense a soon-to-be city in which all people have free license to shape their own fates. You enable a society in which ordinary, nameless, untitled men may advance beyond roles that have restricted them for eons. Where princes never again sit upon the throne as a presumed right of their inheritance."

Don Francisco de Leiva was so overwhelmed by his nephew's analysis that he applauded. "Precisely, child. You may prance as a fop, but you are no flop. These are the very aspirations that drive me day and night. The only slip I must set right was your mention of *princes.* You intended to say that *kings* never again shall sit upon the throne."

"No, I chose that word precisely. Princes will not thrive here; kings shall. The modern monarchs of the New World shall accede to their thrones not by blood right, but by *buying* their way onto them. And I predict that you, dear Uncle, shall purchase the very first golden chair."

"Ha!" de Leiva snorted. "You have a way with scheming, Cristó. For all these years, perhaps I was mistook. Perhaps you are no ward, but an actual son of mine."

Proenza, finding himself sidelined, inserted a topic that long had troubled him. "Patrón, why do you chase after His Majesty King Felipe of Spain, when he never favors our island but rather turns a cold cheek toward Jamaica?"

Although he bore no fondness for Proenza, Cristó nevertheless jumped to his aid. "Come now, Uncle. A fair card has been played. The King never includes you in his inner circle, in spite of how you beg, year after year, for an invitation. I commend your high threshold for humiliation."

De Leiva's face descended through spectrums of scarlet. "Tis true, I streak toward the future whilst His Most Catholic King dawdles in antiquity. But I have no choice. I must continue chasing his favor like a dog chasing his tail. At least for now."

"But why?" Proenza puzzled. "This I do not comprehend, *Señor*. With your own and God's brilliance, what need have you for His Majesty? *For with God no thing is impossible. And this is the confidence that we have in him, that if we ask anything according to his will, he heareth us.*"

Finally, de Leiva unveiled the reason for his continued reliance upon the Crown. "A seafaring vessel is composed of more than merely wood. Absent a forge upon the isle of Jamaica, this shipyard cannot provision ships with ordnance, nor can we rebuild them to the degree that I envision. Without iron, smiths, hearths, furnaces, and bellows, we must harvest every bit of metal possible. If the shipyard truly is to boom, we must commission twelve forges at least. Then there is the conundrum of cordage for the running rigging. Hemp is forever in short supply throughout *Las Islas de Barlovento*. In other words, my life's passion will shrivel unless we receive an outpouring of aid from King Felipe IV. By a simple nod of his scepter, he might confer upon us all the resources we require."

Proenza had long since abandoned the lecture. Absent-mindedly, he picked bits of lint off his immaculate military costume.

Cristó, on the other hand, had listened with a steadfast gaze. "Your list of ambitions is longer than Solomon's beard, Uncle. But I concur whole-heartedly. King Felipe sees only the immediate future. He enjoys mining easy money from the ground. But what happens when the mines run dry? You, on the other hand, aim to create an economically independent domain."

"Your grasp of the subject is precise," de Leiva nodded, linking arms with Cristó in excitement.

"But there is another way," the young man suggested. "Already the Low-Dutch have demonstrated the profitability of a concept they call *capital venturing*. We might adopt this system in order to grow your enterprise. By collecting funds from moneyed men who stand to earn a percentage of our profits, we might free ourselves from reliance upon the monarchy. No longer would we have need for the King of Spain."

"Tis a curious suggestion…" de Leiva puzzled, stroking his locks. "But first, we try financing the shipyard my way. Already I have composed an *aviso* to the king, warning him about the forces that conspire to oust him from power upon our island. It is of paramount importance that this message is delivered safely into his hands. If my game plays out as intended, his resistance to my demands will prove futile. I will squeeze King Felipe for every silver piece he is worth, and then I will cast him aside as so much rubbish. My triumph is assured, however, only if I can reclaim the strongbox. If it had not been stolen," he clenched his fists, "by that cursed—"

"Maroon queen," Proenza snapped, suddenly showing interest in the conversation again.

De Leiva tightened his jaw to match his fists. "Yes, she. Nani. And all the Maroons. They must be wiped from the surface of our island. Every last one of them."

"For what reason?" Cristó protested. "The Maroon tribes keep tight amongst themselves deep within the hinterland. They do not play into your schemes… or do they, Uncle?"

"They do. Nani has impeded my monumental aspirations. By stealing my *aviso*, she has put my plans at risk," de Leiva seethed.

"Have you not contemplated the possibility of allying yourself with the Maroons? Could they not align with your cause?" Cristó argued.

"I maintain solid relations with Lubolo, chief of the Mocho Mountain Maroons. But even the tenderest alliances end when objectives collide," de Leiva replied.

Proenza, seeking his advantage, piped up. "*Patrón,* I have a scheme by which to eradicate these savages."

"Of course you do," de Leiva said with a creeping smile. "Which is precisely why I plan to speed your advancement to the post of Jamaica's *maestro de campo*."

Proenza could not conceal his glow at the prospect of being granted Jamaica's highest military position and winning don Francisco's everlasting approval.

"However," inserted de Leiva, "before I adorn the sterling crest upon your lapel, dear Paco…" He stabbed a finger into his nephew's skinny chest. "You must take Cristó here alongside you as one of your militia. He will join you as a soldier until the Maroons all are hunted – but especially, Nani."

The two men erupted simultaneously in protest. "God's wounds, *Patrón,* you ask me to carry a bee into battle against a thunder bolt?" Proenza argued.

"Surely you do not speak seriously, Uncle," Cristó complained. "Why would you include me in your militai? I will only cockeye your efforts. I have no military seasoning, nor am I shaped from the same clay as Proenza and his disciples. He colonizes Hell with a gun. I touch Heaven with a quill."

"Curse of Adam's rib, quit your whining!" de Leiva cried with venom in his eyes. "You shall embark at once."

"I cannot. I have not the stomach for it," Cristó moaned.

"Ock! You say you like to play characters? Well, tis past time for you to play the conqueror and not the coward," de Leiva ordered as he clenched his ward by the shoulders. "Brother of my wife, yank your lapping face away from every quim – or every cock, if that is your preference. It matters not to me. But you *must* defend your bloodline. Fight, Cristóbal, as a soldier of this island, before Godless meddlers end our rise to prominence."

Flummoxed, Cristó slunk off to his carriage. Paco de Proenza delivered angry kicks to his snowy mare. Both men were propelled by acid.

IN WHICH A LOVER IS ASTOUNDED

Don Francisco de Leiva relaxed in his office upon the upper floor of the *cabildo*. Inside his lair, he researched the philosophies of capital commerce, stayed abreast of the master movers in Europe, and sketched sophisticated schemes to execute at home.

When it began, the night seemed predictable. Three constables rounded the main plaza with customary lethargy. Their batons tapped a steady rhythm against the brass horse and wagon hitches attached about the square's perimeter. De Leiva travailed at his escritoire, which stood under a massive painting of Mars, Venus and Vulcan. Occasionally, he glanced out the vast windows offering views over La Vega.

In the small hours, he finished his work and moved to his private abode via the door hidden discreetly in the wall. The bedroom displayed tapestries, frostwork, and gilding both decadent and seductive. As was her fancy, Maxi Supa readied herself the moment she laid eyes upon her lover. She beckoned her servant maiden to strip away her bodice and corset, then shooed the *criada* from the ravishing chamber. De Leiva, meanwhile, readied himself at the bedstead.

Maxi Supa loved to flaunt her naked body. She relished the power in it. As she ran her fingers over her subtle curves, meteors exploded in de Leiva's mind, undoing him. Without any preliminaries, she approached, spun around, and offered him her perfectly heart-shaped arse. De Leiva gasped as she forked two fingers around his rock-hard organ and slotted it inside her. His engorged sex thrust into her womanhood. As stiff as a pistol's ramrod, he drove into her. Watching her flesh bounce and gyrate, he was whisked to the edge of madness.

Maxi, meanwhile, controlled the bucking of his staff from tip to balls. Between her groans, she exerted absolute dominance over the cadence of their path to rapture. He was about to spew glistening beads across her backside when a noise dislodged them both from gasping bliss. Someone was banging on the mighty doors of the *cabildo* over and over again, pummeling with the force of 9-pound cannon shot.

"Saint Medusa! What is happening?" Maxi shouted, infuriated.

Within seconds, de Leiva reclaimed his breeches and navigated them over the peak of his erect cock. With pistols in both hands, he raced to the atrium and flung the doors wide. The moonless night was hushed. The constables obliged to guard the plaza were nowhere to be seen.

He looked around, straining his eyes into the darkness. Then he noted an ugly heap laid before the door – a battered leather sack exceeding the size of a coffin. It took several seconds for him to comprehend what lay before him. He tested the sack with a stern kick. Deepening his investigation, he emptied it of the carcasses of a dog, two rodents, and a rooster. The racer snake was nowhere to be found. It seemed the serpent was one of two beasts to have escaped the trial by drowning as commanded by the Seven-Part Code. The other was Owen Butler.

De Leiva marveled at Throat's achievement. Immediately, he reinstated the *bravo* to his previous position, the highest-ranking amongst his servants.

Illuminated briefly by the candlelight emanating from a nearby window, de Leiva detected a figure strutting southward. The creature was no specter, although his pale skin defied natural color. Throat passed beyond the glimmer and strode boldly in the direction of The Other Side. It dwelled, as did he, in a realm between living and dead.

Chapter 7

JAMAICA

IN WHICH A MONKEY IS A MAN

Sweeping limbs through the air, the creature came to rest atop a mahoe tree. He clinched his legs about the stupendous trunk, panting. The breeze disbursed his crushing aroma – a blend of fish guts, boar dung, and sweet tamarind.

A troupe of 30-odd lemur-sized monkeys with dingy fur, snubbed faces, and beady eyes came leaping behind him. The Pathfinder accounted for each one. As they swung, their claws served as grapnel hooks and their long black fuzzy tails acted as ballast. None stood higher than their leader's kneecaps.

The island crossing demanded two days. Once they committed to the canopies outside their safety zone, risks multiplied. To avoid being spotted by humans, they had to remain in near-constant motion. The Pathfinder was thankful that Jamaican monkeys required little sleep, for they also had to eat frequently. They supplemented a light diet of succulents and fruit with worms, beetles, and other grubs.

Recognizing his own hunger, he nibbled upon piquant pimentos stowed conveniently within the matted locks atop his head. Then, clambering across the broad system of mahoe branches, he harvested an egg from the nest of a potoo bird. Prank spat out a mouthful of breadfruit and reached over to steal the treat. The Pathfinder snarled. Prank retorted by wagging his genitals before skittering away.

When the sun slumped and the air cooled, the hour of flight was upon them once more. The Pathfinder whistled. He was the sole constituent of his band capable of producing such a sound. The others screeched and whimpered. As their leader soared, they pursued him like wind rifling through the foliage. Although he was not the fleetest amongst them, he was beyond a doubt their unique spark.

The monkey's home territory was a treacherous wilderness called *Los Poros*, the Pitted Country. Eons of erosion had birthed among the Jamaican highlands a topography of mammoth sinkholes, sheer cliffs, and constricted passageways. In decades ahead, it would come to be known as Cockpit Country. Precisely because it was so difficult to traverse, the terrain proved an ideal refuge for those eager to avoid human company.

Every Jamaican monkey bowed to their elders' mandate to isolate within this remote location – save for those who belonged to the insubordinate segment led by the Pathfinder. He possessed an alarming fascination with humankind, one which had ignited a tribal crisis.

Enlightenment does not arrive equally to all individuals. For some, it emerges gradually. For others, it bangs, squawks, and shits upon everything until it is finally noticed.

A naïvely capering juvenile, at age five the Pathfinder had confronted the absence of a tail. At age eight, he had learnt that he was the only one in his family incapable of identifying distinct tangs and aromas. His growth spurt at age 13 had resulted in a 30 percent gain in size, landing him a foot taller than his friends. But his brawn failed to develop to match his stupendous height. During forages, his harvests were surpassed even by those of Slower, whose generous paunch and stubby limbs leant her the look of a sloth. That same year, the Pathfinder surrendered for good the hope that he would ever sprout fur. In shame, he took to coating himself in mud and excrement.

"Everyone is different," the elders had justified, dismissing his angst.

Fortunately, when he reached 16, characteristics started to emerge that he felt might counterbalance his liabilities. His thoughts leapt beyond the present moment. He started to perceive patterns. From the habitual flood of primal cravings, there emerged a voice. It seemed simultaneously separate from and buried deep within his mind. It talked to him in dreams, fantasies, and plans. It offered him intricate emotional experiences, such as wonder, embarrassment, and melancholy. Already by age 20, he was ancient by monkey standards; none of the elders surpassed 22 years. Yet he displayed no signs of decay. On the contrary, he appeared in peak physical form.

Given these realities, the Pathfinder had felt called to meander beyond the Pitted Country. Eventually, he was spied by people subsisting at the edges of society. Taíno villagers called out to him, but he scurried away. He became obsessed with humans, who resembled his monkey friends yet behaved as none.

Over and again, the three elders warned him to stay away from the war addicts. *They slay animals for no reason, slay one another for any reason, and slay their own selves when reason is no more,* the wisest monkeys said. Frustrated, Guide gaped his mouth at the Pathfinder more than usual, baring his teeth. Answers expressed her glands. Most excruciatingly, Giver, who had suckled him at her breast for nearly a decade, distanced herself from him.

When murmurs of ultimatums harangued his ears, he strained once more to abide by their stiff commands. Henceforth, he vowed, he would spurn Jamaica's human settlements and remain within the bounds of monkey territory. But that promise had been tossed to ruin only weeks later, upon a single night in spring.

He had been resting atop his favorite guango tree pondering the night sky. *Are the stars above me?* he wondered. *Or am I falling into the sky whilst dangling upside-down?* Then, all at once, the sounds coming from the creatures of the woods – their lulling trills, drones, clicks and hoots – had snapped into meaning.

The Pathfinder had flipped forward in order to dangle inches from the undergrowth. He could, he had just realized, interpret the squeaking and sucking patterns of the hutia moseying beneath him. "Trouble here. Trouble there," the rodent rambled. Next, he heard a swallowtail beating a message from out her wings. "Mine, mine, mine!" Moments later, he comprehended the communications of a frog. "Bug!" it celebrated with a low laugh.

Unable to resist the drive to wander again beyond the Pitted Country, he discovered that he could decode human languages quite easily, as well. By the conclusion of the soaking rains of spring, he had grasped the Spanish tongue upon the lips of a sugar cane laborer, the French of a ruddy-faced curate, and the English of a buccaneer. His entire existence felt recast by this ability to penetrate animal and human communication.

And so, the Pathfinder had mustered his splinter troupe and soared away from home. They frisked thoroughly the island, from the far-flung reaches of El Morante, to the outskirts of the southerly capital of La Vega, to the northern barrens of buccaneer territory. Outcasts, provokers, and misfits, these were primates who dared to lock step with a strange companion. Mesmerized by the Pathfinder's intelligence, they were willing to abet him in any act – even as he steered them toward the flagrant abuse of their tribe's staunchest commandment.

They would, he told them, intervene in the affairs of a woman who had named him *Sasa*. He had read her entreaties upon the wind. She needed his help. But it was more than Nani's plight that compelled him. Not ever had he encountered a human with so deep a talent for communing with the spirits. He felt an urgent desire to connect.

IN WHICH A MAN IS NO LONGER A MONKEY

Lashes of sweat raced down Sasa's denuded and blood-drenched body as he aimed for the rocky heights of the Pitted Country. Nearly two weeks had passed since he had led his renegade monkey troupe in defense of the Maroon queen Nani, helping her defeat the violent gang of Spaniards led by the knife-handed man. At last, he was journeying homeward.

The Pathfinder bore no doubt that this time he had depleted utterly the elders' patience. They awaited him with some dreadful punishment. His troupe members had returned from the skirmish with the humans many days ago. But he had not. He had lingered about the battleground, struggling to comprehend what had occurred and gathering the courage to face his family.

Nearing the congestion of trees that for two decades had been his village, he witnessed a dozen vultures circling on high, anticipating their next meal. From a distance, in spite of his lack of olfactory prowess, he could smell death.

The moment he set foot within their territory, some 300 slushy brown and grey monkeys began accosting him. Tree limbs jerked, fronds tumbled, and a siren of screeches spewed forth from the lungs of his lifelong companions. A group of females aspirated chemicals into his face. Even members of his own renegade troupe renounced him with lewd wiggles. When Prank and Snatcher began bombarding their former friend with anal effusions, it sent the entire crowd into a frenzy. They hurled at him any projectiles within reach – fruits, nuts, rocks, and branches.

He shielded his face. The upbraiding bruised his arms and hairless chest. Soon, blood trickled from wounds covering every part of his body. Yet the tribe continued to throw, spit and bare their fangs at him.

Behind them, he perceived the funerary mound.

"Merciful Lord," he uttered, because these were words he had heard humans whisper when confronted with horror. The monkeys had piled eight carcasses upon the dramatic conical-shaped hillock that arose from the forest at the center of their homeland. Guide was moaning and knocking fists against his brow as he paced around the decaying corpses. These were members of the Pathfinder's sect who had been killed during the battle – and he alone bore responsibility.

He felt an endless fall of his gut. Answers sprouted from behind a jacaranda bough, face twisted. "Grief. Pain. Disfigured decency," she accused.

Giver swept forth and escorted the Pathfinder aside. She supped the perspirations that sheeted his forehead and peeked into his mouth so as to discern the scent of his breath. About his being, she sensed deep sorrow vying with a yearning for independence. It fired forth from his soul.

Giver had no means by which to express the woe she felt as a mother whose child has defrauded her of hope. Ordinarily it would be rage that followed. But the tribe's matriarch withheld her brute instinct. By *not* combusting, her despair was spoken. A void had opened between them. The Pathfinder understood the truth – that he had forever alienated her heart.

Staring at his toes, he considered several responses but rejected each. Eventually, without meeting Giver's eyes, he spoke aloud to her in human language for the first time.

"Did you know that the two-leggeds believe gods dreamed this world into being purely for *them*?" he said. "So that they might bring into reality their every caprice, every wish and desire? This is why they war against one another."

He looked directly at Giver now. "Who are these gods of which they speak, to whom they pray, in whose name they kill? Mother, a*m I one of them?*"

Flummoxed, Giver wobbled her head from side to side. She gazed at her adopted son and he comprehended what she saw – a being imprisoned by curiosity and self-importance. The Pathfinder doubted he ever would find her eyes upon him again.

Chapter 8

IRELAND

IN WHICH ORPHANS JOURNEY HOMEWARD

They flung themselves across the moors, shadowed by the dark terror of being hunted by Venables and his English brigade. Aisling and Fintan O'Lorcan chose the terrain because it was fixed into their essence. Rory had educated his younger siblings in the art of bog tripping. Even now, his voice chaperoned them, reminding them to identify the peat banks and low heather that offered more dependable ground.

But they refrained from sharing words about their brother. They did not speak of family at all. When they did talk, they bickered, divided in purpose and direction, lost in sorrow. Fintan favored journeying into the Pale with the eventual goal of reaching Dublin. But that city, Aisling rebutted, was a Protestant stronghold dating back to the rebellion of 1641. The seat of English governance, it embodied the nucleus of their suffering.

Fin countered that Dublin boasted the paragon of Irish sea ports. There, they might finagle a passage to Catholic

Spain, where many an Irish had encountered ease. "Oliver Cromwell himself has named Spain a foreign haven for those of our *unwelcome faith*," he argued.

"Mind yourself, brother, lest you forget that the maggoty king-slayer has also ordered every Catholic Native Irish to dance a jig beneath the gallows," she shot back.

Ash preferred Galway. In addition to its significance as Clan Lorcan's family seat, the borough was known to shelter English Royalists and Irish Confederates. Moreover, she trusted that Athair and Rory would speed there. As yet unaware of the fates of their father and eldest brother, each maintained a stubborn hope. For days, they quarreled, sparring over which routes and regions better defended against English perils, dreaded highwaymen, and hubs of disease, particularly those corners of the country rumored to be overrun by the Black Plague.

Their trajectory was veering eastward when the siblings had the good fortune of encountering a sweet-water *lough.* Fin convinced his sister to halt their breathless journey for a day or more so he might go angling in the lake. Aisling deliberated with her fears. A prolonged retreat would mark them as ready prey. But in the end, the voice of starvation prevailed.

Decades of war and the horrid indignities it had imposed upon the folk of Ireland had extinguished the meaning of life for many. Otherwise tender men transformed the tragedies inflicted upon them into evil toward others. Yonder, Ash noted scattered fires twinkling amongst the outcrops and caves of the hillocks. Within these limestone bunkers, shattered souls huddled in the rags, abandoned to bottomless despair, poised to pursue their sole remaining calling as spiteful marauders.

Wolves heckled them at twilight. Nightfall stamped a cold, hard moon atop the raised bogland as Fintan kindled a turf fire. The pair set upon smoking a respectable haul of brown trout, which Fin, through inconceivable effort and skill, had snagged with no instrument other than the spearing blade of his skene. For a lad of 12 years who had been born into this world with an insatiable affinity for impulsive behaviors, he could, when immersed in the hunt, command impenetrable dedication and focus, be it on the field, the stream, or at sea.

The sustenance slayed the ogre in their bellies. But even as the gnawing hunger receded, their clarity widened. The reality facing Ash and Fintan came into unbearable view. No matter their haste and courage, unfathomable miles of peatland stood between them and any hope of embracing their family ever again.

When at last they reached a woodland at the southern end of county Leitrim, Ash spun a heartwarming vision of uniting with their distant relations in Galway. Fin caved, agreeing to set a course to the west and away from Dublin.

"Ock! Tis a shabby land, where Galway lies," he nevertheless grumbled.

"And also our homeland," she said, taking his hand in hers.

By day, the fog rose thick and the heather rustled like a conspiracy. When darkness creeped around them, they hunkered beneath their mantles amidst chambers of willows and alders. Their fish long gone, they shared morsels of mushroom, dined on the lichen scratched by their finger nails, and nibbled the paper-thin bones of the trout.

"Tis like feasting on spindles of moonbeams," Fintan joked.

"And as pleasant as chewing on a pyrate skeleton," Aisling added.

"Or on the fingernails of Poseidon."

Ash spat out a fish splinter. "It dries out my mouth worse than hearing Cromwell preaching God's will."

"But in all faith, it tastes like the salted tears of Irish sorrow," said Fin.

She flicked him a glance, then betrayed a playful smirk. "Brother, you may have a poet in you. Wish we had an inkwell with us."

"Should you gift me an inkwell, by God's fact and my famishment, I'd eat it!"

It was Aisling's turn to giggle. "Behold, the orphan's way for digesting Shakespeare."

They both succumbed to giddiness, as if the dam controlling their worries had broken all at once. Tears streamed down their cheeks.

Knocked on their backs, huffing and panting, Aisling suggested, "We might start afresh and set out for the New World."

"God's wounds, Ash! The West Indies?"

"The Spanish Americas, yes! I read of a land known as Jamaica. Warm water, green mountains, and all the fruit and fish you could ever eat."

Fin scoffed. "You broadsheet-quaffer. Jamaica happens to be an island, not a land."

"Same as Ireland, you cod! And on this Caribbean rock, the pamphlet said, thrive Jews, Lutherans, Indians, free

Africans, and a grand crowd of Irish folk that reeking old Cromwell has tossed over as indentured bonds."

"Body of blood, Ash!" he exhaled anxiously. "Is this how you hammer home a good point? You are one sorry persuader."

When they wagered their fortunes upon the depopulated roads of Connaught, they encountered mud huts and thatched dwellings. Watchers tracked the strangers with uneasy eyes from within. A smattering of *spalpeens* or landless peasants periodically joined the route, but the siblings were met by silence rather than the customary greetings or invitations for news.

Upon the warth road of the Shannon, they were hailed by a boy shuffling along with cankered toes nudging out the holes of his shoes. Puss racooned his eyes, and his nose dripped like a cistern spout. The infirm adolescent cautioned the O'Lorcan siblings about the *Night of Zounds*. It had been given that name, he disclosed, on account of the frantic cries that pierced the night every new moon, when no light graced the heavens. On such eves, a huntsman with a wagon prowled for human quarry.

"*God's wounds!* the wretched will shout. *Tis him. Zounds and have mercy!*" the boy reported. "The Butcher snatches stragglers and deadens their shrieks by cramming iron pins into their mouths. Sometimes his wagon is laden with as many as a dozen souls before daybreak."

Fin shook off a shiver, but Aisling sneered. "Pshaw! We ain't toddlers falling for your nightmarish tale."

"Upon the love of Lord, I speak the truth," professed the boy.

"Cap your druid smoke!" she snapped, tugging her brother away and veering into the anonymity of the tree-line.

"Sister, do you believe this tale of the Butcher?" Fintan asked, eyes wide.

"Tis all piffle and shite."

Fin persisted. "And how about the way the diseased lad described the savagery of this human-hunter upon moonless nights?"

Ash would not suffer the question. "We ought manger," she proposed instead.

"My hunger *is* snarling."

"Aye. And my belly has tightened into a stone," she agreed.

"Lord God, my body is spoiling!" he groaned. "I taste death in my mouth. I hear a tea-kettle hooting in my ears. My every last sense has gone to tatters. And as my gallant pole, why, that rascal molders in my trousers, never again to show his pertness—"

"Crike!" Ash swatted at him, the wrinkle of her lips betraying amusement. "You are the smallest package of insolence!"

Fin laughed.

She giggled, too, hooking her arm with her brother's. His degeneration could not be denied, however. Fintan's blue eyes had turned milky, his complexion waxy. She smiled, but anguish overruled her momentary cheer. "True enough, we have hardly a prospect. Yet I can propose one method by which we might douse our hunger." She delivered a larcenous look. "Do follow."

Slipping from out the woods, they prospected the closest farmland. Any scant tillage that had not yet been burned by the English had been commandeered by their forces. Ash and Fin hid in the skirts of a barley field occupied by five Parliamentarian soldiers. At night, they darted on cat-paws toward the livery. Fin shadowed his sister into the stable, and they both startled as an owl clapped her wings from the rafters.

"This is a bloody daft plot, Aisling," Fin protested.

"Quiet, you," she hissed.

"Dig my grave with a spoon," he muttered.

Ash went to task assessing the personalities of each of the five horses who stood undressed of their tackle. The sable had a festering lower lip. The gelding, ganting by his lonesome, returned a queer expression. The bay stamped a foot. Ash targeted the two docile mares who ogled her with sallow eyes.

With tender footsteps, she closed upon the darker one. She tossed her hand in his direction and Fin understood. Her brother passed his skene to his sister, who secured a perfect fix upon the traditional Irish dagger. With her other hand, she stroked the animal's black mane.

"I give you good eve, Duchess," she wooed. "Are you not a handsome treasure?" She eased the blade through the mare's hide, notching her neck. Blood sprang forth, slickening the coat. Ash snaked an arm round her brother's head and urged him to consume the warm red nourishment. When he pulled back, she placed her own lips upon the horse's wound. The fluid tasted of steel and sweat. Its richness caused her starving belly to ache. She nearly vomited before recollecting Rory's instructions to respire strictly through the nose. After easing her mouth from the mare's neck, she snuffed the bleeding by an index finger.

This was not the first occasion upon which an O'Lorcan had ferreted sustenance from a horse. In the past, however, Rory had sliced open the correct vein. Ash never once had partaken due to her fondness for horses. Now such a choice seemed as distant as wedding bells. Her indifference to the vulgarity of the act surprised her.

IN WHICH ORPHANS ENCOUNTER AN OLD ENEMY

Closing in on Galway, Aisling and Fintan entered a region of more populous tenements along the Shannon. Yet each parish was as eerily quiet as the last. Sickness and starvation stalked together. Those people most deplorably struck by disease stumbled down to the river. They foraged watercress and shamrocks, crawling on all fours with mouths tinted green.

"Oh faith, our country has come to be a walking graveyard," commented Fintan.

Not one village would part its gates for them. Outsiders were not at all welcome.

"They're all shut in with their dark secrets," muttered Ash.

"Cagey as a bishop's penis," Fin agreed.

"Insensitive to our fate."

At one parish fence, Fin opened his mantle to reveal a lack of weapons and Ash tendered a pleading word. Yet the two waifs were driven away by sentinels crutched upon muskets, their faces masked by kerchiefs.

When they came upon another town, Fin stifled a scream.

"What vexes you, Brother?" Aisling asked.

"Beezers! Look there," he gulped, tugging at his sister's ragged sleeve. "What manner of bugbear is that?"

Cloaked entirely in black, the alien figure had emerged from one of the dismal dwellings. He stood the height of a man but bore the head of a bird. A hawkish beak, some four inches long, projected from his head, which was domed by an absurdly wide-brimmed hat. One gloved hand lugged an apothecary case, while the other swished a rod at the barraging blowflies.

"God to you, children!" the monstrous form called, his voice betraying a bookish authority. "I say, beg off these parts. Hearken and heed me!"

Dumbstruck, Aisling and Fintan froze.

The birdman moved toward the next hovel. But before he had slipped indoors, Fin's curiosity bested his fright. "Sir, what beast are you?"

"A plague doctor," the fellow replied.

"A medicine man frocked as a bird?" Fin asked, steeped in disbelief. "Good stars!"

The doctor extricated his head from the mask. His spectacled eyes displayed the first warmth they had encountered from another human in weeks. "The beaked apparatus is laden with herbs," he explained, sounding to Ash like Rory when he would teach them letters. "It freshens the air so as to shield me from the poisoned miasma that conveys the black pestilence." He aimed his rod, marking the road onward. "Be done now and bustle forth. You shall greet naught but death here."

The siblings returned to the roadway. The wind lashed and the wolves circled. Ash cowered beside her brother, singing a ballad that reflected her plaintive mood. Her voice seduced the darkness.

Cold and raw the wind did blow,

Bleak in the morning early;
And all the fields were covered in snow

And winter came severely…

The following afternoon, Fin mounted a hillock, eager to determine how much further lay their destination. Aisling trailed behind. When Fin attained the summit, he looked back at her with mouth agape. She raced to join him. Greeting the sight before her, she nearly fell from her heels.

Not ever again had they expected to lay eyes upon Seneschal the Black. Yet here he was, dangling from the branches of an elm tree. Two additional corpses swung beside him – those of his female consorts. Their eyes had been plucked out and their flesh clawed away by scavenging creatures.

"I ought be gladdened, but…" Fin muttered. "Tis a fearsome picture."

From the mud, Ash took hold of a fallen branch. "Look here," she pointed. The right hands of the Seneschal and his mistresses had been amputated at the wrists. She fed the stick into the Seneschal's mouth, stretching it wide so as to gain a gruesome view, then performed an examination of the women. "One and all have had their hands and tongues cut away."

Fin meditated on the evidence. "Tis a totem."

"Aye," she concurred. "A stamp left by our kinfolk. But which family? MacDermot? O'Connor? O'Rourke? They all are seated in these lands."

"Means nothing to me. Cheers to them for ridding us of that flaming dildo Seneschal the Black!" Fin stabbed his fist into the air.

"I would abstain from praising the savage executioners," Ash admonished. Surveying the still-distinct tracks in the wet earth, she conjectured a party of three to five sell-swords. "The murderers could not have ventured far afield. Though torn, I say we sally forth rather than seek out these blood-letters."

"Ash," Fin squawked, "what other verdict is there? We ought convene with them. They are our kin."

She did not hear him. "The marks press deep. These men are stocked with broadswords and battle hammers aplenty."

IN WHICH ORPHANS ARE ASSAULTED

The siblings did not bank a fire that eve. Although English Parliamentarian troops lacked wilderness acumen, the ranging Gaelic clans could sniff out the faintest smoldering of peat. Wrapped together under their mantles, Aisling and Fintan huddled beneath the glow of the full moon. The wind toyed with their nerves, jolting them every time it spoke through the willow branches.

Hours just after midnight, the thickets rustled. Ash touched a kiss upon her brother's hand before slithering into a den of brush. Rory had taught his younger siblings a simple lesson: The person who confronts a strange party first ought be the least threatening. All others, in this instance no more than a solitary girl edging into adolescence, should calculate the peril before facing untrustworthy figures.

Four men appeared on the hilltop. Fin was steady on his feet. Exactly as his elder brother had trained him, he widened his stance, communicating frankness. His discarded his mantle, disclosing an absence of weapons. His voice creaked nervously despite his attempt to masquerade confidence. "My service to you. It is I, Fintan of Clan Lorcan, seated in Galway."

Ash monitored the clansmen from her hideaway as they hulked closer to her brother. Cloaked in filth, their glibs and beards clumped with vile, they resembled *idle boys*, armed bandits who adored conflict. Such gangs were known to roam the countryside sporting in extortion and murder.

These Gallowglass had painted their faces with coal and blue woad. Two slung broadswords. The other two veiled their blades under heavy mantles.

"A son of Lorcan?" questioned the tallest man, his Gaelic jangling with an Ulster brogue. His black sable coat looked like a colossal set of dark wings. He resembled a monstrous raven with eyes veined with a blood-blaze. The brute beside him, who had ginger hair and pox scars across his face, shuffled forward, a hand secured atop his broadsword.

"On my oath, I am blood-kin of the fearless and noble Cormac the Younger," Fin said.

Raven spat upon the ground. "Aye, the maggot who steered us into that bloodbath at the garrison? The one and same chieftain who advised his own clansmen to trust the lying, craven Seneschal the Black? He who hangs dead beside us now?" He gestured at the corpse swinging from the tree. "By the shining providence of Cormac the Cunt, we suffered our cousins butchered and our wives and children crisped to ash!"

The other men grumbled. Aisling's hope of finding true-hearted companions sank in one dry gulp.

"Have you have food, boy?" Raven asked.

Fin shook his head.

"Coin? Arms?... A scrap of worth?"

"No," Fin mumbled.

"Are you a tiny idiot?" Ginger inserted.

"Same like his kinsmen," commented the eldest of their collection. His back was curved like a question mark. The others cackled like boar fat in a fry skillet.

Raven peered round. "Not a single ally do you have tucked in these here woods, eh boy? For as we know, every member of your clan of shame got minced to pieces by English gun and sword."

"Ain't your brother Rory?" Ginger asked. "He was pissing bloody terror when last I spied him. The poor coward was scrambling up the garrison walls till – BAM!" He curled his hand into a finger-gun and mimed a shot between Fintan's eyes.

"The Puritan hordes plugged that scaredy-cat Rory in his fleeing backside," said the one with a harelip. "Your da and that cunt Cormac, too."

A bomb of anguish combusted within Ash's heart. She emitted a smothered screech. Hers and Fintan's most abominable fear had been pronounced. Their family were dead.

Raven poked his sword into the brush where she squatted. She raised herself, temper aflame. Every rude eye swung upon her. "You are correct," she said. "We have not a thing. We beseech your friendship and aid by the traditions of our kind, the venerable Clan Lorcan, and the many hundred years of our alliance."

Studying her, Raven chewed his lip. "Say you heist up your smock, chatty girl," he proposed. "We might make ourselves a bargain that doesn't include your certain death."

Ginger's massive arms pinioned her from behind. She clenched her teeth against the pain.

"You also," Raven commanded, nodding toward Fin. The other two men pounced upon the boy.

"What be?!" Fin howled.

"Your dungy garments have no worth if we bloody them," Raven sneered.

Ginger dragged Ash into the scrub under the dead bodies dangling from the elm tree, where he flung her upon the cold grass. Raven eyed her youthful body. Ginger lent words to his leader's thoughts. "Such a sumptuous morsel."

"Pray, have mercy upon us," Ash beseeched.

Raven leered at her budding breasts. "You are a maiden yet, still intact?"

Terror jammed her mind. She could not process the situation.

"Are you?" he pushed.

"My blood has not ever flowed," she rasped.

Ginger grimaced as he slapped Raven upon the back. "Just the sort you fancy."

Raven knelt upon Aisling's shins, immobilizing her legs. The rest of the brigands stormed Fin.

She thrashed, her every muscle defending. Raven knocked her hard in the face. She felt a sting of frigid air as he hoisted her ragged saffron smock.

Fin repelled his attackers with stones. His resistance was in vain. Harelip and Ginger set to pounding him senseless. Hook-back stopped them for a breath, but only to collect Fin's mantle and lacquered *croisette,* a family heirloom that dangled from his neck.

Raven's breath was fermented with *usquebagh.* Ash whipped about like an eel. He snarled, strengthening his grasp. That second was enough for Ash to fetch Fin's blade from where she had stowed it in her cloak. She slashed the man's jugular. Blood jetted from his neck. She opened his esophagus further. His eyes widened as he crashed upon her, his breaths disgorging a bubbling foam.

Ginger was the first to realize what was happening. "Jousting cocks!" he bleated, racing toward them.

Pinned beneath Raven, Ash groped through the dead man's heavy mantle, searching blindly. By the time Ginger managed to heave up the sagged body, a pistol marked his face. She had located it in her assaulter's mantle, and she hesitated not to compress its trigger. The shot burst open Ginger's forehead, decorating the sky with his brains.

Aisling affirmed her possession of pistol in one hand, skene in the other. Instinct born from the countless drills

Rory had required of his younger siblings guided her. Slinging her arm back, she launched Fin's knife. It whistled across the moonlit clearing and landed directly in Hookback's chest. He collapsed into the moss.

Tacking toward Fin, Ash targeted the final enemy. Harelip glowered, twirling his broadsword. When he flew upon her, she leveled the small arm. But it clicked softly, barren of shot. By a last-second dive, she shirked the incoming blow. Harelip's sword slapped into the mud.

Her gaze darted. The pistol was worthless. Fin's skene was yards away, buried deep in the heart of another. Harelip lifted his sword and rushed her. Suddenly, she caught a gleam of Ginger's great sword orphaned in the brambles just three paces afar.

She pounced upon the weapon. The monstrous chunk of steel stretched four feet in length and weighed half a stone. She drove all her strength into lifting it, but it defied her slight stature. She tipped over into the heather.

"You frantic gnat," Harelip said.

A shadow swept over him. Fin crashed atop Harelip, clawing and biting. Ash attempted again the great sword, but the blade outdid her.

Harelip kicked it away. In his next breath, he yoked a forearm around Fin's neck. He held the peak of his own broadsword against her brother's pulsing mortality

Fintan locked eyes with Aisling. "Run, Sister!" he roared. "Fly quick as the Lord's ghost. Never peer back."

The brute pressed his blade, squeezing drops of blood from Fin's neck. "Don't be smart, girl. Bring yourself hither or I hurt the boy."

"Be gone, Ash!" Fin cried.

A tear stole down her cheek. It was the first she had shed since her family had taken flight from the English Parliamentarian troops two years past. Her misting gaze remained fixed upon her brother's face.

Fin shook off his look of dread and smirked foolishly. "*You must insist upon living*," he said.

Harelip dropped him upon the earth and began pummeling him, kicking him in the ribs and stomach.

Ash launched into flight. But cycling three bounds into her sprint, she stopped, turned about, and faced the murdering that was about to befall her brother. She lunged into one last attempt. By the power of all gods, Gaulish and Catholic, she dislodged the broadsword from the peat, dragged the ponderous weapon across the dank earth, and hefted it with the incalculable strength of her willpower. Harelip was so certain that she had fled, and so caught up in pummeling Fintan, that he did notice her. She muscled the blade skyward and plunged it into his spine. It was a deep thrust, but he did not register the sensations of an oncoming death. He simply could no longer feel his legs.

Ash yanked Fintan away as Harelip inventoried the jarring circumstances. It seemed the steel had condemned his lower body to paralysis.

The O'Lorcan siblings took off with maximum speed down the hillock. They fled in the grip of panic, alone and powerless. The earth itself seemed to collapse beneath their feet with desperation. Aisling grasped Fin's hand, tears washing down her face. The bleak trees upon the hill derided them.

When they spilled onto the roadway, a wagon awaited. They had delivered themselves straight into the Butcher's clutches.

"But it mustn't be the Night of Zounds! You hunt only on nights with not any moon…" Ash quaked in confusion.

IN WHICH IRISH ORPHANS ARE CAPTURED

Each second turned elastic like cold jelly. When the Butcher's cane shocked Aisling in the ribs, she did not fight. Terror had severed her spirit from her body. Afloat in detachment, she observed her legs fly out from under her. Perched in ghostly suspension, she witnessed Fintan roped like a runty hog by two henchmen. The elongation of time illuminated unlikely details. Their highborn waistcoats and embroidered linens had been consigned to smutty tatters, demonstrating the shared ordeals of Ireland's trauma. Rude hands bound her own ankles and wrists by the same cordage.

"Make one screek and I shall feed your chopped tongue down your throat," the Butcher warned Aisling. "And no sniveling. I loathe lily feathers."

The Butcher's stiffened brogue betrayed old English ancestry. Ash scrutinized the marauder's combative outline. A fine-woven muffler masked all but gold-dusted eyes. Russet tendrils tipped with gray, and tinged with the fragrance of balsam and burdock, peeked from out a hooded cloak. And the hands… Why the hands tapered into wrists slenderer than her own. A bolt of realization struck:

The Butcher is a woman.

No sooner had Aisling groped this fact than the two young scoundrels hurled Fintan into a covered carriage like a sack of oats. They tossed her likewise moments later. The first boy crushed her against the slats. His childish eyes and grimace indicated subnormal intelligence. The second one, a pudgy, freckled accomplice, pressed a vial of tart liquid into her mouth before shoving a dose down Fin's larynx.

Within seconds, her senses wobbled. She squinted at the other captives trussed in the bed of the wagonette. Four were girls who looked as filthy and hopeless as she. Fin had been added to three boys to complete the spoils of the hunt. Ash's green eyes widened at the sight of the lad sniffling beside her brother. He was the same dreary boy whom she and Fin had encountered along the road edging the River Shannon; the very same child who had warned them about the Night of Zounds.

Aisling awoke from a sepulchral slumber to the imprisonment of a stone keep. From the evidence of the circular crumbling walls, she determined that she had been shut up in a defensive pile that had stood for the better part of two centuries. Referred to as *tower houses* by the nobility, such constructions laced the Irish countryside, melding a fortress with a home. In ways a blunt castle, the bottom floor was an inhospitable cavern. Cold hounded Aisling's bones and rainwater wept down moss-covered rocks. Whistling draughts of wind forced the ten other women to huddle beneath horse blankets that vibrated with leaping fleas and greedy lice. She searched the chamber, but Fin was nowhere to be discovered. In abject misery, she curled upon herself and sunk back into sleep.

After many hours, perhaps the next day, the two young wardens of the tower house, one vain and the other vapid, startled the hostages awake. "Food!" the podgier of the lads shouted as the taller one chucked dense loaves of bread at each of the girls. Ash nearly cracked her teeth devouring hers within seconds.

This routine unfolded for several days, possibly as long as a week – Ash really could not say. In truth, unafraid of being assaulted in the night, and with a solid chunk of bread in her belly, she slept better than she had in months.

Then one day, the podgier boy announced, "Bath!" The taller one pressed Aisling and the others into a single file and jostled them outside. There, near folds containing half-starved goat and sheep, stood a row of similarly sickly and terrified-looking boys. She scoured them in search of her brother as her mind hammered out one objective: *escape*.

When it came time for Aisling's bath, she removed her shift as commanded. The bucket of mountain water that the larger, dafter boy flung at her struck like a board of nails. Yet Ash remained stoic in her drenched nakedness. He alleviated her humiliation by offering her a woolsey cloth.

As she swabbed herself with a toweling sheet so well-used it was sure to populate her hide with novel parasites, her gaze fell upon the maiden who had bathed before her. Emaciated as fading twilight, she had stringy flaxen hair. Ash ventured a question. "Who is the Butler and what is she doing with us?"

"Don't you know?" Flaxen shuddered. "She fattens and cleans us for slaughter, the Lady Cathryn Butler."

"*Lady* Cathryn Butler?" sputtered Ash.

"Yes, Lady Butler – the Butcher," the maiden repeated, absorbing Ash's reaction. "You don't know, do you?"

"And you do?" Aisling reeled.

"I do."

"Cough it out, then."

Flaxen surrendered her meager trove of knowledge. For hundreds of years, she said, the Butlers had been the most important English family in the region, with castles scattered across counties Kilkenny, Tipperary, and beyond. This tower house, distant from the family's seat of power, belonged to Lady Cathryn Butler. The two lads who looked after her prisoners, according to speculation, were likely her sons. "But the grandiose dame has become a ghoul who feasts on human flesh," the blonde waif explained, her expression flat. "Fallen on hard times. So, she nabs guttersnipes to fill her barren larder."

Aisling glared. "You're speaking tongues. Tis devil-dung, not more."

The maiden lowered her voice to a conspiratorial volume. "Listen you, Lady Cathryn plumps us up like hogs, scrubs us to a rosy sheen, then roasts us on the spit. Tis fact."

Aisling leaned away, ever dubious. "Tis not."

"Hand on God's wounds, *tis*," Flaxen avowed. "Better take wise. And you may want to shove off your attitude, too, or you'll be the first to get eaten."

"Grace be to God, you yellow-haired lass! You just handed me the keys to the prison!" Aisling exclaimed. Without a flicker of hesitation, she shouted to every ear in the vicinity, "Our kidnapper is a meat-monger. Who here has not faced the dreaded truth that there is no nourishment to be found across our ravaged lands? Pray then, permit me to speak it to you straight: The Butcher, the master of this keep and her brain-withered lads, intend to eat us *while still living*. Tis why they are disinfecting us. Get some sense in your heads, friends! No wealthy carnivore wants to chew on a filthy rump!"

She had scripted her ploy in seconds and performed it in a heartbeat. It worked perfectly. All the captives gathered in the courtyard for their baths erupted into panic. Aisling spotted Fintan just as the file of boys dismantled into chaos. Admiring her handiwork, she slipped to his side and stole her younger brother away by the elbow before anyone could take notice.

Together, they again flung their fates into flight.

IN WHICH PRISONERS DARE ESCAPE

Aisling and Fintan whisked themselves beneath a hovering portcullis, sprang into a pumping stride, and veered for the *bawn* or outer courtyard. Hugging the tower house's mortared curtain walls, Ash strained her vision toward the upper floors of the tower house, where she noted square windows cut into the stone façade. These offered commanding views upon the yard and out over the landscape.

"She's keeping an eye on us," Ash concluded.

"Who is the *she*?" Fin asked, peeping at the ramparts.

"Lady Cathryn. The Butcher. Who else?"

"The Butcher is a lady!?" Fintan blurted. "That news is as crooked as a warlock's cock."

"Hush, wee peg. I swear there'll be plenty of explaining later," she assured her brother. "For now, our only commandment is to run!"

Ash hastened Fin toward the bawn enclosure. Fintan wheezed, clutching his bruised ribs. At the six-foot high wall, Ash clambered up first, her sibling boosting her by the foot. She fumbled atop the ancient barrier, spun about, and dangled her arms back down to help haul him upward and over. With a ferocious yank, they crashed down the other side, banging against rocky earth.

"My thrumming brain," groaned Fintan.

They disentangled, then froze. There must have been ten soldiers securing the perimeter of the tower house. Lady Cathryn Butler clearly had conscripted a segment of unemployed English Royalist troops to operate as her private sentinels.

Without ado, two of the soldiers closed in on the Irish orphans. When Fintan kicked at one, he slammed the butt of his ten-pound iron musket straight into the boy's eye. Ash screamed, but Fin passed into oblivion. The soldier dragged the boy like a puny plough sled back into the tower's courtyard.

The second guard hauled Aisling in a different direction. "Where are we going? What have you done to my brother?" she cried. In silence, he used his gun to direct her inside the tower house, then up a flight of steep, narrow granite steps. They scaled three more flights until they reached the uppermost floor. Here, the soldier shoved her into the grand chamber and shut the oak doors behind her.

The apartment was stupendous in size yet forlorn in its sparsity. Aside from a monumental fireplace blazing with flame, no other mark of luxury or prestige endured. The only furnishings were a common featherbed, a writing chair at an escritoire, and an embroidered settee. Upon one of the four small window seats, attired in a plain blue cotton dress, Lady Cathryn Butler sat gazing across acres of pasture drenched by rain. She scanned for the burgeoning smoke of raiders who violated properties weekly.

"If you are startled by the bleak scene of my dwelling chamber, allow that ten years of war has burdened me with debts." She spoke without turning to face her visitor. "I have been forced to peddle much of my estate whilst the demon Cromwell impounds my holdings."

"What's been done to my brother?" Ash demanded.

"He has been shackled in the dungeon where he might contemplate his missteps." Lady Butler turned her glower on Ash. "Approach, Irish."

Ash moved with careful steps.

"I have been studying you," the lady disclosed. Rising from the window, she walked across the round room and pointed toward a feature in the flooring. She swung open a trapdoor, revealing a square shaft that extended down the entire 50-foot height of the circular stone tower. It was rigged with mirrors, which served to grant a small but intelligible view of the prison.

"This *machicolation*, or drop chute, was mortared as a defense tactic, whereby we might hurl stone, boiling oil, and pails of human excrement at despoiling berserkers," the lady explained. "I summoned my carpenters to modify the mechanism into a shaft for spying. Monitoring my captives, I determine whose antics warrant punishment."

"Such an ingenious schemer you are," Ash tutted. "The heiress of wobbling English trickery, Devil take my name!"

Lady Butler shifted to face the window-glass defended by iron grills, which admitted slivers of sallow light into the otherwise dark tower. "By what name are you called?"

"Aisling of Clan Lorcan. From ancient times, our sept holds its seat in Galway. A onetime *biatach*, we were landholders whose bailiwick dominated miles of Connaught."

If ever a tone could convey a sneer, Lady Cathryn mobilized it. "Well, are you not the genuine article of Saint Patrick, bleeding emerald green and standing ten-foot tall on the pride of your Native stock? You're full of tongue for a lass who claims as her homeland a province of squalor and hopelessness."

Ash held fast. "Ock, why exclude Connaught's legend as a paradise for famine?"

"I admire your spirit, girl, much more than your tact." She gestured now at the spy-hole, which reflected a view of her brother's confinement. "Considering your appalling upbringing, are you literate?"

Ash shot back an icy look. "My father was a fairly unlettered man, but he sowed in us children his most precious belief: *With an education, a person can turn the world over-end*. He drilled all my siblings in words and numbers."

"You will cost me, Aisling O'Lorcan," the lady admitted enigmatically.

Ash discarded her patience. "What is your purpose with me and the rest of the orphans?"

The Lady sidestepped the question. "With your slippery quick-silver wit and blasting attitude, you are a *liability*. Do you grasp a word so advanced, dear?"

"Cease your riddles. What do you mean I am a *cost* and *liability*?"

"Is it not obvious, you naïve wastrel? You will be marketed as indentured servants," Lady Butler said matter-of-factly. "Forsooth, you are no fetching beauty, as is my preferred catch. But with a brother counteracting your lacking, I ought coax a tolerable purse for the likes of two that nears the value of one. At least you possess a symmetrical face and burgeoning figure."

"Like your own darling self," taunted Aisling.

"Pish!" Lady Butler waved her off. "Cruel years have eroded my vitality. Still, I do carry the stamp of a pure English strain, whereas you bleed the tainted serum of the barbarous Irish Catholics. Our pedigrees are universes apart, girl. May God forbid they ever mingle."

Ash pulled away, hot with indignation. She took several breaths before responding. "Indeed, we may not pulse with common blood, but our hearts are entwined in a common cause. You and I battle to rescue the same land: Ireland, our home. We may not be allies, no. But we are not enemies, either. That cock-suck Oliver Cromwell and his Parliamentarians have won that status."

Lady Butler winced at the breech of manners, but then her expression melted into a thin smirk. Her pretension ebbed for the first instant, affording Aisling a glimpse of the woman beneath the noble camouflage. This served to diffuse Aisling's loathing and defiance. She abated her armor, recognizing in Lady Cathryn the immortal resolve of a woman whose spirit refused to succumb to tragedy. No matter her ancestry, she maintained unflinching, unyielding, and unbreakable dignity.

Lady Cathryn stepped before the hearth. The flame-light painted youth into her greying brown tresses. "In these years of trials, I have graved a husband, four sons, a daughter, and a little one – a who graced this world for no more than 10 weeks. My middle two sons, Ewart and Gareth, are the only family that live still – and they are the least adept at enduring these grim times."

Ash did not respond. She granted space for the Lady's confession.

Lady Cathryn fixated upon the fire. "Famine and plague have cut down thousands. There is no work to be found, no land to sow. Lord General Oliver Cromwell has confiscated for his English cronies every acre of fecund soil. By his impending Act of Settlement, only sand-blown, bony earth shall remain for us. What grows in these counties be naught but shame and gravestones."

Her inconsolable rumination broke like a spell when she realized that Ash stood there, listening. "I had it wrong. Your kind and mine are not so distant. Lord Cromwell shall sentence us both to execution. Is that pleasing to you?"

"I wish it were, but nay, it is not." Ash rehearsed several sentences in her mind before venturing them with complete sincerity. "We must cast aside our legacy of quarrels and stand united. We are one Irish!"

As she spoke the last word, a quick pain intruded. Her belly clenched. The twinge released for the briefest moment, then double-knotted her abdomen. She teetered two steps.

Lady Butler hastened to the girl's side. "What ails you?"

Aisling grimaced. "A sudden pain. Tis barely a worry, my Ladyship." She mustered an apologetic smile that was awfully lopsided, and weakened to her knees atop the oak floorboards. Her body grabbed its innards into a fist. This was no distress prompted by the morsels of the latest meal. The lurching sensation arose from deep within, from a sacred place.

Then she saw a thin file of blood dripping down her leg. "Crime of saints," she gasped.

The Lady's demeanor transformed. "Your first flow?" she asked gently.

At first, Ash didn't understand. When she did, she gave a faint nod.

"How many years have you?"

"Fifteen."

"The pain is natural," Lady Butler reassured her.

"Am I dying?" Ash wondered aloud.

"Nails of Christ, no, child. You are more living than ever! Tis a feminine peeve. Not pleasant, to be sure, but no *curse*, as some imbecilic men might suggest," the lady lectured. "A man has a gun to take life. A woman has a womb to make it. Your blood marks the day you have crossed into womanhood. It avows your sound health. It proclaims your ripeness for bearing children. It should be celebrated, never scorned."

"But the blood?" Ash hardly dared ask, staring at the small pool that had formed on the tower home floor.

"I shall demonstrate how to use a belt and linen stitch to catch the purge." Lady Butler leaned in closer. "Anyway, you should be grateful you experienced your first flow under my watch so that I might teach you these things. Because soon, you depart this place."

IN WHICH PRISONERS ARE BOUGHT AND SOLD

The very next night, Lady Butler's two sons gusted into the chamber with three soldiers following. They wrested from imprisonment Aisling and her faction, along with several more from the storehouse of boys. Amongst their selection was Fintan, who sidled up next to his older sister as shackles stifled their ankles and the Butcher's wagon lurched into motion.

Bounding onto the roadway with springs yelping and wheels growling, the vehicle streaked westward across fallow farmland for two days, until the horse team nickered and stomped its conclusion at the port of Galway. Lady Cathryn Butler aimed directly for the houses of commerce. An agent inventoried her lot and finalized the contracts. Her affairs of business transpired with the cadence of a well-oiled event. Ledgers were recorded and promissory notes secured by a dance of feather quills.

Roustabouts bustled Lady Cathryn's human inventory into a skiff. Butcher-paper packages were bestowed upon each of the captives. The girls' contained a pristine white chemise and a linsey-woolsey dress; the boys' a stiff linen shirt, a short-jack, and a set of clean hose.

"Where are you sending us?" Aisling shouted at the Butcher, who stood statuesque along the quay. Lady Cathryn's countenance remained as impassive as a brick wall.

Even as the ferrying craft launched, Ash would not succumb. “For the wailing of hell, is it to some brothel that you’re auctioning us?”

But the skiff already had harnessed Galway’s rambunctious currents, and in seconds Aisling and the huddle of Irish strays were separated by 100 yards from shore. Lady Cathryn drew her mantle close against the spitting drizzle as she disappeared from sight.

The skiff oared toward a shabby fluyt, one of many working vessels idling in the bay. Evening had deadened the green of the hillsides until the land resembled stone and the water appeared as a cursed tomb. Aisling, Fintan and their fellow oppressed were consigned to the ship’s hold, where 40 other cowering souls already had been gathered.

The fluyt put out the following dawn. A spear of light pierced the sky as a number of captives began vomiting from sea-nausea. With adequate concern for the merchandise, the prisoners were shuffled into open air atop the weather-deck. Thankful to escape the noxious fumes of the vessel’s bowels, Ash and Fin watched as they sailed past the legal houses and took to sea.

The littoral of Galway faded from sight just as the heavens shattered open with rain. Ash noted a cruel irony. She and Fin had been struggling to attain Galway. Yet just as they had finally achieved the destination, its shores were perishing from their sight. The pair were being ejected from their homeland by way of the rightful place of their provenance, the Lorcan family seat.

Fintan edged beside Ash. “What lies ahead, do you suppose?” he asked in their native Gaelic tongue.

Ash turned her attention to her brother's wounded eye. The Butler's soldier had cracked the pupil, so that it resembled a broken egg. "Your seeping eye needs to be tended. It could lure death," she said.

"Take a fuck," he quipped. "I shall always insist upon living."

"You're a mouthy sprat," she heckled.

Fin shrugged. "With but one true eye, I see still same how the infinite ocean mocks our brittle existence."

Aisling arched a brow. "Are you yammering poetry again?"

"Every Irish word is a poem," he declared.

The waves shifted, shaping an unknown story.

Aisling threw her arms around her brother, securing Fin in an embrace brimming with her complete love. "By the Lord's mercy, brother of mine, at least we are bearing these travesties together."

Chapter 9

JAMAICA

IN WHICH TRICKS ARE PLAYED

At the southernmost tip of La Vega stood the lawless and neglected *Cayo de Carena* or Careening Cay. No more than a spit of land, the narrow peninsula sheltered Jamaica's principal harbor of Guavayaya, which later would come to be called Kingston Harbor. Within decades, the Cayo de Carena would rise to infamy as the most debauched city in all the world – a Gomorrah known as Port Royal.

Presently, the cay was heaped with decaying ocean vessels begging for restoration: galleons, frigates, pinnaces, barques, corvettes, and sloops. Dozens of men worked as salvagers, carpenters, and joiners. Their employment was *careening* – the cleaning and mending of ships.

"Heave her down, lads," the once-renowned mariner who called himself Portugal advised. After so many years with scarcely a day spent indoors, the sun, salt, and wind had transformed his skin into a blotched parchment.

"Rub off, you crank," replied a youth with white-gold hair.

"Arr, leave us be, you nob-nosed Jew," his brother added. They nevertheless obeyed the older man's instructions, urging their hired oxen to turn the capstan further. As the ropes strapped about the vessel tightened, she moaned. A nearby collection of Spanish drudgers, slapping tar upon the hull of Governor Ramírez's corvette, glared at the foreigners.

Portugal harbored fondness for the twins, who hailed from Amsterdam, in spite of his plans to swindle them. They were obligated to repair the merchant ship in order to pay off debts. This work included removing every barnacle, mussel, and shipworm, that was chewing away at her hull. Portugal had offered his decades of experience to the novices at no charge.

Suddenly, the vessel toppled. When she did, a monstrous crunching sound erupted. The twins blared curses in Dutch. This was no ordinary event. The ship had fallen upon an anchor concealed in the sand. Her starboard frame had split wide open.

The Spanish tars erupted into laughter. The twins gurgled with panic. Then they began to scream at their unsolicited advisor. "Twist a river up your arse, Portugal!"

"What have you guided us to do, you rejected, worthless old man? She popped her gut!"

"There is a method for solving this, fear not," Portugal assured them. "I shall have words with your captain. Kindness compels me to help you. Together, we shall repair the damage done by this immense stroke of ill fortune."

The lads continued to decry their fate as Portugal turned to walk inland. A quarter mile's journey down the peninsula, a wiry youth ran up to greet him. "Aye up, Luka. Tis concluded," Portugal reported with a grin.

"Egads, Master Portugal! Is it true?" Luka gasped, regaining his breath.

"Yes, the comely duchess smashed her hull to smithereens upon the same rusty anchor that you veiled in the sludge yesterday. For your exertions, I will give you a percentage of the remittance I win from the ship's captain. I shall promise him a restoration of his precious vessel for a mere 1500 pieces, the lucky fellow." Portugal grinned with self-satisfaction.

"Huzzah!" Luka celebrated. "A sea of earnings!"

Portugal smoothed his worn, grimed doublet and breeches. "Better to wait a day or three before we begin, however. First let the lads and their captain stew in their troubles."

IN WHICH TRICKS ARE TURNED

Portugal ambled ten minutes further down the path until he came to a huddle of clay huts. The bawdy house within betrayed its humble exterior. When he parted the thick, soft curtain of red Kashmiri velvet, he entered a realm of dream fulfillment.

The brothel mistress was a *morisca* – a Muslim who had converted to Christianity under threat of death. "You are overdrawn from the before month," she hassled in Spanish, nevertheless escorting Portugal into a waiting room enhanced by 200 candles and burning coils of incense.

He gave the whore-broker a blank look. He had no recollection of the sum he owed. Amnesia was a boon, he had determined in recent years. Brimming with excitement over his latest caper, he fished through his haversack and forked over a leather pouch. "One hundred pieces of eight satisfies the debt, and a fresh hundred in advance of the coming days."

The morisca snapped up the coins, but he seized her wrist before they vanished into the folds of her frock. "This amount accommodates as well any physics I demand: mandrake, Indian purge, black leaf, grog, and so forth. Savvy?"

She nodded, but Portugal had not yet finalized his requests. "Also note that I aim to enjoy the enchantments of both Fatima and Aisha."

The brothel madam waggled a finger under his nose, but her eyes were smiling. She was accustomed to his immoderate appetites. He pecked a kiss upon her wrinkled cheek.

She led him to his favored den, where his two preferred harlots lounged upon a pile of dense rugs and silk pillows. Both women were of Moorish strain. The sight of their bronze skin glistening with oil drove his cock erect. Their generous bosoms rising and falling, rosebud nipples peering from beneath sheer gowns, full lips, smoky painted almond eyes – well, the scene alone nearly delivered him to ejaculation.

He crouched upon his knees. Gently, he guided Fatima's legs apart, revealing the dusky pasture that lay between. He was hard as a rock and throbbing with desire.

"Come aboard, my lordling," Fatima teased, her voice greedy.

Aisha wriggled up from behind. Her breasts tickled his back. "We have missed you," she breathed into his ear.

They removed his waistcoat, stripped him of his linen shirt, and peeled away his breeches. There he stood, belly jutting out. Once, he had been a strong man, thick-boned with keen eyes and a crop of boyishly charming hair. Actually, the curls were the one proud feature that remained.

"Ahhh, my depraved Gopis," he sighed. "But first…" He rubbed his palms together like an illusionist excited to perform his next act. Giddily, he rifled through his haversack. His fingers flew with manic speed, unfurling a bundle of beetle leaf, flattening a half-dozen jade green petals, then twirling them into conical pouches. A powdery pinch of a stimulant trusted by the Amerindians he loaded into each of these leaf funnels. He allocated four for future use before hastening to inhale the inaugural dose. It blazed a path through his nose and straight into his brain.

Two heartbeats later, Portugal bolted to his feet, pupils saucered. Tremors rocked him for 15 minutes until the entirety of his pain – from the pit in his gut, to the ache in his heart, to the agues in his bones, to the crippling memories in his head – vaporized. The powder delivered him into a state of bliss. It assured him that he was loved. The truth mattered not. For the next few hours, he would be a decent man.

"Come here," he grunted, drawing Fatima close. "And you, Aisha. Do my balls the French way." He slid one hand between Fatima's legs and stroked her velvet opening whilst savoring with the other Aisha's breasts. He could withhold his wild prurience no more. Mounting Fatima, he shoved his animal-hard length inside, deeper and deeper, pounding a route to rapture.

His wits disintegrated. When the orgiastic spike wore thin, he reached again for a leaf funnel, flung back his head, and snorted more of the mesmeric powder. No longer could he comprehend if he were snuffing a whore's cunt or fucking a mushroom.

IN WHICH TRICKS ARE TROUNCED

Some unknown number of hours or days later, Portugal was stirred by a sound that stomped upon his heart. It was a voice connected to a man he had hoped never to encounter again.

"Truly, an extraordinary sort of degenerate," Throat observed half-aloud.

The whore den, Portugal saw, had been transformed into a lair of excess. Sunlight flared through cracks in the clay walls, revealing smashed cruses of grog, piles of smoked black leaf, and crumbles of beetle leaves. Recoiling to shield his nakedness, he scrambled for his shirt and breeches. In so doing, he noted that Fatima and Aisha had long since exited. He was alone in the fuck sty.

"How is it that each time I fix my eyes upon you, you seem all the more fervently mounted on Death's horse, trotting at full speed towards Hades?" Throat wondered.

"Perhaps you named my very mission."

"You're one queer Jew, Portugal," Throat clucked. "You might consider a more expedient work-around. I have a handy spear of steel here." He brandished the blade bound to his right wrist. "Ask politely, and I can oblige, delivering you without delay into Death's embrace."

Portugal tossed him a look balancing disgust with potential. "But Throat, why should I forgo fantastic galas of debauchery *before* collecting my place in Hell?" With no other intoxicant remaining, he scooped from the floor a tankard and sucked down its last dregs.

"Breakfast, is it?" quipped Throat as he tossed Portugal his waistcoat. He chased that favor by hurling at him iron manacles. The chains crashed into Portugal's face.

"Bah!" the mariner cried out. "What piss was that?"

"It appears that *you*, Baltazar Mesquita, happen to be one further piece of refuse my *patrón* seeks to collect."

Portugal had not heard his proper name in months, years perhaps. He shifted back into the pillows, examining Throat. "Don Francisco de Leiva demands an audience with me?"

Throat nodded.

"For what reason?" Portugal pressed.

Throat offered a snort in reply. "Do something for me? As you were once more expert than any other in clasping iron chains upon human property, lock your own wrists. I'd rather not rub up against your slew of diseases."

IN WHICH A SEWER IS A GAOL

Iron Eyes felt his mind spinning off its gears. After days encased in a dank stone tomb, he battled starvation, hypothermia, and exhaustion. A vulgar stench wafted beneath his nose. The water escalated and retreated at intervals, sometimes rising as high as his chest, but always immersing his feet. It was maddening. His skin had begun to fail and threaten infection.

Of his faithful cohorts, he was the only one chained within the irregular gaol. He had no idea what may have happened to them. And yet an hour past, El Mulato had imprisoned alongside him a stranger. The fellow spewed a constant discourse that seemed devoted to irritating him. More than once, Iron Eyes wondered if the man had been planted here as another form of torture.

"Tis an unused sewer? A dissolute crypt? A dungeon? Oubliette even? Catacomb perchance?" the stranger babbled in Spanish. "Or aye verily, a quarry initiated with a craving for executing the most visionary stonework, but renounced gradually due to the convergence of simony, larceny, incompetence, faineance, and insolvency!" He cackled as though he had lost his God – or was clever enough to comprehend that his dilemma mattered not to any supreme being.

"Oy, for the sake of Caesar, seal your trap!" Iron Eyes howled in English.

"My name may not interest you, but amongst the shipyards, I am known as Portugal," the man offered in the same language.

"Aye, then. Halt your pondering aloud, Portugal," Iron Eyes said, gnashing his teeth. "I swear, your unceasing prattle is more awful than any punishment put forth by the Holy Inquisition."

At once, Portugal's expression turned even more unstable. "Are you so educated in matters of the Tribunal that you can jape about their catalogue of horrors?"

"What is this new topic of blathering?" Iron Eyes complained.

"*Nothing* agonizes human flesh more than being burned at the stake," Portugal gruffed.

"Jesus Christ Lord on Roman sticks."

"Aha! There it surfaces: Your galling prejudice," Portugal accused, jangling his fetters.

"What the God? By those words, I express nothing more than a furious desire for you to shut your mouth!"

"Y*ou* reached for the emphasis on Christ!" argued Portugal. "Plain as day, you're unrested by my Jewry."

Iron Eyes threw up his hands until his shackles banged against their lashings. "Split my skull. How might I possess any knowledge of your faith? And what does it matter, since we both are crimped in irons?"

"Frightened of me, is that it?" Portugal replied.

"For all the kipper's dick, I care not a bloody crack what you are, Jew or not!" Iron Eyes boomed. "With your mug masked in snot and clothes all tainted, I am incapable of diagnosing what species you might be."

"So now you liken me to an animal?"

Iron Eyes did not reply right away. He stalled for a moment, sizing Portugal up carefully. "Bloody skittles. You're taking the piss."

The mad man grinned crookedly. Then his shoulders bucked with a guffaw. "And did I! That face," Portugal stammered, tears pouring from his eyes.

Iron Eyes was incapable of withholding a response to the knavish mirth. He, too, found himself engulfed by laughter.

When at last Portugal recaptured his breath, he surprised his prison mate by saying, "I know exactly who *you* are. Iron Eyes. Captain Damien Baines."

The pyrate stiffened.

"Am I spinning circles around you?"

Iron Eyes did not answer.

"I have a talent for learning between the cracks," Portugal grinned. "All the poor, subservient, outcast, and oppressed peoples struggling here amongst these isles of the West Indies have been chanting your name as though Yaweh himself had arrived to save them. Tis not that I am more salty than sunny, but *me*? Well, I reckon you are no more proven than this here rodent." He gestured at a bloated rat carcass floating past.

"You sport daringly, stranger," Iron Eyes warned, his smile sinking into a frown.

"Hear me," Portugal taunted. "If you are a renegade captain, and if truly you seized a flagship of the Spanish Treasure Fleet, and if actually you had a bully complement of pyrates at your command, and if verily you were rich with a head spilling out schemes of forming a free nation at sea… Then why *ever* did you bumble about the shipping lanes, your vessel plain as day, begging your enemy to hunt you down for the pleasure of destroying you?"

"No other option presented," Iron Eyes refuted. "We were but a single vessel carrying scant provisions. We had no abetting ships. What other route could we have taken?"

"Aye, now we get to the heart of it," the bewildering man sympathized. "You're dimwitted. See, if it had been me, we might have sauntered upon a more pygmy Spanish port – Margarita, say, De la Trinidad, or this here Jamaica even. La Vega is wanting for any manner of fort and boasts not one brass growler to scrape your broadsides. Me and my fellows, we would've laid-to squarely withinside the harbor and sworn a bother of shot upon any vessel that encroached. Soon enough, the port would have come to recognize itself hostage and *voila*! The rewards of victuals, ordnance, and rum would have been poured all over us."

"How now, there's a mighty idea. Except I've heard it once before… How many points for mimicking the feat achieved by Wim Jackson?" Iron Eyes shot back.

"Ain't partial to ideas being yours or his or any original masterpiece. Only what works."

"Yet you strut as a lion."

"No, captain," Portugal returned. "The lion leaps the fence. I'm more akin to a dog – I dig under it, acting as a secret marauder. I'm not ashamed to fight my way through dirt to steal the prized bone."

Iron Eyes considered Portugal's words. Only moments earlier, he had anticipated no such wisdom from the mad man. He was considering confessing as much when the iron gate at the far reach of the tunnel lurched open. Two figures bearing torches approached.

Iron Eyes distinguished the form of El Mulato. But when, by the firelight, he caught sight of the second figure, he feared he was hallucinating. For in place of the man's right hand, a dagger grew. His neck was disfigured by scars, his complexion cadaverous. His appearance induced a gallop of chills up Iron Eyes' spine.

"That scapegallows? You can call him Throat," Portugal muttered with spectacular enmity.

IN WHICH A QUEST IS UNDERTAKEN

Within the grand room of the *cabildo* house, Portugal honked malodorous gas. Iron Eyes was seated upon a chair beside him. Both were stifled by manacles about the wrists.

"For the love of guns!" ached Iron Eyes. "Cease itching your arse-worms, Portugal. The stench!"

The mariner steered their discourse to matters outranking his gastrointestinal eruptions. "He is no Castle and Lion gentlemen. Rot no. A self-made conniver is more like it." Consternation owned his face. An enormous toot announced that he had freed even more gas into the chamber. "One mean puzzle of a man, don Francisco de Leiva rubs lemon into every wound and licks the sugar off any opportunity."

"Bung your blurting mouth hole," Throat grumped. "And your farting arse hole, also."

The door swung open. Throat retreated into a lagoon of shadows. Don Francisco de Leiva gestured at the two soldiers who trailed him, indicating that they ought remain outside the door with El Mulato. "Secure this room at any cost," he commanded.

Circling throughout the chamber, de Leiva ensured that only three other men were present – the two prisoners and his most senior *bravo*, Throat. Then he seated himself upon a chaise with a cushion of crimson velvet. The wooden chair was carved with scrolls and bedecked with silver nails like a throne.

Iron Eyes evaluated his rival. Don Francisco de Leiva equaled him in age but prevailed in princely allure. The Spaniard's features were cut with impeccable symmetry. A flurry of burgundy curls spilled to his shoulders. The pyrate clicked his tongue, impressed.

From a cruet, de Leiva poured rosewater into lead cups. With flawless etiquette, he distributed the refreshments. Then he raised his cup, saluting his two prisoners. But his nose twitched in disgust when his gaze landed upon the mariner. "Señor Baltazar Mesquita, you appear as you smell – like the discharge of a loose gut."

"And you, *Jefe*, as always, enjoy the dapper appearance of a whistling Boabdil," Portugal quipped in refined Spanish.

"God's blood, Jew. You dare compare me to a vanquished Moor?" De Leiva turned to Throat. "He likens me to an infidel. Such cheek!" They snickered.

Portugal responded with more flatulence.

"It is my obligation to hand you," de Leiva said, turning his gaze upon Iron Eyes, "and this *Lutherano* traitor here, to the tribunal of the Holy Office of the Inquisition, which sits at Cartagena. You both are enemies of Christ. If verily the interrogators pronounce you heathens, then you shall fester in prison until your day of damnation. Then, your souls shall be consigned to the Act of Faith… the *auto-da-fé*."

Iron Eyes tightened against his chains. Portugal further ground his teeth. De Leiva luxuriated in their dismay.

"If you aim to deliver my death, then bustle to it!" Portugal blasted a simultaneous chorus of words and gas.

"Rarrgh! Clamp your beak and quit your ass quacking!" Throat carped at him from the rear of the chamber. "Tis torture to share a room with you."

Having made the same critique of Portugal only hours earlier, Iron Eyes could not suppress a smirk. He guessed from Throat's accent that he hailed from the Plymouth colony.

De Leiva scraped his chair across the mahogany flooring. "Hmm…" he murmured as he inspected up close the face of Iron Eyes. "My foremost concern is the murky nature of *you*. Your demise was proclaimed as definite. Sworn to me, it was, by Captain Araña Sangrienta, the first squadron commander himself. He composed an affidavit to the King stating he had perforated your chest with shot."

"Mercy, Saint Cock! Do even the *guardacosta* reside within your pocket?" Portugal shouted.

"Counter to you, Señor Mesquita, I am no prodigy in the sport of buying and retailing African souls," de Leiva retorted. "I dabble in advantages and vulnerabilities. My trade is in plotting, *not* slavery."

Iron Eyes fired wide-eyed surprise at Portugal, who endured the heat of the pyrate's condemnation with a clenched jaw. Then he turned his attention back to de Leiva, primed to tackle the topmost mystery in his mind: *Why does this man not kill us?*

"When all is said and done, we are quite alike, the gang of us," de Leiva announced. "We seek opportunity, we make our way by plot and predation." He rejoiced in his shrewdness by patting Portugal patronizingly upon the knee.

"Yet here I am, slung in irons and stinking of ripe bowels," argued Portugal. "My name carries all the esteem of a dog's breakfast."

"Ha! Forsooth, our faiths and manners are hopelessly incompatible. Nevertheless, we are, by grace of having arrived at this frontier of the globe, sympathetic in spirit. The possession of this New World takes hold of our hearts. The possibilities it throws before us are unlike any other affair of civilization," de Leiva asserted.

Iron Eyes and Portugal swapped perplexed looks.

With a sup of the rosewater, Iron Eyes cleared the limestone grit from his throat. Braving his rudimentary Spanish, he said, "You blow a big gale, Señor. But I figure not your meaning. I would rather break my neck than wade through so many fancy words. Speak plainly your intentions with us."

De Leiva moved to the windows facing the king's plaza. The church bells tolled the hour of the Sext. Horses clomped and barkers marketed mangoes and guava. "Does the name Gaspar Carvalhal trigger your memory?" he inquired.

"A sizable smuggler. Not a minnow, but not a barracuda either," Portugal replied with a shrug.

"Can you furnish me with additional information?"

Portugal squirmed as he gathered his thoughts, straining to disentangle de Leiva's motives. "Gaspar is the nephew of don Antonio de Carvalhal, the White Oak – a supreme trading power and wealthy Jew who promotes England as a new refuge for our people."

"Your people? Jewry? Say more," de Leiva prodded.

"Rumors siren that Señor Antonio imports into London 100,000 Spanish *reales* of bullion a year. And that the full guild of Jewish merchants already has endowed English Parliament with one half million in coin."

De Leiva balled a fist but restrained his compulsion to drive it through the window. "Ejaculators of sin! They bed one another? But *why*?"

"Arrr, why else but shared revilement of Catholic Spain and the jaws of her Holy Inquisition?" Iron Eyes retorted. "Beyond that, I reckon, a swooping lust to win a slab of these isles of the West Indies?"

De Leiva thought on these suppositions. "So it is. Oliver Cromwell and his Protestant Parliament befriend the devilish Jew so that they might conquer a piece of Spain's New World. As an Englishman, Señor Baines, what more can you reveal?"

"Actually, I am a Saxon child of Wales with a flimsy tolerance for English dogs. Lord Oliver Cromwell is a born conqueror, shrewd as a tomcat. He longs to brand his name upon history's flesh. It is thus exquisitely pragmatic for him to ally with the Jews, who possess coin and trade in information."

"The benefits of reciprocation are clear as crystal," Portugal added.

"This, then, is the so-called *Western Design*," de Leiva considered. Gazing out into the square, he observed a troupe of adolescents tormenting a lame dog with a bamboo switch. "May I be sure, then, that Oliver Cromwell is King of England?"

"Nay, nay," scoffed Iron Eyes.

De Leiva cocked an eyebrow. "But he beheaded the king who came before him."

"Har! And about London these days, it is said that Lord Cromwell uses the skull of King Charles the First as his chamber pot!" Portugal snickered.

"Regicidal jackal," Iron Eyes bemoaned. "Oliver Cromwell seized the instrument of government, ousted from Parliament his opponents, and put to execution His Majesty King Charles I. Forthwith, he sailed an army to Ireland and brutally conquered those lands through starvation and carnage. Of this you may be certain, Señor de Leiva: His Excellency Lord Oliver Cromwell is a warlord and *not* a king."

"Thing of it is, Oliver Cromwell gets celebrated by many as an icon in the battle against sovereignty," challenged Portugal.

"True," Iron Eyes said. "For as many men who deride Cromwell as a monster, an equal number proclaim him a messiah."

"The infernal blasphemer! Oliver Cromwell poses the greatest peril on earth to God's beloved Catholic Spain," de Leiva said, glaring.

Long moments passed. Sounds of barkers, creaking wagons, and flirtatious volleys between maidens and militiamen rising from the square alleviated tensions within the chamber.

Moving past the oratory, de Leiva slowed before the painting of Vulcan, Mars, and Venus. "Tell me, *Damien Baines*, about the shame of your betrayal," he asked rhetorically, fingering his chin whiskers. "Of what age now are the children you rejected? I wager you hold tight the possibility that *she* has wed again, and that your abandoned son and daughter live in the care of a more decent man than you. Do they think you dead? Or do they, in fact, realize that your pledge of a two-year absence aboard a merchant vessel was but a ruse? That you crafted a permanent escape from the drudgeries of a farmer's existence?"

The Boatswain sensed jeopardy. Dread struck him like a mallet in the ribs. *How, in Christ's punctured feet, does this Jamaica islander know so much about my former life back in Wales?* he fretted. *How, from the other side of the globe, has don Francisco de Leiva rooted out my true identity? The dark secret I deemed safe with myself and Tiburon and none other?*

De Leiva admired the results of his inquiry, smiling at the angry expression upon the face before him. "I purvey in intelligence. My spies blow whispers into every crossroad, every station, every corner of humanity. There is no dodging me. You do best to remember that."

Iron Eyes felt as though he would vomit. Portugal exploded once more with venomous vapors.

From a cabinet, de Leiva ferreted out a key. This he handed to Throat, who used it to remove Iron Eyes and Portugal from their iron constraints. Next, he sprung forth the pyrate captain's beloved double-barreled French pistol.

Surprise flashed across Iron Eyes' face.

Lingering his fingers upon the weapon, don Francisco de Leiva demonstrated his approval. Then he offered it to the pyrate. Contact with the cherry wood stock infused Iron Eyes with a sense of wellbeing.

"Your band of hunters – each and all nine of your men – are, as we commune, paying seams, sheathing nails, rigging sails, and certifying every solid beam of a modest sloop, thereby crafting it into a full-rigged ship of war," de Leiva announced.

The two prisoners were stunned for a minute. Iron Eyes gauged the Spaniard judiciously.

"As I spoke before, we are more similar in our designs than contrary," de Leiva continued. "We are, all three, plain men driven to flourish. I cannot submit to authoritarianism when I dream of autonomy. Like you, I prefer to steal the opportunity from every occasion."

"You have a plan for us," Portugal stated dryly.

De Leiva turned to Throat. "It is terribly adorable how clever these Jews are."

Throat snorted.

"Why offer a task to us heretics? Why not assign the job to one of your numerous Spanish trusties?" Portugal asked.

"Seems a fine question to me," Iron Eyes concurred.

"The pair of you," de Leiva replied, shaking his head. "Have you ended your smart remarks of the day? Try, now, to listen."

Duly admonished, Iron Eyes and Portugal sat straight as reformed pupils. De Leiva continued. "The dilemma is this: Not the Crown, nor the *cabildo* members, nor the governor – none beyond the four of us enclosed in this room and a sprinkling of well-proven soldiers is aware of your presence here. My sensitive errand cannot, for *verboten* reasons, be consigned to any Spanish vessel indexed by the *Casa de Contratación*."

Iron Eyes ushered in the obvious. "You underestimate me as a pyrate, *Señor.*"

"Harr," Portugal snickered. "How goes that proverb about the frog accepting the promise of a scorpion?"

"Pardon Mother Goose, here," Iron Eyes said to de Leiva. "The issue I am consider—"

But de Leiva already had sped ahead. "Is that you're ripe with cunning enough to nick a barge by your own talents? The answer to that is simple: Even so, you need me. Do I speak plain enough?"

"Forsooth you do," Iron Eyes smiled, confident he had won the upper hand.

But De Leiva savored his own aplomb. "If you were to play with me, to shun my proposal in favor of sailing as rogues by your own measures, then for the remainder of your days you would be hunted with no respite by the entire scale of the *guardacosta.* The Crown and the *Casa de Contratación* have ordered your death with the inducement of a sizable bounty. The writ has been posted in every port."

Iron Eyes sat mute.

De Leiva effaced any doubt that may still have been poisoning the pyrate's thinking. "You have witnessed what I can achieve. You ranged in peace for three months with Mota Sinan upon the North Coast thanks to my volition alone. You would not have lived a week were it not for my beneficence."

Bested, Iron Eyes cast his gaze downward like a lamb on a chopping block. It was Portugal who spoke next. "And say we agree to forming a furtive society with you. What do you offer us?"

"A vessel. Yours everlasting with not a single encumbrance." De Leiva gave a mock bow. "Every treasure, every prize she takes belongs solely on you."

"In return for…?" Portugal asked, ever distrustful.

Deviating once more to the window embrasures, de Leiva relished a breeze that had scurried up from the sea. "My single plea should not aggravate you, given as it appeals to your genuine natures. You need only display a passion for indecent trespasses. Commit galling felonies. Engage in criminal ransacking. In other words—"

"Pyracy," completed Throat.

The chamber fell so quiet that they could hear the chatter of ladies in the square addressing the turn in the weather. Captain Damien Baines stood for the first time. "Speak the demand in English, please."

"There is a frigate christened La Beduina. It is imperative that you plunder her," de Leiva said, complying with Iron Eyes' choice of language. "I arm you with every gem of intelligence my spies have gathered. With the ship I provide, you venture to sea. When you take the vessel I seek, you ravish all her wares – except one. Aboard La Beduina, there is hidden an item at once singular and simple in nature. It is of utmost importance to me. You are to return it exactly as is. All this you must accomplish within the next six months, else the Spanish forces shall rush to destroy you."

"Seems simple enough," Iron Eyes said. "But this item. What is it?"

"That information cannot be entrusted to you," de Leiva responded.

Portugal cackled, directing his next words at Iron Eyes. "Aye, so here's a puzzle. By what matter of witchery do you imagine we might discover the magic item if we know not *what it is*?"

"By virtue of my insights. One and all, we venture to sea together," Throat answered.

Iron Eyes impaled him with a glance. Portugal grimaced.

"Portugal, do not feign disinterest. My spies report that you hunger to return to sea," de Leiva said. "You shall function as navigator. Owen Butler, Throat as many prefer to name him, shall act as quartermaster."

The ladies in the square dispersed. De Leiva watched their dresses flutter in the breeze. "Since you are sparse in number, Throat will bulk your force with a body of trusted sailors and ruffians. When he has determined that your assignment has been achieved, you, Iron Eyes, shall once more be a free man. And we shall not swap words ever again."

IN WHICH PYRATES SET SAIL

The pyrates could not shake the sensation of a waking dream. Having defeated impossible odds, their entire lot – Iron Eyes, Tiburon, Zemi, and the eight buccaneers from Mota Sinan's clan – had been reunited. Their feisty vessel had been donated by don Francisco de Leiva, who had demanded nothing more in return than the retrieval of a strongbox. Iron

Eyes was captain, and Tiburon was the ship's pilot. No longer were they men of the land. They were *pyrates.*

De Leiva's threat to toss him into the jaws of the Inquisition had convinced Portugal to overcome his initial objections and join the crew as navigator. Tibbs and Iron Eyes felt outright clobbered by the man's transformation in the week since. The Portuguese Brazilian degenerate had scrubbed himself immaculate, docked his hair to a smart length, and resurrected his face from the wilderness of its beard. He had changed out his previously revolting attire for an Oriental *changshan* that was canary yellow and even, one might say, daringly fashionable. He wore spectacles that endowed him with a professorial bearing, as if pyracy were but an adjunct pursuit to solving mathematical equations.

Portugal had recruited from his days of scratching out a criminal existence upon the *Cayo de Carena* his devoted sidekick Luka Fly. Though only a lad and thin as a blade of grass, Luka demonstrated a ready talent for ship repairs.

In addition, Portugal had squired aboard their vessel a reluctant yet experienced seaman called Yellows to serve as boatswain. Portugal intimated that their relationship had hardened some three decades past when they had pioneered slave trading at Ouidah, a factory on Africa's Guinea Coast, but he would say no more.

Throat, the quartermaster as commissioned by de Leiva, had been tasked with keeping Iron Eyes on target with his mission. The knife-handed *bravo* had bulked the complement with 15 chums. Every one exhibited signs of criminal histories.

Along with Tibbs and Throat, Portugal had designed a course for Saint Christopher, better known as St. Kitts.

Although it possessed but a few stunted townships, the island boasted a population of rough men whom they might solicit to join their crew. Furthermore, Tiburon pointed out, amongst the French and English settlers, they would be unlikely to intersect with Spanish *soldados*.

"Let go topgallant clewlines, lee braces!" Yellows shouted.

Arms flexed and bodies rounded into boulders. The pyrates loosed sails into the wind. The breeze punched and all 65 feet of the sloop's length lurched forward. Toulouk the shipwright smiled broadly, thrilling at her speed and grace.

Originally, the vessel had been christened *La Nuestra Señora de Magdalena*, after Mary Magdalene. Prior to their departure, Iron Eyes had broached the subject with his men, and they had voted to reject the divine appellation. Due to being sea rovers, they felt the name should pay homage to the infidel nature of their campaign.

Dario Colón, whose advanced education made him ideal for the role of purser, had submitted a suggestion. The pyrates had saluted it with hoots and torrents of *kill devil*, rum supplemented with gunpowder and arsenic. With two cannon shots fired from the bow, they had rebaptized the sloop-of-war *La Negra Magdalena*, the Black Maggie. Dario believed this to be a perfect statement about the hypocritical prejudice they faced in their lives, for it cast the only female disciple of Jesus – a Jew by origin, a saint as worshipped by the Catholics, and a whore by trade – as a dark-skinned heroine.

Zemi strode with confidence about the ship, nose turned up to scent the wind. Tiburon bent to scratch her just above the tail, causing her crooked hind leg to bounce like a woodpecker's beak. Directing his gaze forward, he watched Iron Eyes pace the quarterdeck. A thing it was to behold his conviction in interpreting the waves, wind, sun, and clouds. He could not be more a sea captain. Tiburon prayed they might finally realize their dream of creating a free nation upon the sea.

He moved beside Iron Eyes, Zemi stationing herself firmly between them. As was his custom, Tibbs rolled, lit, and inhaled a cigarette by the nostril before offering a toke to Iron Eyes.

"Aye, Cap'n. Tis done!" he declared, clapping an arm around Iron Eyes' shoulders. "It was an inconceivable task, even for great minds such as ours. But lookee!"

Iron Eyes responded with a barely audible sigh.

"I know you have your gripes with de Leiva, but you can't deny his hold over the Spanish forces. Already we have traded sights with two coastguard ships – one a roving patrol vessel, no less – and neither paused to scrutinize us."

"Aye," Iron Eyes grumbled, scratching his beard contemplatively. Together, the two friends gazed upon the sea in silence.

Tibbs picked a baccy leaf from beneath a fingernail. "What ghost has you?"

Turning to face his friend, one blue and one green eye glistening, Iron Eyes said, "Simply the burden of such a calling, grand as it may be. Having dedicated ourselves to pyracy, it is certain now that Death will barge through our door without the courtesy of a knock. We shall not hear the gunshot coming, nor anticipate the cutlash chop that ends our lives. Yet sure as the sun sets each eve, death at the hands of the enemy is our fate."

Chapter 10

JAMAICA

IN WHICH MAROONS SEEK MAROONS

With a metronome of heavy breathing, the Windward Maroons scrambled past trees, around boulders, and over thickets, making their way through the strangulated terrain of Jamaica's interior. Their progress was unencumbered by their scant personal effects, which they carried upon their backs. The two mules, however, hauled the substantial load of weapons gifted them by the smuggler Gaspar Carvalhal. These animals demanded cautious guidance up the rugged cliffs.

When they arrived upon a triple set of waterfalls that tumbled from 100 feet above, two red-tails took flight. The birds alarmed Alzo, the militia strategist. He aimed his musket into the tightly-fused tree branches.

Nani also scrutinized the towering peaks. "They're tracking us," she announced. "Raptor-sighted sentinels hide in the forest, reporting our movements back to their camps."

By looting don Francisco de Leiva's prized strongbox, the Maroon chieftain knew, she had lit a grenade and shoved it into the lion's mouth. Before long, retribution would come lunging at her and her people. The question was how to carry forward.

Following her brief but torrid rendezvous with Gaspar Carvalhal, she had conducted Obiya ceremonies for three nights and days without sleep. As intended, she had loosed occult visitations. The spirit voices had counseled her to form an alliance with the other two Maroon communities of Jamaica. If they warmed to the scheme, they might encircle and protect her tribe.

Nani did not ever eschew the guidance provided by the ancestral chorus. She had propelled her people directly into the perilous Pitted Country, *Los Poros*. They had marched vigorously ever since. Yet she quailed at the hostility she felt filtering through the ravines. News of her theft of de Leiva's prize had taken flight across the island. Without doubt, the rival Maroon leaders would rage at her selfish act, for she had summoned Spanish ire upon them all.

Rainbows sprouted from the waterfalls where sunlight touched mist. Patiently she waited. When she sensed that danger had receded, she urged her followers to continue in the footsteps of Wol.

The Miskito man led them up an onerous track. He flitted through the foliage with the levity of a feather, his grace all the more noteworthy due to his broken gait. He was stubborn in his concealment of a gimp, but it was belied by the swaying motion of his shoulders. He had to compensate for injuries incurred from twice having had his hips smashed to bits.

Former *encomienda* and enslaved persons like himself could recite every beastly method of punishment employed by their masters. The drovers who presided over his ranch had favored the lash to spur workers to a faster pace. For more severe punishment, they employed the knout or cat-of-nine-tails. But they inflicted the greatest harm for any show of blaspheme averse to the One True Faith. *A fumigation of sin*, they said, *was necessary for a genuine return to the Lord.* This was handled by smashing the hip bone with a maul.

Forever fueled by the threat of being captured and forced again into such dreadful circumstances, Wol traversed every trail with lunatic grit. Bustling up behind him, the group was in short time sloshed in sweat. How they would have managed had Wol not met the fate of two maimed legs, they did not know.

They halted only when darkness descended, erecting a minimal camp for the night. At the base of a mahoe tree, Sipopi, a Taíno woman, awakened the fire that sleeps inside dried kindling. Along with her beloved friend Anapa, who was of Yoruba descent, she began to chant prayers over the meat of a hog they had marinated in lime and wild ginger five days prior. They honored as well their staple foods – *cazabi* and breadfruit.

The two spoke no word of *killing.* Rather, their feminine devotions praised the magnitude of *the cycle*, reminding all gathered of the compassion they must show for every living thing upon Earth. The Maroons memorialized the creatures of land and sea for their sacrifice, which in turn granted life to the next mortals in the cycle.

Nani, to the surprise of none, declined to nourish herself until each member of her renegade family had dined. Only then did she tolerate a morsel passing her lips. It was Anapa, with modesty detaining her direct gaze, who nudged the Maroon leader to partake. Smacking her tongue, Nani slurped from a calabash containing pork and root foliage stewed in a lake of rum. She fastened upon the tribespeople her earnest eyes.

"YoYo," Nani said, calling her renegades by the name she had invented some years past. Derived loosely from the assorted dialects of her tribe – who traced their ethnic roots to Guinea, Angola, Kongo, and Akan realms, as well as islands throughout this region – the word *YoYo* encompassed for her the true sense of family. "All must understand what we face, or else most will die."

She took a deep breath. "The hour of our demise nears. The smuggler Gaspar Carvalhal related to me that already don Francisco de Leiva has gathered the island militia in La Veja, where the armory gorges them with weapons. If we go forth unaided, he will crush us within the fortnight."

Sipopi added more branches to the fire to better illuminate Nani's discourse. The chieftain continued, "Juan de Serras, leader of the Los Vermejales Maroons, feeds upon distrust. His forces, four score strong, rig guns, pikes, pits, rock chutes, and other insidious traps about this territory. Beware! Do not get caught. No man is more ice-blooded than he. Like a raven, he watches and waits. Then and only then he decides whether to raise us up upon his wings or consume us like mice."

Nani gestured to Anapa, who granted her a calabash of fresh water infused with ginger, a stomach-soothing tonic. She swallowed several mouthfuls before resuming her lecture. "Lubolo takes a different tact. He wears his colors like a strutting peacock. His tribe of Mocho Mountain Maroons is more than one hundred strong, but they bow to the Spanish lieges with honey-coated *Yes-sirees.* By scraping himself upon the dirt before de Leiva, Lubolo has won a rickety peace with the Spanish islanders. He has X'ed his mark upon treaties with the *cabildo.* They donate weapons, drink, and livestock to him in exchange for not bothering their settlements. Lubolo is not ashamed of this. Likely he will flaunt over us his rightful footing with the *baccara,* the white man. Pity."

"My fear," Nani stood in order to ensure that her follows still were listening, "is that they plot to blockade an alliance – thereby denying that they, too, have much to gain by gathering into a singular army. They may rather watch us be killed than build with us a stronger Maroon nation. Why?" She paused. "Due only to my condition of being a woman."

"How are we to draw sympathy from these chest-beaters, Nani?" asked Alzo.

"Dirt-skirmishers," grumbled Santo, his voice a serrated blade.

"Their pride is hatched from the cod flaps they string between their ass-cheeks," Wol concurred.

With a wave of her bandaged hand, Nani dismissed their complaints. She had macheted her way through the overgrown pretenses of men many times before and always remained dignified, strong in her convictions yet without delusion.

But the others were not appeased. Santo spat into the fire. Sipopi grunted her disgust. Alzo thumped his ever-present spear against the earth.

"Destiny dictates that we convert the snide prejudices of Lubolo and Juan de Serras. With only our few people, our weapons, our pounding will, and speedy wit, we *must* convince their two Maroon tribes to join with us," Nani said." As one, we can defy the Spanish rulers. As one, we can win freedom for our peoples for generations to come. This the spirits tell me."

"But with your words, you also pour burning oil upon them! You tell us they are not trustworthy, then ask us to trust them. I argue against your plan," Alzo declared. Their confederacy encouraged all individuals to speak their opinions boldly. "We should take a less reckless path."

"For the good of us all, get to showing us, dear Alzo, your treasure chest of fancy choices!" Nani fired back, bridling with vexation. "You recommend another path, but can you cough up a plausible alternative?"

Pin-drop silence followed. Alzo retreated. "I spoke it clearly once, but I shall speak it again," Nani proclaimed. "Either we risk an alliance with Lubolo and Juan de Serras, or within the next two moons, we welcome de Leiva's guns blasting out our brains."

Nani's daughter JoJo inserted herself. "I understand your hesitation, my friends. Trust holds no appeal for those forever hunted. Yet we must remember that these renegades are Maroons, too. All of us have suffered horrors at the hands of our masters. Now, we all rage to keep safe our loved ones. We are chased by the same nightmares. We fly in the same dreams." She finished with a long sup of ginger water from the calabash.

No one spoke. The mules flicked their ears. The frogs trilled. The cicadas scratched notes they had rehearsed for eons.

Finally, Sipopi smiled. With reverence, she rested a hand atop Anapa's swollen belly. "Anapa and Wol are sanctified with child. Here comes the first *true-born Maroon*!"

The others let out a small cheer. Sipopi continued. "Even if Juan de Serras and Lubolo have faced horrors no different than our own, still the pursuit of this alliance burdens my heart. Will they do right by the first sacred baby of our kind? Juan de Serras roars a message of hate and suspicion. Lubolo scrapes his belly before the enemy. Trees, when planted in poisoned soil, cannot grow. No decent thing can come from this union."

"*No decent thing*? Are you certain of this, Sipopi?" Nani scolded. "On countless occasions during my enslavement, I spat at the gods. Some days, I would lie face down in dirt, covered in defeat. *No decent thing can come from this*, I thought. But look at me now. Did *no decent thing* come to me? I am the leader of a tribe of free and noble people. Me, a woman! The spirits led me here. They shall lead us to this Maroon alliance and triumph over the Spanish invaders of this island."

Several of the Maroons, including Alzo, Santo, and Sipopi, continued to squirm. Nani further perforated their doubt. "You who are gathered here. You follow me. *Why?*"

Alzo, the military captain, was quickest to respond. "You're a warrior stronger than crocodile teeth, and a leader more steadfast than a mule."

"Nani, our queen, you also are a priestess," said Sipopi.

"An heir to forbidden knowledge," Wol concurred. "Spirit worker, keeper of the *Obi*, you have a wizard's cunning."

"We trust you," Anapa added quietly.

Every member of the tribe echoed her sentiment.

IN WHICH MAGIC IS DEBATED

At daybreak, Sipopi revived the fire in order to warm a pot of manioc and parched corn for breakfast. Anapa went to harvest guava. The nearby groves were bursting with ripe fruit.

"Ayiiii! Help!" a cry of agony rang out from the woods. Wol flew like an arrow in its direction. Steps behind him raced Sipopi, Alzo, and Santo.

Anapa lay upon the ground writhing in pain. Kneeling beside her, Wol cradled his beloved's head and secured her pregnant belly.

"A trap," snarled Alzo. Just a few inches from where Anapa lay quietening her breath in her husband's embrace, a hole had been dug into the earth.

"It was covered by leaves…" Anapa gasped through gritted teeth.

"Juan de Serras, that prong-tongued snake," Sipopi cursed.

Moments later, Wol and Santo set Anapa by the fire. With water fetched from the nearby stream, the Miskito man delicately cleansed his wife's leg before massaging into it the viscous juice of an aloe leaf. Sipopi, meanwhile, mashed medicinal herbs – soursop leaves, moringa seed, kola nut, and turmeric – into a gourd for the patient to drink. They fretted as Anapa's ankle inflated and the skin purpled.

"She is crippled," Wol said, his mouth turning down. "No more walking for a week, perchance two. Three or four weeks beyond that, the baby comes."

"De Leiva's militia hunts us. I shall not bury two great friends and the first true Maroon. We move," said Alzo.

"But how?" Wol's voice was filled with fear born from a father's heart.

"Scrape the mold out from a worn-out manioc," Santo suggested. "Have Anapa take it by mouth, and press more upon the injury. She will heal quickly."

The others spun upon him. None had been aware that Santo, too, was enriched with knowledge of plant medicine. Sipopi began searching for a rotting manioc.

With a start, Nani cleaved from behind a tree. Wordlessly, she perched herself beside Anapa by the banked fire. Imprisoned in her hands was a *potoo*, an Jamaican owl. With warlock-yellow eyes, it glared at its captor. The other Maroons dropped their activities and collected by the fire.

Nani seemed transformed, her features turned to stone. A hypnotic gaze frosted her eyes. Doubtless she was performing an Obiya ritual. She grappled the owl into submission and, with clinical dispassion, wrung its neck. Her bare hands tugged, and the creature screeched hysterically. With a nauseating *pop* that echoed across the clearing, the raptor died.

Not one person present displayed shock. This gruesome act was not in any way discordant with the stringent demands of their daily existence. They raised brows with unease only when Nani began tearing off feathers and ripping the owl's body open. Bloody suffusions streaked her shift – the single decaying piece of fabric that dressed her from shoulder to knee. Forcefully, she kneaded raptor guts into Anapa's ankle as she prayed, "Spirits, grant this woman healing. Mend her wounds so that we may continue our journey and unite all Maroons."

The pregnant woman's violet bruises did not transform. Her flesh remained swollen. None gathered had a notion of what to do. Doubt taunted them.

A minute passed. Anapa broke the silence with a gasp. "Haaah! That numbs the agony."

"The mind leads; the body follows," said Nani. "When the body believes, the mind need only open to the flow."

Anapa dared her first step upon a leg that appeared too impossibly damaged to sustain her weight. One ginger step lent confidence, and quickly she gained many more. "I am cured!" she cried, embracing Nani and Wol at the same time.

When next dawn streaked from the east, Nani ordered them to decamp. They were seamless in habit as they gathered their spare provisions, expending most of their efforts upon preserving Carvalhal's weapons. With fresh commitment to Nani and her remarkable Obiya skills, they ventured ever-deeper into the Pitted Country upon unshod feet.

Nani, however, felt increasingly suffocated by their circumstances. Chased by Spanish soldiers and traced by rival tribes, she longed to embolden herself with volatile action. For many long hours that night, she sat cross-legged before a tangled mass of tree roots, ruminating instead of sleeping. The undertaking she was considering was so reckless that it just as easily could save her Maroon community as it could deliver them unto death.

Upon the African continent from whence Nani and the majority of her followers came, a sovereign reined over the land's most profound and mysterious realm – the woodlands. His name was *Sasabonsam*, and he was Lord of the Forest. He evinced reactions of fear due not only to his supremacy but also his appearance. Folktales described a terrifying figure with wild eyes, a lean form, sharp teeth, and hooked feet. Christian missionaries, upon encountering stories of Sasabonsam in Africa, translated him immediately into a character they recognized: The Devil. He was, they declared, the personification of evil.

Nani believed no such nonsense. She subscribed not to notions of good and evil, preferring to envision the cosmos as a dance between creation and devastation. Several times already she had bridged communications with this deity, as when she had called him to aid in the theft of de Leiva's strongbox.

Still yet, the mere pronunciation of Sasabonsam's name sent an icy wind blowing through her people's hearts. He was notoriously unpredictable, a trickster who sometimes aided humans, and at other times toyed with their misfortune for his amusement. At his most destructive, the ancient lore professed, he punished people for overconsuming their share of the forest's bounties by biting them in the neck, sucking their blood, and gorging upon their flesh. Inviting him to meddles in their affairs seemed an idea two steps beyond sanity.

Can I control the turbulence of a divine force? she debated, listening to the messages in the rustling leaves. *Are my Obiya powers strong enough to manage a god with license to indulge his every instinct?*

When she opened her eyes, she concluded that the summoning was inevitable. She would invite the Devil himself into their company if he might help them win their freedom.

IN WHICH A GOD IS SUMMONED

Nani gathered the Windward Maroons around the cooking fire at dusk. "YoYo, the day has arrived. We dwell in the ethereal habitation of Sasabonsam – the emperor of chaos, the icon of fertility, the Lord of the Forest. Tonight, we call him forth."

JoJo scratched a mosquito bite on her arm. She debated for a breath before speaking. "I cannot, in good faith, support this desperate decision, Mother. The Lord of the Forest must not ever be trusted. You toy with a fearsome power, risking all that we have strived for many years to build. He might, merely for the sake of his twisted delight, destroy us."

"JoJo, my only certain-living child, my heart of joy, fear not," Nani replied, placing a hand delicately upon her daughter's face. "Sasa *can* be mastered. Thus sayeth the old-world practitioners of our homeland. Aside which, if my magic enlists a god by our side, it will deliver a dazzling kick in the crotch to Lubolo and Juan de Serras!" she laughed.

"Surely it shall inspire their deference towards you – *if* you succeed in calling Sasa unto us and *if* you can control him," JoJo conceded with a reluctant smile.

"Ah, but JoJo, my sweetsop, my winged hawk, my daughter of sky and earth," Nani replied, "there's the rub. I already have."

JoJo flapped her mouth like a trout gasping for breath as Nani recounted the complete story of what had happened when she stole from the Spanish *bravos* their master's prized strongbox. Until this moment, she had safeguarded a vital detail: That she had summoned Sasa to her aid. She had felt that her followers were not ready yet for that knowledge, she explained. Now was the appropriate moment to reveal to her YoYo the entirety of the truth.

Commanding the men, Nani requested an awakening of the *gumbé,* square goatskin drums the Maroons carried with them at all times, even when on the run. An instant later, the warriors were pounding the instruments with a deafening but cadenced rhythm. The women, Nani invited to begin a ritual Myal dance. The pulsing ecstasy of sound and movement would communicate in primal language their urgent call.

Mother and daughter settled themselves a short distance from the others at the base of a magnificent cotton tree. Its branches rose to a height of 100 feet. A model pupil, JoJo possessed imperfect knowledge of Obiya as yet. Nevertheless, in order for Sasa to be summoned, Nani sensed that her daughter must participate.

The Maroon cheiftain accelerated flames within a crude bronze vessel, producing a *cold fire*. Obeying her mother's orders, JoJo cast into the lashing tongues of flame bitter root, dirt, a surge of rum, a pouch of human ashes, and a sprinkling of pimento pepper. This transformed the fire into the very blood, body, and spirit of existence.

For the first eight years of her life, when she and her mother had travailed within their master's home as domestic servants, JoJo had accompanied Nani to church thrice weekly. She therefore could recite long Bible passages with ease. As soon as Nani sensed spirits inserting themselves into the slender veil between worlds, she commanded JoJo to speak aloud verses from the Book of Ezekiel.

Thus sayeth the Lord God: An evil, an only evil, behold, is come. An end is come, the end is come, it watcheth for thee, behold, it is come. The morning is come unto thee. O thou that dwellest in land: the time is come, the day of trouble is near.

Without breaking the rhythm of their spinning dance, Nani herded the women of the tribe into a circle around the cotton tree's nine-foot diameter trunk. "Your arms are clubs!" she bellowed. "Soon, your naked fists shall be complaining and your knuckles shall be bloodied. But do as I beseech. Pummel this tree without interruption!"

As the women beat feverishly upon the trunk, the men continued rattling their drums, the sound traveling to the distant horizons. Even when their bodies begged for rest, they focused with singular purpose upon their queen's demands. They would not collapse until she had accomplished her sacred task.

Leaves sobbed to the ground. Boughs thrashed. Nani repeated Obiya prayers, her entire essence aimed at agitating Sasa out of his netherworld hideaway. She would win him over. She would call him permanently into the flesh this very night.

Their head-splitting undulations reached the ears of scouts from the nations of both Juan de Serras and Lubolo. They judged Nani's cacophony repugnant to all reason. Did she not realize that she was broadcasting to de Leiva's militia her exact location? She must be in the grips of madness, they concluded.

Sunlight began to leak its first rays into the pitch-dark canopy of the cotton tree, and still Sasabonsam had not arrived. The Windward Maroons, exhausted to the point of hysteria, slowed their drumming, fist pounding, and dancing, but they did not quit. Locked they were in a wide-awake dream.

Then, an omen displayed itself. Nani looked to the heavens for guidance and spied a glowing blade slashing its way across the brightening firmament. She gaped at the comet, tears leaking from her eyes. JoJo raised an index finger to point at the cosmic event.

The drumming and dancing halted. Alzo dropped to his knees. Wol traced the sign of the cross over his chest. Sipopi trembled. Anapa laced fingers protectively over her belly.

"Why the sky broke?" inquired an unfamiliar voice.

The tribe members burst into terrified gasps and startled babbles. But the fear on their faces quickly was overcome by awe. Each one felt completely unprepared for the sight of him, the target of their implorations.

Sasa analyzed them with a concoction of interest and exasperation. The blood-shot spheres of his eyes suggested he had spent the night crossing the river Styx. Stark naked yet appareled in organic filth, he displayed limbs wound with cords of muscle, hair in a mass of matted tangles, nails grown long for grappling, and feet twisted into hooks. As well he scraped the branches with his height, trumping six feet. It mattered not that he was decorated by scars and abrasions – in fact, these only compounded his allure. No man or woman could unglue their gaze. Brutal strength, cleverness, and holy sex permeated his being.

Nani was the first person to take steps closer to Sasa. Without fear, she craned her head upward, soaking in the breathtaking outcome of her Obiya diligence. As she absorbed the miracle that was him, his amber eyes softened, nay, melted with the vulnerability of a child. She reached up to touch his hair and chuckled. "Your locks have been groomed by a cyclone."

A smile ransacked Sasa's face. His entire body rejoiced at her attention.

JoJo, standing beside her mother, realized suddenly that she had witnessed the disheveled monkey-man spying on their community before. Periodically, he had observed their doings from the highest canopies of the forest. This was Sasabonsam, beyond doubt. Abruptly, her thoughts scattered like pebbles on hard earth. The more she appreciated him in the flesh, the more her mind refused to move and the louder her heart banged against her breasts. She was caught by the spell of terrific attraction. With untamed desire, she hungered to consume every inch of him.

The other Maroons appeared dumbstruck, as well.

Sasa, a novice in human etiquette, waved his elongated fingers at the heavens. He grinned even more widely than seemed possible and announced into the silence, "Look on it! The sky done got dinged. The Creator of Mysteries be a sorry sight tonight. That quirk marks a not regular sky." He considered his next words over the span of a heavy pause before exclaiming, "Wooohooo, donkey dung! That there also be my first try at speaking human to humans."

Chapter 11

ENGLAND

IN WHICH SERVANTS ARE PURCHASED

Despite his tender age of 19 years, Lucien Gunn already had risen to the rank of *sailing master* or ship's navigator. He was loaded with brass and slippery wit. To these natural talents, life had added another stroke of good fortune: the dawning of an innovative era. He belonged to the first generation to reap the rewards of the Age of Sail and its capacity to impart windfalls of wealth upon the common-born.

In the past decade, a groundbreaking concept born of Dutch genius had welcomed any individual with spare silver to partake as *shareholders* in companies whose ships sailed regular routes that stretched as far as India to the east and Las Indias to the west. This system, labeled capitalism, sparked an explosion of ambition throughout every corner of Europe. Humble men who invested their capital profits wisely were ascending to previously unimaginable societal heights.

Eager to join their ranks, Lucien Gunn had begun directing his own enterprising wiles toward the quick-selling of indentured servants. Whenever the Gallant, a frigate of joint investment between English and French agencies, anchored in the Great Poole of London's Thames, he rushed hungrily into the purchasing of human cargo, his greed set to the ticking of his sterling pocket watch. He had to move fast, haggling for bonded laborers to sell, while also appeasing the crew's non-negotiable demand for a *striker*, a term employed by seafarers to mean hunter.

A lengthy voyage could not be sustained even by a pen of livestock and larder filled with salted beef and stone bread. Sailors depended on a hunter to *strike* fresh game – animals poached from woods, fish angled from rivers and oceans, and birds downed from the sky. An infusion of succulents augmented the crew's strict rations, and could be attempted every time a vessel anchored at a coastal landing. Intermissions of this type were necessary for tall ships devoted to traversing grueling leagues of the high seas.

Lucien Gunn wound his way to Execution Dock. A row of gallows stood at the river's edge and decomposing corpses marinated in the tides. He muscled a path through the hawkers, besotted throngs, and lords of luridness. Venturing deep into the sinister district, he carved his way to a squalid emporium of fetid stalls where, if he were attacked, his robbed and slashed remains would never be found by friends, family or any force of the law.

Apart from the random Amerindian, a few blackamoors, and several exotics from the Orient, vendors traded in Irish and Scottish thieves, debtors, murderers, and refugees of war. Their lot was fated for exile in Barbados, a doom known as *getting Barbadazzed.*

"Find your properties here!" a voice cried over the crowd. "Am teeming with labor contracts, but every last one will be snatched up by a shrewder enterpriser if *you* ain't on the jump!"

Lucien recognized a middle-aged peddler whose pumpkin-shaped belly advertised his success. They had swapped business on numerous occasions. The seller purchased his goods from a most reliable purveyor, one who conducted business under the title of the Butcher.

"Seeking a lad with indisputable hunting skills to serve as striker," Lucien declared.

"Tis *me* you're hankering for! My shot aims surer than that of the legendary Herne of the Wild Hunt!" blurted a whelp with a heavy Irish brogue. He had sprouted from behind the corpulent servant-seller with a grin. "The finest striker you ever shall find stands straight before your face."

The boy was not only frail, but also disfigured. He bore a freshly healing gash across his left eye socket, and his shoulders and arms were embossed with bruises. Yet somehow, Lucien marveled, he sparkled. "This piece of debris is all you have on inventory?" he questioned, pressuring the merchant for a bargain. "But a wee bairn, and one with a bad eye at that?"

The seller grinned beneath his ostrich-plumed hat. "Hand me the coins in advance. You're aware of the policy for cripples. No taking a labor contract, selling him at auction in Barbados, and *then* returning to me a percentage of the sale. Pay now. Savvy?"

"Quite the quaint promotional style," Lucien snorted. "Are you or are not you aspiring to entice a buyer for this corroded child?"

"Aye, but hear this," the merchant replied. "There are no greater hunters upon God's green earth than the Irish."

"I hunt, fish, and wrestle grub for the gut-foundered better than any other!" the whelp bragged, tugging at Lucien's waistcoat.

The sailing master took a step back before judging the lad's impudence as a mark in his favor. "I prefer a wayward Scot Presbyterian over an Irish Papist," he hissed.

The merchant judged his customer's hesitation. "Fret not, my friend. The price reflects the product." He tossed in a wink, "Aside which, you understand the benefits of acquiring the lame."

Lucien grasped his insinuation. He kneeled to examine the child's defunct eye. Most servants aboard a ship who exhibited some manner of physical ruin were assigned the lowest and meanest labors. They were treated as refuse and once drained of worth, tossed to sea. None were expected to arrive at the journey's destination, for no lawyer ever would treat the untimely death of a half-blind urchin as a crime. There was good reason, therefore, to purchase inferior humans.

Lucien silently reckoned the boy's worth. "Permit me to verify the runt's skills prior to purchase," he proposed, tossing the merchant a shilling as collateral.

The bedraggled child shadowed Lucien to the foreshore at Wapping Wall. The air was thick with coal dust and redolent of varnish. Lying 20 yards away was the victim of a waterfront robbery – a cadaver that had bloated into a gaseous balloon and blackened in the silt of the Thames. Lucien handed over his pistol and dagger, and armed himself with nothing more than his pocket watch. He imposed his directive. "You are hereby entered into a race against the clock. Demonstrate your hunting abilities as best you can. Three, two, one – and off you go!"

Fintan frittered away several seconds in a state of confusion. But upon seeing Lucien's reptilian glower, the make-or-break moment became clear to him. He plunged into crazed effort, the defect of his broken eye cast aside by the vision of his determination. Grasping the dagger, he tore into a bank of sludge, dropped to his knees, and snuffled like a swine hungering for truffles. In the decomposing sediment, he located his first catch, speedily digging out a dozen cockles. Even as he extricated the prize, his senses remained glued to the frothing Thames, where he spotted the undulation of an eel. Sucking in a breath, he pounced and snatched the river-serpent with his bare hands. Drenched and panting, he snapped the creature's spine, bolted to his feet, and embraced Lucien's pistol. He fired into the soot-glazed clouds of London, dropping a seagull like a stone. In less than a minute, he reloaded, loosed another round, and felled a prized black grouse.

"That'll do," Lucien decided. He snapped shut the timepiece. "Well done, lad. You retrieved a meal sufficient for a family of six in seventeen minutes."

"So, I'm hired?" the lad inquired

"*Purchased* be the name of this game. You're a servant, and you'd do best to remember that," Lucien corrected. His tone softened at the boy's radiant grin. "But yes, the deal shall be done." He began a swift march back to the seller's stall.

"Then you must purchase my sister also," the lad begged. "Her fortitude surpasses that of any other woman. Not only can she cook and mend, but also read and write, and also she possesses hunting and fighting skills even keener than mine!"

"Aren't you the cheeky one," Lucien smiled. "How are you called?"

"Fintan. Fintan of Clan Lorcan," the boy replied. "And my sister is Aisling."

Upon their return to the market, Lucien assumed the boy's cost in full. He also agreed to review the pot-bellied man's other servant stock. With glee, the seller set forth his copious wares, bolstering Lucien with confidence that these pieces had indeed been harvested by the same purveyor as Fintan – the Butcher.

Included in the chattel was the striker's sister. The boy pleaded relentlessly on bended knee as Lucien surveyed the girl. Though plain, he sensed at once the strength emanating from her spirit and the fight in her grass-green eyes. He had to admit that he had fallen into a pit of curiosity. If Aisling possessed any of Fintan's unique qualities, she might serve as a tempting consort for his captain, Josiah Gladstone.

When purchasing servants, one of Lucien's primary tasks was to secure a female companion for the master of the ship. And yet Gladstone generally wore these playthings to ruin over the course of the trading voyage. More often than not, the young women would be tossed overboard along with the cripples before they arrived at port. If this girl were anything like her brother, with an inexplicable knack for craft and courage, Gladstone might encounter a budding woman unlike any other – and Lucien would be handsomely rewarded.

Acting on instinct, Lucien daringly purchased from the vendor the entire collection of servants with scant inspection: a score of Irish girls and boys from the Butcher, and as well two Scottish adolescents from another purveyor. Lucien judged these two lads as premium commodities, given that they already had grown into pimpled hulks before reaching the age of fifteen.

As soon as the contracts had been inked, the vendor helped Lucien deliver the servants, tied together and shackled at the wrists, to the flat-bottomed barge that awaited him. This vessel would transport them to the ship, which was moored amongst a crowd of other vessels in the London Poole.

The light barge was oared by Billy Creed, the Gallant's master of arms. He had matured in this very dismal neighborhood, amongst the taverns, dicing dens, and brothels of Wapping High Street. Even so, his hard-bitten face bore an amicable twinkle. "The Gallant is topped and freighted. Mechanic urges us to return to the merchant at once."

The crew had taken to calling their boatswain, whose given name was Haskell Thackeray, *Mechanic* on account of his black moods and violent impulses. He was a tree-trunk of a man with an eternally pitiless expression. Lucien avoided crossing him. "Did he divulge the hour she warps out?" he asked.

"By the long hour," Creed grunted.

Lucien understood this to mean the slack tide at midnight, which left little time indeed. "Best you speed to," he warned.

Rallying Creed's sinewy brawn, Lucien organized the human cargo atop the light barge. The two sailors and their indentured thralls embarked down London's legendary Thames toward the floating prison of the Gallant.

IN WHICH SERVANTS JOURNEY THE THAMES

Fintan was crammed into the stern between the two Scottish miscreants, brothers with bashed noses and broken teeth. His own sister squirmed on the thwarts, compressed between a dozen girls. Fin beamed at her, feeling a glow of pride at having arranged for their joint purchase. Thanks to him, they would remain united.

Aisling, meanwhile, twisted about to gain a view over the gunnels so that she might steal a glimpse of the capital city's glory. The barge, gliding low in the water, slipped past the notorious Tower of London. The castle was known to all Irish as a place where their kinsmen, cursed as traitors by the English Protestants, were tortured upon the rack. Further down current, she saw butchers in bloody aprons. Colliers unloading coal appeared dipped toe to crown in grime.

Fintan, on the other hand, inspected the nearer scene. Some of the hopeless indentureds drowned in sobs. Ohers stared into nowhere. The remainder sank their heads in prayer. He watched as the young sailing master with butter-blonde hair, the one who had executed their purchase, wedged himself beside Aisling.

"Lucien Gunn," he announced, smiling broadly. He was vainglorious of his teeth, and rightly so. Only slightly tarnished, they were straight and evenly spaced. He also boasted a rare complete collection.

Aisling abruptly resumed her inspection of the river's bank. Endless stacks of cargo were being fed into the bellies of immense sailing vessels. Even with their sails folded, they inspired awe. Having spent all her years living inland, she had never imagined tall ships to be such stupefying creations.

"Where are we?" she asked Lucien, incapable of hemming her thirst for learning.

Lucien Gunn was pleased to avail her. "This area of London they call the Lower Poole. Tis renowned the world over for the number of merchant ships that clog it. Last year, a thousand trade vessels embarked from here."

They encountered next an endless stretch of warehouses, along with a dumpsite of renounced and decomposing vessels. Her eyes fell upon a prison.

"Marshalsea," he said.

She winced.

"Aye," he sighed. "Some dub it *the Debtor's Palace*. It is the epitome of unjust affliction." Lucien shook his head."Heard say that the bailiffs even try to arrest the corpses of deceased defaulters."

As they drifted past a shimmering district dressed in prosperity, Lucien swooped toward the gunnels to secure a better view. He was magnetized by the bustling commerce and the spectacle of the city's professional elite garbed in their fineries.

Further onward, another gaol imposed itself upon the shore. Its outer stone vault swarmed with captives. "Alack, the horrid Newgate Prison. Dates to the eleventh century. *The oubliette of despair,* it is called. The hangman's rope is the only way to freedom, or so they say," Lucien recited. The he revealed, "In this very hole, my own father is confined."

Aisling blinked, moved by his admission. Never did she figure an Englishman would act so guileless with her. But Lucien, chagrinned at his confession, instantly turned to humor. "Legend has it the ghost of a monstrous coal-black dog stalks the prison feeding on convicts. Can you stomach that?" he chuckled bitterly.

Ash pivoted, as well. "What is your intention, Lucien Gunn? Will you carry the entire trove of us to Barbados?"

"Ah no," he half-smiled, wagging his head. "Only four of you will travel with us. We venture in the buying and selling of many servants at once, so as to turn a neat profit."

"But Fin!" she gasped.

"Fear not," Lucien touched her arm delicately. "You and your brother are two of the four who remain. As well, those two Scottish lads," he pointed to the massive boys who sat on either side of Fintan.

Aisling breathed with relief. Before she could follow with another question, her words were stopped cold. In the contracting light, she saw five bodies swaying from the gallows.

"There by Wapping Wall and Black Friar's Stairs, those are pyrates," Lucien said. "Lord General Oliver Cromwell does not favor sea rovers who plunder our English vessels. Tis sure that when caught, the rogues will find themselves dancing in the breeze."

Then, just 100 yards beyond, a full-rigged merchant vessel emerged from the twilit haze. "Ah, look at her," Lucien said, his voice reverent. "The Gallant."

Ash could discern a Herculean hull and three masts extending upwards from the deck. The ship made a moaning sound that resembled an aging matron griping about her brittle joints.

"She's warping out this hour by a process called *kedging*," Lucien said, educating his newfound maiden. "A portion of our crew oars a light vessel several hundred yards down the Thames. When they drop anchor, the afterguards harvest the line and coil it round the capstan, drawing the Gallant forward. They wage this battle all the day through, until the Thames widens and the wind reinforces her sails."

Ash turned to locate Fin, and they both observed 30 Gallants toiling, their bodies lit by the magenta sunset. Reaching the absolute limits of their force, they pressed beyond their stamina under the chorus of a shanty mingled with spouting blasphemes.

Before being hoisted atop the Gallant, the servants were loaded into a longboat. Watching the other captives step aboard the small craft, Ash locked eyes with Fintan. The shore was so close. London was within reach. Pressing closer to her sibling, she murmured, "Now?"

"How exactly do you imagine we might escape?" Fin grumbled.

"We might snatch that little boat," Ash said, pointing to the skiff tied at the Gallant's side. "Devoted as they are to kedging and loading, the sailors won't notice our departure."

"You think not?" Fintan sneered. "What of your fresh companion, Sir Yellow Toad himself? The one who has been gabbing at you for hours?"

"His attention faces elsewhere," she replied. It was true. At that moment, Lucien Gunn was stalled aboard the Gallant, squabbling with an imposing sailor with a crude face.

"And what then, Aisling? Do you expect we might waltz that scrap of wood to the bankside and sashay our way to freedom? With but a few swift strokes, that brute over there, the one hollering at your chum Lucien, will track us down and scourge us to tatters. Or suppose we topple into the water. Can you swim?"

Ash shook her head. "Curse the quims of every mother who breached these harsh men." Gazing at the floorboards, she accepted defeat.

When eventually they were delivered to the Gallant's hold, Ash and Fintan were shackled together along with their original lot of orphans, the two Scottish boys, and an additional 65 captives already in the hold. The entire population was a mass of sinking bones suffering from the cruelty of starvation. When Ash tallied their total number, she understood Lucien Gunn's sordid business. He was amassing a fortune.

IN WHICH A SERVANT MEETS A CAPTAIN

The Gallant anchored at Halfway Reach – the midway point between London and Gravesend. It was here that the Thames widened upon the English Channel. Six other vessels also lingered, bolstering their provisions and awaiting the appearance of their captains and officers. The indentured servants remained fettered in the hold, the sailors feeding them occasional hard bits of rusk and cups of water.

Two days later, Josiah Gladstone was shuttled aboard his frigate by Billy Creed. When he clambered into the hold to inspect the merchandise, Aisling gawked at the captain's rakish appearance. His statuesque physique was spruced in fashionable attire – an immaculate white linen, embroidered doublet, satin breeches, and silk hose. His finely-sloped nose and broad face were framed by tobacco-brown locks, which he kept bound at the nape of his neck. Although well-muscled, he ambled about the Gallant with the grace of a deer.

Mechanic heard the faint bells of Hornchurch ringing, counting twelve tolls. The tide at last was rising. "The headwater be upon us, boys!" the boatswain hollered.

At daybreak, the sky was shuttered by clouds. Aisling and Fin, who had curled together in an exhausted slumber, were jounced awake by footfalls from above.

"Gravesend! Ready cargo for market!" barked Mechanic.

"*Allez*!" echoed a voice in French accent through a speaking trumpet.

The sailors ushered the captives to deck. Amidst the briny waters of a marshland, several vessels floated with canvas unfurled. "Ash, look there," Fin tugged his sister's smock. The Gallant was approaching another ship.

The sailors began bulldozing the indentureds aboard the longboat and skiff for transfer. Josiah Gladstone sidled up to Lucien Gunn and whispered in his ear. The sailing master obliged, plucking Aisling from the chaotic procession. Gladstone's sultry eyes undressed her. He gave Lucien a silent nod, and the sailing master whisked Ash away to the captain's private quarters, locking her inside.

Fintan was wrenched away by the French quartermaster Septime Devign, who kicked the lad back down to the hold. He skipped like a pétanque ball, bowling into the two Scottish boys. They welcomed the Irish urchin with a carnivorous appetite. The churl named Malcolm, whose face erupted in ulcers, threatened to bite off Fintan's ear.

When the transfer of servants was complete, the men of the Gallant were rewarded with sacks of ready money and papers denoting labor contracts. These certified their future gains once the indendtureds had been sold at auction in Barbados. In the space of a few days, Lucien Gunn had finessed a shower of honey for the crew that added up to a greater than half of a commoner's lifetime salary.

The Gallant caught a gust by her topsails and leapt upon a southward course. From the captain's quarters, Aisling's eyes misted. Her endlessly uplifted spirits at last had reached their limit. She trembled, imagining the fate that awaited her now. Was she meant to be a whore? Was the handsome captain a brute? Would she be confined within this chamber forever? Even though she and Fin had boarded the same boat, would she ever lay eyes upon his again?

God, why do you smite me? she beseeched, grief choking her until she gasped for air. *Am I Job, to be tried by you? I am weary, oh Lord. Empower me!*

Just then, Lucien entered. "You ought eat," he advised.

She said nothing. The strictness of her shoulders and the grating of her fingers upon her smock informed Lucien that he ought not touch her. "Follow me to the gun-deck," he proposed instead, cajoling.

The galley lay adjacent the livestock pen. Its clucking, and bleating residents were incorporated into the crew's dinners by dint of an iron stove. Generally, the tars gobbled their stewed meals quickly. This eve was special, however. Inaugurating the Gallant's launch upon the high sea, Captain Gladstone had invited the full complement to dine together on a special feast prepared by Chef Zanzibar. The hammocks had been tied up and wooden benches had been placed between the cannons that lined either side of the hull.

The Gallants, attired for the English clime in wool coats and tarred breeches, pounced upon the repast. While several warded off the chill with knit Monmouth caps, none bothered with shoes. As they gorged on freshly baked bread, smoked herring, and roasted beef spiced in a wine sauce, they were quick to top their tankards with ale and even quicker to lob insults at one another.

Lucien benched himself and his ward away from the action. Immediately, he ravaged a plate of hot bread and marinated eel with pickled eggs. "Fetch the strikers," he hollered as his belly swelled with glee. "They ought fatten themselves likewise."

Above the din, a voice protested. "Fuck me on the spot. Are we to dine with Irish dogs now?"

An older sailor with a bald head spanked him with a filet of cod. "They're Scottish lads, you flatulent dolt."

"And what does that matter? Enemies to England are enemies for me!" scoffed his chum.

"Oy, mates, did ever you hear the one about the Irish cook?" posed the balding man.

A dozen tars stalled their quaffing.

The seasoned sailor stood to accentuate his performance. "Just after the dog watch tolls, and the basic crew is rumbling with hunger, a round of yardmen ask the Irishman, *Hey, old cook did you get to cleaning the chicken? Nah fellas,* the cook replies, *but I tried to. It's just that I have not any soap in the galley!*"

The sailors cackled.

Another shouted, "Hard by Hell, an Irishman would leap into the mouth of the Devil if he weren't too blasted by drinking, lying, and living with his beasts in one house in one room, all sleeping in one bed!"

The complement doubled over, roaring out guffaws.

Ash cringed. The men alongside her, the Gallant's two carpenters, clogged their mirth with spoonfuls of buttered cabbage and reverted to trading whore tales and pining for the warmth of the Caribbean.

Lucien pitched a tear of rye bread across Aisling's lap. "The cook, Zanzibar, will not likely provide fresh-fired bread again," he warned. "Tis a severe diet from here forward. This feast is designed to elevate our spirits, so that we despair not at being estranged from home for a year."

Ash gagged on the tiny bite she had taken. "An *entire year* fixed to this ship? Bloody faith on a crucifix! How distant lies Barbados?"

Lucien continued to chew. The two carpenters quietened. After heaving a sigh, the thick-set one said, "Takes a mere six weeks to reach the island. But that be neither the hope nor the will of us."

Lucien gulped a long minute of ale. He wiped his lips with the back of his hand, and leaned closer to Ash, his honey-colored eyes rubied by the liquor. "First, we aim for the trading ports of the Guinea Coast," he confessed. "Only upon leaving Africa do we sail for the Caribbean Sea."

Noting the incomprehension blanching her face, the carpenter added, "This here frigate is a *Guineaman*, girl – a slave ship with a capacity below for 175 Negros."

Aisling felt bile rising in her throat. Never could she stomach the enterprise of enslavement. Pressing her palms flat against the table, she struggled to her feet. Vomit gathered in her mouth. Unable to contain her revulsion, she stumbled backwards.

The nearest outlet to the top deck was barred by three tars crooning a miserable version of *Cromwell's Panegyrick*, a broadside ballad. She forced herself to walk to the opposite end of the galley as their praise for the Lord General shifted into a lampoon.

Nay rhymes with treason; and with nonsense too.

To justify what ere you say and do…

As a few of the sailors took notice of the young woman, their sozzled faces churned with curiosity and their voices grew louder. One tar kicked his leg out to trip her. She sickened further when she saw beneath him a floor pasted with chicken bones and tobacco plugs. He yanked her arm in order to reel her into his lap, but Lucien Gunn fell upon him at once.

"Mitts off, mate," he growled. "The lass been marked for our captain."

Marked for our captain. That announcement added to the quantity of nausea already squeezing her throat. She gagged.

When at last she reached the swinging boards of the fore-galley, Ash lifted her head and confronted a pitiful tableau. The three strikers, including sweet Fin, were crouched upon tackle blocks, slurping the food with their hands. They had been provisioned with neither a place at the common table nor the dignity of a spoon.

Aisling raised Fin to his feet and rushed him outside the galley. Upon the top-deck, her composure shattered. She tripped to the gunwales and retched into the sea. When each tiny morsel of the bread she had consumed had been expelled, her gaze skipped over the craft and searched the water racing past. The entire ship was a prison; it proffered no hope of escape.

In her pale green orbs, Fin read her despair. He could sense her desire to pitch herself overboard and drown her endless heartache in the sea. It was his turn to reassure her. "Ash, we are together still," he said. "After no less than every darling of our family has been destroyed. After no less than every kind soul we ever have met has parted ways with us. We endure as two, alone before the world yet united. I insist, Sister… *I insist.* You must stay living."

Ash turned and fell into his battered body, ribbons of sorrow threading her cheeks. Fin felt as frail as a bundle of dry autumn reeds. He embraced her with arms sapped of strength. The security he offered amounted to little more than a ghost's touch.

IN WHICH TERMS ARE DEFINED

Always the captain preferred to dine alone and not with the men, barbaric as they were. As he contemplated the year ahead, he stabbed at the remnants of his private evening repast with his trencher – a nine-inch dagger immoderately suited for dining. He must remember to tell the cook Zanzibar that this dish of pan-fried grouse finished by a glaze of onion and giblets was a culinary masterpiece.

He jumped at a bang upon his door.

"How do, Cap'n?" the sailing master called. "I have a dainty tribute for you."

Lucien escorted into the cabin the lass he had selected for the captain's pleasure. Her white cheeks blushed. Her rosebud lips trembled. From the puffiness about her face, Gladstone guessed that she had been crying. Nevertheless, she fixed upon him eyes the color of clover that carried a warrior's furor.

"Let us be," Gladstone said. Lucien shut the door behind him. A second later, the captain locked it from the inside by a sliding plank.

The young woman with untamed brown locks typified, in his mind, the simplistic, bog-hopping Irish. Even so, he felt captivated. She appeared to him a maiden, as yet blameless, as basic, benign and fresh as crisp linen.

"Hand me your cloak," he rasped. Ash wavered despite his benevolent tone. "Well? What then, girl? You prefer to stand in a corner all night impersonating an oil lamp?"

Strictly maintaining her gaze upon him, she slipped the woolen cloak from her shoulders. Beneath, she wore naught but a simple white shift. Candlelight from the dining table etched in shadow her slender form. Gladstone, taking in the delectable depiction of perk breasts and gently sloping hips, felt his desire rise like a rogue wave.

"I shall not steal your virtue, if that is the source of your terror," he reassured her. "You look exhausted. I imagine it has been a trying journey, weeks in the wearing?"

She offered the slightest nod.

"Would you like to eat?" He invited her to dine upon his half-consumed meal.

She declined by a shake of the head.

"Off to bed with you, then," he proposed, directing her across the great room to the plush featherbed. In the darkness, she could not recognize all the chamber's contents, but she knew for certain that never had she encountered furnishings so lavish.

"Wait." The captain's voice stalled her footsteps. "How are you named?"

"Aisling," she whispered.

"I give you greeting, Aisling. I am the Captain Josiah Gladstone," he returned with a bow. "A joy to make your acquaintance. Now I bid you good-night. Upon the morn, we shall resume our friendship."

She obeyed. However, she inhabited only the tiniest corner of the sprawling mattress. Her instincts questioned the captain's intentions. At the same time, following the events of the past days, she had not one jot of energy to spare. She slipped at once into an impenetrable slumber.

Rays of sunlight woke her. Ash opened her eyes to a commanding view of the sea through the immense windows of the captain's great room.

Gladstone invited her to sit at his regal dining table, where already breakfast had been delivered. Ash stayed put, bundling herself against her knees.

"Why is it that I inspire such fright in you?" he asked.

"What a crazed question," she snapped.

"Then I must confess, the condition is mutual. You also inspire fear in me. I bear a deep suspicion of the Irish."

Ash said nothing. She canvassed the broad apartment with the benefit of daylight. Oil landscapes of London and two other seaports spanned the walls. The floor by the bed was warmed by felted rugs. The great room was decorated by the striped hide of a strange beast.

"Obstinacy is the weapon of the martyr and the nincompoop. If you aim to mount a resistance to your captive condition, Aisling, then you ought arm yourself with good health," the captain teased with a cheery grin. "Come. Eat."

She conceded to his argument. Shuffling across the lush rugs, the sensation upon her bare feet was divine. She sat before a dish of suet pudding. Plunging a spoon into it, she asked, "Are you confining me here?"

"Are *you* planning to swim a hundred miles across open sea to reach the nearest land?" He smirked again.

"I am speaking of the four walls of this room," she shot back.

Gladstone laughed. "Certainly not, my little snowdrop." He stood, rummaging for his stockings, belt, and pistol. "You're free to roam this wooden kingdom as befits a queen."

Scraping a chair forward, he cocked his leg upon it so as to button his breeches at the knee, aspiring to impress her with the noble shape of his calf. He then rolled his red neckerchief, placed it behind his head, and beckoned her favor in tying the knot.

She obliged, although the task required her to stand quite near to him – so close that her breath tickled his chest. She admired his thick curls. She wondered if they felt as silky as they looked. Before she realized what she was doing, she had twirled an index finger through a lock of hair above his right ear. Embarrassed, she snatched it away.

Though he topped her by a head, he lowered himself to ensure their faces were just inches apart. His teeth flashed white as he bestowed upon her a lopsided grin. Ash could not withhold a shudder of excitement when his gaze darkened with desire. She held her breath, hoping that he would not observe the accelerated beating of her heart. But he did not initiate a move. Seeing that her chemise had slanted off her shoulder, he only squared it with a confounding degree of tenderness.

Her breath caught in her throat in confusion. She could not sort through the feelings bombarding her. She felt at once manic with a need to consume the man who stood before her, terrified of what act he might at any moment commit upon her, and ashamed that she desired her captor at all.

Josiah Gladstone stood with chivalrous perfection, watching the waves of emotion cross her face.

Finally, she claimed a rational thought. "I wish to see my brother, Fintan O'Lorcan. The youngest of the three strikers."

"Your *brother*, is he?" Gladstone sniffed, taken aback. A scowl spoiled his face. Abruptly he stepped away. "You may visit him. My one regulation is that you do not ever explore this vessel alone. The master of arms will serve as your escort."

Ah, she mused, *so there the penny drops. The insincere terms of my so-called freedom.*

At the sealed portal, he turned to face her with steely eyes, his voice edged with menace. "When you reunite with your kindred, please solve this riddle. As Lucien Gunn reports it, your brother volunteered you both into indentured servitude upon this vessel. He begged Lucien to take him on as striker. And what plans did your brother have in store for you? What role did he imagine his sister, blossoming into womanhood, would serve aboard a merchant vessel populated solely by men? What sort of pickled clod is your Fin?"

She took note of the abrupt shift in the captain's mood. "One who faces but two choices," she fired back. "Either you insist upon living, or you resign yourself to lying forevermore under six feet of earth."

IN WHICH STORIES ARE SHARED

Only moments after he had exited the chamber, a knock came upon the captain's door. Ash remembered Billy Creed from their barge trip down the Thames. Lucien Gunn had divulged to her that Creed was a ruffian raised by London's most brutal gangs. A grunt sufficed for a greeting, and a flick of his head towards the door consummated the formalities.

From the stairs, Aisling stepped into the clarion blaze of the sun. Upon the open deck, three dozen tars harmonized their labors to the rhythm of a sea shanty. They demonstrated agility upon the hazardous sails aloft, and strength upon the wrenching rigging below. She was mesmerized.

"...if not, we run her free," Mechanic's voice blasted. "She's moving no better than a sow in shite." A flurry of seamen vaulted up the ratlines in response to the boatswain's command.

Ash pressed against the balustrade and peered into the frigate's recessed waist. There, she spied her brother and the other two strikers receiving a stern lesson from a burly English tar. "You flush out the bilge so the seawater swamping it day and night don't threaten the hold," he said, demonstrating the task.

The chain pumps, as they were known, were hollowed elm trunks extending from the top deck, through the hull, and down to the ballast. Throttling the three-foot iron levers so as to draw the bilge water up all three stories and propel it out the scuppers required exceeding effort. The sailor struggled in spite of his superior size.

Now the strikers went to work. The one with the russet hair and copper face, named Angus, harnessed his miserable temper to deliver astounding results. Malcolm, the even brawnier youth, was best suited for the labor's strain. But Fin was not equipped with the height nor the muscle to prise the pumps. He was but a starving boy aged twelve years. The two Scots, impelled to compensate for him, grew acrimonious. Ash worried as Angus took to knocking Fintan with his elbows.

Lucien Gunn was charting the ship's course by his cross-staff when he noticed the Irish lass upon the quarterdeck. His greeting was cut short by shouts. Angus was screeching at the boson while jabbing an indicting finger at Fin. "Mechanic, sir, this puny grub is of no use!"

Mechanic sauntered closer, wearing a petrifying grin. Glancing about, Angus realized that he had attracted an audience. The scraggly Scot played to the spectators. "This blood-drinking Irish pagan – piss perfumed in a smock dyed yellow with his own urine – this reptile who slaughters innocent Protestants, why, he ought to be cast to the currents. Elsewise, him and me," Angus jerked a thumb at Malcolm, "cannot complete a stitch of work."

"How's it, then, if I say you're a sharp-nosed rat for squealing on one of your own?" Mechanic struck the lad in the face. Angus greeted the planks with a crack.

Septime Devign, the French quartermaster, sprang from the forecastle. He suffered from gout, which forced him to scurry like a crab. "Still same, the blame resides with the Irish," he argued, overruling the boatswain and reinforcing his superior rank. He glared at Fin. "Unless you perform every labor for this ship without flaw, the bottom of the sea awaits you, *comprends*?"

Fin nodded.

Raising his voice, Septime Devign delivered an address intended for the full complement. "My office of quartermaster places me also in position as master of accounts. Need I remind you that it is not worth the cost to feed and tenant one single man of dead weight."

Ash observed Josiah Gladstone processing the fractious events from the port bow, aloof. With a faint nod from across the deck, he validated the quartermaster's actions. Forthwith, Fin was demoted. Septime sentenced him to labor in the hold – the deepest part of the frigate, where the chain pumps originated. His penance was to unbunge the bilge machinery, which periodically became clogged with filthy sea dregs.

Fin scowled at the quartermaster. Ash was familiar with her brother's brazen character. All his life, he had played the jabbing prankster, master of the mischievous. But at this moment, his anger seemed birthed from another world. As he climbed down the ladderway, Ash moved to follow.

She had forgotten that Billy Creed had been assigned to track her every move. She was surprised when he came to her aid. "Speed there," he advised, pointing to the forecastle scuttle.

One flight down, the cavernous aura of the gun-deck had been restored since the prior night's feast. The long benches and batten-board tables where the complement so merrily had dined had been shoved aside. The area appeared dreary now, threatening even. Six cannons were chained to either side of the hull. Beside each one stood a locker harboring roundshot. Swaying above was a forest of hammocks. Some two dozen snoring tars comprised the opposite watch – those sailors currently exempted from duties. As soon as the sun set, the clang of the *first dog watch* bell would summon them to toil.

Creeping further down, she found herself sloshing through a rank lagoon. The shipped water intruded into the vessel through gaps in her seams or at times when waves broke over the boards. The fragrance of decay, feces, and carrion met her nose, generating a spell of nausea. She feared she might vomit again. In this nethermost region of the ship, the sound of the surf was dull and distant, yet its Biblical power felt even more immediate.

Billy Creed pointed Ash to the place where the massive column of the main mast met the floor of the hold. Fin lay prostrate in the putrid slush. He heard her footsteps squeak across the dank planks, but did not relent in his travails, which involved fishing slough and sea manure from the pumps.

Billy Creed excused himself to the opening above. "I'll await you there. Beware of a prolonged stay at this depth. The diseased air and infected wood bring black bile into your humors, then agues, and then death." With that blunt admonition, he clambered out of sight.

Her escort withdrawn, Ash met her brother at his humble level. Lying beside him in the filthy stew of seawater, she dwelled upon his injuries and the insult of his present labor. Disregarding her still, Fin's hands swam inside the pump. When he unplugged a nest of drowned rats moving with maggots, Ash retched. "How can you bear it?" she asked.

"You heard the man. I contribute my worth or am tossed to sea."

She gritted her teeth in silence, already plotting how she might sway Gladstone to ameliorate her brother's position. Though given the captain's harsh tone this morning, the granting of such a favor would likely demand a wily approach. And time.

Her brother cocked his head. "At least we schemed a way out of Ireland."

His lyrical Gaelic and jesting tone offered an aching deliverance of comfort. She laughed. Even after every hardship, Fin's drollery still was intact. A smile sneaked across her face. "The truth, though," she asked. "How did you set your bumbling mind to volunteering us as indentureds aboard the Gallant?"

"I am no soothsayer. I knew not what fate awaited us. And yet I had my reasons," he wiped his hands upon his frock and sat upright. "While in captivity with the Butcher, the other lads told me that the trade in servants offers hope. There are those Irish, they say, who earn their freedom and build a whole new beautiful life in the New World."

"Ha! Tis as I told you when we were traversing the bogs. And you called me a *broadsheet-quaffer*." She tossled his hair, inhaling every detail of his delightful presence.

Aloft, the muffled peal of the watch bell declared five of the clock. He lay back down in the muck, bidding her *au revoir*. "Visit me again tomorrow?"

"And every day, be sure of it!" she promised.

Aisling figured she ought return to the top-deck. But rather than aiming herself upwards, she decided to explore the profusion of objects closeted there in the hold.

She struck first upon a whopping volume of hogsheads, casks, and chests teeming with brandy, iron tools, and hundreds of pounds of cowry shells. Next, she discovered scores of lockers ladened with muskets, blunderbusses, matchlocks, and gunpowder. In her unexperienced view, the supplies seemed enough to arm a battalion. Stepping further round, she stopped, spellbound. Towers of fine cloth rose to the ceiling. The fabrics were dyed with ornate patterns – floral, striped, marbled, checkered, calico. One pile consisted of a white fabric so enchanting that Ash envisioned angel wings.

"You are beholding a hundred varieties of the most superior silks, linens, calicoes, and chintzes from India,"

Captain Gladstone announced with cultured diction from behind her.

Ash spun round. His invasion had been utterly silent – no easy feat when the wooden vessel broadcast every tred upon its timbers. Josiah Gladstone, it was occurring to her, was no average man.

"The unforgiving task lies in selecting, without error, the precise styles and colors that will be in demand this season along the Guinea Coast," he said with easy mirth. "For there sashays not one lady in the most fashionable district of Paris more fussy than a tattered, rawboned, sweaty Negro trader."

IN WHICH LADDERS ARE CLIMBED

Hardly ignorant of the craft of subjugation, Josiah Gladstone preferred to practice seduction. Returning to his quarters, he bid Aisling sit at his regal mahogany table for a banquet. A commencing course of *salmagundi* fashioned from boiled eggs, anchovies, olives, and onions was followed by potatoes and filet of dolphin sautéed in butter. The captain crowned the feast with a bottle of Bordeaux culled from his private stock.

Competing against her instincts to demolish the food with her fingers, she used the knife to part a morsel of dolphin and harnessed the fork to deliver it to her mouth. The delicacy struck her as ambrosia. Soon, she was reveling in the luxurious meal.

They were serviced by an ordinary sailor who functioned as the captain's steward – a bright, fidgety boy named Zosime Montfort who seemed to Aisling the same age as Fin. As Gladstone explained it, Zosime had been wrenched from Senegal, enslaved aboard a French ship, and then passed by fate into his hands. He had adopted the boy's debt and liberated him from his demeaned condition.

As Gladstone picked at his food, he regarded Aisling with nonchalance. His outward presentation of decency appeared to be winning her trust. "Zosime and Zanzibar both contribute to my good humor," Gladstone remarked. "But why that pinnacle of a chef stays with me is an enigma. It must be an act of celestial intervention." He lifted his gaze skyward in mock prayer.

Suddenly, his expression flagged. She puzzled at another radical shift in mood. He sighed. "Of truth, these blessings stand in opposition to the ill stars that have plagued my journeys in recent years."

He dismissed Zosime Montfort with a wave. Once the boy had exited the chamber, he continued. "At sea, we are untethered from society. We drift in a solitary vastness where the laws of countries do not touch us." He stood and began the bothersome task of unleashing the clasps from his doublet. "We will voyage upon the blue for nigh a year. It is my practice, during these long and weary months, to take a lover."

Ash burst out breath. "So, you have no wife abiding in London, caring for your brood?"

"Tis of no relevance. As I just informed you, the rules of landlubbers do not impact us." He shirked his doublet and worked next to divest himself of his ivory shirt. She felt her anxiety increasing with each clothing item he discarded. "Upon the sea, there is but my law, the rules made by the captain of the vessel. I alone act as lord and executioner.

Weaker men in my position have been known to abandon societal regulations entirely. Many captains perpetrate heinous offenses, which no court on land might repair. We are, as of here and now, dwelling upon our own planet."

She shot an instinctive glance at the chamber door, which was bolted shut. When she turned her gaze back, she saw that Josiah Gladstone had tossed his waistcoat and shirt upon the wardrobe. He was bare from the hips upward, revealing a torso dense with muscular striations. When he loosed the tie upon his sandalwood-shaded hair, a mane of curls spilled forth. He resembled, Ash thought, a god dropped to earth. She inhaled deeply and exhaled tremors. It troubled her how alluring he was to her. "To speak it all in a word, you desire me to be your whore," she remarked.

He walked to his bedstead, yanked the draperies apart, and sat upon the feather mattress. The padding conceded a sensual sigh. "Peddle your body, your mind, your heart, your integrity, your convictions… from patrician to peasant, we all are prostitutes. If you yield an asset without personal gain, you are conquered. If, however, you extricate yourself from your ideals, your antiquated religious convictions, your societal mores, then you might climb the ladder to the very pinnacle and become the conqueror." With a flair for the dramatic, he fell backward upon the bed.

Ash was paralyzed, dumbstruck like a starling that has smacked against a window glass. Arousal flashed through her body. A torrid wetness exploded between her legs. At the same instant, her mind was thrown into a war of conscience. She stood from the table, both fearful and desiring.

Without another word, Josiah Gladstone swept the draperies surrounding his canopy bed closed. Before a minute could elapse, he had fallen into solitary slumber.

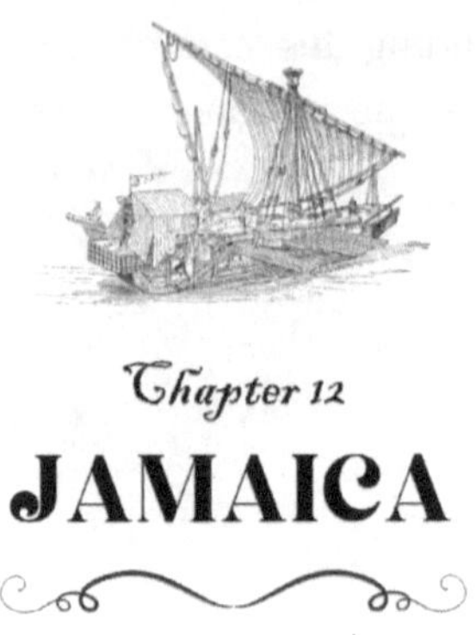

Chapter 12
JAMAICA

IN WHICH WATERFALLS ARE SCALED

Mired in commanding a regiment nigh 100 strong through the treacherous Pitted Country in search of the Maroons, don Paco de Proenza, *sargento mayor* of the Jamaican militia, nibbled on a slice of cassava bread. He assayed the nearby limestone palisade, where waterfalls had carved an enormous stairway into the earth, creating steps fit for a giant.

The opportune tactic, he deduced, was to hoist their one dozen dismantled light cannons to the summit. The manual labor required to accomplish this mission in a short time would guarantee the demise of several servants. Proenza decided to task a group of infantrymen with excavating a mass grave whilse the others hauled the load, congratulating himself on this clever solution.

He was grateful to Cristóbal de Ysassi for correctly advising him against lugging great guns into the Pitted Country. Indeed, those larger cannons already would have been abandoned. The manner in which the youth had asserted his opinion had troubled Proenza, however. The sergeant would have snipped the tongue off any other soldier who did not happen to be don Francisco de Leiva's nephew, ward, and heir.

Cristó had questioned Proenza's strategy before the entire company, calling it "an exercise in insanity." The very reason why Maroons settled within this malicious territory, Cristó argued, was because it provided natural fortifications in the form of hidden sinkholes, contemptible switchbacks and crags, as well as outcroppings that offered views over the entire landscape. Already the militia faced a tremendous challenge in tracking and eliminating the rebels. Toting weighty artillery would make their mission impossible.

Accepting this lecture had led Proenza to gnash his teeth so vigorously that his jaw had throbbed for a day. Yet even though he had wished to knock Cristó to the ground, he had uncurled both fists. For Proenza had to confess that the youth, more than any Spaniard on the island, possessed a rich knowledge of Maroon traditions, tactics, and ploys.

For years, Cristó had frequented the monthly bacchanals hosted by doña Joana de Fuentes, an obscenely affluent widow. The young mistress was notorious throughout Jamaica for her parties involving music, theatre, orgies, and illicit intoxicants. Cristó and his elder sister Zorayda, de Leiva's wife, were both acclaimed guests.

Often when Cristó exited these gatherings, he would saddle a mule and venture alone across the island's hillsides, cavorting with every drudger, Spanish *criada*, *ladino* peddler, African *horras*, and Maroon he encountered. He never turned up his nose at any person – no matter their class, creed, or color. He was not merely considerate of all he met; he was deeply curious to learn of life outside his family's circle of celebrity.

Regardless of whether or not the young heir offered solid advice, Proenza was obliged to endure his presence. Days prior, de Leiva had charged the *sargento mayor* with two monumental assignments: One, command an island militia to inflict upon Nani's Maroon society a mortal wound; Two, guarantee that Cristó live.

Within hours, Proenza had surmised just how challenging Cristó would make the latter assignment. This was the youth's first ever military campaign, which already placed him in jeopardy. Furthermore, the young man was prone to gratifying his every whim. He would glimpse a succulent mango or an enormous bunch of apple bananas and veer off course. Even though many of the *soldados* enjoyed Cristó's mirth, he quickly earned the reputation of a *worm in the wig,* a troublemaker.

The strife of drawing hundreds of pounds of cannon-works up the precipice commenced. Proenza called upon Cristó to join him at the top of the cliff, where noise from the agonized workers was less deafening.

"War is not as infantile as scoring operas," he shouted at Cristó above the din. "Here, we do not pretend to illuminate universal truths. Rather, we aim to mystify."

"A show of *legerdemain*…?" wondered Cristó, utterly secure in his inexperience.

"Of a sort, if your audience has monkey-nuts for brains," jeered Proenza. "Combat is a show that delivers death, anguish, terror, and pissing confusion – with no illusion whatsoever of revealing cosmic truths."

Cristó's voice jammed.

"Excellent," Proenza concluded the lecture. "Now aid in the transport of the guns. These ledges are monstrous and punishing. Nani shall inherit our pain, I vow it."

IN WHICH *QUARRY* IS TRACKED

By the time the light guns had been hauled up the falls, the moods of the militiamen were sour. As predicted, two drudgers already had died. Several more had fallen ill. Then, as Proenza initiated the second stage of their operation, the sky opened its bladder. Rain pissed upon them for days.

They ventured into enemy territory under the guidance of a blackshot. From hands and knees, TokTok decoded messages in the woodlands. An escaped bond turned buccaneer turned mercenary, he captured Maroons for money. Yet he was not loyal to pieces of eight, nor was he faithful to any patrón. TokTok's religion was revenge. In his view, the world never once had offered him a crumb of hope. The freedom he enjoyed as a sell-sword was well worth the price: Betrayal of his own kind.

Proenza was enamored of TokTok's skills. He relished observing an artist at work. By detecting delicate impressions upon the earth and a single break in the branch of a ginger patch, TokTok was able to determine his quarry's path. With a series of rapid clicks and hisses, he marshalled the Jamaican militia into a bowed formation known to poachers as *a crescent moon file*. With foot-long intervals between each *soldado*, the offensive line flowed forth in silence, the pounding rain masking any accidental noises. To leverage the play of surprise, Cristó had only to abstain from announcing, at the top of his lungs, his latest epiphany.

But of course, the novice soldier ignored Proenza's commandment to remain silent. In an outburst that awoke a kaleidoscope of macaws, he asked, "Why do we travel in this direction?"

"TokTok tracks the Maroon encampment to that ridge," Proenza snapped, pointing. "Now shut your face, boy, or I'll make your mouth fuck a ball of stockings."

"How is that?" shouted Cristó, cupping his ear. "You wish me to wear stockings upon my face?"

Proenza bit his lip. The youth prattled with all the nonchalance of someone enjoying one of doña Joana de Fuente's parties. He ignored completely the fact that death grinned at them from behind every boulder.

"Sir, with one neat shot, I might spray his brains upon that rock," muttered Proenza's faithful subaltern, Captain Julian de Castilla.

Proenza sat a grateful hand upon Castilla's sodden shoulder but declined. His inward voice replied, *And control somehow the testimony of 95 men who witnessed the wanton assassination of don Francisco de Leiva's nephew? I think not.*

But Castilla was unable to stomach the novice's insolence. He smacked Cristó on the back of the head. "I advise you to slip the tampon from out your musket this instant," he hissed.

Cristó glanced at his weapon. The tamp indeed clogged the weapon's barrel. With a sheepish grin, he yanked it out.

"That way, don Cristóbal, your hands will not explode into dolphin flippers when next you fire," Castilla quipped.

The other soldiers laughed. Trembling at his carelessness, Cristó discovered finally his ability to stuff his own mouth with nothing but silence.

IN WHICH SOLDIERS ATTACK

Forced to hunker within a cave for refuge from the sobbing skies, unwilling to kindle fire at risk of revealing their location, the Windward Maroons awaited an attack by the Jamaican militia. The hardy warriors pined for the sun's warmth and light. Each sound that rattled the hillsides seemed a conspicuous event.

Alzo, Santo, and two other men alternated sessions serving as lookouts. They observed Lubolo's village, just one league afar. However, given their discovery of Spanish *soldados* clambering up the cliffs several miles away, Alzo recommended delaying their congress with the other Maroon chiefs.

Santo argued that they ought abandon this treacherous rendezvous entirely and flee into the wilderness as usual. But Nani held firm in her choice. Furthermore, Anapa's belly was near bursting. Wol demanded they remain sedentary in order to safeguard his wife and their unborn child.

Only Sasa remained unperturbed. At the moment, he was busy evicting lice from his matted locks. Pausing to adjust the scrap of cotton that Nani had given him to conceal his crotch, he reengaged with scratching at his scalp. Seconds later, he rejoiced when his fingernails returned a tiny, wriggling form – which he promptly ate.

Nani spoke to the spirits, asking them to reveal the hour of her people's soon-coming battle against Goliath. Finally, an answer came slipping through the barrier between worlds: *They shall attack upon the first hour after noon.*

"Fetch me a flurry of coconuts, Sasa," she commanded.

He brightened at his queen's injunction. Always he jumped to complete any task she requested. In a flash, he scaled a palm tree. Minutes later, he arrived within the cave cradling a dozen rotund nuts. Nani prompted him to break their rigid shells. He employed the two tactics familiar to him: hammering the coconuts against his forehead, and squeezing them under his armpit. Soon, a wealth of fibrous shards, pulpous flesh, and white fluid slunk down his face and nearly nude body.

Most of the Maroons watched Sasa with a combination of fascination and fear. Only JoJo eyed the alien being favorably – and in secret, libidinously. Painstakingly, she memorized every detail of his dripping torso, noting the way the coconut milk sluiced across his sinewy chest, down his jutting hips, and into his loin cloth. She could hardly restrain herself from pouncing upon him and licking it up.

She was about to speak when Sasa encased her mouth with his caterpillar-like fingers. "No sound!" he gruffed in a low voice, his demeaner suddenly sober. "The *soldados*. They breathe nearer," he warned, spearing a finger at the closest peak. "Thither. Very near, very here. Your folk soon to be returned to Maker. Howling Spaniard guns fix to blow you into leaky bits and make breakfast from your giblets."

The announcement knifed trepidation into their guts. They stabbed Sasa with looks of icy distrust as they collected their spears. Wol distributed the muskets and pistols showered upon them by Gaspar Carvalhal.

Nani hewed to her task with single-minded urgency, knowing she must bridle the runaway panic splintering her flock. She gathered JoJo and Sasa to prepare Obiya magic.

Just then, from the opposite side of the woodsy valley, came the call of Maroon *abengs*. This was followed closely by bursts of cannon shot. Cries of horror, agony, and comprehension erupted. Muskets blasted. The vale reverberated with the sounds of death.

"Ayah!" cried Alzo as he came crashing into the cave drenched in rainwater and sweat. "De Leiva's men have begun their attack – but not upon us! They aim their canons at Lubolo's *palenque*. Soon they will find their true target. With fury in their hearts, they seek our unsparing annihilation. We must prepare at once."

Nani harvested select ingredients from her *jege*, the oracle sack of Obiya priestesses, which she carried always. Sasa she commanded to mash the coconut flesh. JoJo added pinches of her mother's supplies: parched manure, pimento seeds, dried caiman heart, and rooster blood, all whilst reciting verses from the Book of Ezekiel.

Now will I shortly power out my fury and accomplish my anger upon thee. And I will judge thee according to thy ways, and will recompense thee for all thine abominations. And mine eyes shall not spare, neither will I have pity.

Behold the day, behold it come, the morning is gone forth, the rod hath blossomed, pride hath budded. Violence is risen up into the rod of wickedness. None of them shall remain, nor of their multitude, nor of any of theirs.

The instant the Obiya medicine met her standards, Nani offered the malodorous concoction to her tribe. JoJo rubbed the paste into both the tops of their heads and the soles of their feet. Sasa aided her. Despite their misgivings about the monkey-deity, the Maroons trusted eternally the transformational powers of Nani's spirit science.

"As soon as this preparation leeches into your life force, you will wash away from eyesight. When the Spanish *soldados* come upon us, we will be vanished as ghosts," Nani declared.

The balm of invisibility alleviated at once their crippling fright. Anapa gripped her belly in relief, Wol's arms wrapped around her. Sipopi relaxed for the first time in days. They saw each other, in the rain-drenched gloaming, as no more than muzzy shapes of ashen color. Sasa glared at his translucent hands, turning them about with giddy squeaks. For a deified being, JoJo thought, he could be enchantingly naïve… as well as downright scrumptious.

IN WHICH A TRIBE IS DECIMATED

Beneath a cotton tree sat a bulky man with a robust brown beard. He wore a jolly expression that befit his large belly. In other words, he exhibited not the vanquished look of the common fugitive. Such was his intention. He wanted all the world to know that he enjoyed an enviable state of affluence – even whilst living as a mountain renegade.

At this noon hour, Chief Lubolo was reveling in a rare moment of solitude at a short distance from his cloud village, where dwelled 137 Maroons. He devoted himself to an ongoing quest for literacy. The thick canopy protected the pages of his primer from the glittering precipitation. He grappled with the letters, bent upon breaking the code. *In A-dam's Fall, we sin-ned all. A dog will bit-e a th-ie-f at ni-gh-t.*

The chief rested in complete confidence that the *soldados*, whom his lookouts had witnessed hauling their small cannons over the cliffs of the Pitted Country, would never harm his Spanish-friendly community. Lubolo had negotiated peace with don Francisco de Leiva himself. Doubtless the Jamaican militia aimed itself at Nani's temporary encampment. His spies had further informed him that the Windward Maroons were journeying to his *palenque* to meet with him and Juan de Serras. Yet having heard tell of Nani's treachery, he had surmised that de Leiva would deliver upon her people the most gruesome revenge. So it was, and he would not interfere. The foolish woman had brought the master's wrath upon herself.

A breeze capered through the trees, carrying with it a foreign stench that captured Lubolo's attention. Seconds later, his scouts sounded their *abengs*. From the traditional Maroon trumpets blared a sequence of alarms that demolished any delusions of security in which he had been wallowing.

The Spanish cannons began their battery. Lubolo gained his feet in an instant and chugged up the steep incline towards his palenque. He watched the elder brother of his third wife roll into a ravine, his back aerated by shot. Next, the father of his second wife tumbled downhill covered in blood. At the hillcrest, two of his warriors fell flat.

Lubolo could not stop running toward his people, even as death whistled past his ears. By the time he reached his encampment, mania had broken over it. It was engulfed in screams, winging cannon blasts, and a barrage of musketeer fire. Every Mocho Mountain Maroon – warrior woman and man alike – searched for a weapon. However, their strategy had rested upon cooperation with the foreign settlers, not warfare. They possessed only 11 muskets, five pistols, and not one cannon between them. They were forced to rely upon pikes, lances, and pronged spears, or *jungas.* It was a battle waged between two companies separated by centuries of technological advancement.

Lubolo watched a roundball shatter the skull of his niece, a girl aged seven years. Livid, he aimed his *junga* at the murderer. He freed it with such force that while the spear missed its target, it bifurcated the nearest tree trunk. Cannons detonated without cessation. The rain continued to pound. All about him, precious souls tumbled to the ground, jetting blood.

Spotting Mariana, a fearless Black Amazon of Dahomey, Lubolo made his way toward her. She hunkered with her back against a boulder, blasting at the enemy with one of the tribe's few muskets. But just as he reached her side, she jerked. Her corpse landed at his feet, legs outrageously awry.

Lubolo snatched her fallen musket and homed wad and cartridge. As he did, he noticed a flag boasting a burgundy cross upon a field of white waving dramatically 100 feet afar. The Castle and Lion leaped just behind that, distinct even in the downpour. De Leiva was sending a message, Lubolo understood. He wanted this moment seared into Maroon remembrance.

Shrieking, Lubolo beckoned his tribe into retreat. The Mocho Mountain Maroons lurched down the hill that he had climbed only minutes earlier, Spanish militiamen hammering carnage upon them. Gathering two of his wives and several children, the chief leapt into the densest part of the wood. With a boom, a swathe of his family was dismembered before he could even shout a warning.

Turning to face the enemy, Lubolo counted six light cannons. He could not fathom the agony of effort the militia had expended in order to port these weapons into the mountains. *How was their sudden zeal for our destruction ignited?* he fumed. *Why did de Leiva dissolve our agreement? Why did he betray me?*

The light guns kicked once again. The remaining Mocho Mountain Maroons fled, but Lubolo felt himself struck in his thick belly. He fell into a bush. In solitude once more, he panted, watching his life's blood trickle upon the rain-soaked leaves.

IN WHICH THE SUN SHINES AGAIN

The following morning, the sun roused the Windward Maroons with warming rays, selling the notion of fresh hope beneath a blue sky. At last the rains had ceased.

Any cheeriness they may have felt at the change in weather dissipated, however, the moment Alzo and Santo returned from their dawn scouting expedition. Although the Jamaican militia had vacated the area and therefore no longer posed an imminent threat, the two lookouts reported, the *soldados* had laid waste to Lubolo's *palenque*. The massacre Alzo and Santo described caused Nani and her YoYo to sink to their knees and weep.

Meanwhile, their tribe had been untouched. This miracle they attributed to Nani's Obiya powers. After all, Lubolo's nation was the sole Maroon tribe to benefit from a friendship with the Spanish islanders. It ought to have been the last of the three nations attacked, not the first.

Humbled around the cooking flame, the Windward Maroons sang mournful hymns to guide the spirits of the Mocho Mountain Maroons safely to the netherworld. Sipopi then led them in chanting melodious anthems of gratitude. "We live another day, you *bakra* chiggers!" she gushed, radiating relief. "The High Creator blesses us. We outlast the others. Let us sing our thanks!"

Later, she and Anapa distributed portions of simmering *busu soup*, *cacoon*, and *thatch-head* – foods they leaned upon during the most difficult periods.

"You must eat more, woman," Wol advised his wife. "Go on, get to it, so that our child might suckle heartily at your breast and gain from you ample *witty*."

"Big man, you are trouble!" Anapa laughed, belly shaking. "When night falls, why do you come to me all floppy? It is *you* who needs my witty!"

"*Tchiip*!" Wol sucked his breath in irritation. "Quit your public trumpeting of my ailment and eat now for strength." The others chuckled, enjoying the inane marital dispute, which delivered relief from their recent stress.

Throughout the morning meal and work hours that followed, JoJo nabbed glances at Sasa. He smiled. He always did, she noted. In fact, his being emanated joy. Deciding to acknowledge her skittish glimpses, Sasa skipped to her side.

"Join me," she said, gesturing to the calabashes and cooking implements she was cleaning. Three warriors daggered her with critical looks. She hissed at them – especially Bermudo, a middle-aged man who petitioned her frequently with hungry eyes.

When JoJo brushed her luscious body against his, Sasa felt his male member stand up. He looked down. His penis jutted straight through the concealment offered by his thin loincloth. He pressed himself against a tree, cheeks pink, experiencing awkwardness for the first time in his life. He understood neither his body's uncontrollable reaction nor the sensation of embarrassment.

JoJo responded by making a zany face. He giggled. "My mother can catch pistol balls in her hand. Is this magic of your doing?" she asked to distract him from his erection.

"I never done catch such a thing," Sasa answered. "Not certain you ought pin that feat on me. The quickest thing I ever snagged was lightning."

"Are you a god?" Her question was firm.

"Are you a dream that I am hosting while asleep?"

"I am not spinning riddles," JoJo said. "My question is a true one."

"And my answer is a truer one. *Truer* or *more true*, which is the precise talk of your tongue?" he puzzled.

"It matters not. I grasp your meaning." She waved her hand to dismiss the question. "During the Spanish attack on Lubolo's *palenque*, did you make us invisible?"

"Me? Not me. Who be the rascal who did? Obiya. Spirit science. Your mother."

JoJo pondered for a slow inhale and exhale, striving to understand it all herself. "We convinced the Spaniards to not notice us. Or perhaps we convinced them to pursue a tactic born of their own initiative, and assault someone else?"

"What importance has it?" he said. "They did not perceive us. That is the vital matter."

JoJo narrowed her eyes. "Speak it now, Sasa: Are you a deceit or a deity?"

He shrugged his shoulders. "The day we understand completely who we are arrives just before death."

"Can you die?"

"I know not. I have not ever tried. Have you?"

She chuckled. "You mean, have I ever been under threat of dying or… Have I ever desired to end myself?"

"Oh no," Sasa raced an apology. "I did not mean that."

"Well, I have never sought out Death. But I have seen him many times walking by my side." She paused. "Are you immortal?"

"I shall tell you when I know."

JoJo sighed in exasperation. "My mother's magic slipped a satyr into human shape. You split the sides of reality, Sasabonsam."

"Yahii!" he smirked, poking her in the ribs. "The answers in this life bewilder us. Is it not so?"

She shook her head in acknowledgement.

Unsure how to proceed, Sasa grasped a tin spoon from their washing gourd. With an elegant motion, he twisted it into a bracelet. This he slid about her narrow wrist. Marveling at the titillation generated by the minimal contact with her skin, he braved his next question. "What is the act among your kind when one wants to show like… wants to be close to another?"

"We offer gifts like these," she said, eyes shining. "Thank you, Sasabonsam."

"I mean..." he hesitated. "Being monkey-kind, I might snuffle your fur, but you have not overmuch. I might lick your teeth, but I guess that would make you go *screak* – or worse, knife me! I observe Wol and Apana grasping hands. May I grasp your hand in mine?"

Eager to master human customs, he took her hand in his. She felt in his grip an abnormal warmth. It was like holding the metal pan of a bed warmer, as once she had done for her mistress upon the plantation. The sensation of toasty coals radiated comfort. She nuzzled into his chest.

The minutes confused her. JoJo lost all sense of time as they snuggled together. She startled when he asked, "What means *witty*?"

"It means... someone with spiritual intensity. A fierce and wise warrior."

"Like you," said Sasa simply.

"Like you," she replied. She touched a hand to his heart and felt it beating into her fingertips.

Sasa said nothing, but his huge eyes glittered with adulation. Silently, he pledged to guard these *witty* Windward Maroons till they reached their goal of freedom, even if it required that he journey to the sun.

IN WHICH STRATEGY IS SPOKEN

Under that same sky of victorious blue, Proenza and his contingent scampered down a slushy vale. Of the 100 men the *sargento mayor* had marched into the Pitted Country, 30 had perished battling Lubolo and hauling small cannons. By some miracle, Cristó still was alive, having suffered but one small knife slice across his forehead. Disregarding collateral losses as he did, Proenza viewed this opening stage of the war upon the Maroons as a triumphant rout.

As they inhaled the sweet air that announced their arrival upon the cane fields north of Guadibocoa, Cristó gained upon Proenza. As usual, the young man burst with questions.

Noting the bloodied bandage wrapped around his head, Proenza congratulated the dilettante. "And just like that, you are a proper soldier."

Cristó did not celebrate. "You did not ever aspire to tussle with Nani and her people."

"You are correct, golden child."

"Do not address me as that again."

"And if I do?" Proenza asked. "Do you prefer that I refer to you as *the human discharge who diffuses the scent of dishonor upon his family*?"

"I, too, carry a pistol in my sling."

"By the time you locate it, I will have punctured your chest a dozen times."

Cristó scowled. He steered the discourse back to the subject that troubled him. "Why did you attack Lubolo, with whom my father, with painstaking finesse, has wrought an agreeable rapport these past years? Why not pursue Nani straightaway? Was that not the *explicit* commandment of my uncle? To decapitate Nani with no mercy as punishment for stealing his *aviso* to the king?"

"You game at child's play." Proenza knelt at a stream. He gulped deeply and purged filth from his face before finalizing his thoughts. "Here is the why: Because Nani is vermin. A plaguey and repulsive rat, even if she styles herself as the pestilential queen. Have ever you learned the name given to a collection of rats?"

Cristó was in no mood for a lecture, yet obediently he shook his head.

"A *mischief*," Proenza clucked. "Nani leads a mischief of rodents. Hours ago, we crushed the infestation with a grim lesson. From now on, if any being upon this island – Maroon, smuggler, blackshot, buccaneer, even Spanish aristocracy," he shot a pointed look at de Leiva's heir, "—if any treasonous person so much as consents to an audience with that foul queen, they can be sure: The holy wrath of our militia will extirpate them."

"Your intent, then, is to isolate her? Make her an outcast?" Cristó clarified.

"Well, well, you have shot the sheep!" cracked Proenza. "Allow me to present the facts to you simply, so that even a dunce such as you can comprehend. Nani strives to create a coalition of Jewish smugglers and Maroons to overthrow the Spanish ruler of Jamaica. All the while, de Leiva allies himself with buccaneers and pyrates. At present, he has commanded Iron Eyes to recover the thieved strongbox that shall, when delivered to His Majesty, sway the Crown to reinforce Jamaica's defenses and bring upon us a fresh influx of investment. When that happens, your uncle shall win his place in this New World, heralded as the most modern ruler."

"Ha, much obliged for the excellent reprise, don Paco," Cristó replied with a mock bow. "Recall that I, too, was present at the shipyard when my uncle prattled on regarding his manifesto. Still, I do not comprehend your reasoning. Why not eliminate Nani straightaway, as don Francisco bid?"

"Because, cousin, clown and idiot, when Nani finds herself estranged from the others, she will, like a starved rat, surface."

"My, you seem smitten with this rodent metaphor."

"Fuck up," grunted Proenza.

"Speaking truth, is all."

"Speaking complex strategies, the likes of which you cannot grasp, is all," Proenza replied, clenching his fists in frustration. "When Nani emerges, we shall nab her and haul her to La Vega—"

"And pike her head upon a pole before the *audencia*, blah blah blah," Cristó interrupted. "You are forever a puppet reacting to the strings jiggled by my uncle."

"Drink a cistern of humble piss, you termite," Proenza snapped. "I am attempting to puncture your cloud-head with the image of an eventual jubilation day. Picture the applause of hundreds of *vecinos* as they enjoy the spectacle: the desecration of the African witch Nani. Their adulation for don Francisco will multiply a thousand-fold."

"And yet you might pause to reflect upon what some islanders are saying. That Nani is a tinderbox whose execution might spark a revolution," Cristó warned.

"A negro woman humiliated and paraded as a dead rat?" Proenza scoffed. "You should control your over-livid imagination."

"Consider this," Cristó tried again. "Nani surpasses flesh and bone, rising to the realm of hope and spirit. You aim to murder a movement. Have ever you assassinated an angel? A ghost? A god?"

Proenza went quiet.

"I wager you are familiar with similar talk passing through the public houses and parties these days? The Maroon Queen is not the only hero we might fail to destroy by death. The pyrate Iron Eyes? You mentioned his name recently…" Cristó regarded Proenza's expression closely. "His name, too, carries a meaning that will live beyond his mortality."

They drew to the edge of a sugarcane field. Proenza strained to reply. Nothing materialized but a limited conclusion. "I suggest you combine your efforts with mine in executing this act for the sake of your uncle, your family, your island, and your own redeeming."

"Ha!" Cristó responded, unhinged by the moment's absurdity. "It seems every person I encounter yearns to deny the tide of history."

Chapter 13
ST. KITTS

IN WHICH A PYRATE IS HANGED

"Oh, how I love a Gallows Sunday," Jonah Profit announced to Splosh, his most cherished chum amongst their flock of ne'er-do-wells. He gazed at a dawn sky whose stars diminished rapidly. "By noontide, some rover will be dancing in the wind."

The governor of their isle of St. Kitts had, for the last two years, embraced a policy of hanging pyrates monthly – even if the crimes were more rumored than substantiated. In his decision, Jonah recognized the fear thriving these days throughout the New World. The true danger of pyrates lay not in their thievery, but rather their capacity to seduce the disenfranchised and overturn traditional hierarchies.

"Heard tell this felon was a genuine mutineer?" inquired Splosh in *the rogue's Latin* – the English jargon of the gypsies and beggars who resided amongst the Lesser Antilles. He scratched furiously at lice inhabiting his brown hair, which was forever singed in patches. The skin of his arms and face was decorated by scars. But he wore these badges proudly, considering them a testament to his bravery; the boy experimented constantly with explosives. "What's the story, Lord Muck?" he pleaded, employing his pet name for his dearest friend.

"The pamphlet gives his name as Wim Jackson, Lemon Squeezy," Jonah replied, addressing Splosh by his own nickname. "Seems that ten years ago, Cap'n Wim took hostage the Jamaican settlement of St. Jago de La Vega, forcing the lordly Spaniards to pay a ransom in provisions and 7,000 pieces of eight!"

"Wish I'd been blessed with reading by a learned mum like your own," Splosh remarked.

Unconsciously, Jonah touched the pendant fixed about his neck. "Point be, since that occasion, not one pyrate has rivaled Wim Jackson's feat in winning demands from rulers of the land."

"Ahhh, but forget not how, two years past, Captain Iron Eyes triumphed at sea, capturing the flagship of the Spanish Treasure Fleet!"

Jonah fantasized for several long moments before smacking his friend on the bum. "Best secure our viewing spot!" he cried, heading up Old Road toward the main plaza. Splosh trailed with broken leather boots clomping zanily, causing clouds to rise from the volcanic dirt.

Jonah Profit had survived the previous six years as an orphan by swindling an existence amongst gangs of highwaymen, cutpurses, drunkards, vagrants, and knaves of St. Kitts. With fetching looks and remarkably pale skin, the 15-year-old bore hardly a dusting of hair upon his upper lip.

He appeared still achingly young. His raven black hair he cinched behind his head with colorful silk ribbons. He had come of age in a nunnery where his mother had been rented nightly as a whore, and thereby had developed a flamboyant style. Yet ever since her pitiless death when he was nine, his black eyes had betrayed a brooding somberness.

As he and Splosh sped to the execution site, Jonah fussed again with his necklace, squaring it at the plunge of his worn linen shirt. The whittled ivory medallion, his most precious asset, spurred universal intrigue. It had been a gift from his mother. She herself had secured two such identical ornaments from a boatswain of the VOC – dubbed in English as the Dutch East Indies Company – after a particularly lusty congress. The sailor had informed her that the amulets were constructed from elephant tusk. They depicted, he said, a magnificent white palace called the Taj Mahal, which recently had been erected in the far away kingdom of India.

Ever since her death, Jonah faithfully had rested the prize close to his heart. His worship of the relic edged toward infatuation. In the small hours of the night, he would huddle beneath the quay tracing its furrows with his fingers. And almost every night, he suffered nightmares in which he witnessed again the hideous murdering of his mother.

By the time the two street rats arrived at the Basse Terre town plaza, a giddy crowd had gathered. They represented a cross-section of the St. Kitts population: housemasters, tailors, farmers, soldiers, merchants, goodwives, younkers, dipsomaniacs, piss artists, plantation owners, and indentureds. Clamped into the pillories were four scoundrels meant to foment their bloodlust prior to the capital event: The *execution of death* of Wim Jackson.

The multitude hushed at the first ring of the English bell, a massive hunk of ore wrought in Bristol. It reverberated like a 463-pound heartbeat. On this day, it tolled precisely 42 times, signaling Jackson's age.

The governor, in the company of three turnkeys, banged up the wooden platform where the hanging would take place. The guards urged Jackson up the steps by a *bastinado*, a cudgel adorned with nails. He shuffled unshod, his footsteps printing blood. A jute sack hid his face.

The hangman yanked the hooded felon atop the gallows. "Neck him by the salt-eel!" the governor commanded. The hangman coiled the noose and fit it snuggly about Jackson's neck.

The dirge of the bells concluded. When its reverberations had washed away, the world seemed terrifyingly still. "Like Wim Jackson, us riff and raff concern ourselves not with the future nor the shackles of the past, but only with the present," Jonah pondered aloud, his gaze fixed upon the pyrate.

"Aye up, Lord Muck," Splosh agreed.

"If only we could mingle *but for a minute* with such a rogue, Lemon Squeezy, we might join his crusade," he said longingly.

"You think we might squire for a true-bred pyrate? By what means, do you suppose? A jig? A bouquet of roses? A ballad of your soon-coming legends?" Splosh teased.

Jonah clenched his jaw. Then there was a gasp, a shuddering hiss, and a bone-cracking burst from the hinged planks. Splosh sucked in his breath, seizing Jonah's hand in his own. "Reckon you shall not ever gain an audience with your hero, Lord Muck."

Jackson did not readily surrender. He had been collared by the short rope. It promised a cruel, slow demise from strangulation, the drop from the platform providing insufficient force to snap a man's neck. His legs danced and his arms quarreled with the breeze for an age. Gurgles leapt from his throat. He drenched his trousers with urine and shit, eliciting chortles from the crowd.

Then it was over. The governor pronounced Wim Jackson dead, his soul delivered to the gates of Hell.

As the mass of people scattered, Jonah took Splosh by the arm. "Thing of it is, they realize not their nonsense. What perishes with a man is but flesh. The cause he devoted himself to survives."

IN WHICH MISTAKES ARE MADE

Beyond the quay of St. Kitts, but seated well below Basse Terre where stood the stately council houses, coiled a lane too constricted to permit the passage of horse-drawn carriages. It led to a collection of clapboard lodgings where settlers and sailors alike journeyed to satisfy their most licentious longings. Amongst these *stables,* or *maisons d'abbatage* as the French settlers named them, Jonah Profit plied his petty vocation.

He was bound, in return for remnants of food and lodging when available, to serve as bar hand at the Punk House. The tavern master dedicated the lad primarily to the craft of *bilking the swill* and *cabbaging the dreg-stew*. In other words, Jonah collected the remnants of rum and cassava mead left behind in the patrons' tankards so that the establishment might serve the vile juice again.

Never had Jonah enjoyed what sailors termed *a 15-minute marriage with a strumpet.* The working ladies, considering him like a son, were partial to purchasing the handsome youngster a roast, mending his buttons, patching his trousers, tussling his hair, loaning him ribbons, and stamping painted lip marks upon his cheeks. For a laugh, new arrivals sometimes unslung their tops to garnish him with a view of their breasts, but they offered nothing more.

Upon this eve, Jonah overheard whispered reports that an enigmatic vessel had moored in the St. Kitts harbor. The next morning, he finagled a spyglass from one of the resident women. Thanks to his obsessive studies of renegade vessels, he determined that this was a *sloop-of-war*, a *frégate légère* in French. Although constructed of lesser timber than some ships and armed by only ten guns, she was nonetheless a beauty. With her three masts cocked fiendishly aft, she looked like a shark come to feast. Fore and aft sails along with square-rigged drivers would enable her to move at more points off-the-weather than most other vessels. And with a draught of less than ten feet, she could maneuver over shallow shoals. In short, she had been designed for wondrous speed and maneuverability.

The tavern chatter grew more fervent with each passing hour, as the crew did not set foot upon the shores of St. Kitts. When, finally, a longboat rowed to the beachhead three days later, the entire populace of the island was bursting with curiosity.

The doorway banged open as though prognosticating a hurricane's approach. Jonah lifted his eyes from the counter where he was sponging blood and vomit into a pink lather to see a dozen men file sleekly into the Punk House. This was a gang of pyrates, to be sure – rough men all. When a stocky man of Taíno origin commanded tankards of mead and bowls of stew, the tavern master nodded obsequiously. Soon, the pub roared. A gaggle of painted ladies leaned over the balustrade, their expressions, for a moment, selling nothing more than the repression of fear.

An awestruck Jonah Profit, on the other hand, marveled at his good fortune. When he overheard an aging rogue with a neatly-trimmed beard and spectacles address the captain as Iron Eyes, Jonah positively jigged in his shoes. Hardly could he restrain himself from racing forward to engage with the celebrated pyrate.

Having a dream come to life before your eyes is like holding the whole world in your hands, he thought, fingering his pendant. *Thank you, Ma, for delivering to me this gift!*

Everything Jonah craved stood right now before him – but queasiness intervened. He nearly regurgitated his lunch onto the freshly-scrubbed counter. Never had life presented him with such an opportunity, a chance to cleave from existence a *purpose.* He had no idea how to respond.

Then the door burst open once more. Every worker and customer, and all dozen sea rovers flooding themselves in mead and mutton stew, careened around. Each one was equally flabbergasted to witness entering into that backwater inn a genuine Spanish commander. Flanked by 13 soldiers, he hushed the tavern from breadth to length.

He strode into the center of the room and boomed in English lilting with Spanish tones, "I am master of the *guardacosta* patrolling *Las Islas de Barlovento.* You have heard my name extolled even in this pig-sty of a foreign province. It is I, Araña Sangrienta!"

The young captain, though short in stature, was long in pride. He swept his eyes up to to the balcony to meet the flabbergasted stares of the whores, down along the bar where the tavern keep's jowls waggled like stirrups, and past Jonah, until they eviscerated the pyrates seated at the far tables.

"The man I murdered claims he is living still!" Sangrienta declared before the rapt audience. "How can that be, when I myself fired the shots that burst open his chest? I stood over him until the Devil within dimmed and he was breathing no more."

In the tense stillness that had descended upon the Punk House, Araña Sangrienta's voice dropped low. "Yet now, to my great perturbation, my patron, don Francisco de Leiva of Jamaica, not only swears that Iron Eyes lives, but forbids me from murdering him once more. Even so, I must ratify his existence with my own eyes."

Swish went Sangrienta's cutlash as he freed it from its sash. "Banner, Crown, and Cross, I summon you, Iron Eyes! Step before me this instant so that I might expose the raving falsehood that is you!" As he slashed his steel through pipe smoke, his 13 henchmen winged out to encircle the pyrates.

Jonah Profit understood, in that spark of a second, the single action that could right the pyrates' unfavorable situation and win him a place amongst them. He knew well the hiding place of the tavern master's primitive musket, the preferred defense against troublesome customers. Moving slowly so as not to attract the attention of Sangrienta and his men, Jonah slipped below the bar, reached past a copper basin of lye, and secured the crude weapon.

Featuring a wheel-lock mechanism and no real trigger, it was a cumbersome apparatus. It was impossible to predict where a shot's voyage might end. Undaunted, Jonah tucked the unwieldy long stock under his arm. He scooped a candle and by its flame livened the weapon's frizzen. It fired.

The powder coughed an acrid haze into the tavern. A scream erupted from the women upstairs. A gaudy oil canvas of Cleopatra traipsing through peonies that hung from the far wall crashed to the floor. Araña Sangrienta staggered. Rapidly, Jonah fired a second shot. The captain of the *guardacosta* dropped with a caterwaul.

For the next several moments, the Spanish *soldados* stuttered. Unmoored by shock, they appeared woefully unprepared to act without the guidance of their leader. It was obvious to everyone in the room that they had been instructed not to kill.

The right side of Sangrienta's face dripped blood from a constellation of puncture wounds. The Punk House musket had been loaded not with costly round balls, but rather with partridge shot – bits of broken glass, rusty nails, shards of crockery, and other refuse. It was intended only to startle, not to murder. Nevertheless, Jonah had inaugurated pandemonium.

Within an instant, the pyrates attacked. Ibra's adze punched a hole in the skull of one *soldado*, Scipio's mallet toppled a second. Yellows' machete spoke for him as usual during such contestations.

"Defend yourselves, you imbeciles!" screamed Sangrienta from the floor. His soldiers unsheathed their weapons and began, at last, to fight.

Like Iron Eyes, Tiburon was an uncanny sure-shot. He downed a rushing soldier and reloaded with aplomb. Iron Eyes sent rounds smashing from his cherry wood fusée and into the teeth of one Spaniard and the head of another. A growling pounce from Zemi made a fourth soldier turn tail and run.

Portugal's blast rescued Jonah from a cutlash that had been looping its approach toward his head. But pistol fire from another *soldado* caught the aging mariner in the arm. He spun round just in time to glimpse the half-blinded Sangrienta being hauled by three of his consorts out the tavern door.

Yellows, Ibra, and Scipio rocketed after them, but Iron Eyes whistled his men back. The captain recognized that any pursuit of the enemy was foolish given their own insufficient numbers upon shore and at sea. As well, Sangrienta had honored de Leiva's directive and left the pyrate crew relatively unharmed. Iron Eyes appreciated that he must do the same, else de Leiva would be unable to protect them. He permitted the surviving Spaniards to beat a hasty retreat.

Although nearly everyone in the tavern cheered, the pyrates could not claim a jubilant victory. Strewn across a foundered bench lay Xiki, his eyes empty. He had enjoyed liberty from enslavement for less than six months. Bequo lay with legs kicking fitfully. To no avail, he clutched both hands at the severed artery in his throat.

Tiburon sped to the aid of his compatriot. Bequo's face showed no fear, nor confusion nor even misery, but only unalloyed outrage. The older Taíno man had shared a few details of the atrocities his former Spanish masters had leveled upon his wife and children. He had longed for retribution. With a bow, Tiburon witnessed the final beat of Bequo's heart.

Iron Eyes perused the five dead *soldados* and acknowledged each of his nine surviving men. He surveyed the patrons and whores, and then rested his piercing gaze upon Jonah. The lad stood motionless, still cradling the tavern master's musket.

Five pounding steps echoed throughout the Punk House as the pyrate captain crossed to the bar. Iron Eyes snatched hold of the crude weapon and remanded the young ruffian by the neck, as though readying a hare for skinning.

IN WHICH A LIFE IS THREATENED

Six miles upcountry of Basse Terre, Zemi cat-footed through elephant grass, her desiccated tongue swishing compulsively across her fangs. Tiburon clutched his musket as he peered into the milky darkness through a tunnel of ackee trees. Yellows and two of Throat's men monitored the other approaches to the makeshift encampment. These four were tasked with guarding the reduced pyrate crew from attack – foremost a potentially vengeful return of Sangrienta and his soldiers.

Just a few hundred feet further into the woodland's deep, torchlight licked at the towering trees. Throat had remained aboard the Black Maggie as senior officer, minding the majority of the crew. He had loaned to the St. Kitts expedition his favored companion, a 17-year-old Zeelander called Comet who previously had labored in de Leiva's shipyard. Presently, Comet tended the flambeaus. He was of ordinary brawn but surly as a pig.

Portugal, Dario, and Ibra observed their captain, uneasily shifting their feet. Iron Eyes was a black nucleus at the center of the scene. "Let it fly," he instructed Scipio as he quaffed swill from his goatskin.

Scipio ignited the captain's musket. The round ball exploded into the loftier reaches of the poxwood tree from which Jonah dangled like bait at the end of a fishing pole. Splinters rained down upon him. Jonah wailed in terror. Iron Eyes had ordered the vagabond jumped up the tree by a halyard, but only now revealed his intention to use the lad as a live mark for target practice.

"What in God's creation?" Comet squealed, spinning his attention away from the torch he had been lighting and racing to the captain's side. "I figured you only wanted to scare him. Pray, Sir, do not kill the boy."

"You dare direct *me*, you itchy dust mite?" snapped Iron Eyes.

Comet did not cringe. "Throat sent our crew to the Punk House. He gave me orders to find this lad, Jonah Profit, and bring him back to the ship."

"Pshaw," Iron Eyes scoffed. Then he hesitated. "You jest not."

Comet shook his head with conviction.

"For what reason?" the captain asked.

"You must ask him yourself," the young Zeelander replied.

The captain raised an eyebrow. "Hmph. Now shy back a step. Have half a mind to string you from the tree next to that one."

Jonah, ears still ringing from the recent explosions near his head, did not overhear their conversation. Instinct drove him to lobby for his survival. "Merely wished to cure your predicament and join your crew, Cap'n! You and your brothers were jammed up with no exit. Was it not *my* aid that rescued you from certain catastrophe? I exhibited such gumption, dousing Sangrienta with iron chuck! Will you not honor me for my display of mettle?"

"Is this so? You're a clever lad, eh? And this act was proof of your intelligence?" Iron Eyes took two steps forward. He yanked down Jonah's tarnished breeches, letting his cock dangle in humiliation. "Listen near, hen fucker: Sangrienta *announced* that he could not touch us, as we benefit from the protection of Jamaica's High Sheriff, don Francisco de Leiva. Further, luck alone meant that musket was loaded with partridge shot. Had you assassinated Sangrienta, de Leiva no longer would have been capable of restraining the Spanish forces, and hotly they would have pursued our sails. Already we would be captured, our bowels unspooled. All you accomplished, you mound of turd, was the murdering of two of our dear-hearted companions, Xiki and Bequo. Xiki was most beloved by this man here, Scipio."

Iron Eyes snapped his chin downward, and Scipio fired the musket once more. This time, the iron shot slaughtered a tree limb terribly near Jonah's face. "Bloody buttered onions!" he screeched. "I swear upon a candied Jesus, I meant you no harm. Pray, Iron Eyes! Hold fast!"

"Quit your gassing, boy. You have no more than three minutes to live." Iron Eyes took another slug of mead.

This time, Dario stepped forward and pulled Iron Eyes aside. "Captain Baines, perhaps we ought spare his life? Grant the child a path to mending his error?" He raised his volume so that Jonah would be sure to hear.

Iron Eyes searched the Colón heir's sincere gaze and just as quickly dismissed him. "Show us another try, Scipio."

"I can be of service!" Jonah cried. "You have need of further men, aye?"

"We do," Ibra muttered. He favored not such theatrics of cruelty.

Scipio, on the other hand, was furious at the death of his friend. He cracked the captain's musket a third time.

"Gaaaa!" Jonah hollered, grabbing his ankle where the shot had skimmed his flesh. "I know of a klatch of men trusty and true, vitalized with brawn and wit. Lick as quick, I can fill out your complement, if only you cut me down."

"Enough with your cowardly begging," scoffed Iron Eyes. As Scipio reloaded his musket, the captain leveled his beloved cherry wood pistol.

That second, a detonation blindsided the pyrates. Zipping and snapping bangs rang out like fireworks, smothering them in smoke. Gagging, they tucked their mouths into their shirt sleeves. Comet's eyes spidered red.

Zemi dashed about barking madly. He was followed by Tiburon, hacking coughs. "A spy swept past our watch?"

Then, through the peppery fumes, they heard a lawless howl. "Behold, Cap'n! This runt has genius skills!"

As the fug uncurtained, Yellows barged into the encampment dragging a filthy guttersnipe behind him. "I have not ever witnessed anyone with more talent for crafting and slinging petards. This wee sprout has a card to play."

"Lemon Squeezy! My hero!" cried Jonah from the tree branches. Splosh looked up with a wild grin.

Iron Eyes narrowed upon the interloper, mulling him over for a taut moment. "Tis you who fashioned these bombs? You and only yourself?" he asked.

Splosh nodded.

"How?"

"Poured powder into a clay pot. Added pitch, tar, and peels of gummy shoe-leather, which same I usurped from these failing boots. Lidded the concoction, fit the flame, and – boom!" The youngster could not contain his enthusiasm. "But fear not, Sir. Though it offends with a stink haze for a while, it delivers no lasting illness."

Iron Eyes replied with a suspicious nod.

"Think on it!" Yellows suggested, unable to bely his exuberance. "Just a few of this fellow's *grenadoes* could provide sufficient time for us rogues to board a ship and rout the prize without ever expelling a single musket shot!"

"Tis true. Splosh is a shaman of explosives," confirmed Jonah from his elevated position.

Dario edged closer to Iron Eyes. "Well now, this be a drop-dead quirk."

Examining the unabashed admiration upon the faces of his men, Iron Eyes granted Splosh membership upon the Black Maggie as assistant to the yet-to-be-named master of arms. Upon the sprout's insistence, combined with urging from Dario, Ibra, Portugal, and Comet, the captain reluctantly agreed to quarter Jonah as well.

Iron Eyes swallowed tightly. He lifted his cutlash out of his belt and sliced it through the rigging lines. Jonah fell like a coal sack to the ground. The captain stepped directly before Splosh, the tip of his sword nearly piercing the boy's chin. "Find us the men we require, or else I shall stuff *your* bowels—" he pointed the blade at Jonah, "with *his* liver."

Although astounded to have realized his decade-long dream, Jonah Profit nevertheless felt roiled by the events of the evening. After all he had connived, it was his sidekick who had earned for them a place aboard a pyrate ship, not him.

IN WHICH GRAVES ARE ROBBED

"Bide a moment," Portugal commanded Jonah and Splosh, halting them before they disappeared into the woods for a morning constitutional. The other Maggies poked about, nibbling jerked meats and fruit as they gathered their supplies for the day's adventure. "Either of you wastrels capable of delivering to us a surgeon?" Rolling up the yellow sleeve of his *changshan*, he divulged a rashly construed tourniquet at his right elbow. "Seems I been nipped during our encounter with the Spanish vermin. Reckoned it scant cause for worry, but—"

"Aye, aye, can do!" interrupted Jonah.

Brushing the youngster aside, Iron Eyes glared at Portugal's bandage. It was oozing puss. "You should have consulted *me* with this matter, you bleeding martyr."

Portugal shrugged an apology.

Iron Eyes summoned Tiburon with a wave and paused, contemplating Sangrienta's bellicose announcement at the Punk House the previous day. Raising his voice so every man present could hear, he announced, "Yay, verily you need only inspect the scars that cover my body to verify the condition the Spaniards left me in upon that dreaded atoll of Zéros. Comes as no surprise that Sangrienta believed me dead. But Tiburon salvaged me. Our friend here is a hand-of-God healer."

When Tibbs inspected the wound, however, he shook his head. "I shall cleanse the wound and dress it with a salve or three to ease the suffering, Portugal, but it lies beyond my skills to remedy so—" he halted.

"So what?" pressed Portugal.

"So fatal of an injury," Tiburon relented, and he set to work, removing a set of small gourds from his supply pack.

"Luck fancies you, Portugal," Jonah proclaimed with a cocky jaunt. "Follow me. I shall lead you to the ideal man to heal you."

Hours later, Jonah guided the pyrates to a site that had gained notoriety less than 30 years prior. During the Kalinago Massacre, united French and English forces had committed genocide, slaughtering 2,000 of the island's indigenous people. Ever since, the area bore the name *Bloody Point.*

By the time they arrived, night had fallen. The rogues anticipated a raucous eve of drinking rum about a banked fire.

Instead, they arrived upon a scene so taboo that even the hardened blackguards swore they were trapped in a nightmare.

Zemi barked menacingly, her eyes mirroring the yellow moonlight. Dario Colón made the sign of the cross over himself, whilst Ibrahim Reis sputtered Hail Marys. Even Comet, who was miles from Catholicism in faith, grabbed hold of Ibra's rosary beads. Others determined the situation would be better confronted with arms. They drew pistols and took aim.

A shovel tossed clods of red clay from a musty grave. In a moment that elicited genuine horror, an undead figure clambered from out the hole, hauling with him a maggoty corpse.

"Tis a curious sport, body snatching," Iron Eyes remarked.

The zombie did not reply. His blonde hair fell in a curtain over his face. Without the slightest concern for his perturbed audience, he began to poke at the human relic. It was as mushy and black as an overripe avocado, yet he examined it with meticulous fascination.

"Good eve on you, Hendrik Boer," Jonah greeted.

"Never before have I met a true resurrectionist!" Portugal confessed, enthralled.

"Eck! Too pretentious a title," Hendrik Boer grumbled. His polished English struck a bizarre contrast with his present appearance and occupation. "I favor the trade name of *grave larcenist*. Besides which, I play not at occultism. My interest in these cadavers is straightforward and purely medical. How else might I study the mysteries of human anatomy, humourism, contagion, and prognostication?"

He fixed his gaze upon Jonah. "I have amassed over 200 case reports promoting my theory that illness derives not from possession by demons. Rather, it might be remedied by good hygiene and salutary climes. Soon, I shall submit a paper on these findings of mine, Lord Muck!"

Jonah beamed at the pyrates. "I present to you Hendrik Boer, master at the arts of a barber-surgeon," he exulted.

"How now?" Iron Eyes puzzled. "True as true, this here resurrectionist is a surgeon?"

Hendrik heard the incredulity tinging the pyrate's voice. "With carving saw, mallet, chisel, trepan, cautery irons, forceps, nippers, and muscle knife, you may test me against any man trained at Leiden University," he defended, immodestly mentioning the name of the best medical school in Europe.

Sensing the captain's rising impatience, Jonah stepped in. "If you please, gentlemen, no person in the world – or at least upon these Caribbean island – is more skilled in human science than this Zeelander, Master Hendrik Boer."

"Feather my foreskins!" the blonde man exclaimed, disregarding Jonah's praise as he explored the dead body further. A perplexing clod germinated from her chin. In a move that caused several of the Maggies to gag, he tugged the growth off her face and tasted it with his tongue. "Manioc slush. She poisoned herself. Suicide is the fact of it."

Tiburon shook his head wearily. Iron Eyes curled his brows in astonishment. Hendrik remained balled over the corpse.

"Have you ever applied your talents to a *living* customer?" Iron Eyes queried. With that, he grabbed Portugal's arm, causing the mariner to cry out in pain.

Hendrik Boer stared at the injury for a long moment. "The round shot intruded here, through the forearm.

Launched from an unrifled barrel, it churned the flesh at the entrance point, caromed off the radius, and shattered the ulna before escaping at the elbow," he autopsied.

The Maggies stood in silence, impressed. Portugal revived himself first. "I imagine you're set upon lopping it off. What a shame. I always favored my right arm."

"Aye, for with his right arm, he husks the cob," Iron Eyes teased, making a lewd gesture.

"Toss off," Portugal said.

"Exactly."

Hendrik Boer's face remained stern. "I shall consider no such action. Amputation is propaganda. Eight of ten people are graved by it, and it would spell certain doom for you."

"All the better," Iron Eyes said. "For I would blast a marlinspike through your brain if you assassinated this jolly fellow."

"*Now* you proclaim your love for me?" Portugal snorted.

"Tis only a practical matter. With you dead, how would we navigate our ship?"

Hendrik Boer intervened. "We shall reconcile the seat of the sore. Due to the degeneration of flesh, it is not possible to purify the wound by common debridement and potions alone, as I see you already have attempted. We must expose the injury to blowflies. After a day, it will be infested with maggots. We shall allow these cheese-worms to feast upon the putridity for several days. By virtue of the revolting pain we shall then find you in, we will know that the decaying flesh has been purged." These last words Hendrik Boer articulated with thinly disguised glee.

"Bah gums, *what?!*" Portugal yelped.

"Lanks a mussy," Splosh cringed.

Even Iron Eyes displayed a curdled expression.

"Be not distressed, for promptly I shall excavate the maggot population and season the lesion. It ought then mend itself willingly," he concluded with a confident puff of his chest.

Only Tiburon appeared convinced. "Please do as much," he requested.

"We would be much obliged if you would join forces with our pyrate crew, Hendrik Boer," Iron Eyes added. "No longer will you lack opportunity to practice your medical skills upon living specimens."

"Aye to it," Hendrik replied with a grin. At once, he freed himself of his breeches and aimed his penis at the patient.

Portugal reared back as though dodging a viper. "By God, what be?"

"The first step is to season your predicament," Hendrik stated evenly. And without further ado, he urinated upon the mariner's arm.

IN WHICH A FIGHT CLUB IS FOUND

It was afternoon upon the following day when the company of a dozen rovers, inflated now by one Low-Dutch surgeon, arrived at the point where the French and English provinces of St. Kitts met. The sun heckled the men ceaselessly. They were denuded to their linens, which sagged with sweat. Their skin was decorated with lacerations. Their beating hands failed entirely to thwart the curtains of mosquitoes.

Tiburon pulled from his pack a carved-out breadfruit filled with hog lard. He passed the bug repellant to Jonah and Splosh. Glancing sidelong at Hendrik Boer, who strode some 30 feet ahead in the company of Iron Eyes, Tiburon asked, "Why didn't he train as a common barber-surgeon?"

"Oh Hendrik… he was a *bona fide* practitioner enrolled at Leiden University," Jonah replied, scuffing the dirt with his toes, "till they kicked him out the door."

"Till they accused him of murder! At which point he beat a rapid escape to St. Kitts," Splosh clarified, relishing his ability to divulge the secret.

Tiburon cast a stern look upon both boys.

"What my counterpart Lemon Squeezy here gobs about is but a tiny matter," Jonah hesitated. He craned his neck upward, as if seeking an explanation from amongst the clouds. "Um, err, I suppose Hendrik butchered, what… seven people?"

"Seven?" Tiburon looked pale.

"But tis not what you fear!" Splosh added rapidly.

"His trespasses were for the sake of *good*, actually," Jonah elaborated. "As it happens, Hendrik operated upon whores."

Tiburon's expression turned even more quizzical. "Curing the French pox? Or what?"

"Ummm…" Jonah fidgeted uncomfortably. "The strumpets, as the case were, well… they were men. But, ahem, they desired to travel through life as women, you see?"

"So, they asked Hendrik to chop off their bits and pieces! Can you even fetch that?" Splosh asked, eyes gleaming.

Tiburon nodded, revealing nothing. Unconsciously, however, he touched his ribs with his hands, feeling the cloth that bound his small yet treacherous breasts.

"Hush now, Lemon Squeezy," Jonah warned, his expression rueful. "The way Hendrik speaks it, the procedures did not take as he desired. The harlots bled out, and the law blamed Hendrik for killing them."

Tiburon, however, was no longer listening. He floated in his thoughts until a rumbling ripped through the trees. Zemi raced ahead, nose twitching. With a wave of his hand, Jonah flagged the men to break their advance. After bending an ear to the woodland, he encouraged them to follow him through a gap in the trees.

Moments later, the pyrates breeched a pasture dusted up by a horde of hooting men who were doused in a fermented mash that stank of shit and vomit. A battle was unfolding. The *mop ringle*, as these gamesters called it, was delineated by a circle dug into the dirt. Within it stood a bald man, solid as a boar and boasting a horseshoe-shaped moustache. Unshod and bare chested, he was garbed solely in a pair of loose trousers. His adversary was of equal size but a far lesser fighter. He soon wilted to his knees, moaning like a sick cat. The conqueror sneered demonically. The crowd exploded in cheers and jeers, exchanging coins and collecting debts.

"That there be your master of arms," Jonah hollered at Iron Eyes above the din, pointing to the winner. "Howler

Dornan. The beast savors abuse. Whether by pistol, blade, or good old-fashioned fist, he delights in delivering a beating."

Iron Eyes said nothing. He assayed the feral collection, his eyes darting from one eccentric man to the next.

Uncertain of the captain's humor, Jonah rushed to explain. "They convene the matches here, upon the border betwixt the English and French colonies, in order to avoid intervention from either government. This way, no official can compel them to share a portion of their winnings. Clever, do you not agree?"

Still Iron Eyes refused to respond. He itched the scruff of his beard, ruminating.

Jonah grew increasingly concerned. "Do you fancy him?"

"Aye," Iron Eyes grunted at last his consent, "and these five, as well." He pointed them out, including the sod who just had been clobbered by Howler Dornan. Presently, the man was spitting out teeth like sunflower seeds. Even so, his hands twitched as though not yet emptied of the desire to wage battle. "How's that one called?"

"Joy de Bones," Jonah replied.

Chapter 14

JAMAICA

IN WHICH A LIFE IS REVIVED

The Cloud Fortress was the ultimate incarnation of a Maroon *palenque* in terms of its natural defenses. Set atop three hillocks that offered views across the south of the island as far as the sea, the village was surrounded by sheer cliffs, dense dells, and cathedrals of trees. A single defile through a narrow canyon afforded entry into the village.

Even so, the Jamaican militia had met with total success in their surprise ambush. Lubolo had not prepared for it, presuming the Spaniards intent upon eliminating the Windward Maroons and no one else. He had trusted in the peace pact he had forged with don Francisco de Leiva years ago. Now, lied to and cast away, the survivors suffered.

As the Windward Maroons approached with their mules in tow, the stench of carcasses sickened the air. When they reached the central encampment at last, they halted, wearied by their efforts and the annihilation that stretched in every direction.

Wattle homes of thatch and palm leaf smoldered. The remaining Mocho Mountain Maroons grieved. Some wandered with vacant expressions. Some bawled with despair. Some screeched at injustice. Some crumbled with humiliation. And some searched for a fissure that might permit them to tumble directly into the afterlife.

"Phantasms," JoJo remarked to Sasa.

"The living who walk whilst unable to be dead," he said.

A handful of Mocho remnants who still could muster their will charged at the fresh arrivals. With a gentle hand, Nani placed herself in their path. Sasa stood by her side. When they realized the legends they were facing, the tumbledown warriors staggered to a stop.

It did not take long for all 40 surviving members of Lubolo's tribe to circle round. A vicious debate ensued, in which they segmented into two factions. The first framed Nani for the carnage that had befallen them: Her theft from de Leiva had infuriated the Spaniards and annulled their truce. The second party, composed mostly of women and a handful of true-born Maroon children, dropped and pasted their foreheads to the earth. These individuals revered Nani's Obiya power, and as well the strange monkey-man with whom she traveled – whether demigod or spawn of Satan.

"Where is he?" Nani asked.

None could answer.

"Hasten to find Captain Lubolo, living or dead."

When they discovered him, he was not either.

It was his fourth wife, Madrileña, who located Lubolo lying amidst the boscage bathed in blood. He wandered the limbo between this realm and the next. Unlike his other three wives, Madrileña was neither *Africana, criolla, ladino*, nor *Yndian*, but rather a *donzella*, a woman of flawless Spanish bloodlines. Less than one year ago, the abuse she had endured as an indentured housemaid had driven her to escape. Although just five feet tall in stature and, at 16, the youngest of the chief's wives, she had equaled the other wives in valor. Now, she was the only one left.

At once, the Mocho Maroons brought Nani to him. They were equipped with healers, but none matched Nani in knowledge of spirit science. She dragged him to a nearby cave to afford him some protection from the elements.

"Lubolo has been assigned a seat upon Death's barge," she announced to the Maroons who had gathered while she examined him. "But the vessel sails sluggishly. We often forget about the strains shouldered by Death. He can be exhausted by his work, especially in times of warfare. This is our opportunity to plead with the Reaper: Allow your leader to disembark from the boat to eternity."

Sasa set to bringing more Windward and Mocho Mountain Maroons to the site. Sipopi lit a fire outside the cave. Nani and JoJo, meanwhile, dove into the incomprehensible task of convincing Death to release Lubolo from his grip. The others offered to gather whatever materials Nani might demand, but she refused, explaining that the Obiya version of the *philosopher's stone* required many unusual ingredients. And so, the curious tribe members simply stood around the fire to watch.

Drawing from her oracle bundle, Nani pinched several powders and herbs. She then extracted from the *jege* a curling bronze thread that stretched to a foot in length. Into the calabash it went. "A strand of hair from our enemy," she announced.

Next, she called Sasa forth and directed him to open his mouth. She fished out the mankey's tongue and, with a blade, nicked its tip. Sasa spat blood into the Obiya bowl. "The blood of a god," Nani explained.

JoJo added *kill-devil* and stirred the mixture with a ladle. Within minutes, it congealed. Nani passed it around, instructing each Mocho Mountain Maroon to sup. The remaining liquid she poured over Lubolo's bare chest.

Minutes passed. Lubolo's face still resembled overcooked breadfruit, yellow and desiccated, but his lungs began to fill with sweet air. The crisis had passed. Madrileña collapsed upon Nani, her gratitude spoken in sobs.

Though she did not admit it to anyone, Nani grieved. Her summoning of Lubolo had placed her in arrears with the King of Tombs. According to the law of earthly mortality, the ledger recording living and dead must always be made even. To win back Lubolo's life, she had given up time from her own hourglass. The sand might run for another year, possibly more, but soon Death would shake through her final grains of sand and take her home.

A sudden spate of rain formed a rainbow over the hills of the Pitted Country. Nani's mind traveled with its colors. She was reminded again, as she had been many times before, that life endures in hearts and thoughts. No longer did her own future feel dark with concern. Intuition told her that she would persist, motivating heroes for generations to come.

JoJo discovered her mother grinning at the vivid sky. She had bided an hour till the crowd had dispersed so that she might engage her mother in private conversation.

"What shy thoughts ail you, my spring swallow, my gem, my star child?"

JoJo cleared her throat. "How does your *jege* include a hair from the head of don Francisco de Leiva?"

"I performed an exchange for it," shrugged Nani.

"I am the daughter of your womb, the only living child not ever kidnapped from your loving embrace. Why do you alienate me? Honesty, Mother, please."

Sliding a hand into the oracle bundle, Nani pretended to inventory its contents. "You and I both are familiar with Señor de Leiva from our years slaving under his sister's roof," she said. Then she released a sigh heavy with burdens. "You may be certain that he, too, preserves a part of me within his secret stores."

Many further questions sprung to JoJo's mind, but Nani's sunken expression halted her inquest. JoJo understood. Her mother had not the vigor at this moment to voice yet another weeping history.

IN WHICH CUSTOMS CAUSE CONFUSION

Sasa crouched at the foot of the eastern hill watching the Mocho Mountain Maroons carve massive rectangular pits out of the hard soil. For all the godhead wits about him, he could not surmise what crops they intended to plant.

"What fruit or vegetable will relieve their sorrows?" he asked JoJo. He knew from the sound of her footfalls that she was the person approaching him from behind.

"They aim not to sprout beginnings, but to honor endings," she said, kneeling beside him.

His eyes crossed. "Huh?"

"They are digging graves," she explained. "For their dead."

Sasa's heart skipped two beats. "Fill me with pistol lead! They smother their beloveds with dirt?"

She was startled by his alarm. "Why, yes. To grave the dead is a noble habit."

"Noble?!"

"Yes. When people die, we bury them in plots as these so that we might return their bodies to the earth. *Ashes to ashes, dust to dust.*"

"No!"

"No?" she returned quizzically.

"No!"

"Yes, I say!"

"NO!" his frustration tripled. "They must not, JoJo. We stop them this second." Sasa fired upright and took a long leap toward the Mocho toilers.

JoJo trailed, swiping at him once, twice, three times before finally grasping his forearm. "A hundred *nos* to that, Sasa!" she reprimanded. "It is *you* who must halt. That which is far from your knowing, you must let alone."

He glared at her with defiance. Meeting the bedrock of her conviction, he snorted before plunking himself back down onto the ground. A furrowed brow betrayed his irritation.

"What is the habit amongst your kind? How do you honor your departed ones?" she inquired, keen to soothe tensions between them.

"In the past with monkeys, mean you?" he asked, turning to her with face alight.

"Yes."

Sasa sniffed, recalling the pain of his final visit and Giver's rejection of him. "In the soil and the water, all beings are consecrated, my monkey kindred say. These give life. So, no beast should place their dead into earth, river or sea. They are for sowing the future, not disposing the past!"

"What do they do, then, when someone passes beyond this realm?"

"Place them atop a hill and send their bodies to the air."

"By burning them?"

"No!" he jumped up and down in frustration again. "Leave them there. Let the vultures and other animals eat them and carry them to the sky."

"I see," JoJo said, sympathy framing her smile. "Numerous human customs must appear unpalatable to you."

Before Sasa found a reply, an *abeng* sounded from the central hilltop, echoed by blasts from the other two summits. The people heeded the code: They must gather at once.

IN WHICH MAROONS GATHER

Juan de Serras had arrived at the Cloud Fortress. He had soared southward the instant he had learned that the Spanish had thrown their forces upon Lubolo and *not* Nani. She observed them closely as they scaled the central hillock of the *palenque*.

The Los Vermejales Maroon tribe consisted of 50-odd people, at least 20 of whom Nani identified as women due to their calico headwraps. They were a diverse party of African, indigenous, and mixed-race warriors. Juan de Serras' gaunt frame, clothed in naught but grimy breeches, was woven with muscle. Strapped to his torso were a musket, a powder-horn, and a bandolier. His copper skin concealed his age; he might be near 70 years or just past 30.

The Mocho survivors rewarded their guests for their arduous journey by leading them to a pond where they might bathe. Next, they served a meal of jerked pig, roasted maize, and mashed yams. Welcoming Juan de Serras and his people to the firepit when night fell, they passed a calabash of rum punch.

During this period of diplomatic overtures, Nani noted that her lot had not been accorded such hospitality. But she cared not. She had instigated this convergence of the three Maroon tribes with the dream of forming an alliance. The rest was irrelevant.

Thankfully, her Obiya magic had not only rescued Lubolo from Death's grip, but also accelerated his recovery. Though not nearly returned to his customary strength, he was nonetheless cogent.

By mid-morning, 120 Maroons had gathered upon the Cloud Fortress sacred grounds, set amongst a grove ruled by the most exquisite guango tree. Nani and Juan de Serras stood just beneath the tree. Lubolo sat propped against its trunk. His wife Madrileña stood by, attending to his needs. At her side, Nani boasted the incarnation of Sasabonsam and her daughter JoJo.

Lubolo opened the congress by sounding the *abeng*. With pain tormenting him, he dispensed of formalities. "The murmurs of your magical prowess appear valid, Nani. I am grateful for your healing."

Juan de Serras was not so gracious. "I heard you caught musket balls with your naked hand. True or not?" His voice was sharp as gravel.

Nani splayed open her fingers. Juan de Serras fished her right hand to within an inch of his nose, authenticating the scar. A jealous vindictiveness swelled his chest and purpled his cheeks. He cast her hand aside. "Even so, no mortal can achieve such a feat."

"Unless that mortal is the queen of Obiya and most trusted beneficiary of spirit science!" Sasa piped up, his untamed mop of hair bouncing wildly.

Juan de Serras whirled upon the monkey-man with a ferocious look. Sasa rebutted the man's suspicion in animal fashion, by a flash of his teeth and wiggle of his bum. The children erupted into laughter.

"So, this rumor stands, as well?" sneered the infuriated Vermejales Maroon chief. "You have summoned a demigod and leashed him as your pet?"

"No, Captain Juan," Nani replied, eyebrows arched. "As you see, Sasabonsam wears no shackles. I dispatched transmissions into the twilight realm. By his own volition he spirited forth, rallying his immortal courage around the banner of our Windward Maroon and volunteering to support our just cause."

"And what is that *just cause*?"

"Our crusade is as straight as a razor drawn across our necks," Nani stated. "We have no tolerance for the Spaniards who occupy our island. We wish to unite our three Maroon tribes in taking up arms against them, so that we might free Jamaica from bondage and claim it as our nation home."

"Garr!" scoffed Juan de Serras. "What childish fancies you speak! We have no means by which to claim a refuge such as you describe – in Jamaica or anywhere else upon this earth."

"Only months ago, I would have bowed to your refutation. But now, we claim a demigod as our ally. Also…" She waved a hand.

Alzo and Santo leapt into action, lugging into the clearing the eight chests they had borne to the Cloud Forest atop their mule train. The Maroon congregation regarded them with wonder as they pried wide the casks, exposing a collection of treasures. Wol and Sipopi aided them in distributing the arms, powder, and shot. When the task had been accomplished, nearly every fugitive present had been vested with a musket or pistol.

"A supply of the highest-quality weapons shall be flourished upon us in perpetuity," Nani announced. "With these firearms, we banish timidity from our hearts. We convince our minds that our revenge against the Spanish invaders will meet with success. We operate as one unit, stronger in numbers, in arms, and in strategies."

Lubolo expressed his delight by noising a sprawl of *ooohs* and *ahhs* that sparked a coughing fit. Madrileña offered him water from the calabash. He cleared his throat and questioned, "But who funnels such riches to you?"

"Gaspar Carvalhal," Nani said.

"The famed Jewish interloper?" Juan de Serras asked, his skepticism evident.

"Aye! Listen, you. Jewish traders clamor to break Spain's clutches upon the Americas, just as we do. Carvalhal instructs us to contest the Catholic Empire from within, whilst he and his cabal lure forces from without. His own uncle, the White Oak, sits upon the right hand of Lord Oliver Cromwell. He tells us that England already has a plan to conquer this region, which Cromwell names *the Western Design*. If we ally with England, the White Oak says, we might conquer Jamaica together and safeguard it as a refuge for Jews and Maroons."

"You tell us to trust these strangers, a king-slayer among them?" Juan de Serras snarled.

"I place my deepest trust in Gaspar Carvalhal," Nani answered. "Like our kind, his kind have been degraded by Old World rulers for hundreds of years. Like us, they have no home. The Jews yearn for a haven wherein each person's fate is determined by self-rule, where thralldom and servitude are banished. *This* is our just cause."

Madrileña offered her the calabash. Nani quaffed deeply. Lubolo and Juan de Serras, meanwhile, shifted uncomfortably. First Nani flaunted her magic, then her weapons. Now she lessoned them on world affairs. They resented being publicly outclassed.

"And who do you propose should lead this crusade of our three united nations?" inquired Juan de Serras after a stilted silence.

"Me."

"A *woman*?" Juan de Serras barked laughter. Lubolo swallowed but said nothing.

"A woman of ingrained might, with support from a weapons smuggler, Obiya sorcery, and a demigod!" JoJo fired back. "Let it be Queen Nani. Never shall she perish. Her spirit is immortal. Even when her body exhales its last breath, her essence will live on. Nani shall lead us for one hundred, two hundred years, incarnated in the flesh of others."

One of Juan de Serras' eight wives, a warrior called Perfecta, bore holes in Nani with coal-colored eyes. "Your merits remain thin," she stated flatly. "Yet you chase these Spanish breeds with great impatience. Are you certain that your present resources equal the demands of such an offensive?"

"Ayii," Nani responded with a sharp nod of her head. She surveyed the heedful Maroons witnessing the parley. "It is time to free ourselves from hereditary monarchy and the enslavement upon which it feeds. We will accomplish this only by violence. To war we go."

"We will play no part in your insanity," Juan de Serras announced, retreating from the sacred guango tree.

"We must deliberate," Lubolo said. He closed the gathering by raising the calabash to all. "Let us congregate upon the morrow, my people. We shall declare our intentions then."

By the time the sun had climbed above the mountain peaks the following morning, Juan de Serras and his tribe had deserted the Cloud Forest. His message was clear: He would not follow a woman.

At their convocation, Lubolo proclaimed that he would not unify forces with Nani, either. However, he was willing to put a choice to his people. Any Mocho Mountain Maroons who wanted to risk themselves by joining her crusade could do so. Twenty presented themselves to the Windward Maroons. Fifteen were women, amongst them Madrileña. Three were children, two men. All were seduced by Nani's Obiya prowess.

Nani faced Lubolo. "You set free your only remaining wife, allowing her to pursue her wants?"

"Madrileña escaped enslavement already. Tis not our way to cage her again. But swear to me this: You will guard her life."

"I swear it," Nani promised, embracing him. "As well, I swear to show you, the wary, the pathway to a better life for ourselves and our children. With each passing day of triumph, we shall inspire more Maroons to join our just cause. You may be the last one persuaded, Lubolo, but I am a patient and magical woman."

Chapter 15

AT SEA

IN WHICH A BARGAIN IS STRUCK

At first light, Captain Josiah Gladstone arose from his bed with a yawn, pissed into his chamber pot, and gazed through the immense window casements that stretched across the Gallant's stern. He kindled the lamp that rested upon his navigational table.

Aisling awoke to his movements with a sudden rush of fear. She had scrounged slumber upon the settee, having resisted lying in bed next to him. He beckoned to her. With furrowed brow, she stepped to his side.

Her mood changed entirely the moment Gladstone floated the lamp across the table, illuminating a four-by-three-foot exhibit of fibrous paper pressed on felt. Upon it had been painted, in excruciating detail, a map. Her infatuation was immediate. The representation of the landmass and its surrounding ocean was marked by myriad nautical measurements, as well as fantastical drawings of dragons, elephants, monkeys, and humans garbed only in loin covers.

"This chart, or *card of the sea*, as sailors term it, was published by the guilds of Amsterdam, whose skill is surpassed by none," Gladstone said. "Tis a work of art."

"Nay," Ash interjected, slack-jawed, "even grander than that. Tis a work of art bound together with the triumph of science." She fell silent. To observe the world from this perspective delighted her imagination.

Gladstone stood apart, admiring the dazzle in her green eyes. He laid his hand upon hers, guiding her index finger over the hundreds of lines of the *waggoneer*, or sea-router. Next, he moved her finger to the compass, explaining how it indicated true north. Her curiosity plunged upon the engravings that marked rivers, lakes, and mountains.

Ash realized that she had been struck giddy as much by the masterpiece as by Josiah Gladstone's touch. The heat of his breath upon her neck made its downy hair stand on end. It set her cravings on fire. An insatiable surge extended from her nipples to her nether regions.

Josiah Gladstone retreated a step. Ash studied his contrasts. His chestnut eyes were tender, yet his muscles strong. His tone of voice could be harsh, yet more often it was benevolent. He carried with ease his expertise, yet also remained curious. Though technically her master, he acted as her suitor. Above all, she could not deny that Josiah Gladstone presented a delectable package. His looks, position, wealth, knowledge, and power combined to both titillate and terrify her.

Ash sank into confusion. *The energy between us is seditious to my very integrity*, her brain argued. *Still*, her body disputed, *such carnal attraction is natural to all the animal kingdom.* Her pining to glide her hands across his belly, to stroke those curls, to feel those lips upon her bare skin, to see him unclothed – it drove a red-hot throbbing deep inside her. Her hands threatened to grope him of their own volition. But in her head, she heard Rory yelling, "Stop!"

She was panting, her heart hammering. The only words she could eek out were, "But which land does it portray?"

Gladstone frowned.

"The card of the sea," she creaked. "Which land does it portray?"

"Ahh… that," he smiled, pushing aside a paper that had been covering the bottom right corner of the map to reveal the title plate, which was delightfully decorated by figures personifying the wind.

"Africa!" she exclaimed.

"You read?" His eyes widened.

"Yes, I read," she huffed in exasperation, pulling away from him. "Why do the English always presume that we Irish are uneducated fools? My father and elder brother taught me letters and numbers – until your kind murdered them both." The lust that had dominated her but seconds prior evaporated, replaced by self-loathing, fluster, and anger.

Gladstone attempted to soothe her spirits by returning to the map. "Laid before you are the Guinea Coasts of Africa," he said, skating his forefinger from west to east. "Here is the Grain Coast, followed by the Ivory Coast. Next we greet the Gold Coast, and just yonder – peer here, child," he nudged her nearer, pointing to a line of ink scarcely thicker than a hair. "The River Volta, the destination of our voyage."

She had tumbled again into torment, lured by the sound of his voice, the smell of his hair, the worldliness he shared with her. Depleted of her wits, Ash appealed to her soul. Then, Gladstone's words from the previous night came to mind: *Peddle your body, your mind, your heart, your integrity… From patrician to peasant, we all are prostitutes. Yielding an asset without personal gain is to be conquered.*

She struck upon a compromise. "If I move forward with this arrangement, I require a return for the concubinage you demand of me."

"Not one thing have I demanded of you!" he protested. "Not so much as one finger have I forced upon you."

"That's half-crack and you know it," she argued. "My fate aboard this ship is certain. If I do not bow to your lust, I meet with abuse and, more likely than not, a watery grave."

"Hmm," he muttered, an amused glow creeping across his cheeks. "What, then, is this *return* you desire?"

"Let us speak as stones, Captain Josiah Gladstone – cold, hard, and blunt. As my freedom is out of question, I shall play my hand such wise: Willingly shall I open my sweet, pristine wares to you *in trade*. You swear, in turn, to educate me in the domain of my choosing."

"Jesus nails! Look how you play the capital merchant!" he replied, his smile swelling into a grin. "I do say, my curiosity has been peaked. Which particular domain do you choose?"

"Tutor me in the science of sailing," she stated.

"I rather would partake in such an arrangement than lapse into the habits of a savage king," Gladstone said with an accommodating bow of his head. "However, the arrangement you propose strikes me as unwise. If you learn the art of sail, will you not enlist that knowledge against me?"

"You *are* a superior ninny!" she cracked. "What do you suppose the likes of me might accomplish aboard this vessel? Conquer all your men as one lowly girl pyrate? Do you figure me for the next Grace O'Malley? Bloody harr!" She stomped her feet and feigned a sneer, but instead broke into laughter.

Gladstone chuckled.

After several moments, she quieted. "No, sir. This ask is innocent and sincere. Being physically imprisoned aboard this ship, I desire the only freedom that remains available to me: a liberation of the mind."

IN WHICH A MAN IS MURDERED

A fortnight upon the sea slipped past with seamless coordination amongst the Gallants. Daily soundings told the fathoms of their course, and readings of the log-line revealed the distance sailed in miles. The men hazarded squalls, gales, hazy conditions, and even sporadic hail. Once, they rounded inshore to take shelter at a trusted port and restore supplies of victuals, livestock, drinking water, and wood.

A week beyond the Canary Islands, the Guineaman experienced her first death. Whilst heaving in the anchor, a novice became entangled in its rope. He drowned at the bottom of the ocean. It was an average calamity for the Gallants, who gathered on deck briefly with their Bibles in hand to bid adieu.

As more suitable breezes spawned from the northwest, the vessel gathered speed and soared upon the north coast of Africa. Ash enjoyed daily tutoring sessions and superb meals with Captain Gladstone, who played the gentleman and refrained from making any sexual demands. Her sole complaint was the captain's refusal to grant her an audience with her brother. Reluctant to permit his men to feast their sex-starved eyes upon her, he had decided to keep her guarded within his chambers, occasionally inviting her to join him for a stroll about the deck.

Fintan's spirits, meanwhile, faded by the hour. During the days, while Angus and Malcolm flushed the bilge pumps, he cleaned rot from the ship's hold. He was never permitted to emerge into the sunlight. At night, the three boys slept bolted by shackles in the orlop, the lowest level of the ship. Here, 50 chain-sets ran from stern to bow, ready to stifle 200 African souls. Their clanging, animated by the pounding seas, haunted his dreams.

As the Gallant crossed the Tropic of Cancer, per sailing tradition, Zanzibar the cook butchered the plumpest goat to celebrate. Upon the gun-deck, the din rose to a fervent pitch as the men feasted and consumed bonus rations of rum. The strikers, crowded in their usual corner, were given naught but discarded bits hurled their way. Gloomily, they gnawed on bones and munched tendons whilst famished cries spoke as always from their stomachs.

The feast concluded, the strikers were returned to chains. Light from a full moon traveled through cracks in the floor above, casting a silver glow upon the prison. Fin waited for Angus and Malcolm to fall asleep before hitching up his trousers. From a garter he had improvised about his thigh, he liberated the skene of his father. He hardly recalled retrieving the blade from the Seneschal's murdering scene, catching its glint upon a moonlight night much like this one and snatching it even as the last of their four attackers had chased him and Aisling from the hilltop. He had succeeded in sneaking the blade past the Butcher and aboard the vessel, just as he had snuck his existence past a world forever dismissing him.

Fintan O'Lorcan freed his glib – a mob of sun-colored hair never before shorn as a declaration of his native Irish pride. Slowly, deliberately, the boy placed the blade to his skull and started to scrape. His locks spilled to the floorboards in tufts matted with blood.

"Rot!" he yelped as the skene bit into his flesh. Yet his resolve did not fade. He scored further divots into his scalp, shedding with each stroke a humiliated identity.

The sound of Fin's occasional cries woke Angus. The forever angry Scot stood over him, eyes twinkling with greed. "Fuck a sickle, lookee here. You look like a condemned crook set for the gallows."

Fin gripped the bulge in his trousers. "Suck on this, you bespawler!"

"Why, you snappy hedgehog!" Angus lunged, grabbing hold of Fin. He tossed the smaller boy about, searching him for the skene. "Hand over your cutter!"

Fin resisted, but Angus was stronger. Feeling up Fin's leg, he discovered the skene in its hiding place. He clasped the blade with a toothsome smile and, with a distinct air of sadism, traced a finger along its stellar edge.

Malcolm's shadow enlarged behind Angus. The mammoth striker spoke covetously. "Easy now, Angus. An appliance as fine as this deserves a skilled hand. Tis a choice prize that belongs in the possession of a gladiator with the brawn and guts required to slay our captors."

"I can sling an edge-tool better than a Turk! Step off, Malcolm. The blade is mine," Angus hissed.

"You're too clumsy to fiddle your own arse," Malcolm chortled.

"Mute your tongue before I cut it into ribbons."

"That so?" Malcolm threated, looming atop his countryman.

"Put a hand on me and I'll sweep you to Hell, you ape!"

Malcolm stomped forward with three meaty steps. He shoved Angus. The lesser boy teetered for a heartbeat, then flung all his mania upon Malcolm. Angus was a seasoned fighter. He knew to strike first, aiming at his opponent's legs. The two strikers tumbled to the floor, wailing punches, butting heads, and ripping teeth into flesh.

Fin receded as far away as his fetters permitted, amusement kinking his lips. Just behind the bulkhead, the cows began to low. Soon, the goats kicked and the chickens screeched in concert.

Angus harvested the advantage for a split-instant. Then Malcolm, the Scottish bear, careened backward, smashing his slighter opponent against the bulkhead with a crack. The redhead slid to the planks.

"Now that's settled," Malcolm grunted, "this here blade is *mine*." He usurped the skene from Angus' limp hand. It dazzled in the moonlight. "A spanking treasure."

With a withered moan, Angus revived himself. He spat a tooth and struggled to his feet. "Give me my steel-edge, you furious fuck!" he wheezed, rushing Malcolm again. The giant sidestepped his attacker and buried nine inches of steel in his ribs. Five times Malcolm drilled the smaller lad's bowels with Fin's skene. Angus died in bloody convulsions.

Fin counted each knife thrust, riveted. "Murder. Murder's been done," he muttered. Then he locked eyes with Malcolm and screamed in alarm, "*Murder! Murder!*"

Malcolm blinked ignorantly, as though innocent of the events he had shaped. He dropped the blood-dripping skene and plunked himself upon the timbers, head in hands.

IN WHICH AN EXECUTION IS ORDERED

As had grown customary over these past weeks, Aisling and Josiah consorted around the map table, pupil and teacher. This evening, Ash planted herself cross-legged upon the opulent rug, listening with a transfixed expression.

Captain Gladstone licked a finger and flipped through the pages of a costly but pivotal sailing tome: *The Young Navigator's Compendium To the Sidereal and Planetary Component of Nautical Astronomy.* He had discovered that he rather enjoyed educating the Irish lass.

"*As the fixed stars afford a ready and infallible method of determining the latitude at sea nearly every moment at night,*" he paused to steal a glance at his enamored student and lost his place, "Let's see, ah yes, here we are *...with faithful* *opportunities for estimating longitude and the variation of the compass-*"

Pandemonium disrupted entirely the gentle scene. "Oy, Cap'n, we must congregate at once!" came a shout from just outside the door.

Ash recoiled behind the bed curtain. The captain unlocked his door and three men burst into the room: Sailing master Lucien Gunn, quartermaster Septime Devign, and boatswain Mechanic.

Trembling, Lucien described the night's bizarre developments. He had been first to respond to the cries arising from the below deck, jack-rabbiting down the hatchway into a lurid scene: Blood everywhere about the orlop, Angus dead. Several other tars had followed just minutes behind.

Upon confrontation, Malcolm had denied all knowledge of his fellow striker's death, swearing to Lucien that he had been asleep until Fintan's shrieks of murder had awoken him. But the brute's appearance belied his testimony. His shirt and trousers were dyed red. He was marked everywhere by scrapes and bruises.

Fin, meanwhile, bore an anaesthetized look. His freshly shorn head was nicked in places, but he had only a few drops of blood upon him. Lucien asked what had happened to his hair. Bizarrely, Fin insisted that Angus had shaved it with the blade that Malcolm had then stolen. In the resulting fight, Malcolm had killed the angry Scottish lad. Listening in, Ash felt gutted with worry that severe punishment awaited her beloved sibling.

Most distressing to the captain, however, was the matter of the murdering instrument: It had vanished. "But where can the blade be?" he demanded. "Things don't simply disappear!" The three standing officers had no answer.

"You must not hesitate to deliver your verdict, *Capitaine*," Septime Devign recommended. "Pronounce now your judgment upon this vile occurrence."

Gladstone chewed his lip, deliberating. "Malcolm shall be executed; Fintan, for the time, imprisoned permanently within the orlop."

"They ought both be executed," the perpetually surly Mechanic argued, his eyes narrowed to slits.

IN WHICH DESIRES ARE FULFILLED

The moment they left, Gladstone poured for himself a brandy and offered as well a glass to the pale, dismayed young woman who floated about the great room. She appeared frail enough to faint. "Tis a regrettable circumstance," he said, downing his dram and pouring at once another. "No, tis beyond mere circumstance."

"What of my brother?" Aisling implored. "Shall he be implicated in the crime?"

"Posh," he replied. "Lucien Gunn reported that the lad played no part in the horrid drama."

She allowed herself to breathe for the first time in a quarter hour. Gratitude multiplied her growing fondness for the captain.

Gladstone did not express similar relief. "A crisis engulfs me," he groaned, pacing. "I hear again the dismal clanging of that black fate who shadows me. I cannot endure yet another round of its curses!"

He banged his crystal to the table. Ash startled. Gladstone seemed depleted of confidence by the turn of events. Uncertain how to respond, she said, "Captain, sir, why such haunted speech? Twas no more than the barbaric work of one scum battling the other. When that boy was strangled by the anchor, you said death was commonplace aboard a ship. You told me *hazard marks the sailing man's occupation.*"

Gladstone did not register her words. He fetched his glass, splashed more brandy into it, downed the pour, and rambled on. "I shall disclose all, Aisling. You may see through me as you see through the window glass of this great room. The thing of it is, I have suffered a series of unjust wounds. And here again, tragedy has set upon me."

He spoke, then, in a dithering stream, confessing how his three most recent voyages had resulted in an unusual number of deaths on the part of both the crew and the enslaved. He exhausted the bottle of brandy and unbunged a second. "Am I scorned by witchery? Damned by God Himself? Each time I dare my ambition boldly, Satan pursues me. My crew is vexed now with some new plague. Dear child, *what is my defect?*" He pleaded like a little boy.

"Trust me, there is no curse upon you, Captain," Ash consoled him. "You're as sacred as any of us in God's eyes."

She watched his expression transmute from grief to desire. His raw vulnerability caused her to relinquish at last her mind's grasp on her body. She was on her way towards him before she fully realized it. Before she could fathom the doing of it, she was placing a kind, securing hand upon his hunkered shoulders and bending her cheek next to his. Josiah grasped her with all the desperation of a mortal being in freefall. His arms encircled her, his breath haggard with desire. She felt her bosom, prickling with a thousand fires, press against his shoulder.

He drew her closer until she fell upon his lap, where she sensed the full pressure of his yearning against her thigh. Softly, he murmured, "Please, Aisling. Come to me. I need you."

It was the humility of the request that compelled her to continue. She raked her fingers through his hair and he closed his eyes with satisfaction. With his rugged hands, he rubbed her back, her shoulders. Then he moved them down to encompass the crescent swells of her firm behind. She inhaled sharply at the warmth that emanated from her wherever he touched.

Yet still some part of her remained disturbed. Mental calculations paralyzed and then released her. She was his concubine, his whore, his slave. He was her master. Being English, he also was the enemy. And also, the moistness of her groin could not be ignored. Soon, it would douse her dressing gown at the fork between her legs and leak onto the captain's lap. She longed for him to take her.

"Josiah," she called softly, speaking his familiar name aloud for the first time.

He moved a hand upward across her belly. She gasped aloud. Then he found her firm young breasts, nipples erect. The drenching between her legs grew unbearable.

She clambered down from the chaise and onto the plush rug, drawing him on top of her and guiding his hands to massage her breasts more forcefully. Moaning louder now with exquisite rapture, she arched her back and raised her lips to touch his. He rolled over so that he lay fully atop her, the weight of his taught body crushing her. Distinctly, she could feel the throbbing of his staff, *like a mouse demanding a nuzzle in a warm nest*, she thought with a grin.

Then, for a moment, she was again beset by panic. How could she do this? Was she betraying her clan? Her ancient and valorous name? Her own character? No, refuted her indomitable spirit. It felt deserved. Necessary, even.

He cradled her face in his hands and, as though drawing a delicate sip of wine from a crystal goblet, lowered his lips to hers. Parting her mouth with his tongue, he began a tentative exploration that quickly turned more passionate. She returned his touch with zeal, pressing the full hunger of her kiss into his. His lips traveled from her mouth to her shoulder to her rounded breasts.

"Take your pleasure with me," she whispered into his ear, just as he swept a finger past it, tickled the nape of her neck, and unleashed shudders down her spine.

He lifted her shift, revealing her supple body. He parted her coltish legs and inhaled her tangy redolence. Her eyes crinkled shut. Her hands grasped the carpet. Some part of her still could not reconcile that she was inviting this intrusion upon her sacred attributes. Yet all the same, she grabbed him towards her and ground her hips against his.

Josiah tore off his shirt and unfastened his trousers, releasing the length of his erect shaft. He gripped his rigid length and with it circled the exterior of her femininity, his manhood rubbing back and forth across her hot core. "More..." she begged with sudden urgency, "deliver me more."

His weight pressed upon her and she felt the tip of his penis enter her. An instant of ecstasy was followed by sharp anguish. A tight yelp sprung from her mouth.

"The hurt shall pass, my dove. Follow those seizing flurries to eruption," he gasped.

As he rocked back and forth inside her, the pain dissipated. The experience that replaced it was rapture beyond any physical joy she ever had encountered. The thrusting ecstasy spiraled higher and higher, until her entire body rippled into spasms.

She screamed, transported. No more was she a servant upon a slaving vessel. She was the master of an armada. She was the goddess of her own realm. Aphrodite birthed from the waves. Powerful, beautiful, and free.

IN WHICH SECRETS ARE KEPT

That same night, Lucien Gunn assembled with Septime Devign in the quartermaster's chamber. "Speak your opinion of the wee Irish striker. Does he seem to you… unnatural?"

"I don't believe he tampers with *le diable*, if that is your meaning. I know others are jittered by him, but he is only a boy with an odd manner," the Frenchman grumbled dismissively.

Lucien tidied his perfect teeth with a splinter of wood. "Reckon he, in some fashion, abetted the murder of Angus?"

"Phssssh," Septime replied. "Lucien, we are seafarers, the first generation of men devoted to science. What you say is but mystic conjuring."

An hour later, having concluded the ship's business, Lucien returned to his tiny cabin. Having secured the door by a plank, he removed from his dressing cupboard the dagger he secretly had purloined from the murder site. Noting the Gaelic engraving upon its bone hilt, he determined that it was a rare ancient Irish skene. It proved, to his mind, that Fintan *had* involved himself in Angus' demise.

Still, the following morning, the Gallant crew awoke to the large Scottish striker Malcolm dangling by his neck from the main mast. But the strange boy Fin lived on, confined by chains within the orlop.

Ash opened her eyes to a glorious magenta sky. For several moments, she luxuriated in evocative images and sensations from the previous eve. Her body lit by desire, she rolled over to invite Josiah Gladstone into another tumble. Moments later, his erection glided into the opening between her legs.

Then she remembered her brother's plight. Divided by clashing emotions, she squeezed Josiah tighter. Their movements grew more turbulent and aggressive. She found that she preferred it, crying out until she climaxed and he finished with a shudder.

With the captain happily expended, she made her delicate but dire plea. "Might I visit with my incarcerated brother?"

Wholly besotted by the Irish nymph, Gladstone agreed, stipulating only that Billy Creed accompany her. As he did upon the first occasion, Creed delivered her to Fin's company in the orlop and then clambered to the level above to wait.

Ash sulked to where Fin huddled in shackles. She leaned next to him against the rickety wall. "Brother..." she moaned, searching for words.

"Terribly glad for your visit, Sister," he said, his lilting Gaelic soothing her disquieted spirit.

"How is it?"

"I have found myself in better conditions," he said, attempting a smile.

She could not resist mentioning a topic that had troubled her since the night before. "I fear the blade employed to murder Angus was yours."

"Aye," he muttered, eyes directed at the floorboards. "Twas our forefathers' skene that committed the act."

"But Fin, speak true. Did you play a part in slaying the Scottish boy?"

"I am unwell," was his only reply. Abruptly, he shifted to face the wall, ending their discussion.

Her heart ached at his tribulations. She leaned over to hug his back, voice soft. "Beyond this dungeon, beyond even what we apprehend, Brother, there are greater freedoms to be found in other realms. Oath to me you shall search for them."

IN WHICH A CRIME IS PUNISHED

Over the next few days, the skittishness of the complement increased. The Gallants applied their seamanship with leaden moods due to the strange incident. One of the tars was so ill-tempered that he poached a bottle of the captain's choice brandy and knocked it back all at once. The moment the drunk was discovered snoring in his hammock, Septime Devign sentenced him to a sound lashing. In part he also hoped to enliven the crew, distracting them from their dour spirits.

An hour later, the Gallant's topmen saddled the upper yards and clung from the shrouds. The remainder of the complement curled round the stage of the quarterdeck, razzing the criminal. Stirred by the banging aloft, Ash could not curb her curiosity. She joined Captain Gladstone and the other officers at the balustrade.

Septime Devign grasped the cat-o-nine-tails and hissed it through the air. A red welt erupted on the sailor's back. He grunted as the whip trounced him a second time. The French quartermaster hurled the lash over and again, until the howls of pain resounded across the deck.

"For how long does the suffering continue?" Ash shuddered.

"40 lashes and one for good fortune," Gladstone answered dispassionately.

She felt nauseated by the cruelty.

The crew, however, exhibited no such chagrin. They burst into the mess for supper more jovial than they had been since crossing the Tropic of Cancer. Septime Devign smiled, triumphant.

IN WHICH A STORM STRIKES

Days later, the crew's spirits restored, Josiah Gladstone exhibited downright cheer during his private supper with

Aisling. He followed dinner by addressing her appetite for knowledge. They gathered at the imperial teak table to commence his lecture on the calculations necessary for navigation. "The network of lines that emanate across a map are called—"

"Rhumb-lines!" she cried. "They spark out from true north and other affirmed observational points. Tis believed they cut the meridian at a constant angle."

"Aye, girl!" Gladstone beamed.

"Yet where is the evidence?" she argued. "Why can we not yet plot longitude? When *will* longitude be figured properly?"

"Perhaps it will be you who first succeeds," he jested, tempted as much by her lively mind as by her body. After two hours, high seas and harassing winds enticed them to resign their studies for the evening.

"Tomorrow, I shall bid Lucien Gunn demonstrate for you the use of a backstaff," he said. "But tonight…"

He lowered his face to meet hers, tempting her into a kiss. He led her to the canopy bed where she lay back, lifting her shift over her head. But Josiah had still more to teach. Instead of climbing atop her, he drew her naked body over his own, enthroning her upon his splendid cock. Ash thought later that if it were possible, she would have died from pleasure that night.

From an intoxicated slumber, they were wrenched awake by crashing seas. A gruff wind thumped the Gallant with hideous might. In the moonlight, Ash could discern immense waves surpassing the height of the windows. She was frozen upon the bed, filled with terror.

Straining to dress, Captain Gladstone was hurled across the room. "Blast this squall!" he cursed. After wriggling into breeches, he surged for the cabin door.

Ash felt more frightened of being alone with the pounding sea than braving the open deck. She chased him aloft. There, she confronted battalions of waves. The seas were a field of foam. Water seemed to explode billows as tall as cathedrals.

"Tis no squall," Gladstone said, his voice bleak. "Tis a colossal tempest."

"God give mercy," she gasped.

Mechanic dashed amidships, barking emergency commands. "Shorten sail!" the boson cried out.

"Refund yourself to my chambers, girl. You will not survive such a tantrum of Neptune on deck," Gladstone ordered her sharply, turning his attention to saving his ship. "Heave to!" he wailed over the shrieking wind.

Just then, a breaker slammed over the bow, pummeled the forecastle, and sheared away the foreyard. Shards of timber whistled across the deck. One massive sliver harpooned Lucien's apprentice in the chest. He would have reached sixteen years in a week.

The pilot, Oliver Riddle, burst from the gun-deck. "Seas are shipping into the hold!"

Aisling's mind went straight to Fin. She fought her way to Oliver Riddle and clasped him by the arm. "What of my brother?" she beseeched.

"Avast, girl!" Oliver Riddle huffed. "Such a battle between sea and sky can tear *all* our lives to pieces." He pushed her aside.

Panic shot through her. She raced her eyes about, calculating. Then she skittered down the ladder into the treacherous, flooding hold, determined to save her brother.

Just as Ash disappeared off the deck, a monstrous rogue wave arose from the sea. It appeared to stall at its peak, as if gathering more power. The most incredible second elapsed as the crew watched the bubbling beast. Then it exploded upon the Gallant.

"Fin! Fintan!" Ash shouted as she labored blindly upon the gun-deck, struggling to open the hatchway that would lead to her brother. When the rogue wave bore down upon the ship, the force of it smacked her head against the capstan so brutally that she slipped into blackness.

Above deck, Captain Josiah Gladstone wrung his hands, despairing once more his black fate. Chaos spilled around him. Yet peering upward, he observed a cloudless sky with the nearly full moon shining bright. The pugnacious wind and surf were offspring of a storm that raged leagues away.

IN WHICH LOSSES ARE CALCULATED

By the time Aisling's senses returned, the seas had calmed. She heard bare feet slosh up beside her. Oliver Riddle's voice echoed in the murk. "Your purpose is evident, you pitiful pup, but remove yourself at once. The flooded orlop is unpassable."

"But my brother… chained below… He battles for his last breath as we speak!"

"Far more likely he's dead," Riddle snapped, dragging her by the elbow to the top deck.

Quartermaster Septime Devign exhorted all hands – including Aisling O'Lorcan, whom he called out by name – to labor through the remaining hours of the night to rescue and inventory whatever wares they could upon the gun-deck. They travailed ceaselessly, conveying from one side of the ship to the other hundred-pound casks of gunpowder, chests of muskets, coffers of linen cloth, barrels of brandy, and hogsheads of cowry shells, pulling aside anything that had not been pulverized and casting the rest overboard.

Throughout, Ash persisted in trying to reach Fin. She shouted his name through split boards, summoned him in silent prayer, and even hazarded a flirtation with Lucien Gunn on her brother's behalf.

When the greater half of their work had been completed, the captain again requisitioned all hands on deck. He had planted the superior ranking men – Mechanic, Lucien Gunn, Oliver Riddle, and Billy Creed – beside him. Shortly, Septime Devign appeared with his day record book and diary beneath his arm. His purpose was evident to all. He was obliged to tally the loss of life alongside any goods wiped out.

Several tars, Septime attested, had witnessed the demise of the assistant navigator John Burgess, speared through the heart by a rampaging fragment of wood. Then he sighed. "Further, we have lost Zosime Montfort, the ordinary. He vanished during the night. We presume the sea swept him away also."

The Gallants lamented the death of the French African boy, whose cheery spirit they had cherished. In the quiet that ensued, Ash expressed her concern. "What of my brother, Fintan O'Lorcan?"

"Reckon he drowned," the quartermaster grunted with a shrug. A few men sniggered, relieved to be unburdened of this striker who had disquieted them so. Ash fumed at their unconcealed relief.

Captain Josiah Gladstone, however, took note of her distress. Forthwith, he commanded a gang of men to work the bilge pumps in order to win back the lowest level of the ship's hold. Some murmured protest, pleading for a spell of rest after their night of hard labor. But Gladstone belittled their fatigue. A meaningful glance told Ash that his enthusiasm for the task had been propelled by more than a sense of duty to the ship.

"The belly of the frigate is near empty of water," attested Alexandre Fauçonberg, the Gallant's gunner, with a slurp. The Frenchman's heavily accented English had grown even more difficult to interpret of late due to spells of incessant drooling. He was overly tinctured with mercury, rumor held. The Gallant's barber-surgeon had prescribed calomel so as to counter the man's repeated eruptions of syphilis. Ironically, Fauçonberg now suffered more from mercury poisoning than ever he had from the French pox.

"A night with Venus, a lifetime with Mercury," Lucien Gunn quipped to Billy Creed as they seized their adzes and began smashing a passage into the stores beneath the gun deck.

As figured, Ash appendaged herself to their exertions. Nigh an hour elapsed before Lucien crawled out from the miasma pasted in sludge and reeking of fish entrails. Impoverished of breath, he sputtered, "Hundreds of biscuit loaves soaked, the livestock drowned and spoilt, and, cells of Newgate, the stink of the chamber pot! It rules beneath."

He turned toward Ash, mindful of the words she yearned to hear. He shook his head. "No signs of Fin," he muttered.

She choked. Her throat felt jammed by a wooden crucifix.

The afternoon watch was about to sound when the deck above crackled with turbulence. Sixty unshod feet scurried to meet a miracle. Soaring cheers followed. "Zosime! Well alive!" the tars hollered.

Along with Billy Creed and Lucien Gunn, she raced to the top deck. The sun had reached its apex, illuminating Fintan with a halo. He had punched a hole through the rear hatchway and lifted Zosime onto the planks. Pale and trembling, the French African boy resembled a ghoul wearied of the grave. Several of the crew hurried to administer brandy. Fin, meanwhile, was ignored save for the smothering embrace of his sister.

Eventually, Zosime's skin regained its pleasant hue. He told the gathered tars in delicately French-accented English, "The Irish boy saved my life. He spent the entire night forging a way out. Not for one moment did he neglect me, not even when my spirit was black as night and I could hardly breathe. Fintan is a hero."

"*You're* the saintly one," Fin responded sheepishly. "Twas you who dared free me of my chains during that storm. Thank baby Jesus for you taking such a risk, elsewise I would be dead!"

Zosime snickered. "How did you depict the storm? Tell it to these fellows."

"Must be Satan banging his scrotum upon us!" Fin replied, and they both roared, punch drunk.

Ash was not the only person perplexed by this sudden friendship between the lowliest striker and the most popular ordinary. Whilst the complement pelted Zosime with questions, Fin quietly reported his version of events to his sister. He had fought like a crazed rodent for their liberation from the rising water, evidenced by the fact that his fingernails had been completely torn off.

When that afternoon Captain Josiah Gladstone was summoned for an audit of damages, Aisling joined him. The bowsprit and foremast were wrecked, Lucien Gunn reported. The chain plates of the standing rigging had been stressed and the mast no longer functioned under proper tension. The fate of the rigging was even more despairing. The foretopsail, topgallant sheets, and lifts all had been destroyed, their canvasses shredded.

Moreover, a thorough evaluation of goods had determined that the trading cloth was ruined by a rank batter of filth and stench. Animal carcasses lay strewn across the floor, and the stores of salted beef, smoked hams, and cheese had been contaminated with unhealthy effusions. Finally, nearly all the freshwater hogsheads were fractured to oblivion.

"Our remaining food and water stores shall not last the week," Lucien surmised grimly.

Several tars, listening in, gasped and began spreading the unfortunate news about the ship. The captain jerked his head and stomped his feet. He inhaled deeply the sea air for a solid minute before addressing the crew. "There, there, fellows. By merely a short rationing, we might surmount these troubles. Rest assured, in a few days we shall harbor in Cape Verde, where we can repair our vessel and restock."

A grumbling scurried throughout the complement. One of the ordinaries challenged, "Are you to nip our water, as well?"

Others shouted, "We won't be handled like animals," and "Forget not the Rare Fox!" This warning spurred other Gallants to whistle and hiss.

The year previous, an infamous merchant ship called The Rare Fox had put out from Barbados. After no more than a week upon the high seas, an accidental fire originating in the furnace had devastated the general stores. The captain, concerned more with profits than fellowship, had decreed the narrowest rationing of provisions. In a mere four days, the company of the Rare Fox had demonstrated their displeasure by mounting the captain upon the mast and employing him as a pistol target. The tale spread across the seven seas told of how the piteous man's wife had been unable to recognize the corpse delivered to her in Bristol six weeks later, so riddled he was by round shot.

Josiah Gladstone's eyes darted about the deck, surveying a minefield of sudden enemies. A mutinous impulse bred quickly at sea; this he knew. Verifying that his pistol remained secured at his breast, he waited for blood.

Then, Fintan O'Lorcan scampered to his feet and strode straight toward Captain Gladstone with impossible optimism. Ash observed him closely, baffled by her brother's transformation. Consternation no longer racked his face. In spite of his maimed eye and multitude of scars, he appeared younger than the week before – nearly as innocent as the child he should have been. It seemed to Ash that his harrowing experience during the storm somehow had lifted a weight from him. *No, tis as if the water purified him. A baptism,* she thought. *He is reborn.*

"Sir, allow me to assist you," Fin blurted with pride.

Gladstone stepped back, looking as though he had just sampled curdled milk.

"If it please you, Sir, I know a method for solving this drinking water problem. It comes to you straight from the noblest sept of Ireland – our own Clan Lorcan, naturally." He swung an arm about his sister's shoulders.

Gladstone maintained a skeptical gaze.

"Upon those days when our kinsmen were impelled to flee across every portion of our homeland, our leader, Cormac the Younger, restored our spirits with a version of *the Irish run-up*," Fin announced with a smirk. "He packaged the last remaining firkins of liquor into flasks and fastened them to the horses leading the march. Anyone who yearned to console their woes with the cure of *usquebagh* whiskey had to advance quickly, no matter their worsening conditions. This method propelled our migration forward. Ofttimes, our clan accomplished the destination swifter than anticipated."

Surveying the furnishings aloft the Gallant, Ash engaged the knowledge she had acquired during numerous hours spent consuming Gladstone's library and absorbing his tutorials. Claiming Fin by the elbow, she pointed a finger at the foremost mast. He gave a wink.

To the captain, Ash said, "There. This same mast ought remain absent of traffic. Tis the ideal spot for the run-up."

Gladstone nodded approvingly at his student. Unexpectedly, he then cozied an arm around Fin. "You possess a sharp mind, lad, alike your sister."

"Huzzah!" Fin cheered. He kissed his sister's cheek. "There ain't a riddle you can't solve, Ash."

The captain engaged the tars in accomplishing Fintan's designs. The topmen hoisted the first of two salvaged casks of drinking water to the zenith of the foremast. From here on, every sailor desiring to a single sip beyond his daily ration would be compelled to climb 65 feet. The men griped, but none could deny the cleverness and fair play. Favor for Fin grew, and steadily the crew's mood lifted.

Gladstone delighted in the outcome. "To what do you credit your brother's renewed vitality?" he demanded of Aisling as the light began to fade and they took a simple supper in his quarters.

She could not, of truth, hypothesize the reason, and so merely shrugged and returned to her meal. The more she nibbled at the bits of dried cheese and beef from Josiah's private stores, the more guilt arose in her chest. "Might I share some sustenance with my brother?" she asked quietly.

Summoning Septime Devign, Gladstone ordered the quartermaster to convey his gratitude to the Irish lad who had saved the life of Zosime, the crew darling, and devised an ingenious game of rationing. Fin would be granted the same scant portions as the rest of the crew - one bowl of gruel and one cup of brackish water twice daily. In addition, he would be permitted to wander free of chains and work atop the open deck, never more confined to the bowels of the ship.

It was a grander gesture than Ash had dared hope for, especially considering both her brother and the captain's somber moods these past days. She slid happily between the bedsheets that evening, devouring her lover's neck as an excuse to travel her mouth down to his cock and feast upon his begging erection. She swallowed his crystalized emissions, sweet as caramel and rich as butter.

Chapter 16

JAMAICA

IN WHICH SOLDIERS ARE SMOKED

"She'll poke you till your patience jumps off a cliff," vowed TokTok.

Don Paco de Proenza responded with a curled lip.

"That Nani witch will put a hood over your eyes and spin you round till you lose your senses," the blackshot omened further.

"Aye," the *sargento mayor* grunted, too worn to summon an argument.

They trudged beneath a springtime sun that left their bodies as heavily drenched in sweat as had the rains of winter. One month into their campaign to eradicate all Maroons from the island, the Jamaican militia had withered with heat and fatigue. Even the light cannons they had used to decimate Lubolo's *palenque* had been discarded. They journeyed now with only a half dozen pack animals, their small guns, and the most necessary supplies.

Ever resentful of the mission his uncle and warden don Francisco de Leiva, for the sake of manly virility, had foisted upon him, Cristóbal de Ysassi lived with great physical discomfort. His boyish chestnut complexion sizzled to a deep mahogany brown. His eyes sunk into sooted circles. He was finished with being cured alive in perspiration.

As well, he felt certain that Nani had augmented her force. Creeping eyes traced their every movement. Yet whenever the young man suggested that Maroon numbers had multiplied, Proenza had a similar reaction. He burst into guffaws and declared Cristó *a soft fig*, a *disgrace to his family*, or *a pity whose weak wits crash under the pressure of a single excursion.*

When at last the sun deserted the western hilltops, a blissful breeze cooled the air in the teak and sandalwood forest. TokTok traced a recent set of tracks into a deep ravine. The Jamaican militia descended through dense vegetation into a clearing. It was filled with a haze that smelled of fern, greenwood, and piquant peppers.

Proenza gestured his men to keep silent, waving them forward with excitement. He anticipated a successful ambush at last. Muskets were loaded and cutlashes swooped as the hushed file filtered deeper into the jungle.

The smoke continued to curl its grip around them. Six footfalls further, the caustic climate thickened, encasing them like a coffin. The militiamen were blind beyond a few feet in every direction.

A spark rasped and shots crunched, anonymous and practically point-blank. One of the pack mules charged into the woods. Soldiers plunged into a state of frantic whirling.

There was shouting; the answering report of pistols; the thud of a body tumbling onto the grass.

Cristó heard blood snorkeled through drowning breaths, yet he could not see past the length of his own arm to help the victim. Smoke laced with capsaicin crumpled him thoroughly. He was forced to brace himself against his musket. He and all the men around him collapsed in racking anguish, unable to breathe through the poisonous, hot pepper-spiced air. Cristó raised his weapon to shoot into the muffled light, but his eyes were filled with tears.

By the time the peppered smoke had cleared, the attackers had long since darted away. The *soldados* surveyed the carnage. Their company had lost one mule, one bonded African man, a soldier, and an eager ensign aged 14. The entire confrontation had been decided in five minutes.

IN WHICH SOLDIERS ARE SURPRISED

Ten days passed with Proenza determined to reverse fortune's tide. The militia sighed relief when they came upon a more genial landscape with fewer pit-ridden, jagged rocks. Tracking a path of discarded coconut husks and plantain peels, TokTok guided them to a campsite so recently abandoned that the embers glowed still within the firepit. A pig and a brace of ringtail pigeons broiled on the spit. Though the food smelled luscious, it was untouched. As well, several skins of rum had been left upon the copper dirt.

"Ha! They abdicated the grounds in haste due to our approach," Proenza concluded. "We shall pursue the cockroaches with fury!"

But the men refused, noting the impending darkness and calling to mind the embarrassment of the recent smoke-out. Having survived on slender rations of dried meat, along with fruit they gathered and any small game they happened to hunt along the way, they ripped into the meal that had been orphaned over the fire. Few of the Spaniards previously had sampled Maroon cuisine. Some rejected the spice, but others delighted in the blend of African, Amerindian, and Spanish flavors.

"Damn the blood!" grinned Cristó, juices sluicing down his chin. "Spirit lives in these edibles. I cannot fully express the glory of them."

As the sky darkened, they cycled the left-behind jerkins of hard drink about the firepit. The Maroon adaptation of rum proved a true fire sauce. Within minutes, it had executed its mission, dousing the soldiers' wits and sailing them into drunken slumber.

Their dreams exploded when a battery of musket fire tore open the heavens. Scarcely one crack of a branch had been triggered; the Maroon footfalls had sounded no louder than a hug. A young soldier fell over while urinating, his skull cratered. Nearby, a snoring youth received a bullet to the heart without even waking.

Intoxicated, Cristó sprang for the cover provided by a small grove of palms. Struggling to load his musket, he cringed as salvoes whizzed overhead. After a few seconds, he gave up and curled himself into a ball.

Then he felt a quiet flutter. He looked up to see, framed by palm leaves, a wiry, dark-skinned woman dressed in a cotton shift, her plaited hair knotted behind her neck. Her eyes pierced his as she reached toward him with a machete in hand.

Cristó wet his trousers. He did not face death bravely. The Maroon woman did not begin hacking him to bits, however. Instead, she reviewed carefully his features, as if deciphering the symbols upon an ancient scroll. Without a word, she leapt back into the moonlit night. An astounded Cristó found himself unharmed.

When the smoke cleared, Cristó crawled from his hiding place to survey the damage. Blood slimed the campsite. A voice called out, "*Socorro… ayúdeme…* someone help me, please…" Proenza fired a pistol to end the soldier's suffering.

The Maroons, upon this occasion, had killed three Spanish militiamen and plucked for their cause one more mule and all three of the baggage slaves. The insult, once more, had been delivered within the space of minutes.

TokTok approached. "You witnessed her," he rasped, his eyes holding Cristó prisoner. "What occurred there in the palm tree betwixt you and Nani? Speak it."

The youth was taken entirely by surprise. Until this moment, he had not realized that anyone in their collection had been privy to the remarkable moment. Nor had he fully nursed his suspicion that the mysterious visitor had been, in fact, the notorious Maroon chief.

Cristó backed away from the blackshot's stubborn gaze. Pregnant seconds elapsed before he responded. "Nothing passed between us, but in good faith I tell you this: She holds an iron grip on her cause. She will continue handling us as readily as she wrings a chicken's neck."

The militia continued its demoralized mission at dawn. Cristó fell numbly into cadence at the rear of the file, lost in thought. *Why did Nani inspect me so?* he wondered. *And why ever did she leave me alive?*

IN WHICH SOLDIERS ARE SPOOKED

Cristó squeaked and squelched. Another body-aching six days had trickled by as the Jamaican force journeyed back into the woodlands in search of the Windward Maroons. He wondered if the sensation of wet ever would end. He stank of mold. "I shall tell you which part of me *is* dry, however," he scoffed.

"Virgin of Sorrows, relieve me of this runt," groaned Proenza.

"As well, our unwavering regime of fruit is hurling explosions out my bowels," Cristó continued, undaunted. "I can withstand being part of your bumbling militia no longer, don Paco. I am abandoning this embarrassment of a mission and returning to La Vega."

Proenza glared. "If you turn tail upon your principles and God-given duties, I shall shoot a gaping hole into the back of your head."

"Tsk, such abrasive language," jibed Cristó. "It would make my uncle frown."

"Not so much as your flaming dereliction."

"Ock! And what of yours? Trounced *twice* now by a small and poorly armed band of mountain rebels?"

"You are a mockery of a man."

"You, the king of privy farmers."

"The blood in your veins is skimmed milk."

"And your head is a shrine of ignorance."

Rain spat upon them. They fell silent, each lost in disheartening visions.

Studying the landscape, TokTok observed something strange – something very strange, indeed. Prickly shrubs called *pínguin* had been tied one to the other, weaving an uninterrupted wall of brambles. It limited quite effectively the troop's movements. Overhead, a black rope was fastened around the branch of a mahoe tree. From it hung a sculpture of a man hewn from wood. A closer look revealed that the noose had been fashioned from plaited hair. He searched the area more closely.

"Sir," he beckoned.

Proenza traced the blackshot's finger, examining the evidence. Talismen were strewn everywhere. Animal bones had been steepled like miniature mausoleums across the forest floor. Pouches plumped with powders had been jammed into tree nooks. Calabashes brimming with snowy pebbles stood at intervals throughout the bizarre site. Closer scrutiny revealed that these were filled with teeth.

"Teeth are thought by many Africans to possess cosmic intelligence. They are used by sorcerers to produce hexes," TokTok informed the others. "Nani practices Obiya magic."

The color faded from the cheeks of the *soldados* as they, too, inspected the omens, pulling their cherished muskets closer to their chests. They were hunched, twitchy figures held hostage by superstition.

"Hush now with your witchery," Proenza scolded TokTok. "Tis blasphemy you speak."

Cristó felt particularly disturbed – but not because he dreaded Dark Magic. Rather, the talismen called forth memorie's of his painful upbringing. His mother had died giving birth to him. No one ever would speak of her, nor so much as utter her name. An illegitimate child, he had been conceived in sin, born into shame, and reared out of sight of society.

His father – who also had fathered a legitimate child, Cristó's half-sister Zorayda – enjoyed the inherited wealth and privilege of the Ysassi name. Intermarriage with the de Leiva clan had woven their two family trees into a single impregnable fortress. Yet Cristó's father had squandered his fortune on gambling. When the boy was just seven, the debtor had been forced to flee Jamaica.

That may very well have been the end of Cristó's story, had not Zora, elder by a decade, come to his rescue. She had married don Francisco de Leiva immediately upon their father's shameful abandonment of them. Shortly thereafter, she had convinced her new husband to take on the guardianship of her baby brother Cristó. Though he forever inflamed his ward and uncle's temper, Cristó had blossomed thanks to Zora's care.

Proenza congregated with his men. "We must not resort to wan trembling, my fellows. We arrive at present upon the banks of victory, I do oath it. No matter the tricks and traps the Maroons lay before us—"

"Or behind us. Or to the side of us. Or atop us," sang Cristó.

"In every case, it shall not daunt us," Proenza continued, piercing the youth with his gaze. "We are the legitimate representatives of Spain. The almighty Himself is on our side. See here, my valiant soldiers, from our thrusting muskets, an ejaculation of great death shall come. *Huzzah!*" He raised an arm skyward.

Cristó palmed his forehead. "*That* is your moment of stirring? Absolutely never deliver such a speech again." Several of the *soldados* snickered.

They shuffled forward, spooked by the scene. Cristó deduced Nani's tactic. At their most vulnerable, she was preying upon the soldiers' irrational fears so as to curdle their judgment and corrode their trust in one another.

Cristó could not identify which part of him was able to repeatedly decipher her strategies. It was an eerie sensation. He felt, actually, in tune with her lessons. This even as the other militiamen clung to the worthless vanity of their Castilian ancestry.

He pressured Proenza into allowing them to gain refuge at the nearest estate. A dozen men voiced immediate agreement. That would be, TokTok calculated, upon the land of one don Jerónimo Tello, the *cabildo* accountant and nephew of the governor of Jamaica. The blackshot reckoned two days' journey to reach the respite.

Although Proenza agreed reluctantly, he berated the young militarists for their hen-hearted failure. He indicted Cristó foremost, condemning the youth for his cowardice, weak ideas, and gassy opinions.

"Suck a pap," Cristó blistered.

"True as the silver under a bishop's bed, you are a wee impetus," Paco retorted.

"And you, unhinged boredom."

"Lick fly spittle!"

"Eat donkey dung!"

"Twiddle a filthy pinkie in the queen's arse!"

Proenza and Cristó circled one another beneath a tree that was hung with braided horsetails dangling figurines, creating a macabre theater. The soldiers closed in around them, enjoying the spectacle of disaster.

Just then, a single primal note swelled across the forest, making their flesh crawl. The *abeng*. The *soldados* shuddered, muskets pointed outward in defense. The Maroon horn blew again.

A mob of ten Maroons stormed the militia, swinging edge-tools. From the opposite tree line, gunfire rained upon them. A militiaman embraced death just before another had his head blown to bits. A third nearly managed a shot at the enemy before the warrior hacked his arm off with one fatal chop. A fourth caught musket fire in the throat.

The Maroons vanished as quickly as they had appeared. Nani's attack had killed four more soldiers and freed yet another enslaved porter. Proenza's total force now hovered just above 50.

"A massacre in slow motion," Cristó declared.

IN WHICH SOLDIERS SPAR

After three further days of trudging through woodlands, Proenza's troops felt themselves no nearer civilized land holdings. Not even the good will of a roadway presented itself. Functioning on fumes, their moods turned ever more brittle. When at last they exited high country and eased into the vale, the ocean breeze intoxicated their spirits.

The adolescent ensigns, Lope de Medina and Jaén de Falcona, lagged at the rear of the line, chuckling. Cristó drifted closer, his curiosity peaked. Jaén had a cherubic look, with an effusion of black locks and a pretty face. Lope made do with rude features.

"Dear cockerels, what puts such sparkle in your eyes?" Cristó asked.

Lope grinned. "Last year, upon an expedition in this country-"

"-we requested respite at this same palatial *hacienda*, the home of don Jerónimo Tello," Jaén jumped in.

"Tis newsed in La Vega that Tello is quite the producer of rum," Cristó commented.

Lope nodded his head vigorously.

"Three score toilers accomplish this enterprise," said Jaén.

"And among them," Lope smirked, "there bustles a slave of finger-licking comeliness."

"An inflictor of the most heavenly torments."

"And throbbing ecstasy."

"The perfection of her bloom!" squealed Jaén.

Cristó rolled his eyes. "Does this temptress have a name?"

"Yes. Juliana," Lope answered.

"She drudges in the boiling house, a sweltering and musty place famous for its dark corners," Jaén grinned.

"Stand fast. Any pretense of chivalry shall disappear when you lay eyes upon her," pledged Lope.

"And when you take her beneath the gutters of molasses!" laughed Lope.

Jaén cupped his mouth and lowered his voice, mocking the sharing of a secret. "It happens that if you lavish upon her a petty token, such as a hair comb, Juliana will coo at you and counterfeit pleasure."

Cristó clucked, judging both ensigns sternly. "My work upon Tello's plantation shall be confined to obliterating my cares with a deluge of rum."

"Pish! Once you verify for yourself Juliana's amply proportioned body, her exquisite face, her black fluffy hair redolent of cinnamon, and her great eyes like that of a doe, you, too, will have her heels in the air," Jaén wagered. He paused for a moment, then added, "It must also be noted that Juliana is a delectable mulatto of Negro and Spanish blood."

At this, he lingered a look upon Cristó. Then, as though realizing it for the first time, he said, "In fact, Juliana is a mirror to you – golden-brown of eye, hair, and skin. Likely a few dollops of African blood besmirch *your* lines, as well. Is that not so, don Cristó?"

Cristó tensed. He counted every soldier's gaze upon him.

"We were led to believe that you were equal to us, of pure Spanish heritage. But now I see that you are not *limpieza*. Your blood is *not* clean," Jaén provoked, resting a hand casually atop the hilt of his poniard.

Lope disconnected from his friend, slinking two steps away as Cristó's discomfort filled the air.

"Despite your dirty blood, you're dignified still by a coat of arms and rights to inherited lands." Jaén swept his gaze across the other soldiers. "Look how this mud-blood ascends over us, the vulgar class, riding upon the golden wings of his family. I challenge you to combat, don Cristó. Raise your sword to defend your puny worth!"

A split second later, the pistol of don Paco de Proenza ploughed into Jaén's cheek. "Blather again, and your pretty little face eats my gun."

Every soldier was startled to find the *sargento mayor* championing Cristó's honor. "Señor Cristóbal de Ysassi's blood is *not* mixed with that of an African. He is confirmed *limpieza de sangre*. Speak it!" he snarled at Jaén.

The ensign stumbled backwards in panic.

"Speak it!" Proenza shouted at his loudest.

"Don Cristóbal de Ysassi..." the young man stuttered, "is not ...mixed with an African."

Proenza dug his pistol deeper into the cherubic face.

"He-is-confirmed-with-*limpieza-de-sangre*!" Jaén spat.

"Now concede that *you* are no more than an insect."

"I-am-no-more-than-an-insect."

Cristó himself was not startled by Proenza's commitment to him. He had heard de Leiva's commandment to safeguard his nephew's reputation. And yet, as much as Cristó appreciated Proenza's defense, he knew it to be devoid of fact. He removed himself abruptly from the scene. As a child, he had cleaved to the belief that his blood was pure Spanish. But of late, he felt certain that his father had conceived him by a Negress, likely a slave. Even more, he did not care. At age 21, he no longer desired the truth of his identity held prisoner to delusions – his own or anyone else's.

IN WHICH SOLDIERS TAKE REFUGE

Fog roamed the pastures of don Jerónimo Tello's estate. It was bound by pigeon-wood, brazilletto, cedar, and fruit trees that served as a gateway to paradise. Throned upon the hillock was the main house, a wooden structure painted sunset pink and orange.

"Perhaps I shall attempt to win a permanent place here," remarked Cristó to no one.

They passed the sugar mills, where each of the three giant rollers slumbered. Proenza's men soon noted a total lack of industry across the entire compound. Not one slave toiled upon 20 acres of cane field. The estate appeared to be a work of art, silent and still.

"Do any of you find this scene odd?" Cristó asked.

They approached with caution. By the garden, tossed chairs and splintered tables squashed the flowerbeds. A rash of garments and bedding littered the front lawn. As they circled closer to the villa, they spied smashed doors and shattered window panes. Brocade and bobbin lace had been trampled into the earth. Further afield, rum cisterns lay exploded next to a collapsed poultry hutch. The drying cabin, hacked asunder, was strewn about like bonfire fuel. The boiling houses snapped and hissed with an expiring inferno.

Yet at the rear of the property, alongside empty stables and pig sties, the wattle cottages of the enslaved stood untouched. Not one palm of their thatch had been disturbed.

Jaén and Lope, who knew this sugar estate better than the others, directed the group to the apartments of the head thrall, a *criollo* named Juan.

"Dead, all dead," he murmured. "Father, mother, children. All the family dead."

Proenza interrogated. Juan explained how a demonic throng of mountain rebels had raided the estate four days prior. Their leader had been a woman. Of the 60 bonded souls who had worked the Tello plantation, only 20 remained. The rest had absconded with the Maroons.

Jaén and Lope inquired after Juliana's fate. "Gone," Juan replied flatly. The ensigns cursed their misfortune.

Back at the dwellings, the thralls who had stayed peeked at the militia from behind closed doors, gripped by panic that they would be blamed for their masters' deaths. Cristó empathized with their unease. Culpability always was determined by the tint of a person's complexion. It therefore surprised him when Proenza boomed his support of the few loyal bonded souls.

"I swear my guardianship upon you," he said. "This is the treacherous work of none other than the Devil named as Nani."

Even so, the Tello fiasco verified for Cristó the verdict he had for a good while been incubating. It was time he reject the militia, no matter the consequences.

Chapter 17
CAPE VERDE

IN WHICH FAITH CRUMBLES

Following the storm, the Gallant was barely conscious. The vessel limped a southeasterly course for the next nine days whilst the crew endured rationing. Aisling, on the other hand, was scarcely affected. Aside from satisfying her appetite with food from the captain's private stores, she indulged every sexual impulse of her teenaged body. Even Josiah Gladstone's long stretches of brooding could not calm her lust. In fact, she found they enhanced his allure.

The sole disappointment she faced concerned her navigational studies. The captain's dark moods seemed to have drained his interest in her education. Yet she durst not complain for fear that he would distance himself from her – and quiet their lovemaking. Meanwhile, she read fervently, every text on history, navigation, and the art of sail.

The standing officers had charted a course to Cape Verde, a ten-island archipelago that lay westward along the same latitude as Guinea Africa. Ash pressured Josiah to tell her why they had chosen this landing. Eventually, the captain informed her that the colony was enjoying a period of prosperity thanks to a robust sugar industry and trade in enslaved African labor. In passing, he remarked also that, being Portuguese, the majority of Cape Verdeans were of Catholic persuasion.

Faced with this fact, Ash had to acknowledge that recently she had soured on religion. The past few years had left her questioning the benefits of belief systems that instigated people to declare war upon one another solely because they prayed to different gods. Or even – in the case of Protestant, Catholic, and Jew – to the same God, only with slight variations in rites and edicts.

Above all, she rebelled against the Bible's portrayal of women. *"Lord said unto the woman that, as punishment for her awakening, He greatly would multiply her woes. In sorrow thou shall bring forth children: and thou desire shall be to thy husband, and he shall rule over thee."*

Great plan of Adam, what a lick of imbalance for women! she thought. *And what of this tall tale about a virgin girl who births a child without ever having carnal relations with a man? Pish! I ought to have words with God.*

Her pondering halted when Septime Devign, the quartermaster, sighted through his glass Porto Praia, the capital of the Cape Verde chain. The settlement greeted them with a stone fort of jagged crenellations that, from a distance, resembled massive teeth. Two foreign trade vessels already were anchored in the sickle-shaped bay.

With a nod, Gladstone initiated the Gallant's bid for landing by firing five blank cannon shots from her bow. The fort returned three empty blasts, assuring her a safe mooring. Soon after, Pilot Oliver Riddle, Mechanic the boatswain, and two further sailors set off in the longboat to extend salutations to the governor of Cape Verde along with an invitation for supper.

IN WHICH A GOVERNOR PRESSES HIS ADVANTAGE

The following afternoon, Governor Pero Mesquinho embarked through the Gallant's hatch and followed Captain Josiah Gladstone to his private quarters. Attired in grease-stained breeches and a top coat of declarative red, Mesquinho was that ridiculous type of European who insisted upon ruffles, brocade, and a talcumed wig even in deplorable heat. His physical health clearly had suffered from a royal diet of meat pies, organ stews, and brandy.

"You must not consume the foods of these islands," he warned Gladstone in a soupy Portuguese accent as Zosime Montfort served him salt beef. "They cause the white man to degenerate. Forsooth, a previously distinguished gentleman – hailing, as myself, from Lisboa – lost his manhood due to his taste for coconut, manioc, sweet potatoes, and maize. First he failed to grow a beard. Then his pecker shriveled entirely!"

Before negotiating, Gladstone entertained a tedious discussion of the latest news, scuttlebutt, and rumor. Hovering behind the bed curtains pretending to be a chamber maid, Ash followed each turn and logged every tidbit.

Eventually, the captain confessed that a supply of trade goods adequate to recompense the Portuguese governor for his assistance had not survived the storm. What proceeded was a flagrant abuse of Gladstone's feeble position.

"In return for the timber and cables you require, I shall issue a bill," Mesquinho declared. "The next England-bound vessel sailing from our shores will deliver it to your benefactor in London, Lord Bloodworth. It will stipulate that in addition to principal, he must repay me arrears compounded on a monthly basis."

"I thought Catholics did not practice usury," Gladstone snapped.

Mesquinho smirked. "The righteous call it *interest* in order to please the ears of God. A rate of six percent seems just."

Gladstone steeled his gaze upon clouds drenching the distant mountains of Porto Praia. He recognized that unless some miracle occurred to reverse his ill fortune, upon the Gallant's return to London, the debt would destroy him. This even after taking into account his and Lucien Gunn's earnings from short-selling indentureds. No longer would he be able to provide for his wife and six children. In all likelihood, the courts would charge him with criminal negligence, gross misconduct, and intent to defraud the shipowners. After enduring a sham trial, he would be sentenced to Marshalsea, the debtor's prison.

"If you offer me what remains of your private stores of middling wines and preserved meats imported from the mother countries, Captain Gladstone, I might as well grant permission for two of your men to poach wild game from our island," Mesquinho offered, enjoying thoroughly his advantage at the bargaining table.

Gladstone kicked the wall with his boot. "Have me suck a plate of bricks, why don't you?" he gnarled. The thought of surrendering his few remaining luxuries spiked his blood to a boil. Yet he was aware of his empty hand. "So be it."

IN WHICH A SERVANT CELEBRATES AND A CAPTAIN SUFFERS

As the Gallants slogged through scorching sunlight and mists of mosquitoes to rehabilitate the foremast, its rigging, and the architecture of the orlop, Billy Creed and Fintan O'Lorcan scurried away each morning in the longboat. In the evening, the two strikers would reappear aboard the Gallant lacquered in dust and perspiration. Much to the crew's astonishment, their small vessel almost tipped over with game and kidnapped livestock.

"You resemble Noah with his arc of beasts," commented Zosime, clapping his friend on the back.

Within days, sunset heralded the most triumphant hour for the sailors. They enjoyed banquets of fresh kill. Fin developed a particular fondness for flamingo, which yielded a lean, black meat. Its tongue tasted like a musty oyster. Cape Verdean rum, a fiery fluid distilled from the dregs of sugar cane mills, also delighted the men.

One moonlit eve, Billy Creed recounted an illegal trespass upon a local farm. "Ain't never seen a boy nab a chicken like this one," he said, spanking playfully the fuzz overtaking Fin's shaved skull.

Fin offered a humble grin.

"Listen to what he does," Creed urged. "Just before daybreak, we prowl by the glim of lanterns into the coops. Fin, he goes like this-" he waddled like a penguin, causing a dozen tars to burst into laughter. "Then he employs his Irish secret: He thrusts the lantern straight into those clucking faces. The chickens freeze, as if facing the Second Coming. Quick as a lick, the lad snatches them over the wings, as easy as plucking tomatoes off the vine!"

The men exploded with cheers. Fin blushed, cheeks aglow with the warmth of long-absent joy.

Gladstone reveled not. In sharp contrast to his men, he succumbed further to dour thoughts each day. One morning, he refused to climb out of bed. "My skull feels trapped in a head-crusher. How is it yet another curse plagues me?"

Ash moved to massage him about the temples, but he shooed her away. "I shall fetch a cup of water," she offered.

"For heaven's sake, at least one time might you prove yourself useful?" he complained.

"What, Sir, is your desire?" she replied curtly.

"Summon Lucien Gunn."

The sailing master's eyes saucered when he entered the captain's chamber at Aisling's behest. "Sir?"

"Venture ashore to inspect the goods the governor said we might purchase for trade along the Gold Coast," Gladstone commanded. "The rendezvous is set upon the docks at ten of the clock. Trust not a fleabite in that dog Mesquinho. Ensure the quality and the price, as it shall determine our livelihood."

"Of course, Cap'n," Lucien replied with a small bow.

Ash cleared her throat. "Might I beg a favor of you, sir? As this island boasts a Catholic church, I thought I might visit? It's been an age since I confessed."

From where he lay propped against the bed pillows, Gladstone scorned. "Have you fouled your good Catholic soul, Aisling O'Lorcan? Are you desperate to seek repentance because, of late, you run about with lascivious excess?"

"Aye, I shall wash away my sins," she responded tartly.

"Even Catholics – whether barbarous Irish or conniving Spaniards – are vessels of God, Sir," Lucien inserted himself into the conversation. "We debate not the condition of Negroes, widely understood to wander beyond the Lord's reach as they possess no soul."

Gladstone narrowed his eyes. "Do not sport with me, Lucien Gunn."

"I do fear heavenly consequences unless we bequeath the lass her quest for communion with Christ," Lucien dared to argue. "We need not tempt further ill fortune."

"Master Gunn gets it correct," Ash said, approaching the bedside with eyes hard as agate. "Hazard not more curses upon us, Josiah."

Vexed, he spun away. Then he launched to his feet, marched to the bay windows, and heedlessly began roughing up his maps. Lucien and Aisling regarded each other slyly without moving. Several sullen moments later, Gladstone conceded. "But keep a watchful eye," he cautioned Lucien. "If there be any skullduggery, I shall strangle both your necks."

IN WHICH AN OPPORTUNITY IS PRESENTED

Lucien tarried not in punting the skiff given the captain's mood. He oared the Gallant's landing vessel to shore whilst Ash, hunched at the opposite end, debated his motives. Vaguely, she feared he might attempt to take advantage of her womanhood. But no, Lucien would not make such a move against the captain. Nor did she believe that he possessed a rapacious nature.

As the distance to the Praia quay narrowed, she noted the commerce congesting it. Three more trading ships had anchored. The dock bustled with dark-skinned local merchants, coffles of enslaved Africans, and ruddy European sailors collapsing in the heat. Beyond lay a beachhead crowded by palm and kapok trees, and from there rose vibrant sugar cane fields, hills covered in lavender, and finally, steep mountain faces. It was a resplendent place, she thought.

"All the colors of this land chatter at once. Even the earth is red like forgotten blood," she observed half-aloud.

"The church stands there, facing the plaza," Lucien gestured, indicating a modest stone steeple. Forcefully, he projected the skiff to shore.

As they stepped onto the rocky beach, Aisling's patience evaporated. "Speak plain your intentions, Lucien. Why did you intervene on my behalf?"

"Trust in me," he replied.

She did no such thing. Yet she had to admit that in her month upon the Gallant, she had known Lucien Gunn to be a reasonable man. Certainly, she could speak better on his character than upon most other tars aside from the captain, Zosime Montfort, and perhaps Billy Creed.

Holding out his hand, he led her up a rugged incline to the roadstead. Here, he veered her vision away from the bustle of Praia and toward the headlands, where the path was decorated by the occasional man on horseback. A group of women ambled by, dressed in brilliantly-dyed fabrics and balancing calabashes atop their heads. Ash was entranced.

"The island missionaries dwell over yon," Lucien said, indicating a series of thatched roof structures nestled amongst the hills. He paused, fidgeting.

"Declare yourself, Lucien," she demanded.

He cast his eyes about sheepishly. "A ripe opportunity presents itself this minute, Aisling O'Lorcan. You might escape."

Her face contorted with emotion as she questioned the ludicrous statement. *What manner of cruelty contrives Lucien for his amusement? This man – who purchased me from the Butcher – this man offers me freedom?*

"Flee for those refuges," he said with not a hint of mockery in his voice. "The Catholic Priests will be kind to you, I wager."

"Why do you say this?" she stammered.

"Because you're a slave, and you might escape and live free." His eyebrows were arched, his tone earnest. "Imagine. You abide with the missionaries, deciding if you remain in Cape Verde or leave. As you yourself can perceive, the bay flourishes with commerce. Easy enough to encounter an obliging vessel. And like that, you are delivered back upon the shores of home. Or off to the New World, if that be your hankering."

"Clap your mouth, Lucien Gunn," she blurted, alarmed. The picture painted by his words was so outstanding that it clobbered her with fear.

"Ain't laying a plot against you, Ash, of that I assure you," he said, reaching a tentative hand to touch her forearm. "Tis possible to fashion a cover for your absence for a day or two. Gladstone, beleaguered by insolvencies, likely will surrender you soon enough. Next, we engage in the treacherous business of buying African captives. I can replenish the ship with a fresh wench for our captain, lickety-do."

"I am without parallel, Lucien. None alive can replace me!" Ash snapped.

"Pray your pardon." He slumped, eyes upon the earth. "Tis true. You are a phenomenon, Aisling. An angel meeting her wings after resurrection."

Her heart banged against her ribs. Desire for the future Lucien painted twisted her with distrust, fear, and outright anger. When at last she spoke, only croaks arose. "I... cannot."

"Fintan?" he asked.

She nodded, tears streaming down her cheeks. Ash could not depart unless her brother were by her side. But that was only a piece of the larger truth. What she did not admit to Lucien was that Josiah Gladstone tethered her to the Gallant, as well. It was possible, it occurred to her in those mosquito-blasted moments upon the dusty road of Porto Praia, that she had fallen in love with the captain.

Suddenly, Lucien regretted his actions. Of truth, he had known that she would refuse – he understood her loyalty to her brother. He had intended only to cultivate her trust and affection. He had not anticipated how sacked she would be by his proposal. Foraging a clout from his pocket, he offered it to her.

She tamped tears with the linen square. Then, she threw back her shoulders and plastered upon her face a strained smile. "Shall we to church, then?"

Lucien guided Ash to port, where she might confess and he might conduct his trade.

Six days later, the Gallant's condition had been righted – sails repaired, orlop restored. Moreover, thanks to the efforts of Billy Creed and Fin, the pen was full to bursting with plundered livestock. Zanzibar the cook had worked tirelessly to salt and preserve the hunting team's windfall.

Upon the morning of their departure from Cape Verde, the Gallants completed their final task: Loading the commodities that Lucien Gunn had purchased on credit in Porto Praia. When bricks of richly-colored Cape Verdean cloth crowded the ship's belly, Captain Gladstone bid a stiff adieu to the repulsive Governor Mesquinho.

Ash was surprised by the shift in her sentiments since the island excursion. Her experience at Confession – *beg forgiveness, cease your sinning, speak your Hail Marys* – had rung hollow, and her doubts about her faith had multiplied. Meanwhile, Lucien's proposal that she escape indentured servitude had served to solidify her loyalty to Josiah Gladstone. If she abandoned him, she doubted she would find a better man. And if she tempted the journey alone, how could she keep safe? She knew how penalizing the world could be – especially to a woman.

Aside from which, she longed only to drown her body in his.

Nestled in the captain's great room, she experimented with new positions for her willing body. She chaperoned Josiah's hands and mouth over her, abandoning herself to ecstasy. She clasped knees above his head and demanded he ejaculate upon her heaving breasts. She moaned for him to drive his shaft more forcefully into her pussy. She begged him to pound her into oblivion.

Always, the captain obliged. But with his own pleasure came the uneasy realization that although he wielded rank over her, she was the commander of his ship.

IN WHICH CHRISTMAS IS CELEBRATED

The Gallant had applied a mostly southwestern bearing around the Iberian Peninsula and the western protrusion of the African continent. Now, for the first time since quitting London five weeks ago, she traveled in a southeasterly direction, pursuing the curve of the Guinea coast. Gladstone gathered the standing officers upon the quarterdeck to plot the next phase of their journey.

"We ought jollify," Lucien Gunn suggested. "The Christ child's birth stands but two days hence."

"Parliament of England be damned – that dour lot may forbid celebrating on land, but they ain't banning Christmas revelry aboard our ship!" Mechanic concurred.

The French Catholic quartermaster Septime Devign sniggered. "Such a *ridicule* piece of legislation, typical of your Protestant lack of *joie de vivre*. To declare a holy celebration too pagan, absurd!"

"Quite right," the captain agreed.

Zanzibar labored to prepare a feast including choice portions of flamingo, tortoise, and iguana accompanied by roasted cassava and sweet potatoes. It culminated with a heavenly dessert he had invented – bananas flambéed with cane sugar and rum. The Gallants spent the better part of Christmas day eating, guzzling grog, and gamboling with dice. Billy Creed produced a fiddle that he had "liberated" from a Cape Verdean farm, and a half dozen tars took turns singing bawdy ballads.

Fin, seeking the company of Zosime Montfort, stumbled across his sister upon the top deck. They had exchanged few words these past weeks, as she had kept mainly to the captain's quarters and he had been occupied by foraging food onshore. As he caught sight of her standing at the gunnels gazing at the stars, Fin sensed her contentment. He stepped near enough that their shoulders touched.

They listened to the howls of laughter and curses at lost coins that scattered across the breeze. "How have you abided, Ash, whilst a servant upon this vessel?" he asked.

Her mouth turned up at the corners. "Well, Fin, well."

"To hear the men tell it, you and the captain have developed quite the fondness for one another." His tone was absent its customary light-heartedness.

"What's it to you?" she snapped, disconcerted.

"What's it to *me*, dear Sister? What's it to all Irish? To each and every buried heart of Clan Lorcan? What would Athair say? Rory? Have you fallen under the spell of the enemy, yes or no?"

"*Enemy?* Do you remain so simple at age thirteen as to consider Josiah Gladstone our foe?" she scoffed, adopting the attitude of a mother scolding her child. "The more I mature, dear Brother, the more I get to realizing: We all are players – like as those tars dicing now – in a mighty game of bones. It dictates, through some choice but mostly chance, our destiny. Josiah Gladstone is of English heritage, true enough. But the enemy? Certes not. He merely plays the game adeptly. Clever and disciplined, he is also patient and generous. He is no adversary; he is an ally."

"You traipse in perversions, playing bed-games with this English captain like a first lady of Shakespeare! What role does he take? That of the prince of House Montague? And you, the tragic young Juliet? You and your Romeo are no star-crossed lovers, Ash. The actual drama you enact is one of mutual debasement."

"How dare you accuse me so!"

"Tis not I who throws accusations. God stands in judgment upon you always, Ash," Fintan chided. "He is with you inside the captain's chambers, observing all. *There is no creature that is not manifest in His sight, but all things are naked and open unto the eyes of Him with whom we have to give account.*"

She trained a firm look upon him. "Aye, and this, Fintan: *Beloved, if our heart condemn us not, then we have confidence toward God.*"

Her brother chuckled more aggressively this time. "Cherished Aisling, do you see not how the captain tinkers with you? For him, you are property and no better. His affection commences with your vulnerability. Say this eve or the next, you utter *nay* to his groping. What, suspect you, happens then? Do you trust he shall oblige your preferences?"

"Aye, he shall. You believe yourself to be a clever lad, Fintan O'Lorcan, but I am a grown woman. My life includes mature happenings, the likes of which a *child* cannot grasp," she defended.

Then she felt her heart soften. She had said it herself: Fin was only a boy. A child forced to cope from a young age with terror, warfare, starvation, and grief. "Let us be glad. We both have adapted to foul circumstances. Just like me, you improved your station aboard this ship by befriending our *enemies*, as you persist in calling them. And at the end of days, we shall face the same almighty Lord." She reached her arm around his slender waist. "My cherished hope is that we meet a God who enjoys forgiving."

Captain Gladstone lurked about, evidently the sole Gallant whose spirits had not been lifted by the festivities. His unraveling escalated when Aisling's moon cycle commenced. He lamented that if the toxic fluid touched him, it would further contaminate his fate. "You shall sleep upon the settee till not one speck of the vile excretions soil you!" he commanded.

Ash rejected the captain's beliefs, recalling the Butcher's gentle words upon her first blood: *Tis not a curse, as some imbecilic men think*. But she sealed her mouth shut.

Another matter was tunneling self-doubt into Josiah Gladstone's spirit, as well. Pestered by thoughts of Aisling, he stared sleepless at the ceiling of his chamber at night, pondering her curiosity, her aptitude for navigational studies, her rapid adjustment to life aboard the ship. She triumphed over any challenge. Then, of course, there was her hunger for him, which was unlike anything he ever had experienced. *Her* passion aroused *him*. It was a confounding paradox.

On previous journeys, the captain scarcely had showed interest in the servants he took as lovers. In fact, throughout his four decades of life, he had felt little esteem for God's subordinate creations – even his wife. But he could not diminish Ash so comfortably. She ambushed his opinions and conquered his convictions, until he began to question his entire world view.

Of late, Captain Josiah Gladstone felt compelled to admit: *Ash is a woman, but a being equal to myself.* And if such were true, then logic obliged him to collide with the following conclusion: *Others I have bought and sold as property – not only indentured servants, but also enslaved Africans – might have stood equal to me, as well.* If such was true, what did it mean for the fate of his soul? What manner of living had he chosen?

As master of a slaving vessel, did he do the Devil's bidding? Perhaps this was the why God had delivered upon him a black curse.

IN WHICH VIOLENCE BEGETS VIOLENCE

The Gallants slipped into 1654 and Aisling past her sixteenth Saint's day with scarcely any notice. A full week after decamping from Cape Verde, the Guineaman encroached upon the Sierra Leone River. Once passed, ocean currents shifted dramatically and vessels no longer could return straight to Europe. The sea would spirit them eastward along the shoreline of West Africa, to the Kingdom of Gabon and beyond.

They were, in other words, overrunning the point of no return. Sensing this, not only the captain but every tar who previously had made this journey turned more peevish. They were haunted by their appointment with a place that terrified them like no other.

"Sailors speak of Africa as a *white man's grave,*" Gladstone babbled to Aisling. "Lethal perils besiege us. Fevers alone might waste an entire crew: malaria, typhus, yellow fever, the bloody flux. Small pox abounds upon the coast, and leprosy pervades the hinterland. As well, infestations torment: parasites, mosquitoes, fleas, lice, chigoes, ringworm. Beyond such unnatural cruelties, we compete also with beasts slinging butchery. The natives of these lands are fast, strong, and adrift from God."

"You speak as a man afraid," she said.

"Mother of Christ, I am. Just as you ought be. Better clasp tight your rosary. For I have yet to remark upon the ships flying Low-Dutch and Portuguese banners that pace continuously these coastal waters. They fire upon independent traders such as us. Nor have I mentioned the *caboceers* – the criminals what run the trading factories, never to be trusted."

"But Josiah," Ash intervened, "this is not your virgin undertaking. Thrice already you have weathered the dark continent as captain."

"Forsooth, my dove, I have survived Africa six times. Even so, I shiver as we reach her shores." From his cupboard, he retrieved a crystal, settling upon intemperance.

Rum spilled across his chin as he gulped. "The Dark Continent is both a mystery of chaos and a monster of contagion."

He poured a second glass, offering it to her. She refused. She had grown weary of his complaints. Standing straight before him, she clasped his two shoulders. "You must quit this gloomy speculation, Josiah. Whatever matter of opposition the wide world brings, you are equipped to face it. Now shutter your infantile whining. No woman hungers for a champion who shrinks before a challenge. Nor does any man follow him! Already your bleak bearing sabotages your leadership. The Gallants murmur. I have by my own ears heard their whisperings of doubt. Mutiny breeds—"

Erupting as a volcano, Gladstone shoved her away so forcefully that she fell to the floor. Blood pounded in his chest. His ears rang. His mind buzzed with alcohol and anger. He raised an arm as if to strike. "Dare not raise your tongue at me! When next I desire the counsel of a whore, I shall toss you two shillings and stuff my cock down your throat."

She pushed back against the wall, the color gone from her face. "Josiah, it is still me, my love—"

"You reckon us partners in thought?"

"Sir, I did not intend a morsel of impudence. My words were drawn from a great well of affection," she argued.

Gladstone spat upon the carpet. "If one man outside this cabin overheard even one phrase of our discourse, I would be the eternal butt of the crew's jests, never to recover their respect."

"Pray, I only meant to help!"

"By *insulting* me, Aisling, Wench of Clan Loran? By suggesting that I am inadequate, incompetent, brain sick?"

"No, Josiah, no such thing. I view you with the Heavenly light of a brilliant mind and a true heart." Tears dashed her pale cheeks.

"Liar! Irish witch-hag! Catholic wretch!" Gladstone's voice boomed with the force of a cannon. "You imagine, insignificant child, that *you* can inform *me* about the condition of *my* ship? You fancy yourself a captain now that your feeble mind has drunk up a few piddling lessons in reading the stars?"

She swallowed and forced herself to stop speaking.

But Josiah Gladstone was not appeased. The damage to his already fragile sense of himself had been too great. He grabbed her by the forearm, lifted her like a scrap of flotsam, and carried her across the great room to the bed.

She snatched at the quilts and scrambled to the furthest corner. With nowhere left to flee, she felt pathetic, powerless. Hauling the sheets to her chin, she braced herself.

"What's the ruin with you?" Gladstone snarled. His eyes flashed with rage and unhinged desire. He pulled her down and lay his body across hers. His hands were cruel. Previously, he had been cautious to conceal their callous strength. But not this time.

"Stop this horror, Josiah! No! STOP!" Ash cried, battling against him. She raked nails across his arms. Then she cocked a knee and launched it into his groin.

A flare of pain sped through his senses, but the bold move served only to sever honor from instinct. Grasping the bedpost with one hand, he dedicated his other to steering his erection into her clenched sex. There was no rhythm, no pleasure, no joy in it; just a gruesome motion repeated over and again. A spike of vomit invaded her mouth.

Upon that shuddering bed, Josiah Gladstone confronted his genuine nature. He was a trader who stole human beings and sold them as beasts. He despised himself. And he despised the woman who had made him see the truth.

Ash could not breathe. Gladstone's palm sealed her mouth. The violence filled her body and mind. What broke her was this: She had come to love this man. She had trusted him, and now he betrayed her. Yet in the midst of the horror, she encountered also a cold calm. A purpose. A warrior within.

A noise startled them both. The plank door banged open – even though Gladstone had sealed it, as always, from the interior. In an instant, Fin had overrun the length of the captain's chamber. In his hand he carried a pistol won from his raids with Billy Creed upon Cape Verde.

Stunned by the intrusion, Gladstone hurled himself forward. But his pants, pulled down around his knees, and sent him crashing to the floor. He thrashed about, searching for his gun slings.

Ash shrieked.

Fin heard nothing. The hatred roaring through his ears deafened like whitewater. Standing over Captain Gladstone, he leveled the shooting iron expertly and snicked the hammer.

The matchlock fired but, ever unreliable, the shot merely skimmed Gladstone's forehead. Bleeding and disoriented, the captain lunged at his dressing bureau, attempting to redeem his cutlash.

Fin flung himself upon the man. Exploiting the hilt of the pistol, he pounded Gladstone's skull.

"NO!" Aisling screamed. She leapt onto Fin's back, wrapping her arms around his.

She underestimated her brother's strength. He had grown these past weeks, thanks to ample nourishment and exertion. He pushed her aside, heaved the pistol high, and brought it crashing down, braining the captain.

"The yearning for freedom is unopposable!" he shouted as he ended Josiah Gladstone's life. "No creature under God is at peace without it."

Even after the captain had ceased moving, Fin continued to swing his arm up and down, using the pistol as an axe. Gladstone's brain splattered every corner of the room.

Responding to the ruckus, Mechanic tumbled in with sleep still in his eyes. He captured the Irish boy and secured him to the bedframe with a belt.

Ash, lashed with bolts of blood, stood stricken and still, momentarily dislodged from awareness.

"You can be certain as sorrow he dies for this," Mechanic growled.

IN WHICH A MERCY IS DONE

"These are unsparing men," Lucien Gunn said quietly. "When a fellow's life is calloused with spite and dashed prospects, it contributes to a way thinking whereby vengeance *is* justice. Men such as they don't deliberate a verdict; they only choose the most repugnant option."

He skidded a chair nearer to Aisling, who jerked back and forth upon hands and knees holystoning the planks of the captain's cabin, attempting to rid it of blood. "Have you ever witnessed a keelhauling?" he asked, knowing that she had not.

She did not acknowledge the question.

"I'm not saying that Fintan doesn't *deserve* an end for murdering our captain," he continued. "But mark me, keelhauling is a torment as gruesome as being hung upon the cross like our Lord Jesus Christ."

She peeked at him through her tresses. Her eyes, red from sobbing, were glowing cinders.

Lucien shifted uneasily. Then he began constructing for her an honest depiction of the reckoning that awaited her brother. "With the rigging clutching him by limb and breast, they lower him over the bow and scourge him beneath the keel, drawing the hauling lines till he makes an appearance again at the stern. Held so long underwater, the boy's lungs get overtaken by saltwater and, generally speaking, his breathing ceases. If, however, he gasps still with life, they repeat the hideous exercise till he breathes no more."

Leaning even closer, Lucien draped his hands over his knees. "But that ain't the worst of it. The bottom of any vessel long at sea gets studded with barnacles jagged as razors. I vow to you, as I have witnessed it before – the condemned, scored all over, bleed from every part of their bodies. Their faces, especially their noses, look as though they've been gnawed off by rats. The first turn alone strips his clothes, peels him red as flank steak, and tears his skin to shreds. Scarcely anyone can bear the sight of it, no matter how devilish the tar may be. Tis not possible, I assure you, to endure the horror befalling your beloved *kin*."

He had her attention at last. Ash gazed with dread rolling over her. She scuffled toward him upon her knees. "Help me," she pleaded.

"I have no influence over his fate," he rebuffed.

Her face warped with dismay. "Then why abuse me with such a grisly tale?"

He steadied her by the shoulders. "I can only figure one remedy." He pressed into Aisling's hand an item he had been concealing.

Sight unseen, she recognized instantly what it was. The forge of the blade was true, the grind sheer, the point a faultless peak. Her gaze held Lucien's, questioning.

"For both your welfares, spare your brother this execution," he muttered. "Tis a mercy." He searched her face for some emotion, but she had vacated the present.

"Get to it, then," he ordered, interrupting her reverie. "You have short of an hour."

Minutes later, the complement gathered upon deck for the funeral honors of their erstwhile captain. Gladstone's body had been laid into a modest casket engineered by the ship's carpenters. Unlike the common tar, whose remains were entombed in hammocks, the captain was befitted with a coffin.

Ash slunk into the orlop, where she reunited with her brother. The boy was leashed in irons. Behind the bulkhead, goats bleated and chickens clucked.

Fin hauled himself to standing, his blue eyes painfully knowing. "Don't be afraid, Ash," he assured her in lilting

Gaelic that sounded to her like a lullaby. "For each ecstatic hour given, life demands a price. Then one fine day, anguish knocks at the door – and the debt is paid in tears."

Aloft, Septime Devign recited scripture. In a raspy voice, Lucien Gunn proclaimed the assets of the departed Josiah Gladstone.

Ash conducted Fin toward a sprig of light breaking through the floorboards and kneeled beside him. Her throat felt crammed with stones. She could not manage any words. She only could throw her arms around her dear brother and weep.

"I'd live this same tortured life again because it gifted me with so many cherished days alongside you and Rory," he sighed. He displayed his best grin. "Never did I crave a thing more than to succeed beyond both you boastful cunts."

She clutched his face. "Yours is a beauty beyond knowing, Fin. A greatness only God can put to words."

Feet shuffled as the crew distributed brandy and rustled their voices into a shanty.

Ash shifted behind Fin and murmured into his ear, "Look now. Envisage Máthair and Athair and Rory. Summon Beatha and little baby Grace. She most especially ought be lavished with robbed years. Older now, she arrives to us with hair of rich gold and eyes, like yours, of crystal blue. Do you see her sauntering over the snow-covered hills of Ulster, decorated in a fox cape and a smock of true saffron? Behold our sister, watching over our lands like the stars watch over all creation."

Josiah Gladstone's final rites were punctuated with a blank shot from the stern cannon. Several nine-pound balls were tethered to his coffin. When the men overturned it from the gunnels, it carried the captain to an unmarked grave at the bottom of the sea.

Ash gripped Fin's skene firmly and aligned its edge with the pulse throbbing in his neck. He drew a sweet, long breath and demanded, "Swear you always will *insist upon living*."

"I swear it," she whispered. Recalling as best she could the words Rory had recited to Cormac the Younger upon taking his position as tanist of Clan Lorcan, she added, "*If I break my oath, may the land open to swallow me, the sea rise to drown me, and the sky fall upon me.*"

Fin draped a hand over hers, steadying her hold upon the knife's hilt. "Arc the grind edge up and then across, just as Rory lessoned us," he instructed.

When the moment came, she did not flinch. She gazed at a thing beyond her, a thing as great and difficult to discern as a secret. Like colors and words and emotions, it was a thing that had no dimension.

And then she unsealed her brother's neck. He wheezed sickeningly before pitching over. She yanked him roughly against her, holding him upright, clutching him to her chest until she bathed in his lifeblood.

She remained bound to him for what might have been a span of minutes or the length of a lifetime. Time was taunting her, just as it had when her mother and sister had burned within the church, and again when she had learned of her father and Rory's death, and again when she had abandoned Fin and been captured by the Butcher. Mourning mutated the running of hours. She had come to regard grief as a poison because of how it urged her to recollect obsessively every intimate detail of the person she loved, whilst simultaneously distancing her from their memory.

The men aloft began to clamber for justice. They called for Fintan's death as they dragged about the rigging necessary to prosecute the keelhaul.

Hurriedly, she staged her brother's corpse upon the floor. As a keepsake, she snipped a lock of his blonde hair with the skene. It was the same blade that once had belonged to her father and to his father before that – an heirloom stretching back generations, as much an eternal spirit as a weapon. Now, it was the only trace of Clan Lorcan that belonged still to her, and she was the only trace of Clan Lorcan that belonged still to life.

This is it, she pledged to herself, *the final incursion. Fin is the last person I ever shall love, cherish, or lament. From here forward, I entrust and uphold only myself.*

Still distant from the young Irish woman's knowledge, though, were happenings that marked her as not so much alone. Throughout the world, legions of *have nots*, hardened from abuse by their lords and lieges, were condensing their resolve into cold lead. By the clink of coin, stick of blade, and punctuation of gunfire, a novel incarnation of society was commencing in the Western Hemisphere. Soon, it would break with all history, rejecting kings and traditions in favor of opportunity for the commoner, rule of law, and self-determination.

Aisling O'Lorcan tidied her blood-soaked frock and swept the tears from her face. With a heaving sigh and slit-mouthed persistence, she staggered away from the devastated remnants of her former existence and into the Dark Continent's unknown.

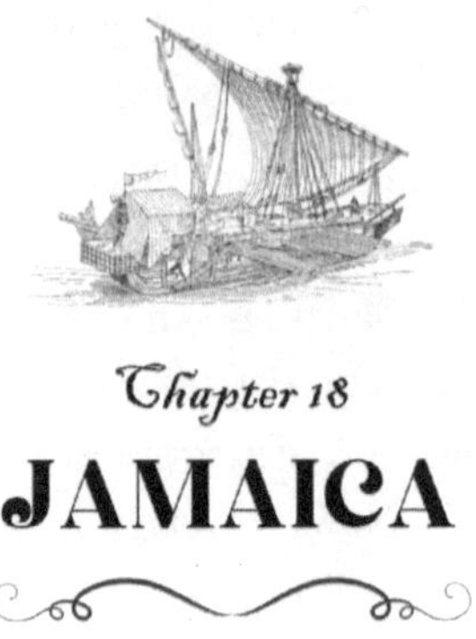

Chapter 18

JAMAICA

IN WHICH WATER BREAKS

JoJo had been struck wan by Nani's bloodletting. She refuted her mother's violent campaign. Moreover – or perhaps more accurately – she could not resolve it in her conscience. Terrorism was not a habit they previousy had embraced. Now, murder attended all Nani's successes as she assaulted don Paco de Proenza's troops and raided estates owned by the Spanish gentry.

Unwilling to participate, JoJo had remained at the Windward Maroon's temporary command post, which stood shielded in the Pitted Country. It consisted of nothing more than a jam of huts hastily forged from thatched palm branches. They had built one to protect Anapa, who was on the brink of childbirth, as well as the wounded and 30 new arrivals from Lubolo's tribe and the Tello plantation. The location boasted a grove of banana trees that provided easy sustenance, and protection by way of rocky precipices on all sides.

The yowl of a cat set on fire echoed through the narrow canyon. JoJo recognized at once the voice of Anapa. "JoJo! Sipopi!"

JoJo tore into Anapa's hut. The discovery she ploughed into trapped the breath in her throat. The usually indomitable woman – who had endured enslavement for a decade and Maroon hardships for the past five years – had been reduced to an incoherent mass. She lay in a puddle, face twisted.

"Her water broke," Sipopi panted as she rushed upon the scene.

"The gravest of earthly trials awaits! And my beloved gone to war," Anapa wailed. "Tis beyond what any might bear!"

"We are here, sweet one," said Sipopi. She propped Anapa to standing and walked her several tentative steps outside the hut into the sunlight. "Recall how Nani selected this place? The spirit blessings abound and encircle you. Wol discovered the birthing stone. Your true-born Maroon baby will be delivered safely into the arms of freedom."

Anapa bent over her belly and moaned.

"Come, come, all is as fated to be," Sipopi comforted. She and JoJo guided Anapa gradually up the hillside. "Get to moving, that we may channel the enchantments of Obiya. Only steps further, sweet one."

Screened in the woods rested a rock smoothed by scores of backs. With a height of three feet, it offered a gently sloping surface ideal for supporting feminine grit. "Ease your body here upon the birthing stone."

Gripping her sides, Anapa howled and collapsed onto the forest floor. "Not possible. Wringing agony grows in waves."

IN WHICH MAROONS PLOT A RAID

Nani and her select group of three dozen hellions readied their assail upon the haughtiest estate of Guadibocoa. For this operation, their leader preferred an elite group that could capitalize upon Maroon stealth. Rallying her people to destruction, her intentions were bleakly fundamental. Under the tutelage of Gaspar Carvalhal, she had remodeled her methods to resemble more closely those of the pyrates and Brethren of the North Coast.

Can you kill, my lovesome? He had asked upon their most recent congress.

Copious blood, Gaspar had explained, reverberated straight into Caribbee hearts. News swept from island to island, passed between innkeepers, fish mongers, carpenters, birds, bawds, and sailors, transforming truth into apocryphal testimony. In manufacturing diabolic fame, Maroon warriors – like rogues and sea rovers – might achieve the one outcome sweeter than defeating an enemy in battle: They might attain surrender without raising a single cutlash or firing a single gun.

Given the nomadic nature of Maroon existence and their lean numbers, Nani had deemed this tactic genius. Yet of truth, her vindictive appetite was further stoked by her loathing for bondage. Having been enslaved at age nine and endured for over two decades the whims of her masters, she believed opening the gateways to freedom necessitated war, cataclysm, and decimation.

When battling in the bush, the Maroons conducted themselves as pinpoint assassins. When assaulting estates, however, they acted as anarchists. In both cases, they followed the tactical commands of Nani and Alzo, their militia captain.

In Africa, Alzo had earned his coin as a captor of humans employed by the kingdom of Kongo. But one day, his greedy Portuguese partner had accepted the high price placed upon Alzo's own head. Sold into captivity, Alzo had endured four grim years of forced labor upon the sugarcane fields of Jamaica before escaping. During this time, he had vowed to harness his combat training to destroy the trade he once had abetted.

The estate they would attack this time was owned by don Francisco de Leiva but leased to his sister, doña Violante de Leiva y Espinoza, and her husband, don Garcilasco de Blas Sánchez. Naturally, the majority of the profits gained from the tobacco and cane fields were shunted directly into don Francisco's treasury.

Nani had travailed here as a house servant, cleaning, cooking and serving meals in the *hacienda*. It was from this estate that she and JoJo had escaped eight years past. Relative to many, they had been fortunate. Doña Violante was a mistress touched by humanity. She had yielded to Nani's excruciating distress and safeguarded JoJo, her second child born upon the estate. But she had not demonstrated the same sympathy with Nani's first infant. With prompt decisiveness, Violante had sold the newborn boy to a human trafficker who operated, she had informed Nani, upon a different island, one called Porto Rico.

As the years passed, Nani had interred the broken portions of her heart and learned to accept the kindness her mistress showed her and JoJo. Yet never would Nani forgive Violante. A jailor was a jailor, no matter how pretty her tea sets and gowns, how warm her occasional words of thanks, or how sincere her efforts to provide her house servants with "a proper education."

In preparation for the attack, the Windward Maroons dwelled for a time in the bushland fringing Violante's estate. Several days prior to raiding any property, they culled the loyalty of thralls who demonstrated a passion for freedom – those whom their owners considered to be *recalcitrant* and *incurable of defiance*. To these acolytes, they revealed their schemes.

Upon this occasion, Nani sent two scouts to pass under the gaze of the Spanish guards and into the slave quarters of the tobacco estate: the loyal Maroon Santo, and Juliana, a beautiful young woman from the Tello estate who had chosen for herself the free name of Jubilee. Nani felt Jubilee would prove most convincing to the fresh recruits, as she herself had been liberated from bondage only two weeks previously. The two scouts gathered 15 people to join the rebellion.

When the designated night arrived, the recruits awaited with trepidation the moment when the Maroon warriors would crash into their estate. Together, under the dim light of a waxing moon, they would whale justice upon the masters.

IN WHICH PRAYERS ARE RECITED

"Heaven above, pity my suffering!" Anapa wailed.

JoJo and Sipopi had heaved her pregnant body upon the birthing stone, but their friend continued to despair. Sipopi gave her a mango seed to suck upon and massaged her back and belly. JoJo recited from the Book of Psalms:

For thou hast possessed my reins: thou hast covered me in my mother's womb. I will praise thee; for I am fearfully and wonderfully made. My substance was not hid from thee, when I was made in secret, and curiously wrought in the lowest parts of the earth. Thine eyes did see my substance…

By now, the other women of the Windward Maroon tribe who had not joined the raid also were arriving upon the sacred site, bringing with them healing balms and calabashes of cotton root to ease the labor pains. They lit a fire and burned upon it branches of cleansing sage. Lubolo's former wife Madrileña followed them. She stood by Anapa's head, bathing her brow in cool spring water.

The diverse collection of a dozen survivors chanted prayers to every god in every language known to them, praising spirits and the lifegiving powers of the female form. Then, gradually, they fell into a single repetitive, uplifting chant: *Hey bomba hey na nana!*

Nothing eased Anapa's torment. Her screams did not end. She writhed and clasped her back. JoJo peered between her legs. Though the sacred channel had opened for birth, no crown as yet could be detected.

"The baby's shoulder is stuck," Sipopi announced, eyes wide with fear. She brushed lips upon JoJo's ear, lest the others overhear. "Pray the spirits save them."

IN WHICH MAROONS ATTACK

The warriors applied the Obiya cloaking and invincibility rubs that tirelessly Nani had prepared as she recited Bible verses, calling forth the holy wrath of the Creator:

Blessed be the Lord my strength, which teacheth my hands to war and my fingers to fight. My goodness and my fortress, my high tower and my deliverer, my shield, and He in whom I trust: who subdueth my people under me…

From out the underbrush, the Maroons entered tobacco fields colored sterling by frost and moonlight. Santo, Alzo and Wol had sheered to perfection the edge of every machete, hatchet, and adze, entrusting the hush of cold steel over the ringing report of gunpowder. This way, no tell would alert the masters' or drovers' ears.

Bow thy heavens, O Lord, and come down: Touch the mountains and they shall smoke. Cast forth lightning and scatter them: Shoot out thine arrows and destroy them. Send thine hand from above, rid me and deliver me out of great waters, from the hands of strange children whose mouth speaketh vanities and their right hand is a right hand of falsehood.

Alzo steered the party single-file through a passage between the stable and the storehouses. Nani instructed Jubilee to remain there to keep watch. The new tribe member protested. Her argument, voiced too loudly, caused the mastiff hounds to begin barking.

Had Sasa joined the raid, he would have pacified the beasts by speaking their language, telling them of their imminent release from imprisonment should they remain silent. Nani, however, had cast him away on a private errand some two days hence. Fortunately, Jubilee demonstrated her own subtle way with animals, calming the dogs with a nurturing hand.

Slinging into the communal residences of the enslaved, the warriors found waiting the phalanx of rebels. Nani humbled herself upon the earth before them. One glimpse of the legendary Queen of the Windward Maroons grew the number of true believers instantly from 15 to 23.

Alzo, Santo, and Wol organized the near 60 total battlers into four teams of 15. As two groups siphoned toward the flanking stables and shelters to steal livestock and assassinate guards and drovers, Nani and Alzo proceeded with their militias to the *hacienda*. The *casa grande* was a regal domicile of limestone foundation, earth-toned timbers, plastered facades, and clay-tiled roof. The second-floor balustrade commanded a view over the sprawling lands.

Let their way be dark and slippery, and let the Angel of the Lord persecute them… Let destruction come upon him unawares, and let his net that he hath hid catch himself; into that very destruction let him fall.

From out the jute packs worn upon their backs, the Maroons drew stakes bound with turpentine-laced rags. These torches would be lit later. They raised a wiggling ladder constructed from bamboo, clicking it atop the railing. Nani was first to climb. The others followed in a flurry. She commanded her pack to follow Alzo, who sent one group to search the house for weapons and accompanied the other to the children's room.

Previously, Nani had demanded to be left alone for this phase of the attack. As she tiptoed toward the chamber of the master and mistress, her breath raced.

After this I saw in the night visions, and behold, a fourth beast, dreadful and terrible, and strong exceedingly - and it had great teeth. It devoured and broke in pieces, and stamped the residue with its feet, and it was diverse from all beasts that were before it, and it had ten horns.

IN WHICH SKILLS ARE REVEALED

JoJo panicked. Her breathing sped to the pace of hummingbird wings. She was paralyzed at the prospect of losing Anapa and the Windward tribe's first True-Born Maroon. She dared not employ Obiya without her mother's guidance, risking some novice error. Yet if she stood by whilst Anapa died, neither Nani nor Wol ever would forgive her.

From Anapa's head, Madrileña stepped beside JoJo. "You know me not," she spoke softly. "But I come from Spain where I served as midwife. I have attended a birth such as this. I possess the skills to deliver this baby."

JoJo hesitated. One breath. Two. Anapa wailed. Sipopi oozed fear. JoJo stepped aside. "I beg you. Save them both. Please."

Madrileña demanded coconut oil. Sipopi raced to retrieve a calabash from beside the fire. Anointing her hands with the oil, the midwife slid them into the birth canal.

Anapa did not screech in pain as JoJo had anticipated. She fell silent and went utterly still.

"Wake up, mama!" Sipopi shouted, shaking her friend by the arm.

How precious also are thy thoughts unto me, O God! How great is the sum of them! If I should count them, they are more in number than the sand: When I awake, I am still with thee.

JoJo's recitation and as well the women's chanting grew more fervid. One newcomer had fetched a *gumbé* and when she began to drum, the sound traveled as far as the sea.

Steadily, Madrileña worked the fingers of her right hand around the baby's shoulder whilst simultaneously pressing at Anapa's belly with her left. She prayed and breathed and prayed.

The volume of chanting resounded through the canyon. A gust of wind sailed through the branches, adding to the rattling rhythms. The tiny bone slipped free. Madrileña guided the small head forward until she could detect the infant's eyebrows.

"Ayiiiii!" Anapa screamed, awake again.

"Push, push, sweet sister, push!" Sipopi commanded.

Screwing her features into a prune, Anapa lifted herself from the birthing stone and squatted directly upon the earth. Out slipped the baby in a torrent of blood. Madrileña scooped up the slime-covered form, whacking it upon the back with an expression that spoke of her pride. The infant choked, wheezed, then let out a mighty cry.

"Miracle of miracles!" Sipopi celebrated. "She lives!"

"A miracle baby girl," JoJo said, smiling. Anapa fell backward upon the birthing stone, face alight with joy.

IN WHICH MAROONS DELIVER VENGEANCE

The door to the bedchamber moaned as it opened, but the sound vanished amongst the master's snores. Don Francisco's sister and Nani's former mistress, doña Violante de Leiva y Espinoza, lay with a plump leg resting atop the quilt, her chest rising and falling with her own far more delicate respirations.

Not ever in her years of serving doña Violante had Nani glared directly into the white woman's face from mere inches away. She luxuriated now in staring at her former mistress with impunity. Unconsciously, she fingered the lady's gown of fine linen. It tickled her like a dream. She both desired and despised it.

With a grunt, Nani heaved the axe skyward. But her mouth turned dry and dew filled her eyes as blurred memories intruded. Violante cradling JoJo after a knee-scraping accident. Violante singing nursery rhymes to the child. Violante bending over the escritoire, teaching JoJo to read. Nani paused for an expansive instant, mind flipping through alternative futures.

At that moment, doña Violante rolled open her eyes. Still dopey from sleep, her mind gradually distilled the image towering above her: an onyx-skinned woman reaching only five foot two inches in height but wielding an immense axe in her muscled arms. The arrival of recognition astounded her like a star searing the night sky.

"Maria, is that you?!" she questioned, brow twisting with confusion as she called Nani by her enslaved name.

Nani remained inert, willing the woman to slip silently away. It would be so easy for her to escape, for Nani to tell a tale of her absence that night. Instead, Violante shattered the night with a maddening shriek that would not stop.

Her spouse shot upright, terror ruling his face. "Heaven forefends! What *disease*?!"

Don Garcilasco de Blas Sánchez wheeled upon Nani, but his night-linen was convoluted about his legs. With a single sling, she cranked her arm toward the ceiling. Plunged it down. Hitched it upward again. Downward and upward, down and up, pumping with a lunatic rhythm.

Violante wailed endlessly.

Nani's checkered headwrap, donated to her by one of Juan de Serras' sympathetic wives, fluttered loose. A scrunched bank of braids burst across her eyes. Sweat pasted the locks against her cheeks.

By now, crimson pulp pelted the Bible, silver pocket watch, and chinaware pitcher that stood upon the husband's night table. It soared upon the looking glass, ivory comb, and dyed ribbons that lay on Violante's side. It freckled the painting of Pope Innocent X that decorated the wall above the marital bed. The chamber pot was whipped with lurid streaks, as was a child's book of woodcut shapes left idly upon the floor.

As if awakening from a trance, Violante leapt over the bed and moved toward the threshold. Nani obstructed her. Reduced to hysteria, the mistress raced to the open window and lifted a leg, preparing to throw herself 20 feet onto rough ground. Nani prevented this as well, slamming the window closed. Violante scratched at the walls as though she might dig her way through them. She attempted to clamber up to the ceiling in a futile clash with gravity. Then, finally, she backed against the cage of her imprisonment, slumping.

A flutter of regret snuck through Nani's heart when she saw her former mistress cowed into a mewling ball atop the floorboards. Yet a heartbeat later, she heard a voice sounding from across the ruined lives of so many treasured family members and friends, across whole villages, entire tribes, nations of once proud African warriors.

Only with unrelenting effort can you win the right to thrive, the voice told her. *Only with the persistent accumulation of stature through terror can you achieve your people's liberation.*

Nani raised the axe once more. Violante, hearing the motion, lifted her gaze. She met Nani with pleading, innocent eyes, eyes wide with fear, soft and unsullied, like the eyes of a lamb before slaughter. "Please," she said. "Please, Maria, spare me."

The Maroon queen brought the axe crashing down upon the lady's bosom. Violante screamed, but only for a moment. Blood soaked her white cotton gown. It coated Nani even further in a slick second skin of gore.

From the nearby bedroom, Nani heard Maroon warriors throwing the diminutive bodies of children about like disjointed dolls. In the spin of an hour glass, every Spanish master, hand, and relation who had dwelled upon the estate had been returned to their Maker for final judgment.

Outside, the torches were lit. Upon the balustrade, the Maroons were scalding angels kissing every structure into flame. Fire burnt the bungalows of the slave drovers. The inferno's wrath grew, devouring the storage houses and huts used for curing tobacco. It writhed atop the cookhouse. It leapt into the barn, where it torched wood and mutilated steel. It gobbled whole fields of tobacco.

A blood-soaked Nani emanated from the ramparts like a demon of revenge. The tiles and timber of the *hacienda* had blistered, and now the window glass began to explode. As the combustion whooshed toward the sky, Nani marched onward. Behind her, the fire's fluid bolts of amber, marigold, and vermillion formed a cathedral born from the depths of Hell.

Chapter 19
JAMAICA

IN WHICH A SOLDIER IS KIDNAPPED

Routed in defeat, don Paco de Proenza's troops slunk homeward. The *sargento mayor* had no choice but to acknowledge the decisive truth: With depleted munitions and dismantled confidence, the Jamaican militia must retreat to the southern capital of St. Jago de La Vega.

Proenza dreaded his impending interview with don Francisco de Leiva. Each step alongside the Rio Cobre deepened his dejection. Silently, he rehearsed justifications to parry the jabs his *patrón* surely would deliver given the militia's woebegone performance in Maroon territory. Yet puzzle as he may, Proenza could not concoct any reasonable retorts.

Previously, the mountain dwellers had been regarded as a petty vexation, which even a neophyte captain ought vanquish. Instead, the Maroons had mounted a defensive strategy more adept than any Proenza ever had faced. Cast with courage and craft, Nani had proven herself an unbreakable adversary. She never duplicated tactics, but rather launched unpredictable ambushes worthy of the greatest annals of warcraft. Inexplicably, her tribe also boasted sophisticated firearms.

Communicating this to de Leiva would be more excruciating than dining on a plate of nails. Standing unshakeable in his hubris, the Jamaican leader would spout obscenities and excoriate Proenza's ineptitude before demoting him to the status of a worm.

The *sargento mayor* felt further discomfited by thoughts that had vexed him of late. He could not fathom the extent of de Leiva's enmity for the Maroon queen. Although she had provoked him by stealing his strongbox, de Leiva's retaliatory crusade was extreme. For what reason would Jamaica's wealthiest citizen, an exalted *alcalde* and High Sheriff of the Inquisition, monomaniacally target a derelict, squalid African runaway and her few dozen conspirators? It seemed there must be some further thread weaving the two opponents together, which Proenza had yet to unravel.

Amongst the forested hills emerged a clearing impeccable for raising camp. The battered retinue alighted their threadbare furnishings from the few remaining mules. As night broadened under a kingdom of stars, the militiamen tumbled into slumber.

The first spurts of cacophony escaped the notice of most men. But with awful quickness, the strange growling crescendoed into snarling wails, startling even the most sluggish troop members awake. Seasoned as they were by this stage of the expedition, the soldiers prepared with unmistakable dread for yet another Maroon ambush. Hearts clanging blood into their ears, they chased for their weapons, livening muskets and sliding Waloon swords from scabbards.

Proenza shouted at them to form a tight circle about the fire pit. Helpless in the night's grip, every eye strained.

An imposing shadow darted across the treetops. Next came a spewing of husky gibberish. The *soldados* blurted oaths and made the sign of the cross, begging God to reinforce their righteousness.

Proenza blasted his musket. Nothing happened. Two soldiers sent shots ripping through the desolate night, but they fired upon nothing other than leaves. The fiendish heckling erupted again.

Cristó pinched his gaze skyward. In the branches, he made out the form of a beast – a genuine monster, towering in height, covered in filth.

"Be still my heart. Tis a chimera!" Proenza shouted. "Bring your weapons to bear. Fell this corruption of God's works!"

Cristó did not budge. On the contrary, he dropped his weapon to the damp earth, observing the animal calmly.

"Why do you hesitate, you stuck minstrel? Make the shot!" Proenza commanded in a fury. He applied his utmost efforts to reviving his own musket, aiming it again at the perversion.

Cristó leapt, pushing the weapon to the ground. "Curb your killing, don Paco," he scolded before turning to scale the tree upon which the creature perched.

"I veto this inclination, child!" Proenza fumed.

Cristó clambered steadily upward.

"Halt your madness! The abomination will saw off your head!" shouted Proenza.

"And decorate his cave with your skin!" added Jaén de Falcona the ensign.

Nearing the beast's scummy feet, Cristó gagged at the stench. But he recognized a distinctly human face and eyes. "Pish… tis only a man."

The *soldados* murmured their disagreement. "That is no son of Adam," the ensign Lope de Medina gasped.

No human incarnation could move so fast, jump so high, nor carry so weighty a burden with such grace. Quick as a blink, Sasa plunged to where Cristó gripped the tree trunk, scooped the young man over his shoulder, and stole him away into the moon-dusted night.

IN WHICH A TRUTH IS TESTED

When the Maroon brigade returned from their raid of doña Violante's tobacco estate, day was breaking. Wol's ecstasy at beholding his newborn child rivaled that of humanity when first it mastered fire.

"The babe Cybella fetched all the *witty* from your belly and bosom," the proud father beamed at Anapa.

Those who had remained at the encampment had prepared for the roasting of the livestock they knew would be poached from the estate. Sipopi, who was of Taíno lineage, served as principal chef. Her Amerindian ancestors had invented the style of cooking known as *jerking*, which later had been appropriated by the Maroons and eventually would achieve fame across Jamaica and all the world. She had guided the others in quarrying pits in the soil. Across these, she spread a quilt of embers, so that the earthen beds exhaled smoke. The slaughtered flesh Sipopi scored, seasoned with pimento, lime, ginger, and rum, then swaddled in elder leaves. These packages she placed in the underground oven. Soon, a heavenly aroma wafted about the ravine.

When they gathered for the celebratory feast, Nani's YoYo numbered 89 souls. Alzo, flush with bottles of rum and Spanish wine, offered up the spoils he had liberated from the *hacienda*. It felt, for a suspended moment, like no greater degree of mirth ever would make their acquaintance.

Yet their blithe cheer crumbled the moment they glimpsed a smutted and untamed intrusion. Half the guarded warriors snapped up their arms. When the streaking form eased to a saunter, they recognized Sasa. Across the prodigious being's shoulders sagged a mass the size of hunted game. As it neared, several Maroons cried out in shock. The captive's moldered uniform imparted no doubt: He was a member of the Jamaican militia.

Sasa plunked his prize aside the cooking ground with a thud that surged panic across the hapless victim's body. The young man thrashed and gasped. Sasa issued not even the faintest reaction. His intrigue already had been captivated by the scent of dripping fat and crisping flesh emanating from the jerk pits.

It was Nani who scuttled to the *soldado*'s aid as he sucked air and dry heaved. Eyes caroming with distress, he pleaded his thirst. She helped him to deep sups from a hide bladder replete with sweet water. Mopping his lips in relief, don Cristóbal de Ysassi gained at last command of his senses.

He stared at Nani. She stared back at him. Cristó was ingrained with Iberian etiquette and tradition. Yet she recognized a youth straining against his nature with mutinous independence. He was a seeker.

The momentary confrontation unnerved him. He could sense that she was reading him for precisely what he was.

Cristó and Nani's intimacy broke as, simultaneously, they sensed the crowd of Maroons pressing upon them. A certain faction spat insults at the Spanish *soldado*. Greater numbers backed away, lest they be polluted by black omens. At Alzo's behest, a dozen warriors grabbed their weapons and formed a wall before him.

Nani shoved herself between their phalanx and the young man, but she spoke first to Sasa. "Well done, you," she praised, bestowing upon his cheek a caress. His complexion glowed with delight.

Only then did she turn to face her YoYo. "This here is no ordinary soldier. This is Don Cristóbal Ysassi – ward to don Francisco de Leiva."

Their expressions grew even icier.

"Our prisoner!" Santo declared, stomping forward to hurl a swift kick at the base of Cristó's spine.

Cristó tumbled to the ground. "Yoww! Smite of hell! What bloody troubles you?"

"Avast!" Nani scolded. She raked a reprimanding glare across the tribe. "None of you are to harm this visitor. If you do, you face the full force of my wrath. For twenty long years, I have awaited this moment."

Alzo scrutinized Cristó. "Having asked *what bloody troubles me*, I shall tell you: You contain not one drop of Maroon blood nor bear a minuscule of Maroon *witty*. Your kind stand completely outside of permission to exert one footfall upon our premises."

"Is your lecture complete, Alzo? Let me remind you I am the last to forget of our laws," Nani rebuked.

Suspicion muddied many a countenance. Santo and Sipopi stood aside Alzo, declaring their outrage.

"I am of a mind to take this Spanish islander at once to the Morro," Nani said. "Upon our anointed Obiya grounds, the ancient spirits shall confirm Cristó's righteousness… or deny it."

A smirk danced across Alzo's lips. "That infantry rat will not win the blessing of our ancestors. They shall judge de Leiva's ward for what he is: Duplicitous and insidious. This Spaniard was birthed from the rectum of the Devil. Dearest irrefutable leader, please accept my enthusiasm when the spirits command us to bury him in the earth — for that will be the verdict of the fates."

Nani sucked teeth to sound her irritation. "Tchip!"

She shifted her focus to Sasa and JoJo, recruiting them for the sacred excursion. With Cristó in tow, their small party mounted the craggy acclivity to its crest, where the Morro greeted them. This particular Obiya tabernacle was no watchtower with turret and fortifications, but only a wee lodging erected from wattle and thatch. Even so, it boasted a commanding view over miles of mountainous territory.

Within, the rasping wind penetrated the woven palm fronds and wooden stakes. As Cristó's eyes adapted, he discovered a shrine decorated with icons of snakes and monkeys carved from bone and woven from twigs. Three human skulls judged him through empty sockets. Two calabashes, one that appeared to brim with blood and the other with rum, completed the haunting scene. Across from the holy table stood a post three feet in girth and reaching six feet high, which had been fashioned expertly from a *kapok* or cotton tree. When JoJo incited a tinder and lit a dozen tapers, the tremulous flames caused the walls to undulate. Shadows fermented. Suddenly, the Morro appeared as a living, breathing entity.

Nani commenced chanting in a tongue unintelligible to Cristó. JoJo alone addressed him, catapulting her directives like pebbles. "Stand with your back against the splinter post. Do not move – not even the faintest flinch. Still as the dead you must keep. Understood?"

Cristó looked for Sasa, who seemed to have absented himself. But an instant later, the monkey-man bounded into the tabernacle with an *afana*. JoJo stepped back. Nani escalated her chanting.

Without warning, Sasa crashed the machete into the pillar where Cristó held himself utterly still, as JoJo had commanded. The blade landed less than an inch from his cheek. The Spanish youth, filled with terror, quieted his breathing so as not to wriggle. Without hesitation, Sasa dislodged the *afana* and struck again, detonating splinters. The next hack pruned a lock of hair from Cristo's head. The following slice nipped his doublet, severing the linen without touching his flesh.

Speeding his blows, Sasa cycled the machete up and down, crashing the wood with each fatal chop. The kapok pillar screeched. Cristó squeezed his eyes shut until he saw constellations. He willed every part of his body to disown the urge to either defend itself or escape. This he did by convincing himself that he was already dead.

With one final burst, Sasa hurled the *afana* directly at Cristó's unshod foot. The blade shuddered as it embedded itself. Yet not one spurt of lifeblood emerged, nor did Cristó, eyes still sealed, react.

Nani ceased chanting, causing Cristó to fling open his eyes. He marveled as she unplugged the blade from his foot. The slash mark closed quick as the wounds of Christ.

"The ancestors give assurance of the truth," Nani announced, gliding her index finger across the *afana*'s edge to verify its fineness. The resulting cut oozed red drops.

"But *how*?" Cristó asked in confusion, his heart only beginning to slow its frantic beating.

Nani's smile evolved into a laugh. "Child, a being begot from gods, with all his unearthly might, struck you. Yet he caused you no damage. By Heaven, *you* are the one I have been seeking."

JoJo, Cristó, and Sasa stared at her in silence.

"As I made known already, I have an immortal desire to unite our Windward tribe with the families of Lubolo and Juan de Serras, that we might conquer this island of Jamaica," Nani announced. "The three of you must come together in order to make this crusade a success. You must keep pushing on with the battle to win our homeland, so that our people can live free as we want and deserve."

"Ock! You expect me to turst this bubonic vulture?" JoJo scoffed, waving an arm at Cristó. "Mother, he spawns from 200 years of avarice, carnage, and oppression. Greater even! How can you speak such toilet sauce? Pray, I plead with all my earnestness: Never ask me to found an alliance with a Spaniard. Tis madness to build a friendship with the enemy!"

"My darling daughter, my sweetsop, my moon and sun," Nani lowered her voice beneath the keening of the wind. "Every person on this island chatters about how don Cristóbal is a bastard child of half-African blood. You have only to lay eyes upon him to verify this fact. Have you ever wondered at his origin?"

JoJo snorted. She was in no humor to indulge her mother's riddles.

Nani raised a taper directly before Cristó's befuddled face. "Are you a zealot dedicated to churning our Maroon race into gruel? Clearly not. Nor are you a drunkard seeking a keg of ale in which to numb your integrity. No. You are a defiant one. You wish to vomit upon your Spanish heritage."

"You know not the truth of it," Cristó snapped.

"Perhaps you ought first listen to what I have to say," Nani retorted. "The father they say sired you, Captain Sanchez de Ysassi, was buried to the chin in borrowed credit. Evading debtors' prison, he absconded to Santiago de Cuba. But they never told you the name or origin of your mother, only that she perished thrusting your bastard self into this cruel world. You became orphaned. Your supposed father's eldest child, your half-sister doña Zorayda, took you up and raised you as her own. Her husband, don Francisco de Leiva, claimed you as his ward. Is this the story they told you, yay or nay?"

"Yay," Cristó muttered.

"A tale they construed to keep the dignity of your house intact. *Limpieza de sangre* is required by Spain for the highborn to wield privilege over those of vulgar birth," Nani explained.

Cristó's face tightened. "Have you seduced the Devil to gain such knowledge?"

JoJo, on the other hand, softened. Speaking with meticulous care, she inquired, "Tell us now that which you wish to relate, Mother. Enlighten us as to the purpose of this conference."

Nani gauged Cristó. His distress was manifest. Sweat pooled at his eyebrows. His hands trembled. His eyes failed to maintain focus. She addressed him directly. "Upon the slave traders' landing in Jamaica, they sold me to the master don Francisco de Leiva. Younger then, he was arresting in appearance and ambitious as ever. He consumed that which he lusted for, ravishing women whensoever his impulses overcame him." She gulped three times before continuing. "When my belly swelled, de Leiva expelled me to the rustic estate of his sister, doña Violante. A tender mistress, she took me as her house servant. But when my baby came, she snatched the wailing infant away. I never even held you. In seconds, they disconnected me from a mother's joy and consigned me to eternal heartache – until this very day."

Cristó's jaw had fallen open, as had JoJo's.

"De Leiva contrived a yarn to defend against rumor, attesting that his wife Zora shared your same father," Nani went on. "But I tell you: That man, Captain Sanchez de Ysassi? He abandoned Jamaica an entire year before you were born. You and doña Zorayda do not share not blood."

She went quiet, drawing even with the trauma that had haunted her these past two decades. "Cristó, your genuine father is don Francisco de Leiva, and I am your genuine mother. Never again shall you lose my love."

None of them could assemble a response. Cristó feared he might suffocate under the load of lifelong premises spun upside down.

Ruled by her pragmatism, JoJo wondered aloud, "So, this Spaniard Cristó… is my half-brother?"

"For very real," Nani emphasized. "And the link between you, Cristó, and Sasa shall strengthen your souls."

The three stunned young people fell silent. Nani doused the tapers so that all were masked by the anonymity of darkness before she spoke again, her voice serene. "Omens pass to me by virtue of Obiya science. My existence races to its end. I shall not witness the precious victory of our freedom, for soon I embark upon the carriage of Death."

"What?" JoJo hiccoughed just as Sasa yowled, "No!"

Nani filled her lungs, cherishing each breath. "Several times, I have traded with the King of Death, haggling for a soul whose quickness already was in his grip. You observed such magic when I revitalized Lubolo. His was not the first human vessel whose inner fire I restored to mortality. But the price of those actions was the sacrifice of my own celestial candle. Now, the debt has grown too large. The banker of souls aims to even our accounts."

"Mother, your words scare me," JoJo stammered.

"Embrace this truth, my fluttering hummingbird," Nani said, fumbling through the murk to forage her daughter's hand. "Our bodies are but frocks of clay. Although my physical form will decay into dust, my spirit shall claim a space within your soul. *Nani* is not limited by flesh. She is an idea that brings hope to the downtrodden. You, JoJo, will rise as the next Nani, styled in her essence. She may be resurrected again by women after you, until finally this almighty dispute with injustice is settled."

"I cannot," JoJo replied, squeezing her mother's hand with tears stinging her eyes.

"Oh, but you can and you will. And finding the means – your *own* way, JoJo – shall be your greatness," Nani argued.

Slowly, shock turned to resolution as the magnitude of Nani's words sunk in. Each of Nani's three offspring stood quietly in the dark, the sound of their breaths mingled into one. JoJo imagined herself taking up the role of Maroon Queen. Sasa felt his chest expand as he contemplated helping her lead. Cristó, though nauseated by the revelations, sensed himself transcend. New truths and visions hurled open a fresh identity.

At last, JoJo reached for Sasa's hand, Nani reached for Cristo's, and they all joined in a circle. Nani made her final remarks. "Before we return to our tribe and communicate to them this extraordinary outcome, my children, you must face one last cruel revelation. The spirits of Obiya have testified to a coming fate: *One of you will execute my death.* This act shall arise not through treachery, but as an imperative for Maroon salvation. Still same, I tell you three standing nearby, whom I love beyond all the wonders of this world: One of you has been chosen by the spirits to murder me."

Although Nani's words were unbearable, she spoke with such conviction that the three young leaders found themselves believing in her prophecies. Drawing strength from their mother's spirit, they prepared to face the course ahead. They knew they would reel, at times, from battles, despair, and hopelessness. Yet they were not alone. They had each other, the blessings of their mother and all their ancestors, and the magic of Obiya to aid in unlocking their unified power. And they had the legend of Nani, which would live on for generations.

Chapter 20

AT SEA

IN WHICH A SAIL IS SPOTTED

Iron Eyes scanned the horizon. The morning sea was filled with silver dust skittering across cushions of blue. He pinched his eyes against the blinding bleach of the sun, and strode toward a haven of shade. Moving toward the half-deck compartment, he observed Joy de Bones, who had been voted into the position of helmsman. The St. Kitts fighter turned pyrate crashed his might into the tiller, steering the Black Maggie faithfully. With his sun-bronzed mane whipping in the wind and his bare chest etched in sweat, he resembled a Viking of yore unleashed.

With the addition of the new recruits, La Negra Magdalena hosted an adequate though not generous crew of 36 rogues. Four days past their departure from St. Kitts, Tiburon and Throat had charted a course for Samaná Bay, a harbor lying upon the northeastern edge of Hispañola, an island also known as Santo Domingo. According to don Francisco de Leiva's intelligence, it was there that La

Beduina, the ship in possession of his stolen strongbox, was being ladened with supplies.

They anticipated a more challenging voyage than the sail from Jamaica to St. Kitts. Traveling southeast, the Black Maggie had profited from the customary Caribbean trade winds. Running the contrary direction demanded harnessing night lees, when warm air rushing off the land met with cooler seawater, generating a wind that might lift their sails. As well, the Maggies were required to await an hospitable *weather window* in crossing from Porto Rico to Santo Domingo. Known as the Mona Passage, this stretch of water was notorious for its boisterous swells, baffling winds, and impulsive squalls.

The sloop began a contest with rough seas, her bow splitting roof-tops of waves when a cry from aloft startled the air. "Darrr, Cap'n," Joy de Bones boomed from the hutch, pointing to the topsail yards. "Tis our vigilant scout Master Winter Seasal screaming the spots off his calico."

"Sail!" the Carolinian man whooped. "Sail!" he elevated his cry from the main-top shrouds. "Yonder east. Four points about, three leagues afar. Can you make light of her, Cap'n?"

Iron Eyes surged to the amidship gunwales. Standing officers, grasping the gravity of the alarm, rushed him from all sides.

"Tis a customary run for a merchant ship trading in cacao or sandalwood," Tiburon resolved, expanding his spyglass.

"Fetch us away in pursuit, Cap'n, for she be a true prize!" Yellows pleaded.

Iron Eyes spoke nothing, his mind weighing merit against hazard.

When their captain delayed his response, the Portuguese-Brasilian boson thundered, "For the quick of the grave, pursue! Even a fowlery of dead hens could take of her."

Iron Eyes peered round, judging the zeal of the greater complement. In his years upon the sea, he had endured a dozen or more chases – albeit mostly from the perspective of the terrorized prey. What the neophytes and the blood-hungry amongst their fellowship could not comprehend was the exertion demanded for *any* chase – even one of such seeming convenience. The moment the quarry surmised pursuit, she would turn heel and haul. The Black Maggie then would press a frantic quest in a direction contrary to her intended destination. Even if she did gain the advantage, the thin numbers of her crew lingered as a worrisome concern.

"We aren't prepared as yet to win her," Tiburon said in a hushed voice.

"Tis the prickly truth," Iron Eyes nodded. "Stand off!" he bellowed across the weather deck.

His unexpected decree vexed the pyrates. Vitality drained from their faces, giving way to grumbles and scowls. Yellow's exemplified their mounting angst.

Tiburon intercepted his captain. "They fail to grasp the burden of our oaths, Damien" he injected. "The capture of La Beduina is our sterling objective – else we risk the wrath of don Francisco de Leiva and the Holy Inquisition, not to mention the onslaught of Araña Sangrienta and the entire *guardacosta*. Yet these groaning fishwives… they'd rather exhaust themselves in a fruitless chase than win the boon promised by our confidential errand."

The captain blinked a weary look.

Tibbs, however, had not finished. "Best you devise a strategy for reinvigorating the complement," he cautioned. "Given their froth at present, the men may get to suspecting that *Iron Eyes* ain't the hero they took him for."

IN WHICH A SAIL IS PURSUED

Three days later, La Negra Magdalena was running through a track of waters just north of Porto Rico when Winter Seasal spotted another sail by the starboard bow. Iron Eyes investigated the ship by his lunette, identifying her as a full-rigged pinnace.

"Coming straight to us!" Yellows hollered from the quarterdeck.

"Stand fast," Iron Eyes ordered.

"No choice of chase upon this occasion, Cap'n," the boson argued with a smug grin. "*She* pursues *us*."

For the two hours following, the pinnace adopted a course parallel to the Black Maggie's, mirroring her movements from an undeviating distance of two leagues. Iron Eyes, Throat and Tiburon devised a strategy. First, they bid the tars strike topgallants and topsails. Then they ordered the fowl coops, livestock pins, and sea chests from the hold placed atop deck. They asked Howler Dornan, the master of arms recruited from the St. Kitts fight club, to select three ponderous swivel-guns, lash them with ropes, and hurl them overboard from the stern.

Now the Black Maggie moaned and yawed. She trudged through the sea as if swimming in syrup. With her weather deck cluttered by trunks, casks, and honking farm-chattel, she appeared a cloddish merchant ship: Quite possibly the most irresistible and simplest of targets at sea.

As soon as Winter Seasal was able to distinguish the pinnace's colors, they deployed another daring tactic. The enemy ship flew the gold and sable lion, the flag of Flanders. Zeelanders abhorred the Spanish, who presently occupied their homeland. Iron Eyes and Tiburon asked Scipio to raise the red and yellow banner of Spain, believing it would further provoke the enemy.

Like a raptor dropping from the sky, the pinnace made her approach. She closed upon La Negra Magdalena with all her teeth – gun ports open. Soon, she sailed a mere 400 lengths afar.

Taking command as captain, Iron Eyes summoned his men to gather their weapons and prepare to board, but ordered them hold fast. "Be not troubled, my hearts! We shall defeat these arrogant raiders in due time."

At a precisely calculated moment, he bellowed at Joy de Bones, "Helm up!" The Black Maggie veered hysterically, as if attempting escape.

The pinnace answered at once, closing the distance between the two ships by a single stay. Her captain, anticipating an effortless capture, brought his great guns to bear and prepared to attack.

But it was too late. The Flemish ship, which the Maggies could now see was christened The Rode Afgunst, had encroached beyond 700 feet – well within musket range. Tiburon led Yellows, Toulouk, Winter Seasal, and Dario

Colón at the fore shrouds. Ibra, Scipio, and Chucho were among those armed upon the main tops. Meanwhile, hidden from view, Splosh and Jonah awaited with a barrel of petards. Howler Dornan and the other St. Kitts fighters, along with Comet, Throat and his men, leveled their barkers from the mizzen and gangway. Strapped by cutlashes and several muskets and pistols each, the renegades let loose a wash of shot that cleared their opponent's decks.

Frantically, the Flemish sailors attempted to protect themselves. But by the time a glint of slow-match flame could be spied upon their gun-deck in preparation for cannon fire, Splosh and Jonah had launched an onslaught of smoke bombs that had blinded the enemy, and other Maggies had delivered from their muskets a hailstorm of lead. Shadows dashed about the Rode Afgunst, howling and yipping as the sailors were struck.

"Stand down or blame yourselves for your death!" Iron Eyes shouted across the span of turquoise.

The Flemish pinnace struck her colors in surrender. The Maggies slung their grapplers, boarded the ship, and without further argument declared themselves masters over the enemy.

The more seasoned amongst La Negra Magdalena's crew were hardly astonished by the succinctness of the victory. They knew that the bulk of contests between ships at sea could be won with not any conflict. Merely brandishing weapons with the guarantee of murder gained submission from all but the most fortified prizes. The common mariner, garnished by scant wages, saw no reason to jeopardize his life in defense of a merchant vessel.

This, however, was no merchant trader. This ship had pursued *them*, suggesting she must be a smuggler. The victory therefore struck Yellows, who had spent decades of his life at sea, as extraordinary. Their captain, he felt, had proved his brilliance as a leader by engaging in such clever tactics. "Bravo, Iron Eyes, bravo!" the boson shouted loud enough for all to hear.

The Maggies muscled the Rode Afgunst population into the vessel's waist, hammering the captives to their knees and binding them one to the other. Iron Eyes regarded them soberly. Most were hostages or indentureds, individuals of sundry cultures whose poor treatment by the officers had degraded them into scarecrows. Small wonder they had surrendered.

Iron Eyes instructed his men to search for the captain and other standing officers. They could not be found. Then Zemi began yawping. Hackles raised, the hound barraged the sealed entryway to the galley. Tiburon collided his shoulder against the door but made no progress in forcing it open.

"Craven ringtums!" Howler Dornan frothed. "We shall bust your cowardly skulls open for hiding in closed quarters."

As Howler prepared to ram the door with his body, Splosh appeared. With a cackle of delight, he plopped a petard made from rank fish, rotten manatee, and horse hoof filings at the locked door. The stink pot sizzled smoke inside the cabin. In two blinks of an eye, six superiors of the Rode Afgunst raced into the open, vomiting and gasping for air.

Iron Eyes pinpointed who was captain by his dapper white linen shirt. Swooping, he aimed his cherry wood pistol at the man as he sucked breath upon hand and knee. The Flemish captain looked up from beneath a tousled wig, eyes filled with terror. But then, as he sleeved regurgitation from his lips, his expression turned sheepish. Iron Eyes felt his own glee evaporate, replaced by dread.

Splosh led several Maggies to defend their noses and mouths with clouts and enter the galley. Others mobbed the ship, claiming prizes. From the stores, they collected casks of brandy, which promptly they gushed down their gullets. Joy de Bones crashed his axe through several barrels purely for delight, spewing the deck with sweet-scented fluid.

In answer to the pandemonium engulfing them, the captain of the Rode Afgunst stood slowly, puffed out his chest, and spat phlegm upon the deck. Face to face, he gazed unblinking upon Iron Eyes. The aged seaman was haggard with a gristled face. He said in English tinged by slight Flemish intonations, "Welter Vandenbosch, captain of this ship and quartermaster afore that. The Rode Afgunst has been my home for nigh twenty years. Many a sailor I have encountered upon my journeys. Do you recall meeting me, friend?"

Iron Eyes barbed his expression, forcing his breath to remain slow and even.

The smuggler flicked a dismissive finger at his indentured crew. "Every glum lad here has heard tell the myth of Iron Eyes, as well the news that he has been dead for months. Tis a mystery, then, how your crew calls you by that name. Witness them, eyeing you lovingly, like the damned looking from Hell into the gates of Paradise."

"Shut your yapper and get to liberating the ship's documents and breaching the captain's strongbox," scolded Iron Eyes, his heart rate increasing by the second.

"Otherwise you'll be the first coward hanged," Howler Dornan hissed, lifting his brace and blade.

"Fancy a listen, lads, if you plan on wagering your lives on behalf of this pretender," said Captain Vandenbosch, a laugh ripening in his mouth. "You look not at all how you ought, *Iron Eyes*. Too golden-haired. Too slight. And far too confused in the paint of your eyes. Seems you have composed a fairytale in order to lure these men into following you. Imposter!"

A crowd of Maggies watched the conversation. Joy de Bones and Howler Dornan murmured to one another. Yellows arched a brow at Comet. Even Toulouk and Winter Seasal's faces exhibited concern. From the huddled group of captured sailors came several daring jeers.

The man who claimed to be Iron Eyes felt fear lunge against his chest. His hands bunched, but he resisted the impulse to smite the jaw of the inciter. "Choke down those words and fuck a gun," he remarked calmly. "Your opinion of me is farfetched. Shan't speak twice on the subject."

"Aye, you dissembler of reality," Tiburon concurred, stepping before them. "Twas I who rescued this man, the heroic pyrate Iron Eyes, from the bloody shores of Zéros, and then nursed him back to health upon the isle of Navassa. Look, he displays the scars of that carnage," he lifted the captain's left arm and pushed back his cotton shirt aside to reveal the twisted flesh. "Also, see how he wields a cherry wood pistol proofed by Brachie and hailing from

Dieppe, France? This he claimed from his greatest prize, the flagship of the Spanish Treasure Fleet."

The Flemish captain looked upon each of his officers. His voice tightened. "Aside from me, others here remember that day, only two months prior to his famed conquest of the Treasure Fleet vessel, when the *true* Iron Eyes purchased from us ten roves of cannon shot and six pipes of claret. *That* man weighed two stones heavier, towered a half-foot taller, bore a thinning halo of dark brown hair, and had matching eyes the color of *iron*, not grass and sea."

Without further thought, Iron Eyes jumped his cutlash forward and tore a gash through Vandenbosch's belly. Horrified, the remaining Rode Afgunst officers exploded for their lives in every direction. Tiburon and Howler Dornan unsealed two throats. Yellows, Throat, Scipio and Chucho punched holes into the heads of the final three.

Dying upon his knees, Vandenbosch creaked to Iron Eyes, "It matters not your deception. This edge of the world is plagued by hoaxes." He coughed blood. "Mouths full of sugar, hearts full of gall, this fresh gift of a *free new world* promised us as a utopia has been turned rancid. A promise made invalid. Dream your way out from the barbarity, pyrate – whoever you may be. Frame a just order from the treachery."

Yellows kicked the Flemish captain with his boot until he drew his final breath. For a moment, the Maggies stood in a hushed circle. Then Howler Dornan, the master of arms, raised himself tall before Iron Eyes. "Why did he allege a false identity?" he demanded.

Iron Eyes felt insubstantial as a shadow. He floundered his gaze about the newly-gathered crew and peeked at the pitiful indentureds huddled aboard the captured ship. These were men of no home, no family, no country — no chance other than *this very one* for forging a life worth living. And every last one was watching him, waiting, hearts full of a tremulous, rapidly evaporating hope.

"Give here," Throat announced, gaining their attention. "Don Francisco de Leiva, High Sheriff of the Holy Inquisition, eminence of enterprisers, wealthiest landowner in Jamaica, and my master for many long years, is one of the most consequential men in all the New World. Do you not agree? His spies collect secret intelligence from the four corners of Earth. None escape his network. *He* discovered Iron Eyes dwelling amongst Mota Sinan and the Brethren of Jamaica's North Coast. *He* bequeathed the famed pyrate captain with this ship. Tell me, do you imagine he was mistaken? Harr! If you do, you have lived not one day scraping for survival within his worldly realm. Gentlemen, if de Leiva speaks it, then it must be so, for his words ring with the truth and power of God. *This* is the renegade pyrate Iron Eyes – and none other."

Iron Eyes stared silently at Throat, confounded by his rival's decision to mount so vociferous a defense. Just then, he caught sight of a gleam in the dead Flemish captain's pooling gut sludge. With a prod of his cutlash, he hooked an item from the muck. From his pocket, he withdrew a clout, which he used to smear away tissue and blood.

The mysterious object was an emerald.

"Jewels… they swallowed their precious jewels…" Yellows muttered. He slashed wide the bowels of the other dead men. One after another spilled pebbles of bright color from their entrails. All the while, Yellows shouted, "Cunting sneaks! They gobbled the gems so as to hide their booty from us!"

Howler Dornan drooled, mouth open. His eyes skipped from Yellows to Iron Eyes. "Weeping wombs!" he exclaimed, stupefied. "*How*, Cap'n? How did you see past that coxcomb's blarney?"

The captain gave an elusive smile. In his mind, he thanked the real Iron Eyes, his teacher, whose presence he felt watching over him. His false identity safeguarded for another day, he fixed a long look upon a calm and friendly sea.

With the force of a dam broken open, the rogues spent the next four hours ransacking thoroughly the Rode Afgunst and celebrating their victory. All concerns about the identity of Iron Eyes vanished, replaced by blatant craving.

From the viscera of the six freshly-murdered principals, the pyrates harvested a pile of precious gemstones. Dismantling the officers' quarters by adze and hammer, they located three hidden strongboxes. When the locks repulsed round shot, Splosh blasted them open, emancipating sacks of ready money and pearls. Before them, heaped upon the Flemish captain's table, lay a spectacular mound of prizes. These riches assured each of the 36 Maggies comfort for the remainder of their lives – should they not squander their wealth upon whores and drink when next they landed a port.

Appetites unappeased, they continued pillaging the pinnace, carrying away everything their imaginations could liberate. They stripped the hold of its stores of logwood, cacao, hides, brandy and other spirits, Spanish cigars and tobacco. They poached the swivel guns, powder chests, muskets, and small arms. They pinched dried viands, blocks of cheese, and firkins of sugar from the mess.

Eventually, they turned their attention to the less obvious booty. For Hendrik Boer, they unearthed physics from an ignored medicine crate. For Portugal and Tiburon, they gathered maps and pilot's guides; for Iron Eyes, the captain's log and moldered books. To service their ongoing pyratical adventures, they collected sails, spars, and cordage, and reveled in discovering a collection of duplicitous national banners. Their delirium continued as they pilfered the officers' wardrobes, pinching trousers, doublets, frocks, scarves, belts, skullcaps, and the odd pair of shoes.

When there was naught else to claim or destroy, Tiburon opened La Negra Magdalena's confederacy to those who had been enslaved upon the Rode Afgunst. He vowed full clemency to any man who elected to become a Maggie, and an easy escape to Porto Rico by longboat for those who declined. Most deserted, but nine sailors befriended the pyrate cause. Among them was Pink, the chef, an Irish indentured. He had earned his nickname because he resembled a pig in both plumpness and skin color.

At nightfall, the fire-monkey Splosh was given as his own special reward: the Flemish pinnace to burn. La Negra Magdalena hauled out, a dragon of flames taking flight behind her. Into the darkness she melted – richer, abler, and more malicious than before.

IN WHICH A CAPTAIN CONFRONTS HIS QUARTERMASTER

"I have questions that demand answers," Iron Eyes said. He had been waiting until the complement had descended fully into intoxicated revelry to confront Throat.

The quartermaster veered away, but the captain trailed after him. "Arr, seeing as how we done poach a hundred barrels of brandy, you'd best settle your interrogation within the hour," Throat said, pointing his knife-hand at his temple. "Following that, alongside all the sweet rogues of this vessel, I shall be soaked in the brains and unable to speak."

Iron Eyes directed Throat to his private chamber. The estate room was an ample apartment for a cruiser of La Negra Magdalena's proportions. The far, canted wall was adorned with a round rose or *Catherine* window composed of multicolored stained glass – a far-fetched garniture. Otherwise, the room was invested sparingly with a hammock stayed to the ceiling beams by chains, a walnut armoire, and an upright chair standing by a mahogany *vargueño* or fall-out desk. Upon it reposed a quill, an inkpot, and a log book.

Throat seated himself confidently at the desk.

"As a first task, get to solving this puzzle for me," Iron Eyes bid, remaining standing. "Why, when the Rode Afgunst officer poured out my false identity, did you defend me as the one true Iron Eyes? You ken I am not he. De Leiva informed you as such upon our first congress at the *cabildo* in La Vega."

Throat canted back in the chair and plopped his bare feet upon the *vargueño*. "Worry not, Damien Baines, or whoever you be. Tis no crime counterfeiting an identity – especially when men plead their need for a noble cause. We wage war against the privileged and entitled. Every person aboard this ship plays a confidence game. How else might we outdo our pitiful pasts and awaken to a bettered existence? Your name brings our crew together under a banner of hope. Would be a tragedy to cast it aside, agreed?"

Iron Eyes offered at tentative nod.

Throat rose, relinquishing the furniture. "No cause grabs power unless its soldiers rally behind faith." Bending over to polish the mahogany table where his boot had scuffed, he added, "*You* are our faith."

The hammering of Iron Eyes' heart was becalmed. "I shall accept those words with sincerity, Throat." He walked to the rose window. "The second matter concerns motivations. With this journey, what do you aim to achieve?"

Throat's face creeped with inscrutable emotion. "Fear not that don Francisco de Leiva has sworn me to his cause. Not by the Devil's scaly tail! The smuggling vessel La Beduina be a prize I covet as much as does our *patrón*."

This revelation did not surprise Iron Eyes so much as the direct manner in which Throat spoke it. The captain felt compelled to close the distance between himself and the spectral-looking rogue. "What, then, are you after, mate? Tis just you and me here, our ears sodden only by the groaning of timbers. Speak."

Throat faltered for the first time, debating his ability to trust the captain..

"How does de Leiva go forward?" Iron Eyes pressed. "What meaning does this strongbox contain, sealed as it is by marks of the Holy Crusade? What does his precious *aviso* to the Spanish king say?"

Still Throat did not speak. The room was so hushed that he could hear the wicks of the tapers sputtering. He had constructed a life with endless escape hatches. Always he left himself a way out, whether fleeing promises, pain, blame, friendship, or even fatherhood. But now, before a man he barely knew, a man who would not admit who he was, Owen Butler considered surrendering the keys to his freedom – and his prison.

"When we conferenced in La Vega, de Leiva revealed to you that he wishes to augment Jamaica's might," Throat said, swallowing his reticence. "He longs to pen his chapter in the chronicles of history. For greater than a dozen years, he has pursued his vision of a thriving empire. None but his wife doña Zorayda has full knowledge of his masterminding. But by my own tactics, knowledge of his *aviso*'s contents has come to me."

Pacing from rose window to cabin door, Throat explained. "What de Leiva seeks aboard La Beduina – the object stolen from him by the Maroon queen Nani, who passed it along to the Jewish smuggler Gaspar Carvalhal, who conveys it now to connivers we know not for certain – is a message woven in the secret Quechuan code employed by all Sheriffs of the Inquisition. It alerts His Majesty King Felipe IV as to Jamaica's vulnerability to foreign attack. No fortifications guard any shore of the island. The North Coast – unsettled by government forces and Spanish landholders – carries the most substantial risk.

"Now listen close, for here comes the trickery," Throat continued. "Negotiating with the *Casa de Contratación* in Sevilla, de Leiva years ago persuaded the House of Trade to veer Spanish shipping lanes *closer* to the unguarded North Coast of his island. This territory remains, with de Leiva's blessing, under the control of Mota Sinan and his Brethren, whose acquaintance you have forged. Few apart from de Leiva and Mota have calculated how intimately the Treasure Fleet hugs the northern Jamaican shallows each year."

"Harr!" In that instant, the colossal nature of the situation crystalized in Iron Eyes' mind. Words rushed from his mouth. "All said, the Spanish armada, sailing from the mainland territories of the New World brimming with silver from the famed mines of Potosí and other riches, passes close by Jamaica each year. At de Leiva's bidding, the buccaneers attack from the North Coast and capture all the dripping treasures the galleons carry. True? Then, in concert with the traitor Mota Sinan, de Leiva straight away spills wealth from out his ears."

"Aye, but his plans stretch even further!" Throat announced, raising his knife-hand. "For in the treacherous *aviso*, de Leiva also demonstrates to the king with what ease any enemy power might capture *all of Jamaica*. For decades too long, Colón's descendants have ignored their island possession. De Leiva understands her most intimate secrets – when to attack, from whence, and with whom."

"He aims to build himself a roaring empire!" Iron Eyes marveled, his face lit. "Capture *both* the Treasure Fleet and the isle of Jamaica for his own glory."

Throat nodded, a leer upon his bloodless lips.

"But why share this precious knowledge with the Crown? Why not guard it for himself?"

"Because De Leiva does not wish to wage war upon his mother country," Throat replied, clucking his tongue. "He moves his chess pieces, plotting exponential steps ahead. He prefers the King of Spain deliver wealth and military might to his doorstep with nary a battle nor any trouble. Enterprising de Leiva may be, but a rogue he is not – therein lies the difference betwixt him and we. With Spain as his ally, he dreams of building the finest shipyard on earth. He wishes to attract the most illustrious traders, so that Jamaica might emerge as a global competitor, a capital of the world."

Suddenly, Iron Eyes' demeanor shifted. He felt weighted again by suspicion. "Why divulge such secrets to *me*, Throat?"

"Simple enough: My heart's desire is to capture the *aviso* in order to harness its knowledge, trounce the Treasure Fleet, and claim the isle of Jamaica for myself!" He turned mad eyes at the captain. "But I cannot accomplish the task alone. Even a masterful renegade such as my own self must bond with other rabble rousers. Trust that degenerate the Catholic Majesty of Spain and his minions? Tis a preposterous idea to me, a man who hails from Protestant Salem and cares not a whit for King Felipe nor his fastly declining Empire.

"As with every Maggie, tis greed that drives me. Greed fueled by an unquenchable desire to live free. De Leiva partners with Old World nations and North Coast buccaneers. We might forge an alliance with the Maroons who rule Jamaica's interior. As a leader, Nani embodies tremendous force. She outwits de Leiva's soldiers. She even has commanded an army of monkeys by her side! Look here: With Nani's aid and de Leiva's *aviso* in our possession, we plunder the Treasure Fleet of Spain. Then, with our wealth unbounded, we win Jamaica as home for freebooters and masterless men, rogues and renegades, outcasts and misfits, the formerly enslaved and the greatly derided Maroons. Imagine."

Iron Eyes paused, conflicted. Throat's sentiments in many ways echoed those of his beloved deceased captain, the true Damien Baines. But some matter gave him pause. "Alas, though it appears you have unraveled his complexities, you played the trusted *bravo* to don Francisco de Leiva for many a year. Why betray him now? Why not sooner?"

"Never has such an opportunity appeared," Throat replied. He approached so that their eyes were even. "Have spent an age beside the man, as you speak it. But never *aside* him, equal with him. Only ever beneath his handsomely-booted feet." He collapsed upon the desk chair, fixing his eyes upon a speck of lint decorating his pant leg. "Since my twenty-fifth year. Twas faintly a man, as yet. Thirteen years of my best life have been stolen from me by that Spaniard. Now is my time. I shall not ever return to him."

"I yearn to trust you."

Throat rose again to his full height. "I have submitted to you all my knowledge and plotting. Pursue La Beduina with all the force you have to muster – with me as your ally or without."

Throat made to leave the chamber, but before he had taken two steps, Iron Eyes snagged him by the arm. As he did, the captain felt a strange shock, as if pricked by a splinter. He had not encountered such a sensation of attraction since the original Iron Eyes had died. The feeling caused him angst. With pinched brows, he asked, "One final conundrum... Why did you send your mate Comet to the Punk House in St. Kitts, instructing him in secret to fetch Jonah Profit? What claim have you on the lad?"

"Not once have I inquired as to your past, demanding either your birth name or tales of the family you abandoned in Wales," Throat responded with a narrowing of the eyes. "Tis fair and reasonable for me to request that you withhold your own questions about my private history."

Iron Eyes offered a tilt of his chin. Then the caption dismissed his confounding quartermaster and readied himself for the following day, when he must rally his crew of rogues to a loftier goal.

IN WHICH A BANNER OF BLOOD IS RAISED

The following evening, every member of the complement gathered upon the gundeck. Iron Eyes had summoned all hands. Hendrik Boer even hustled Portugal into the chamber. A sling mantled the patient's right shoulder, sheltering his maggot-infested wound. The surgeon had commenced his noxious treatment, and Portugal now suffered from a grinding pain that sent him into daily trances.

Once he could account for every last man, Iron Eyes inventoried them. None but Tibbs, Throat, and Portugal could recite the truth of his identity. Yet in spite of Throat's recent reassurances, his fraudulent identity forever locked panic around his heart. For a second, he stalled, recalling his previous existence. He heard the voice of his beloved, the original Iron Eyes, issue a warning: *A lie is like a disease. You cannot flee an affliction that dwells within your own self.* But he breathed himself into a place of confidence, embracing his role as the leader of this ship, a true pyrate vessel.

Having shoved a quartet of chests into the center of the room, he raised himself atop them, whistling for attention. Forty-six sets of eyes stared back at the captain, awaiting a speech. "We have vanquished our first prize! A vast treasure we have won, and without bloodshed. Ra-haar and huzzah!"

"Huzzah!" bellowed the Maggies.

"We ought sweeten our triumph!" Comet howled from the stern.

Iron Eyes evaluated the young Zeelander with eyebrow cocked. "Tell us, Comet, what do you propose?"

"Dear Captain, permit me to paint a picture for the 16 and one score rogues gathered here. Upon this ship lies the glittering fruits of our mischief. Tis right proper to laden our wealth into skiff and longboat, so as to touch upon the first convenient port and put our coin to use. Pyrates all the seas over travel a common road. We seek rebellious pursuits, wicked employment, strong liquor, and binging upon women, is that not so? Or are we a guild of haberdashers, cobblers, and tooth-doctors?" He paused to allow the Maggies a moment to exclaim their yowls of protest. "Nay, nay, we are not! Sea-wolves are we!"

"Aye, we must pursue deviltry!" Howler Dornan declared, racing his agreement. "And our barbarity at port serves a further purpose. Tearing through a settlement as patrons of the Devil, venting a million curses, we spread cold fear throughout the Caribbee. Our reputation will assure that no gunship will chance to chase us – not even the wretched Spanish *guardacosta*."

Yellows contributed an additional aye. "We might release our primal tensions and—"

"Forsooth, what is there to debate?" Joy de Bones interrupted. "Needs must take a woman with terrible force at once, else my jammed scrotum shall blow with such force that you shall drown!"

Iron Eyes allowed the guffaws and cheers to continue for several minutes before clearing his throat. "Alas, my mates. This shall not happen. For if we deny our compact with don

Francisco de Leiva, then the Spanish *guardacosta* will hunt us for the remainder of our days. Tis not possible to dice, whore, and drink from under six feet of earth."

"As pirates, we pledge our lives to a brief yet starry existence," Yellows argued.

"Live for the day!" Comet seconded.

"Or live *but* a day," Iron Eyes blared in return. He jumped down from the chests to position himself aside Tiburon. "We have set our course for the Bahia de Samaná in pursuit of La Beduina, the vessel that bears the prize don Francisco de Leiva seeks. Only upon capturing her treasure might we venture forth as true pirates upon the seas, unencumbered by obligations and free from pursuit by the Spanish *guardacosta*."

Many of the complement moaned loudly. Seditious whispers arose faster than winds in a hurricane. The majority of fighters from St. Kitts and Throat's original crew moved together, forming a coalition against one wall. Tiburon, Jonah, Splosh, and a handful of others grouped behind their captain, signaling their support.

"Hey ho, Iron Eyes!" called Toulouk. "Once you accused our buccaneer leader Mota Sinan of possessing no more valor than the dirt beneath our feet. You compared him to a grub trampled by don Francisco de Leiva's boots. And yet now you display similar meek obedience?"

Hissing, Yellows, Howler Dornan and Joy de Bones unsheathed blades. Hulking forms amassed into a giant shadow. Iron Eyes felt his grip over the Maggies slipping.

"We stand a complement of free men," Comet challenged. "We might put your captainship to a vote and hail a different leader, one who champions *our* pyrate cause. Is that not so, Iron Eyes?"

"Shut your shit hole, you fool," Throat uttered with a ferocity that quieted every voice on deck. Comet startled to hear his former companion denigrate him so. Throat leapt atop the chests, scanning the eyes glued upon him. "I'll tell you true: Protection from the Spanish forces is no small promise. When bested by the *guardacosta*, the Heavens spin in reverse. Capture by them outdoes your worst nightmares, for they be a hideous fact of *real*."

The men watched him with eyes narrowed and blades ever ready.

Throat stroked his intact hand against the scars encircling his neck. "Caught at sea, the Spanish *soldados* won't put you straight to sword. Especially not if your lot has offended them by, say, betraying their master don Francisco de Leiva or disfiguring their captain Sangrienta's pretty face with partridge shot." He turned a glare upon Jonah. "If they figure you hold secrets, they'll lash a slow match round your wrist and interview you as it burns. Supposing you do not reveal a worthy tidbit? Well, the flame will take to peeling your flesh straight down to the bone. Tis startling how the charred hand just snaps off." He lifted his knife-hand towards the mesmerized eyes.

"Of course, there always exists the possibility of hanging," he remarked. "But see here, no suitable gallows exist about Santo Domingo or Jamaica, so the *cabildo* officials employ a cottonwood tree and horse cart for the task. That makes for macabre comedy. The condemned man might thrash and kick his soul away for the better part of an hour without dying. Upon one famed occasion, after the offending party was certified dead, the wagon rolled off and… *wham*!

The brute sprang back to life alike Jesus himself!" Throat guffawed, an unnerving sound. "It was nearly worth the agony endured to mock the panicked executioner."

The men stood motionless. Then a cough was expelled from where Portugal rested against the gunwales, his sweaty skin devoid of color. "Villainous though she may be, the Spanish Empire and her dependencies uphold a law that no man may be double hanged," the sickly mariner said in a low voice. "Kindly edify us, Master Throat. What happens when a fellow owes the kingdom his life but refuses to die?"

Throat's shoulders hunched forward, as if defending against a nippy breeze. "You be made a slave."

Gauging the disheartened expressions of the assembled tars, Iron Eyes climbed aside Throat on the chests. He stalled a hand upon the hilt of his prized pistol before crying out, "But once we have trounce every last man aboard La Beduina and over-ended their corpses into the seas, we shall rip the vessel apart till she is spoiled utterly of her hidden wealth, same as we did just yesterday when we won our prize. Our purses then will burst with one thousand times the treasure you now possess — more than a common man has the possibility of earning in a million lifetimes!"

"And how can you be certain that we may win vast riches by capturing La Beduina?" Comet questioned.

"Why do you think don Francisco de Leiva has commanded us — and without question, a dozen other vessels — to capture La Beduina? For this simple reason: She contains the keys to more wealth and power than your pygmy imaginations ever might conjure," Throat said.

"Your life upon your oath, Iron Eyes: On the other side of this errand, you shall cease your belly-scraping? We shall find freedom for every sea rover, with no further biddings from Spanish nobles to fulfill?" Howler Dornan demanded.

"None. As Throat spoke it: We shall enjoy riches and freedom more extreme than you can conceive," the pyrate captain promised.

"The mother countries of Europe will not allow us to forge onward," Comet argued. He pushed himself to standing aloft the carriage of a nine-pound brass cannon. "Across the Western Ocean, commoners are meant to endure the condition of hopelessness forever."

Iron Eyes strolled closer to the fledgling rover. "A truer word cannot be spoken. Europe is beyond hope."

"But this New World," Throat argued, "this New World shall overthrow her colonial yokes. We shall be commanded not by kings, but as rascals we shall rule over ourselves."

"Aye," Iron Eyes smiled, "this corner of the globe offers the venue wherein the low-born may at last trounce history."

He held his breath, seconds passed as he gauged the impact of the debate upon the complement. Temporarily, at least, they seemed appeased. An idea sprang to the top of his mind. "Fetch a bolt of light cloth," he asked the shipwright, Toulouk.

As if speaking from the supremacy of a pulpit, Iron Eyes addressed his crew once more. "Wish to innovate our gang of rovers beyond what Mota Sinan has achieved with his Brethren of the North Coast. His forces consort only when undertaking an exploit, like our recent spoiling of the Rode Afgunst. Elsewise, they stay loyal to their own free will. In the condition we find ourselves, however – living together in spare quarters aboard a ship-of-war – we cannot come and go as we please. We unite at all times under a common purpose. During the lulls in action especially we must remain bound together. But how?"

He clapped his thighs with both hands and removed his cutlash. Opening his palm as though begging for coin, he hissed across it the foot-long edge of his blade. Blood flowed. His arm he held aloft till a vermillion streaked from hand to shoulder.

"Now," Iron Eyes said, his gaze pinned upon Toulouk. The shipwright flung to the captain a bolt of broadcloth used to repair sails. It was as white as seafoam until Iron Eyes grasped it and donated to it his life force.

Suspended in silence, the tars fixed unwavering eyes upon their leader. Without a word, Tiburon gestured for the cloth. Dagger in hand, he sliced his own palm and sponged up the blood. When he peered up at Iron Eyes, a smile danced between them brighter than the North Star.

Throat came forward. His knife-hand skated a line across the other palm. He grasped hold of the linen cloth. Then Comet slid beside his mentor and mimicked the act, harnessing Throat's blade.

Knocking their way to the front of the crowd came Jonah and Splosh. Soon, all of Mota's men fought to participate, : Scipio, Ibra, Chucho, Winter Seasal, Toulouk, and Dario. Following along without hesitation came Portugal's recruits, Luka Fly and Yellows, then the men of St. Kitts: Hendrik Boer, Joy de Bones, and Howler Dornan. The rest joined till every sailor excepting Portugal had added his vital fluid to the broadcloth. Not a word was spoken as the wounded, aging mariner stumbled to his feet to contribute his own blood.

The bolt of linen was sodden now with crimson poured from their veins. Snagging the salacious fabric by the peak of his cutlash, Iron Eyes lifted their would-be flag to the ceiling. His voice bore grit when he made his pronouncement. "*Dignity demands freedom.* Let the world know they can expect no quarter from the pyrates of the Black Maggie whensoever we fly this, our banner of blood!"

EPILOGUE

England

IN WHICH A CONQUEST IS ORDAINED

"Reckon but minutes after the bishop placed his hands upon your floppy head and bid you welcome to the Church of England, you sprinted out of the cathedral set upon bedding a woman," sneered the captain of the yeomen at Whitehall, the palatial London residence that served as the seat of governance for Oliver Cromwell and many an English monarch before him.

Father Thomas Gage suppressed his frustration. Tall and lank with bowed shoulders, his swarthy complexion had suffered from nearly a decade of adventuring as a Dominican friar beneath the corrosive Caribbean sun. Yet in spite of how the Yeoman captain's remark rankled him, Gage could not deny the level of truth it bore. The disgraced progeny of an Old English Catholic family, he had, in recent years, cast aside his black robes in favor of the white-collared black cassock of an Anglican priest. This man was not the first to question whether Gage had converted solely because the Church of England authorized clergymen to marry – which promptly he had done.

"I present this missive, which has traveled forth from the quill of our Lord Protector himself. Hearken now," Gage declared, taunting the scarlet and black-clad yeoman with a slip of paper. "I am, on this day, programmed for an audience with Sir Cromwell. We join minds in matters of statecraft. The first who hinders me in this duty shall be the first to have his head unlinked from his neck!"

"Why should His Highness the Lord Protector include *you* amongst his trusted advisors?" the yeoman captain scoffed, ever dubious of the convert's sincerity.

Six years prior, in the year of our Lord 1648, Thomas Gage had published *The English-American: A New Survey of The West Indies*. It lambasted the Spanish monks who proselytized throughout the New World, accusing them of debauched and sinful lifestyles, and thereby laid bare the hypocrisy of the Inquisition. Prone to aggrandizements, plagiarism, and outright falsehoods as Gage's book was, it nevertheless had capsized Protestant England's worldview by championing a holy crusade to bring about a new global order wherein Spain no longer reigned supreme.

The text even had attracted the attention of England's self-proclaimed Lord Protector. A few months past, Oliver Cromwell had pressed a fresh edition of the polemic. It was the reason why Thomas Gage had been invited to attend the Privy Council this gloomy April morning. Cromwell was intent upon tipping the scales of geographic supremacy in favor of England through his preferred method – a religious war.

The yeoman captain investigated over and again the certificate Gage had handed him, which professed to have been published by the Privy Council. He could identify no errors. The seal authenticating the clergyman's admission to the palace was full-proof. With a reticent sigh, the captain granted Thomas Gage passage into Whitehall.

Just then, a *coach and six* finalized its approach. Five years hence, before Cromwell had beheaded King Charles I, the majestic vehicle had been termed a *royal carriage*. With England since established as a Commonwealth, the coach belonged now to the republic. Nevertheless, it remained festooned with elaborate decorations, including a champagne lacquer and gold leaf trimmings. Signature emblems of a lion and a unicorn declared it without dispute the chariot of the Lord Protector himself.

Traveling toward Whitehall, the coach had corked the roadway, thwarting the flow of wagons, merchants, traders, and the working poor who thrust from every direction of the capital city. The clock tolled nine and still the predicament had not resolved. A torrential rain commenced, causing gutters to flood, currents of rubbish and mud to leap beyond the curbs, steaming heaps of animal dung and human waste to wash through the streets, and besieged bystanders to cram against the walls of nearby houses and shops for protection. Meanwhile, coal and wood embers sagging from the London sky assaulted their weary lungs and eyes.

As the carriage concluded its journey by making its way through the massive wrought-iron palace gates, a guard chaperoned Father Thomas Gage through a labyrinth of imposing archways, columns, and gardens pruned into art. Gliding like a jailor with a ring of keys, he unlocked and locked a system of doorways.

They moved deeper into Whitehall and its secrets until they arrived upon the council chamber, where the Privy Council convened regularly to decide matters of utmost consequence to the Commonwealth of England. It possessed, Gage thought, an air of grandeur second to none. This was a place of power. The rectangular room boasted a vaulted ceiling. Gage gaped with amazement at the massive depictions of Greek and Roman gods dominating the oak-paneled walls. The portraits of English monarchs that previously had glared down upon attendees had been replaced by these immortal judges.

Overwhelming the chamber floor was a war table covered by maps charting the Spanish Main, Caribbee Sea, and its windward, leeward, and Antilles isles. Around it, three men huddled like the witches of Macbeth adding mysterious ingredients to a potion. Only one of their party did Gage not recognize.

The officer in the pristine crimson waistcoat, who crowned his head by a wig and his shoulders by epaulets dripping with silver fringe, he knew to be General Robert Venables. Across from him, Admiral William Penn shifted miniature sterling ships over a map of the New World. Debating softly with Venables, he landed the model vessels along the narrow isthmus connecting the southern and northern continents of the Americas, which accessed the Darién Province. Penn stood tall, clean-shaven, and resolute, his scheming eyes bearing no hint of kindness.

Two further men occupied the chamber. Upon a chaise in the corner sat Thomas Modyford. The prominent lawyer and colonial administrator of Barbados wore a black coat trimmed with white lace and topped by a ruff collar that advertised his rank as a member of the skeletal Parliament.

He was renowned for piercing the fog of distraction to obtain his objectives. With lips set thin, it seemed to Gage that God had not contrived Barrister Modyford for idle talk.

Secretary of State John Thurloe had ensconced himself in a carved mahogany chair at the opposite corner. Decked in a doublet of deep plum, he wore a close-fitting waistcoat and breeches. With an inscrutable snuffle, he acknowledged the clergyman's entrance. "Well so, *you* are the fellow who summons theology into our military enterprises, oathing that God's favor is necessary for England to triumph."

"Were not identical holy objectives transmitted to the New Model Army afore its landing upon the shores of Ireland?" Gage pointed out.

Although the other men abstained from a riposte, Modyford the barrister cast upon Gage an arched eyebrow. Gage ceded to his inferior status by standing against the wall. From here, he studied the only figure he could not identify.

Despite his youth, the stranger had forced an equal place for himself aside the two senior statesmen gathered round the map table. Gage approximated the handsome, green-eyed, sun-bronzed mariner's age at 20 years. Ignoring the momentous nature of this meeting, the outcast had remained loyal to the accoutrements of a sailor, donning a leather jerkin and musty wool trousers.

Animated by a gut impulse, Gage crossed to him. "Afternoon to you. Father Thomas Gage, I am."

The jolly dissident responded with a toothsome smile backed by cunning and mischief. "Greeting you now is Captain Henry Morgan."

"Your brogue suggests you are a man of Wales," mused Gage.

"Guilty as indicted."

"Doubtless you have been compared to another Welsh sea captain whose name keeps every resident of *Las Indias* awake at night with sleepless anxiety?"

"Aye, you speak of the pyrate called Iron Eyes," confirmed Morgan.

"I do," Gage nodded. His brows bunched into ridges. "Pray, I beg God, you are not of his filthy substance?"

"Rarr! Keep your hair on, sir," Morgan chuckled. "The pyrate you speak of and I are not cousins. Hand on heart. We are as chalk and cheese. My integrity outshines his as noon outdoes dusk."

Perspiration skidded down Gage's face, but Morgan's reassurances calmed his thoughts. "Glory to Lord on High!"

Captain Morgan patted his arm, taking care to quash an inflating smirk. "For sooth, I am not Iron Eyes, but *I am* the next generation of him. The pyrate captain acts as a spark, and I am the fire he ignites."

Gage stepped back, unsure.

In hushed tones, below the notice of the others, Morgan explained himself. "The world is about to break open."

"With whose mission are you aligned?" Gage questioned.

At that second, the grand doors of the chamber hefted open and the supreme figure strode into the council chamber, shoes clicking as softly as the ticking of a second hand. *How can an individual be so ponderous and simultaneously so light, as though fashioned from both mountain and cloud?* Gage wondered. Few ever encountered Oliver Cromwell on such intimate terms. Those who did were mesmerized by him.

Cromwell appeared an elegy to loss and survival. His face and hands were scarred by battle. His meaty shoulders sloped from years exhausted upon a horse. He carried, as well, a mass of belly. Notwithstanding the sterility of his Puritanical faith, he was recognized as a man of sincerity – as long as his guests upheld proper deference, manners, and godliness.

Gage, Thurloe, Modyford, Penn and Venables bowed in sequence before the Lord Protector. Henry Morgan, it became evident, never had attempted a motion of such imaginary importance. His inaugural effort was inept. A prickly silence followed, during which Secretary Thurloe denigrated the sea captain by a look.

A noted opponent of inefficiency, Cromwell forged on, distributing curt salutations before bounding headfirst into the critical decisions facing the Privy Council. Gesturing toward the maps covering the immense war table, he proclaimed, "Noble peers and honorable advisors, we session upon this day to determine our actions against the Catholic Kingdom of Spain. Let us not falter in dominating by righteous crusade all that lays now before our eyes."

He sprung his dress sword from his scabbard and nudged the model ships away from the isthmus and into the Caribbee Sea. "The Lord God demands we cure the New World of the diseased delusion of Catholicism. Despite five years having passed since our crushing of the Irish savages, I cannot shake from mind the terrifying quality of the Papists. Their souls are taken by the Devil.

The fate of the world hinges upon our English valor. We must set our designs upon the Western hemisphere."

With patrician inscrutability, Secretary of State John Thurloe looked at the charts and tokens, which illustrated an arena of warfare that stretched thousands of miles from the continents of *Terre Firme* to *Las Islas de Barlovento*. This would prove the most ambitious and costly military expedition England ever had undertaken. "Tis true, then. You aim to make war on Spain?"

"Not Spain herself, John," Cromwell clarified, "only her unjust holdings in the New World."

"Whatever the genuine impetus of your *Western Designs*, you ought not compare them to Ireland," Secretary Thurloe argued. "That war was won nearly a decade hence. These days, it would be impossible to summon an equivalent force. Our men, horse, and sail are unregulated. Some are novices, others imbeciles. Our present military strikes an ugly contrast to the New Model Army with which you swarmed Irish shores."

Cromwell sidled up to his Secretary of State with his sterling dress sword tucked behind his back. He stood two feet superior and one foot broader than his councilor. "Dear John, there is no halting my murderous designs upon the West. The reason is the same as that which roused me against Ireland: Curb the deformed faith of Catholicism. Only *we* may bring about the day when any individual is entitled to reach God and know His grace directly." He turned to Gage, pressing a palm against the clergyman's shoulder. "As his book states."

"Aye, we all have memorized it," grumbled Secretary Thurloe.

"Not I," Morgan commented. "I am not even aware of it."

Cromwell gave a clenched smiled as he inventoried the mariner with prejudice.

"Captain Henry Morgan is my guest," Barrister Modyford interjected. "During the period when I governed Barbados, I found him unsurpassed in harassing Spanish ships. Reckoned his attitude might refresh our stifled ideations upon this day."

Cromwell accepted the defense with a nod. To Morgan he said, "Father Thomas Gage's publication is titled *The English-American: A New Survey of The West Indies*. You may desire to upgrade your intelligence by reading it."

"Oh, doubtless, sir," Morgan replied. "But as of yet, the book has not circled amongst those of my station. May I ask, what thousand eggs does the father chuck at the Catholics?"

"He tells how Spanish friars poison the New World with toxic immoralities," Cromwell attested before Gage had an opportunity to respond. The Lord Protector's memory for books, discourses, dates, and battles usurped that of most humans. He recited from the polemic. "*The Catholic clergy acted as wretched imps garbed in such unsuitable pieces of finery as orange silk stockings and lace-trimmed drawers, whilst they wantonly diced, gamed, and swore oaths.*"

"Sir, I concur with your designs upon the West," Morgan chuckled under his breath. "But it be a blasted fact that, lacking any forces like the New Model Army, England shall not triumph over Spanish America. Trust me, this campaign will bear no resemblance to the child's play of contesting Ireland."

Cromwell stopped to appraise the young sailor more carefully. "How is it that you, a lad with hardly a dusting of whiskers, proposes so rugged a review of my plans – and with such polished confidence?"

"He plies the Caribbean waters with great gusto," Modyford interjected, shedding light on the enigma. "He has analyzed the features of the region and understands it second to none. Henry Morgan, sir, sails with a roving commission."

"Privateer?" Cromwell asked.

"Faithful in your command, sir," Morgan answered.

"Well so, Captain Morgan, with your *letter of marque*: Lay bare your concepts. If your vision is as sharp as a spy glass, then speak plainly. What am I missing? What doings must I undertake? I covet nothing less than total conquest."

"If your quest be to plant 1,000 English banners across the Americas, Lord Cromwell, then I must urge you to take heed. The Spanish Islanders sizzle as a lot of dare-and-be damned warriors," Morgan replied with a cock-sure grin.

"Ha! Verily, you jape with me!" Cromwell rebutted. "The population of *Las Islas de Barlovento* is comprised of naught more than a handful of milkweed *alcaldes*, regiments in satin hose, unwashed ranchers, and inbred settlers. How might they dismantle England's irrefutable military?" He cast his gaze about, soliciting support from the thus-far hushed military commanders, Penn and Venables.

Morgan swept an arm across the charts of Spanish land holdings, sending model ships sailing through air. "In the year of our Lord 1648, Ireland already was fractured by generations of English settlers, as well as competing cabals quarreling over kings and republics, religion, and rightful heritage. The Spaniards of the New World suffer no such disjointedness. They are rife with patriotism, having built a rugged identity over these 200 years past. The Mother Country lives as distant from their hearts as the moon. They stand strong as the original pioneers of America."

"Say more," Cromwell ordered.

"No matter where you land your ships, you will face the furious blades and gunfire of *hidalgos*, regulated militias, master *caballeros* of the horse, and hog-hunters who have claimed these territories as their own. Forget not, as well, their snarling mastiffs, trained to eat the hearts of their prey."

The realization struck Cromwell between the eyes. "Aye, faith. I do well know the ferocity of such devotion. Never will they suffer the disgrace of surrendering what they call their homeland."

"England possesses not the resources nor the stamina for such a war," Secretary Thurloe stated again.

"You underestimate the sheer grit of our countrymen!" Cromwell snarled.

"You underestimate the fight that shall ensue within these far-away territories," Morgan argued. "The Spanish Islanders will battle with ten times the heart of any English trooper."

At last, Venables stepped in. "But the local populace is weakened by impoverished weapons, and as well lacks scholarship in military tactics."

"Yet they are skilled smugglers, nor are they short of military wiles," Morgan countered.

Cromwell's gray eyes had turned the hue of winter. "You have outlined solid facts, Henry Morgan, but I am wise to cunning men such as you. I reckon you have an offer ready in your pocket."

"You figure me well," Morgan chirped.

"I know you not at all," returned Cromwell. "Simply do I read you like I read a book that bears similarity to a hundred others. Now out with it."

Henry Morgan swallowed the insult and, with a huff of fresh breath, unveiled his plot. "The only way to snatch victory in the New World is to team with parties who yearn same as you. You must share with them your deepest wants. Partner with those who battle *already* your Spanish foes, desperate in their desire for freedom and agency."

"And who might these societies be, pray tell?" inquired Secretary Thurloe.

"Privateers such as myself, for one. Those who have evolved their trade into an independent industry."

"Pyrates," Thomas Gage clarified.

"Aye," confirmed Morgan. He scoped a room of dubious looks and added, "As well, those forcibly imported from Africa."

"Enslaved negros?!" Penn squealed.

"Maroons in particular."

"Gun me in the mouth! Do you speak seriously, lad?" Penn questioned, squeezing his temples.

The Lord Protector, on the other hand, remained still, absorbed in thought. After several seconds, he spoke evenly. "As well we might recruit those expelled from Europe."

"Terrific sooth!" Morgan smiled. "By engaging the Jewry, who operate throughout *Las Indias* as smugglers of both goods and intelligence, we shall gain allies of wondrous wit and daring."

"Tis true. Such an arrangement I have spoken of at length with don Antonio de Carvalhal, better known as the White Oak," Cromwell confessed. "He boasts of his nephew and protégé, whose name carries already the status of a shark in the region – one Gaspar Carvalhal."

The disruption of tradition had proved too unsettling for Secretary Thurloe. "You hope to team our glorious English forces with bands of miscreants, dissemblers, and criminals?"

"Criminals, eh?" Morgan chuckled. "You set yourselves upon robbing half the globe from Spain. Should you succeed, your actions shall be considered the greatest larceny ever to embolden the pages of history! If tis your intent to conquer a prize for the ages, must you recruit an army of true believers willing to pitch their bodies before bullets on behalf of your unified cause. Believers, mind you, who as well possess intimate knowledge of every port, cave, hilltop, and battleground throughout the West Indies. Do you not concur, Lord Cromwell?"

"The Western Design is proclaimed!" Cromwell announced, thudding the maps with a fist. "England shall steal America from the Spanish. Captain Morgan, you and Thurloe secure our alliances. Penn and Venables, you assemble sail, horse and 10,000 foot soldiers before six months pass. Gage, you continue flaming our holy crusade amongst the citizens of our kingdoms. Modyford, you restore to Barbados, whereupon you set ears to the ground so that no subterfuge slips past us."

The five older Privy Council attendees stood silent and stunned. Morgan, however, cheered. "Huzzah, Lord Protector!"

"So it is war?" gasped Secretary Thurloe at last.

"Truly, yes!" rejoiced Cromwell. "War it shall be!"

"But sir, upon which location ought we land our terrific forces?" Modyford inquired.

Cromwell turned to Captain Henry Morgan. The privateer skated eyes across the chart of the Caribbee Sea, landing them nowhere. The Lord Protector gazed toward the heavens. "By God, that shall be a surprise reserved for the final hour."

CAST OF CHARACTERS

IN ALPHABETICAL ORDER BY FIRST NAME

JAMAICA

- **Alzo** – Chief of the Windward Maroon militia.
- **Anapa** – Windward Maroon. Wol's wife.
- **Araña Sangrienta** - Chief naval commander of the Spanish *guardacosta* in the Caribbean.
- **Bequo** – One of Mota's men.
- **The Boson** – Boatswain of the pyrate ship under Captain Iron Eyes.
- **Chucho** – One of Mota's men.
- **Comet / Komeet Jutte** - Throat's trusted ally aboard the Black Maggie.
- **Cristó / Cristóbal de Ysassi** - Ward to don Francisco de Leiva and younger brother to de Leiva's wife Zorayda.
- **Dario Colón** - Columbus heir. One of Mota's men.
- **El Mulato** - Spanish mercenary employed by de Leiva.
- **Francisco de Leiva** – Spanish Jamaican landowner and High Sheriff of the Inquisition.
- **Gaspar Carvalhal** - Jewish smuggler.

- **Hendrik Boer** – Surgeon aboard the Black Maggie.
- **Howler Dornan** – Master of arms aboard the Black Maggie.
- **Ibrahim Reis / Ibra** – One of Mota's men.
- **Iron Eyes** – Pyrate captain.
- **Jaén de Falcona** – Soldier with the Jamaican militia.
- **JoJo** - Nani's daughter.
- **Jonah Profit** - St. Kitts resident who joins the Black Maggie.
- **Joy de Bones** – St. Kitts fighter who joins the Black Maggie.
- **Juan de Serras** - Chief of the Los Vermejales Maroons.
- **Juliana / Jubilee** – Woman enslaved upon the Tello plantation.
- **Justo de Leiva** – Don Francisco de Leiva's son and Cabildo member.
- **Kempo Sybada** - Captain of Gaspar Carvalhal's smuggling vessel.
- **Lope de Medina** – Soldier with the Jamaican militia.
- **Lubolo** – Chief of the Mocho Mountain Maroons.
- **Luka Fly** – Portugal's trusted assistant.
- **Madrileña** - Lubolo's youngest wife.
- **Maxi Supa** - Mistress of don Francisco de Leiva.

- **Mota Sinan** - Leader of Brethren of the North Coast.
- **Nani** – Chief of the Windward Maroons.
- **Paco de Proenza** - *Sargento mayor* of the Jamaican militia.
- **Pink** – Cook aboard the Black Maggie.
- **Portugal / Baltazar Mesquita** - Navigator aboard the Black Maggie.
- **Santángel** – Child guide to Throat.
- **Santo** - Windward Maroon warrior.
- **Sasa** - Monkey man.
- **Scipio** – One of Mota's men.
- **Sipopi** - Windward Maroon woman warrior.
- **Splosh** - St. Kitts resident who joins the Black Maggie.
- **Throat / Owen Butler** - De Leiva's most trusted *bravo*, hailing from Plymouth colony.
- **Tiburon / Tibbs** – A Taíno Jamaican scavenger.
- **TokTok** - A blackshot, or bounty hunter.
- **Toulouk** - One of Mota's men. Shipwright aboard the Black Maggie.
- **Winter Seasal** - One of Mota's men.
- **Wol** - Scout for the Windward Maroons.
- **Xiki** - One of Mota's men.
- **Yellows / Helles LeCat** – Boatswain aboard the Black Maggie.

- **Zacuto** – One of de Leiva's bravos.
- **Zemi** - Tiburon's dog.
- **Zora / Zorayda de Ysassi** – Don Francisco de Leiva's wife and Cristó's elder sister.

IRELAND AND ENGLAND

- **Aisling O'Lorcan / Ash** - Second eldest child of the O'Lorcan family.
- **Angus** – Indentured servant aboard the Gallant.
- **Billy Creed** – Master of arms aboard the Gallant.
- **Catheryn Butler / The Butcher** - English Protestant landowner in Ireland.
- **Ewart** – One of Lady Butler's sons.
- **Fintan O'Lorcan / Fin** - Younger brother to Rory and Aisling.
- **Gareth** – One of Lady Butler's sons.
- **Jezebel / Jez** – Captive of the Butcher.
- **Josiah Gladstone** – Captain of the Gallant.
- **Lucien Gunn** – Sailing master aboard the Gallant.
- **Malcolm** - Indentured servant aboard the Gallant.
- **Mechanic / Haskell Thackery** – Boatswain aboard the Gallant.
- **Oliver Cromwell** – Lord General of England, soon to be anointed Lord Protector.
- **Oliver Riddle** – Pilot of the Gallant.

- **Pero Mesquinho** - Portuguese governor of Cape Verde.
- **Robert Venables** – Major-General of Oliver Cromwell's New Model Army.
- **Rory O'Lorcan** – Tanist of Clan Lorcan. Eldest brother to Aisling and Fintan.
- **Seneschal the Black** - Irish warlord.
- **Septime Devign** - Quartermaster aboard the Gallant.
- **Zosime Montfort** – Ordinary sailor aboard the Gallant.

BIBLIOGRAPHY

BOOKS

Alpern, Stanley B. *Amazons of Black Sparta: The Women Warriors of Dahomey*. New York: New York University Press, 2011.

Appleby, John C. *Women and English Piracy 1540-1720: Partners and Victims of Crime*. Boydell Press, 2015.

Arbell, Mordehay. *The Portuguese Jews of Jamaica*. Kingston, Jamaica: Canoe, 2000.

Arnold, Janet. *Patterns of Fashion 3: The Cut and Construction of Clothes for Men and Women c. 1560-1620*. Drama Publishers, 1985.

Bailey, Beryl L. *Jamaican Creole Syntax: A Transformational Approach*. London: Cambridge University Press, 1966.

Ball, Erica L., Tatiana Siegas and Terri L. Snyder (Editors). *As If She Were Free: A Collective Biography of Women and Emancipation in the Americas.* Cambridge: Cambridge University Press, 2020.

Barreiro, Jose. *Taino: A Novel.* Arte Publico Press, 1993.

Bellamy, R. Reynell (Editor). *Ramblin' Jack: The Journal of Captain John Cremer 1700-1774*. S.l.: S.n., 1936.

Bilby, Kenneth. *True-Born Maroons*. Florida: University Press of Florida, 2008.

Binney, Marcus, John Harris, Kit Martin and Marguerite Curtin. *Jamaica's Heritage: An Untapped Resource: A Preservation Proposal*. Kingston, Jamaica: Mill, 1991.

Black, Clinton. *Tales of Old Jamaica.* New York: Pearson Schools, 1988.

Block, Kristen. *Ordinary Lives in the Caribbean: Religion, Colonial Competition, and the Politics of Profit.* Athens, GA: University of Georgia Press, 2012.

Breverton, Terry. *The Pirate Dictionary*. Gretna, LA: Pelican Pub., 2004.

Brooks, Andrée Aelion. *The Woman Who Defied Kings: The Life and times of Doña Gracia Nasi, a Jewish Leader during the Renaissance*. St. Paul, MN: Paragon House, 2003.

Brown, Vincent. *Tacky's Revolt: The Story of an Atlantic Slave War.* Cambridge, MA: Harvard University Press, 2020.

Brown, Vincent. *The Reaper's Garden: Death and Power in the World of Atlantic Slavery.* Cambridge, MA: Harvard University Press, 2008.

Burnard, Trevor Graeme. *Mastery, Tyranny, and Desire: Thomas Thistlewood and His Slaves in the Anglo-Jamaican World*. Chapel Hill: U of North Carolina, 2004.

Carpenter, John Reeve. *Pirates: Scourge of the Seas*. New York: Barnes & Noble, 2006.

Carrington-Smith, Sandra. *The Book of Obeah*. Ropley: O, 2010.

Cassidy, Frederic Gomes, and Robert Brock LePage. *Dictionary of Jamaican English*. Barbados: U of West Indies, 2002.

Choundas, George. *The Pirate Primer: Mastering the Language of Swashbucklers and Rogues*. Cincinnati, OH: Writer's Digest, 2011.

Cockayne, Emily. *Hubbub: Filth, Noise and Stench in England 1600-1770*. New Haven, CT: Yale University Press, 2007.

Cook, Judith. *Pirate Queen: The Life of Grace O'Malley, 1530-1603*. Douglas Village, Cork: Mercier, 2004.

Cordingly, David. *Under the Black Flag: The Romance and the Reality of Life among the Pirates*. New York: Random House, 1996.

Courlander, Harold. *The African*. New York: Holt, 1993.

Crichton, Michael. *Pirate Latitudes: A Novel.* New York: Harper, 2009.

Cundail, Frank. *Historic Jamaica: With 52 Illustrations.* London: The Institute of Jamaica, 1915.

Dallas, R. C. *The History of the Maroons: From their Origin to the Establishment of their Chief Tribe at Sierra Leone*, Volumes 1 and 2. New York: Routledge, 1803.

De Laurence, L.W. *The Obeah Bible*. S.I: 1915.

Diaz del Castillo, Bernal. *The True History of the Conquest of New Spain*. London: Hackett, 2012.

Druett, Joan. *She Captains: Heroines and Hellions of the Sea*. New York: Simon & Schuster, 2000.

Eaden, John. *The Memoirs of Pere Labat, 1693-1705*. NY: Routledge, 1931.

Einberg, Elizabeth. *William Hogarth: A Complete Catalogue of the Paintings.* London: Paul Mellon Centre for British Art, 2017.

Emmer, P. C. and Germán Carrera Damas. *General History of the Caribbean*. Paris: Unesco, 1999.

Equiano, Olaudah. *Sold as a Slave*. London: Penguin, 2007.

Exquemelin, A. O. *The Buccaneers of America: A True Account of the Most Remarkable Assaults Committed of Late Years upon the Coasts of the West Indies by the Buccaneers of Jamaica and Tortuga, Both English and French.* London: Allen & Unwin, 1951.

Faber, Eli. *Jews, Slaves, and the Slave Trade: Setting the Record Straight.* New York: New York University Press, 1998.

Facey, Valerie. *Busha Browne's Indispensable Compendium of Traditional Jamaican Cookery.* Kingston, Jamaica: Mill, 2008.

Fereal, M.V. de. *The Mysteries of the Inquisition and Other Secret Societies of Spain.* Philadelphia: J.B. Lippincott, 1845.

Fraser, Antonia. *Cromwell, the Lord Protector.* New York: D.I. Fine, 1973.

Frazer, James George. *The Golden Bough: A Study in Magic and Religion: A New Abridgement from the Second and Third Editions.* Oxford: Oxford University Press, 1998.

Frisvold, Nicholaj De Mattos. *Obeah: A Sorcerous Ossuary.* S.l.: Hadean, 2014.

Fukuyama, Francis. *Origins of Political Order: From Prehuman Times to the French Revolution.* New York: Farrar, Straus & Giroux, 2011.

Gambrill, Anthony. *In Search of the Buccaneers.* Oxford, OX: MacMillan Caribbean, 2007.

Gaskill, Malcolm. *The Ruin of All Witches: Life and Death in the New World.* New York: Penguin, 2021.

Gradner, John. *Grendel.* New York: Random House, 1971.

Graeber, David and David Wengrow. *The Dawn of Everything: A New History of Humanity.* New York: Farrar, Straus and Giroux, 2021.

Gent, B. E. *A New Dictionary of the Terms Ancient and Modern of the Canting Crew*. Middletown, DE: Leopold Classic Library, 2015.

Gerber, Jane S. and Miriam Bodian. *The Jews in the Caribbean*. Oxford: Littman Library of Jewish Civilization, 2014.

Glascock, William N. *The Naval Officers Manual: For Every Grade in Her Majesty's Ships*. London: G. Phipps, 1923.

González, Justo L. *The Story of Christianity, Books One and Two*. New York: HarperCollins, 2010.

Great Britain Hydrographic Office. *The African Pilot, or Sailing Directions for the Western Coast of Africa, Volume 1*. BiblioBazaar, 2009.

Green, Jonathan. *Cassell's Dictionary of Slang (2nd Ed)*. London: Cassell Publishing, 2006.

Griffin, Nicholas. *The Requiem Shark*. Abacus, 2000.

Hall, Douglas and Thomas Thistlewood. *In Miserable Slavery: Thomas Thistlewood in Jamaica, 1750-86*. Kingston, Jamaica: U of the West Indies, 1999.

Hansen, Ron. *Desperadoes*. New York: Alfred A. Knopf, 1979.

Hansen, Ron. *The Kid: A Novel*. NY: Simon & Schuster, 2016.

Harari, Yuval Noah. *Sapiens: A Brief History of Humankind*. London: Harvill Secker First, 2014.

Herne, Robin. *A Dangerous Place*. Winchester: Moon Books, 2013.

Hogarth, William. *80 Prints and Drawings*. Narim Bender, 2015.

Hughes, Ben. *Apocalypse 1692: Empire, Slavery, and the Great Port Royal Earthquake*. Westholme Publishing, 2017.

Hurston, Zora Neale. *Barracoon: The Story of the Last "Black Cargo."* Amistad, 2018.

James, Marlon. *A Brief History of Seven Killings: A Novel.* New York: Riverhead, 2015.

Johnson, Charles. *Pirates: A General History of the Robberies and Murders of the Most Notorious Pirates.* London: Conway Maritime, 2004.

Johnson, Steven. *Enemy of All Mankind: A True Story of Piracy, Power, and History's First Global Manhunt.* New York: Riverhead, 2020.

Karlsen, Carol F. *The Devil in the Shape of a Woman: Witchcraft in Colonial New England.* New York: Norton, 1998.

Kehlmann, Daniel. *Tyll: A Novel.* New York: Pantheon, 2020.

Kerigan, Thomas. *The Young Navigator's Guide to the Sidereal and Planetary Parts of Nautical Astronomy.* London: Baldwin, Cradock, and Joy, 1821.

King, Dean, John B. Hattendorf and J. Worth Estes. *A Sea of Words: A Lexicon and Companion to the Complete Seafaring Tales of Patrick O'Brian.* New York: Henry Holt, 2000.

Kohlenberger, John R. and Alfred W. Pollard. *The Holy Bible: 1611 Edition, King James Version.* Peabody, MA: Hendrickson, 2010.

Konstam, Angus and Tony Bryan. *The Pirate Ship: 1660-1730.* Oxford: Osprey, 2004.

Kupperman, Karen. *The Jamestown Project.* Boston: Harvard University Press, 2009.

Kurson, Robert. *Pirate Hunters: Treasure, Obsession, and the Search for a Legendary Pirate Ship.* London: Elliott and Thompson, 2015.

Lane, Kris. *Potosi: The Silver City That Changed the World* (Vol 27). Oakland: University of California Press, 2021.

Latimer, Jon. *Buccaneers of the Caribbean: How Piracy Forged an Empire*. Cambridge, MA: Harvard University Press, 2009.

Law, Robin. *Ouidah: The Social History of a West African Slaving Port, 1727-1892*. UK: James Currey, 2004.

Leeson, Peter T. *The Invisible Hook: The Hidden Economics of Pirates*. Princeton, NJ: Princeton University Press, 2011.

Little, Benerson. *Golden Age of Piracy: The Truth Behind Pirate Myths*. Skyhorse, Inc., 2016.

Lynch, Paul. *Red Sky in Morning*. NY: Little Brown, 2013.

Mann, Charles C. *1493: Uncovering the New World Columbus Created*. New York: Vintage Books, 2012.

McFarlane, Milton C. *Cudjoe of Jamaica: Pioneer for Black Freedom in the New World*. R. Enslow, 1977.

McLaughlan, Ian. *The Sloop of War: 1650-1763*. Barnsley: Seaforth Publ., 2014.

Mohr, Melissa. *Holy Sh*t. A Brief History of Swearing*. Corby: Oxford Academic, 2013.

Moorman, George J. *The Latin Mass Explained.* Charlotte, NC: TAN Books, 2007.

Morgan, Kenneth. *The Bright-Meyler Papers a Bristol-West India Connection, 1732-1837*. Oxford: Oxford University Press, 2007.

Muldoon, Sylvan Joseph and Hereward Carrington. *The Projection of the Astral Body*. York Beach, ME: Samuel Wesier, 1973.

Newman, Simon P. *A New World of Labor: The Development of Plantation Slavery in the British Atlantic*. Philadelphia: U of Pennsylvania Press, 2013.

Offodile, Buchi. *The Orphan Girl: And Other Stories, West African Folk Tales*. Northampton, MA: Interlink Books, 2001.

Padrón, Francisco Morales. *Spanish Jamaica*. Kingston: Randle Publishing, 2003.

Payne-Jackson, Arvilla and Mervyn C. Alleyne. *Jamaican Folk Medicine: A Source of Healing*. Jamaica: U of the West Indies, 2004.

Peek, Philip M. and Kwesi Yankah (Editors). *African Folklore: An Encyclopedia.* Routledge, 2003.

Pestana, Carla Gardina. *The English Conquest of Jamaica: Oliver Cromwell's Bid for Empire*. Harvard: Belknap Press, 2017.

Powers, Karen Vieras. *Women in the Crucible of Conquest: The Gendered Genesis of Spanish American Society 1500-1600.* Albuquerque, NM: University of New Mexico Press, 2005.

Powers, Tim. *On Stranger Tides*. New York: Harper, 2011.

Pugin, A. Welby. *Glossary of Ecclesiastical Ornament and Costume (2nd Edition)*. Charleston, SC: Nabu Press, 2011.

Raffaele, Herbert A. and Wiley, James W. *Wildlife of the Caribbean*. Princeton: Princeton University Press, 2014.

Ranston, Jackie. *Belisario: Sketches of Character: A Historical Biography of a Jamaican Artist*. Kingston: Mill, 2008.

Ranston, Jackie. *The Lindo Legacy*. London: Toucan, 2000.

Rediker, Marcus. *Between the Devil and the Deep Blue Sea: Merchant Seamen, Pirates, and the Anglo-American Maritime World,*

1700-1750. Cambridge: Cambridge University Press, 1987.

Rediker, Marcus. *The Slave Ship: A Human History*. New York: Penguin, 2008.

Rediker, Marcus. *Villains of All Nations: Atlantic Pirates in the Golden Age.* New York: Beacon Press, 2005.

Robertson, James. *Gone Is the Ancient Glory: Spanish Town, Jamaica, 1534-2000*. Kingston, Jamaica: Ian Randle, 2005.

Robson, Martin and Mark Myers. *Not Enough Room to Swing a Cat: Naval Slang and Its Everyday Usage*. Annapolis, MD: Naval Institute, 2008.

Rodger, N. A. M. *The Command of the Ocean: 1649-1815*. London: Allen Lane, 2004.

Roth, Cecil. *A History of the Marranos*. New York: Sepher-Hermon, 1992.

Rutherfurd, Edward. *New York: The Novel.* New York: Ballantine, 2009.

Sackville, Amy. *Painter to the King.* London: Granta Books, 2019.

Sears, Stephen W. (Editor). *The Horizon History of the British Empire.* New York: McGraw-Hill, 1973.

Seeman, Erik R. *Death in the New World: Cross-Cultural Encounters 1492-1800*. Philadelphia: University of Pennsylvania Press, 2011.

Seeman, Erik R. *Speaking with the Dead in Early America.* Philadelphia: University of Pennsylvania Press, 2019.

Simpson, John. *The First English Dictionary of Slang 1699*. Oxford: Bodleian Library, 2010.

Socias, James. *Daily Roman Missal (7th Edition)*. Grove, IL: Midwest Theological Forum, 2011.

Sommer, Elyse. *Similes Dictionary.* Visible Ink Press, 2013.

Spenser, Edmund. *The Present State of Ireland*. Oxford: Clarendon Press, 1970.

Stapelberg, Monica-Maria. *Strange but True: A Historical Background to Popular Beliefs and Traditions*. Crux, 2014.

Stedman, John Gabriel, Richard Price and Sally Price. *Stedman's Surinam Life in Eighteenth-century Slave Society*. Baltimore: Johns Hopkins University Press, 1992.

Steinbeck, John. *The Log from the Sea of Cortez: The Narrative Portion of the Book, Sea of Cortez*. New York: Viking, 1951.

Talty, Stephan. *Empire of Blue Water: Captain Morgan's Great Pirate Army, the Epic Battle for the Americas, and the Catastrophe That Ended the Outlaws' Bloody Reign*. New York: Three Rivers, 2008.

Tibbles, Anthony. *Transatlantic Slavery: Against Human Dignity*. Liverpool: Liverpool University Press/ National Museums Liverpool, 2005.

Trouillot, Michel-Rolph. *Silencing the Past: Power and the Production of History.* Boston: Beacon Press, 1995.

Van Vechten, Carl. *Nigger Heaven.* Chicago, IL: University of Illinois Press, 1926.

Waddell, Gene. *The Taino in 1492*. Middletown, DE: People of One Fire, 2015.

Whitehead, Colson. *The Underground Railroad: A Novel*. New York: Doubleday, 2016.

Will de Chaparro, Martina and Miruna Achim. *Death and Dying in Colonial Spanish America.* Tuscon: University of Arizona Press, 2011.

Worsley, Frank Arthur. *Shackleton's Boat Journey*. New York: Norton, 1998.

JOURNAL ARTICLES

Aceto, Michael. "Ethnic Personal Names and Multiple Identities in Anglophone Caribbean Speech Communities in Latin America." *Language in Society*, Vol. 31, No. 4 (Sept 2002), pp. 577-608.

Achinstein, Sharon. "John Foxe and the Jews." *Renaissance Quarterly*, Vol. 54, No. 1 (Spring 2001), pp. 86-120.

Blake, Lady & Edith. "The Maroons of Jamaica." *The North American Review*, Vol. 167, No. 504 (Nov 1898), pp. 558- 568.

Brown, Vincent. "Spiritual Terror and Sacred Authority in Jamaican Slave Society." *Slavery and Abolition*, Vol. 24, No. 1 (April 2003), pp. 24-53.

Bryan, Patrick. "Spanish Jamaica." *Caribbean Quarterly*, Vol. 38, No. 2/3, *Caribbean Quincentennial* (June - Sept 1992), pp. 21-31.

Buissieret, David. "Studying the Natural Sciences in Seventeenth-Century Jamaica." *Caribbean Quarterly*, Vol. 55, No. 3 (Sept 2009), pp. 71-86.

Bush, Jr., Harold K. "A Brief History of PC, With Annotated Bibliography." *American Studies International*, Vol. 33, No. 1 (April 1995), pp. 42-64.

Canny, Nicholas. "The Ideology of English Colonization: From Ireland to America," *The William and Mary Quarterly*, (1973), pp. 575–98.

Carrió-Invernizzi, Diana. "Gift and Diplomacy in Seventeenth-Century Spanish Italy." *The Historical Journal*, Vol. 51, No. 4 (Dec 2008), pp. 881-899.

Chaplin, Joyce E. "Natural Philosophy and an Early Racial Idiom in North America: Comparing English and Indian Bodies." *William and Mary Quarterly*, Vol. 54, No. 1 (Jan 1997), pp. 229-252.

Cray, Ed. "The Rabbi Trickster." The Journal of American Folklore, Vol. 77, No. 306 (Oct - Dec 1964), pp. 331-345.

Danachair, Caoimhín Ó. "Irish Tower Houses and Their Regional Distribution." *Béaloideas*, Iml. 45/47 (1977 - 1979), pp. 158-163.

Detweiler, Robert. "The Jesus Jokes: Religious Humor in the Age of Excess." *CrossCurrents*, Vol. 24, No. 1 (Spring 1974), pp. 55-74.

DjeDje, Jacqueline Cogdell. "Remembering Kojo: History, Music, and Gender in the January Sixth Celebration of the Jamaican Accompong Maroons." *Black Music Research Journal*, Vol. 18, No. 1/2 (Spring - Autumn, 1998), pp. 67-120.

Domowitz, Susan. "The Orphan in Cameroon Folklore and Fiction." *Research in African Literatures*, Vol. 12, No. 3, Special Issue on Oral Traditions (Autumn 1981), pp. 350-358.

Earle, Rebecca. "If You Eat Their Food: Diets and Bodies in Early Colonial Spanish America." *American Historical Review* (June 2010), pp. 688-713.

Echols, Edward C. "The Art of Classical Swearing." *The Classical Journal*, Vol. 46, No. 6 (Mar 1951), pp. 291-298.

Eden, Trudy. "Food, Assimilation, and the Malleability of the Body in Early Virginia." *A Centre of Wonders: The Body in Early America*, eds. Janet Moore Lindman and Michele Lise Tarter (Cornell, 2002), pp. 29-42.

Ennis, Elisabeth Logan. "Women's Names Among the Ovimbundu of Angola." *African Studies*, Vol. 4, No. 1, (1945), pp. 1-8.

Gerhard, Peter. "The Tres Marías Pirates." *Pacific Historical Review*, Vol. 27, No. 3 (Aug 1958), pp. 239-244.

Goebel, Jr., Julius. "King's Law and Local Custom in Seventeenth Century New England." *Columbia Law Review*, Vol. 31, No. 3 (Mar 1931), pp. 416-448.

Grubb, Farley. "The Market for Indentured Immigrants: Evidence on the Efficiency of Forward-Labor Contracting in Philadelphia, 1745-1773. *Journal of Economic History*, Vol. XLV, No. 4 (Dec 1985), pp. 855-868.

Hahn, Steven. "Slave Rebellions and Mutinies Shaped the Age of Revolution." *Boston Review*, April 23, 2021.

Jackson, Rachel. "The Trans-Atlantic Journey of Gumbé: Where and Why Has It Survived?" *African Music*, Vol. 9, No. 2 (2012), pp. 128-153.

Jamieson, Ross W. "The Essence of Commodification: Caffeine Dependencies in the Early Modern World." *Journal of Social History*, Vol. 35, No. 2 (Winter 2001), pp. 269-294.

Klein, Herbert S. "The English Slave Trade to Jamaica, 1782-1808." *The Economic History Review New Series*, Vol. 31, No. 1 (Feb 1978), pp. 25-45.

Kroeker, Ron. "Xenophon as a Critic of the Athenian Democracy." *History of Political Thought*, Vol. 30, No. 2 (Summer 2009), pp. 197-228.

Kupperman, Karen. "Fear of Hot Climates in the Anglo-American Colonial Experience." *William and Mary Quarterly* (April 1984), pp. 213-240.

Livingston, Thomas W. "Ashanti and Dahomean Architectural Bas-Reliefs." *African Studies Review*, Vol. 17, No. 2 (Sept 1974), pp. 435-448.

Lobingier, Charles Sumner. "Las Siete Partidas in Full English Dress." *The Hispanic American Historical Review*, Vol. 9, No. 4 (Nov 1929), pp. 529-544.

Lovejoy, Henry B. "The Registers of Liberated Africans of the Havana Slave Trade Commission: Transcription Methodoloy and Statistical Analysis." *African Economic History*, Vol. 38 (2010), pp. 107-135.

MacMullen, Ramsay. "Christian Ancestor Worship in Rome." *Journal of Biblical Literature*, Vol. 129, No. 3 (Fall 2010), pp. 597-613.

Martin-Casares, Aurelia and Barranco, Marga G. "The Musical Legacy of Black Africans in Spain: A Review of Our Sources." *Anthropological Notebooks*, Vol. 15, No. 2 (2009), pp. 51–60.

McDaniel, Lorna. "The Flying Africans: Extent and Strength of the Myth in the Americas." *Nieuwe West-Indische Gids / New West Indian Guide*, Vol. 64, No. 1/2 (1990), pp. 28-40.

McEwan, Bonnie G. "The Archaeology of Women in the Spanish New World." *Historical Archaeology*, Vol. 25, No. 4, Gender in Historical Archaeology (1991), pp. 33-41.

Montero, Raquel Gil. "Free and Unfree Labour in the Colonial Andes in the Sixteenth and Seventeenth Centuries." *International Review of Social History*, Vol. 56, Special Issue 19: The Joy and Pain of Work: Global Attitudes and Valuations, 1500-1650 (2011), pp. 297-318.

Morgan, Jennifer. "'Some Could Suckle over Their Shoulder:' Male Travelers, Female Bodies, and the Gendering of Racial Ideology, 1500-1770." *William and Mary Quarterly*, Vol. 54, No. 1 (Jan 1997), pp. 167-192.

Murphy, Eileen M. "Children's Burial Grounds in Ireland (Cillíní) and Parental Emotions Toward Infant Death." *International Journal of Historical Archaeology*, Vol. 15, No. 3 (Sept 2011), pp. 409-428.

Ordoñez, Margaret T. and Welters, Linda. "Textiles from the Seventeenth-Century Privy at the Cross Street Back Lot Site." *Historical Archaeology*, Vol. 32, No. 3, Perspectives on the Archaeology of Colonial Boston: The Archaeology of the Central Artery/Tunnel Project, Boston, Massachusetts (1998), pp. 81-90.

Phipps, Frances. "Drinking Vessels of the Colonists." *The New York Times*, (Oct 18, 1981), Section 11, p. 8.

Pocock, J.G.A. "What Do We Mean by Europe?" *The Wilson Quarterly*, Vol. 21, Issue 1 (Winter 1997).

Özveren, Y. Eyüp. "Shipbuilding, 1590-1790." *Review* (Fernand Braudel Center) Vol. 23, No. 1, Commodity Chains in the World-Economy, 1590–1790 (2000), pp. 15-86.

Pestana, Carla Gardina. "Early English Jamaica without Pirates." *The William and Mary Quarterly*, Vol. 71, No. 3 (July 2014), pp. 321-360.

Radin, Max and Nichols, Madaline W. "Las Siete Partidas." *California Law Review*, Vol. 20, No. 3 (Mar 1932), pp. 260-285.

Robinson, Willard B. "Colonial Ranch Architecture in the Spanish-Mexican Tradition." *The Southwestern Historical Quarterly*, Vol. 83, No. 2 (Oct 1979), pp. 123-150.

Rucker, Walter. "Conjure, Magic, and Power: The Influence of Afro-Atlantic Religious Practices on Slave Resistance and Rebellion." *Journal of Black Studies*, Vol. 32, No. 1 (Sept 2001), pp. 84-103.

Rudolph, Jessica. "Rape and Resistace: Women and Consent in Seventeenth-Century English Legal and Political Thought." *Journal of British Studies*, Vol. 39, No. 2 (April 2000), pp. 157-184.

Rugemer, Edward B. "The Development of Mastery and Race in the Comprehensive Slave Codes of the Greater Caribbean during the Seventeenth Century." *The William and Mary Quarterly*, Vol. 70, No. 3 (July 2013), pp. 429-458.

Schmitt, Casey. "Centering Spanish Jamaica: Regional Competition, Informal Trade, and the English Invasion, 1620–62." *The William and Mary Quarterly*, Vol. 76, No. 4 (Oct 2019), pp. 697-726.

Schmitt, Casy. "Virtue in Corruption: Privateers, Smugglers, and the Shape of Empire in the 18th Century Caribbean." *Early American Studies*, Vol. 13, No. 1 (Winter 2015), pp. 80-110.

Sharples, Jason T. "Discovering Slave Conspiracies: New Fears of Rebellion and Old Paradigms of Plotting in Seventeenth-Century Barbados." *The American Historical Review*, Vol. 120, No. 3 (2015), pp. 811-43.

Shawcross, John T. "John Milton and His Spanish and Portuguese Presence." *Milton Quarterly*, Vol. 32, No. 2 (May 1998), pp. 41-52.

Smith, Roland M. "The Irish Background of Spenser's 'View'." *The Journal of English and German Philology*, Vol. 42, No. 4 (Oct. 1943), pp. 499-515.

Sorrenson, Richard. "The Ship as a Scientific Instrument in the Eighteenth Century." *Osiris*, Vol. 11, Science in the Field (1996), pp. 221-236.

Stampa, Manuel Carrera. "The Evolution of Weights and Measures in New Spain." *The Hispanic American Historical Review*, Vol. 29, No. 1 (Feb 1949), pp. 2-24.

Thornton, John. "Central African Names and African-American Naming Patterns." *The William and Mary Quarterly*, Vol. 50, No. 4 (Oct 1993), pp. 727-742.

Wilder, JeffriAnne. "Revisiting 'Color Names and Color Notions': A Contemporary Examination of the Language and Attitudes of Skin Color Among Young Black Women." *Journal of Black Studies*, Vol. 41, No. 1 (Sept 2010), pp. 184-206.

Wright, Irene A. "The Spanish Resistance to the English Occupation of Jamaica, 1655-1660." *Transactions of the Royal Historical Society*, Vol. 13 (1930), pp. 117-147.

ADDITIONAL SOURCES

Demonstration of a 17th C Ship Cannon. Smithsonian Channel, April 16, 2020.

The 1619 Project. *The New York Times Magazine*, 2019.

ABOUT THE AUTHOR

KIRAN is an author and award-winning filmmaker with extensive experience as a Hollywood writer, director, editor and photographer, as well as a branded content producer.

A rare left and right-brained creative, KIRAN's journey began with an MFA in Directing from the USC School of Cinematic Arts. His thesis film was selected by the highly competitive 546 Committee to be fully funded by the University. This first short film won student honors at the Kennedy Center. Honing his craft, KIRAN wrote and directed the short film KID BANG, which earned him a three-picture writing and directing deal with Fox Searchlight. He also won a Directors Guild Award for editing and directing the short.

In the years following, several of KIRAN's screenplays were optioned by the major entertainment studios. He directed TV, internet media, short films, documentaries, music videos, and advertisements. His commercial spot clients included Coca-Cola, Beats by Dre, Major League Soccer,

Hydrolab, Pepsi, and Mike's Hard Lemonade. His films were screened worldwide at festivals including Sundance, Slamdance, Berlin, Cinevegas, and SXSW. His still photography appeared in print and on the web.

Following Hollywood, KIRAN was captivated by the digital innovations revolutionizing the world of advertising. He founded his own branded entertainment company, aalleyoop which sold for seven figures to a larger agency. After that, he joined the top-tier advertising agency Ogilvy. Here, he specialized in marrying entertainment with commerce, creating short films that engaged consumers in a manner prescient of the entire rise of social media-related branded content.

Upon discovering from Nicholas J. Pritzker, a venture capitalist, the true story of CONQUEST—the banding together of escaped formerly enslaved Africans, Irish indentured servants, Jews rejected from Europe, and other outcasts in order to topple Spanish dominance of the New World—KIRAN immediately was intrigued. For the past decade, he has enjoyed exploring the themes of strength in diversity and the battle for freedom from authoritarianism. He has been neck-deep in researching and writing, earning an informal PhD in history ever since. KIRAN has completed one novel with the second following soon and the third outlined in detail.

www.ingramcontent.com/pod-product-compliance
Lightning Source LLC
LaVergne TN
LVHW041053080826
845145LV00007B/1560